IT'S A BIR...
IT'S A...WHALE?

Ufa, Russia—July 1636

Olga Petrovichna went into the tax warehouse with her slate and her charcoal stick. Her worthless husband was supposed to be doing this, but Stanislav Ivanovich Polzin was drunk again. He was usually drunk by noon and it was late afternoon now. Olga sighed. She had long since regretted marrying him, even if he did have a secure post and the family connections to keep it.

"Look up there!"

Olga looked around, even before she identified the voice. It was Sergei Sergeevich, one of the *Streltzi*. It took her only a moment to recall that he would be on guard in the west tower.

She went out the door again, and looked up to see Sergei Sergeevich gesturing at the sky, still yelling. She followed his pointing arm and saw a whale flying through the sky. For a moment she was sure it was a whale. Not that she had ever seen a whale, but her grandpa—who had been a sailor—told her about them. Then, as she watched it, her memory caught up with her. There were stories from back west about great flying machines. And the whale had markings. In fact, it had the imperial crest clearly visible on the bottom of the thing. And it was coming right at them.

Olga wondered how Sergei had failed to see it till it got this close. Maybe because it was silent. Then she heard a faint noise. The thing wasn't silent, but it was quiet.

Olga turned back to the tax warehouse and yelled, "Someone go to the tavern and get my idiot husband! Mother Russia has remembered we're here."

ERIC FLINT'S RING OF FIRE SERIES

1632 by Eric Flint • *1633* with David Weber • *1634: The Baltic War* with David Weber • *1634: The Galileo Affair* with Andrew Dennis • *1634: The Bavarian Crisis* with Virginia DeMarce • *1634: The Ram Rebellion* with Virginia DeMarce et al • *1635: The Cannon Law* with Andrew Dennis • *1635: The Dreeson Incident* with Virginia DeMarce • *1635: The Eastern Front* • *1635: The Papal Stakes* with Charles E. Gannon • *1636: The Saxon Uprising* • *1636: The Kremlin Games* with Gorg Huff & Paula Goodlett • *1636: The Devil's Opera* with David Carrico • *1636: Commander Cantrell in the West Indies* with Charles E. Gannon • *1636: The Viennese Waltz* with Gorg Huff & Paula Goodlett • *1636: The Cardinal Virtues* with Walter Hunt • *1635: A Parcel of Rogues* with Andrew Dennis • *1636: The Ottoman Onslaught* • *1636: Mission to the Mughals* with Griffin Barber • *1636: The Vatican Sanction* with Charles E. Gannon • *1637: The Volga Rules* with Gorg Huff & Paula Goodlett • *1637: The Polish Maelstrom* • *1636: The China Venture* with Iver P. Cooper (forthcoming)

1635: The Tangled Web by Virginia DeMarce • *1635: The Wars for the Rhine* by Anette Pedersen • *1636: Seas of Fortune* by Iver P. Cooper • *1636: The Chronicles of Doctor Gribbleflotz* by Kerryn Offord & Rick Boatright • *1636: Flight of the Nightingales* by David Carrico (forthcoming)

Time Spike with Marilyn Kosmatka • *The Alexander Inheritance* with Gorg Huff & Paula Goodlett

Grantville Gazette I–V, ed. Eric Flint • *Grantville Gazette VI–VII*, ed. Eric Flint & Paula Goodlett • *Grantville Gazette VIII*, ed. Eric Flint & Walt Boyes • *Ring of Fire I–IV*, ed. Eric Flint

To purchase any of these titles in e-book form, please go to www.baen.com.

1637
THE VOLGA
RULES

ERIC FLINT
GORG HUFF
PAULA GOODLETT

1637: THE VOLGA RULES

Copyright © 2018 by Eric Flint, Gorg Huff and Paula Goodlett

A Baen Books Original

Baen Publishing Enterprises
P.O. Box 1403
Riverdale, NY 10471
www.baen.com

ISBN: 978-1-4814-8407-7

Cover art by Tom Kidd
Maps by Michael Knopp

First printing, February 2018
First mass market printing, June 2019

Library of Congress Control Number: 2017052474

Distributed by Simon & Schuster
1230 Avenue of the Americas
New York, NY 10020

Pages by Joy Freeman (www.pagesbyjoy.com)
Printed in the United States of America

To John Huff, Harold Huff and Stephen Huff

Contents

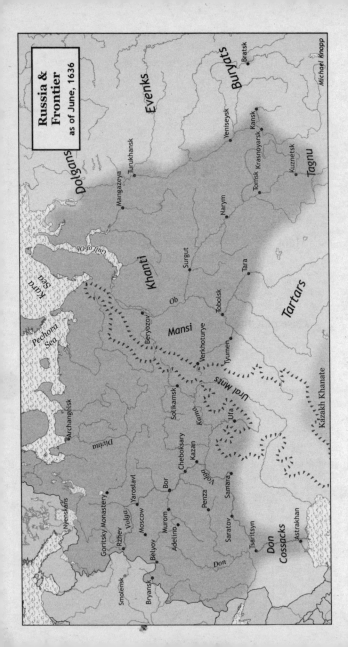

Russia & Frontier
as of June, 1636

Michael Knopp

Evenks

Dolgans

Buryats

Bratsk

Kansk

Krasnoyarsk

Kuznetsk

Yeniseysk

Tomsk

Tagnu

Turukhansk

Mangazeya

Narym

Tartars

Khanti

Surgut

Gulf of Ob

Ob

Kara Sea

Tobolsk

Mansi

Tara

Verkhoturye

Tyumen

Pechora Sea

Archangelsk

Beryozov

Ural mts

Kazakh Khanate

Dvina

Solikamsk

Kama

Ufa

Nyenskans

Goritsky Monastery

Rzhev

Yaroslavl

Volga

Moscow

Bor

Cheboksary

Kazan

Volga

Smolensk

Belyov

Murom

Adelino

Penza

Samara

Saratov

Don

Tsaritsyn

Astrakhan

Don Cossacks

Bryansk

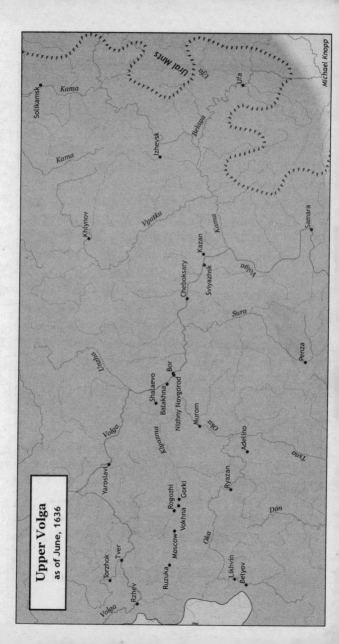

Upper Volga
as of June, 1636

Michael Knopp

Ural Mts

Kama

Solikamsk

Kama

Izhevsk

Belaya

Ufa

Ufa

Khlynov

Vyatka

Kazan

Sviyazhsk

Kama

Cheboksary

Samara

Volga

Sura

Penza

Unzha

Bor

Volga

Shalaevo

Balakhna

Nizhny Novgorod

Klyazma

Murom

Oka

Adelino

Yaroslavl

Tsna

Rogozhi

Vokhna

Gorki

Ryazan

Torzhok

Tver

Ruzuka

Moscow

Oka

Don

Rzhev

Volga

Likhvin

Belyov

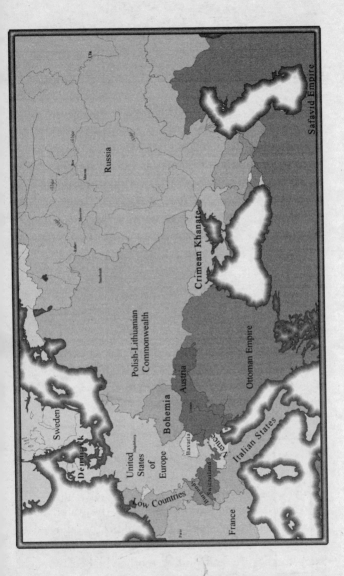

Go East, Young Man

Factory in Poltz, Russia
February 1636

Stefan Andreevich wiped off the sweat, then motioned for Nestor to turn the crank. While Nestor cranked and the weight lifted, Stefan checked the irons in the fire. He had plenty of time. It was a stone forge with a leather bellows, newly made last year with little regard to appearance. The stones were quarried, but not shaped, and the mortar was not of good quality. The sparks flew up as Stefan used the tongs to check the color of the wrought iron globs in the glowing charcoal, while Nestor cranked away.

Once the hammer was up, Stefan used the tongs to pull the plate out of the stamp forge and set it on a scorched wooden shelf. Then he pulled the mop from the bucket and ran it over the bottom and top molds. The molds steamed and hissed with the water, but it was an important step. They couldn't be allowed to get too hot or they would start to deform. He turned back to the fire and pulled another blob of wrought iron. It was yellow hot and would take off a limb if he allowed it to touch him. He placed it in the mold and signaled Nestor, who pulled the lever that dropped the weight.

Over five tons of lead-weighted stamp dropped almost six feet. *Wham!*

Torn between admiring the efficiency of the system and resenting the labor, Stefan repeated the process. Then he repeated it again. There was little discussion. The men at the bellows were from Poltz, where he and about half the men of Ruzuka had been sent to work. It made things much harder, because if they were here stamping out plates they couldn't be back home weaving cloth, which was the main winter craft of Ruzuka. After a long day, the men were given a poor meal and sent to bed in a barn. Just as had happened yesterday and would happen again tomorrow and the day after, six days a week for the last three months and another to come.

Stefan wouldn't be making cloth if he were in Ruzuka. He would be making iron parts for the looms and the plows and other needs of the village. He looked back into the fire of the forge and checked the color of the blobs, then waved for more pumping. Then he thought about how fast he could stamp out various parts if he had a drop hammer.

Nestor would be making cloth if he were in Ruzuka. Like most of the villagers in Ruzuka—and like most of the peasants in Mother Russia—Nestor had two professions. Farmer in spring, summer, and fall, but in winter he was a weaver and made cloth.

Stefan was an exception. A blacksmith was needed all year round, as much in winter as in summer. He was here because, as a blacksmith, he was a skilled craftsman. Colonel Ivan Nikolayevich Utkin, the man who held Ruzuka as *pomestie* from Czar Mikhail, would get paid more when he rented Stefan out.

Ruzuka, Russia
March 1636

Vera pulled Stefan to her and kissed him vigorously, then pulled back and looked into his eyes. "Was it bad?" she asked, her greenish-brown eyes shining.

"No worse than usual," he told her stoically.

She hugged him again. "The women have been working at the weaving, but we don't have nearly as much cloth as last year. Still, the colonel insists that we owe him the same amount of cloth, in spite of the extra work you're doing. And Kiril Ivanovich has told him how much we made, so we can't hide any away. The colonel is going to take almost all of it." Vera's usually pleasant tone was harsh and angry. Then she hugged him again, as though trying to use his strength to hold away the world.

Stefan wished he could hold away the world, but they were serfs and Colonel Ivan Nikolayevich Utkin controlled their lives. The colonel was a *deti boiarskie*, which literally meant "child of boyars," but really meant a retainer of one of the great houses. Someone who served a member of one of the great houses or who owed their position in the bureaus or the army to the influence of a great house. The colonel was both. He was a retainer of Director-General Sheremetev himself and had gotten his position in the army due to

Sheremetev influence. The village of Ruzuka was part of the colonel's *pomestie*, payment in land with serfs. As a serf in Ruzuka, Stefan had little say in how his life or the lives of his wife and children would unfold.

A thought that had been slipping around in the back corners of his mind for the last couple of years came to the fore. *We should run.* He had his wife and children to think about, and though he wasn't overfond of Father Yulian, the priest had said some things in his sermons that struck Stefan as worthwhile. That God and the angels had intended men to be free, but men, in their weakness and fear, had given over their liberty to the strong and the vicious, in hopes of protection. Well, the strong and the vicious had taken the liberty, but they didn't seem overly concerned with protecting Stefan's wife and child from hunger and want. Maybe it was time to try a little freedom. But for now Stefan kept the thought from his lips, even with Vera.

They sat down to a meal of stewed beets with just enough grease to make you think there might be some ham in there somewhere, and talked about the goings-on in the village. Vera's friendly manner made her everyone's confidant and mostly she didn't share what she was told. Except with Stefan, but Stefan was a taciturn man. He didn't talk much, being the sort who thought of just the right thing to say . . . a day or two after the conversation.

That night, with Vera snuggled against his chest, Stefan looked around the small room and thought about what they would need to take if they ran, and how they would carry it. Their house was next to the smithy and not in great repair. Stefan was good with metal, not so good with wood. But small as the house was and as little as they had, they would have to leave a lot. If they went. And if they went, where would they go? Vera hugged him in her sleep and he hugged her back.

Izabella smiled like a cat as she saw her mother leaving Father Yulian's cabin. She knew what was going on there and she decided that if Mother could do it, she could too.

Three days later, she sat in the quiet room that Father Yulian used to take confession. "I have these urges, Father Yulian. Even while in church, I feel these strange new feelings." Izabella was five foot three with golden blond hair, blue eyes, and a curvaceous figure. She knew she was desirable. She only needed Yulian to notice. And she paid attention in church and understood the doctrine. Besides, she had seen him with Mother and heard what he said. "They distract me from the contemplation of faith." She considered mentioning that she had seen him and her mother. Perhaps confessing her snooping would be a good way, but she held that in reserve. She really wanted Yulian to want her, not to be forced into her bed.

Father Yulian was most understanding and instructed her that the best cure for lustful thoughts was satiating them. Then the mind was left clear for the deeper concerns of the faith. "Also," he said, "the realization that our desires can distract us from the worship of God makes us humble and more willing to welcome the Holy Spirit."

By the time he had finished ministering to her, Izabella felt so calm as to be called languid.

Life went on in the village, with Father Yulian ministering to the needs of his flock. To those with a need to learn, he taught reading, writing, mathematics, and other things. Increasingly, political philosophy found its way into his teachings, both from the pulpit and during his private counseling.

Ruzuka, Russia
April 1636

Stefan looked out at the fields. The crops were in the ground, but the children weeding the fields had a gaunt look about them. With the end of winter, the men had finally gotten to come home from the factory in Poltz to do the necessary work in Ruzuka.

Stefan stayed busy at his forge, and whenever he could he made the bits and pieces for a wagon and hid them away. He looked around again. Anatoly was working in his shop, making handles for the new reapers. It was a hot day for April which was part of the reason Stefan had stepped outside. Vera waved as she led Vasily and Eva to the well. He'd almost told Vera about his plan a dozen times in the last few weeks, but he held back. The truth was that he was afraid that she would not want to leave her friends. Afraid that if he gave her time, she would talk him out of it and they would wait till it was too late to run. They were one of the wealthier families in the village, in part because Stefan had built his own drop hammer and that had saved him a great deal of time in the repairing of farm equipment, which in turn meant that there was more time to gather the iron ore and make the wrought iron. It let them trade for more food, more clothing, and they would be even better off if Vera didn't insist on feeding half the village children.

Things were especially bad this summer. Sheremetev had taken power in Moscow, apparently with the acquiescence of Czar Mikhail. And the colonel, as one of Sheremetev's *deti boiarskie*, wanted to prove himself by making the village produce. The only good news was he was doing it by mail, being busy in the army and his son, Nikita, with him. That meant that only his wife, Elena, and daughter, Izabella, were here. Father Yulian seemed to have a great deal of influence with them. Stefan grinned at that thought, because Vera had told him how that influence came to be. Father Yulian was a man who had plenty of stamina, Stefan had to admit. He'd been ministering to the women of the village for a long time. Even to Vera, back before she had decided to marry Stefan.

There was one other thing that Stefan had to respect about Father Yulian. He didn't coerce the women of the village. They went to him. Once Vera had decided that she didn't want to play anymore, Father Yulian had been fine with her decision.

Ruzuka, Russia
May 1636

"Might I have a few words with you?" Father Yulian asked Stefan as he was leaving the church one Sunday.

"I guess so, Father. Do you need new hinges for the church door?" Stefan looked at the door in question. The hinges were a bit rusty, but seemed in good enough shape.

Father Yulian just smiled and waved him toward the cabin next to the church.

"So," Yulian asked, in his deep baritone, once Stefan was seated on a wooden bench by the stove, "when are you planning on running and where do you intend to go?"

Stefan blinked. "What?" The priest was grinning at him, his left eyebrow raised. He had dark hair and rough-hewn features. There was just a touch of gray at his temples. His beard had a little dash of gray too.

"I'm not blind, man," Father Yulian said as his grin mellowed into a smile. "You have been making extra parts for a wagon and squirreling away dried meat and vegetables. At first I thought you were just preparing for the winter like any industrious man should, but then it came to me that your choice of goods are as light and compact as you can manage. You want things that you can carry with you."

Stefan's hand, almost of its own accord, crept toward his belt knife. This was a disaster. The priest might tell anyone—the colonel's wife, the headman, Kiril Ivanovich. And Stefan would be strung up and beaten half to death, maybe all the way to death. Then what would happen to Vera and the children?

"You realize that leaving would leave the whole village in peril? Your debt would be applied to everyone left in the village. How do you think that's going to make Vera feel?"

"Better than burying our children would," Stefan said angrily, but his hand had stopped its creeping toward his knife.

Father Yulian nodded, but continued. "Probably.

But better is not the same as good. Wouldn't it be best to take the whole village?"

"The whole village! You're crazy. There is no way. Besides, what makes you think that they will all want to go?"

"You don't give me credit for knowing my flock, Stefan. There are a few who will actively oppose any attempt to leave. Kiril Ivanovich, for instance. Aside from the fact that he hates me personally, he believes that some are made to be serfs and some to be boyars, and that as a serf, his goal should be to be a good serf. At least, that's what he tells himself. The truth is, he is a horrible coward who will yield to anyone with a whip."

Father Yulian went through the village, telling Stefan who would be willing to run when the time came but couldn't keep their mouths shut, who wouldn't want to go but would continue on if they started, and finally those who he thought they could trust to be a part of the preparations. Mostly women, Stefan noted, in that last group.

But, in spite of it all, Stefan wasn't convinced. "Look, Father, that's all fine, but how do you expect to move a whole village through Russia without anyone noticing? And the ones that we force to go along . . . they will turn on us the first chance they get. How do you plan to deal with that?"

"No, not most of them. Once we leave, their only choice will be to go with us. They will already be Cossacks, runaways, according to Moscow. Especially with Sheremetev in charge. You know what the colonel has been doing since Sheremetev 'retired' the czar."

And it was true. There had been whippings on each visit by the colonel since Sheremetev had taken power, and two girls of the village had been forced by the colonel's son, Nikita.

They didn't come to any agreement that day, but when Stefan got home, there was Vera waiting for him, and it was clear that Father Yulian had told her of his suspicions before he had brought the matter up with Stefan. She had many of the same questions, but she also wanted to know just where he planned on dragging her and the children.

"I'm not entirely sure," Stefan admitted. "The Cossacks to the south, or east to the goldfields. I figure I can make us a good living making mining tools. The Cossacks are closer, and once I prove I can take it, they will leave you be."

"We are not going to live with those animals. They have no law but strength and that's not how I want Vasily growing up."

"East to the goldfields then," Stefan agreed. "After the harvest."

"And we will take the looms and spinning wheels. The miners will need clothing as well as tools."

"Are you crazy? Do you know how big a loom is?"

"No, tell me. I spent all of last winter in front of one. Do tell me how big they are. A loom may be taken apart and the parts can be stowed in a wagon, just like a blacksmith's tools."

Life moved on. Gradually, other villagers were brought into the plan, each one adding to the chance of discovery and making Stefan more nervous. He was still arguing for a small group. But Vera seemed to be assuming that the whole village would be coming.

"We don't have enough wagons for the whole village," Stefan insisted. "And if we start building wagons, everyone is going to know that something is up."

"Well, think of something," Vera said.

Stefan's mouth fell open. *What does she expect . . . ? Never mind. . . .* He knew perfectly well what Vera expected. She expected him to come up with some device or plan so that the needed wagons would just appear when needed.

She gave him a hard look. "That's your job."

Grumbling, Stefan went off to think of something.

Izabella failed to notice the first period she missed. Her cycle wasn't all that consistent. She had a tendency to notice them when they happened, but was able to mostly ignore them. When she missed her second, she stopped and counted back. Her last period was over sixty days ago. And she had had no appetite in the morning for the last month and more. She didn't want to believe it, but she was adding things up and they were working out to a baby on the way. Izabella didn't panic.

She started thinking about how she could get out of this mess. Papa wasn't going to be understanding. Part of the reason she had started up with Yulian was that Papa was so busy trying to figure out where he was going to sell her virginity to get the most value out of it. That, and the fact that Mama was already fucking Yulian. She paused in her thinking. That, in a way, was good news. There wasn't much Mama could do, considering that Papa would likely just send Izabella to a convent . . . but he'd kill Mama. She mulled the whole matter over for a day or so, then went to talk it over with Yulian.

❖   ❖   ❖

"Father Yulian?"

"Yes, my child?"

"You're going to be a father."

Father Yulian felt his eyebrows lift. Izabella had come over to relieve herself of lustful thoughts, so that she might free her mind for more spiritual matters and they had spent an enjoyable hour on that endeavor. She was lying on his bed with a blanket half over her and giving him a very straight look. This wasn't the first time that Father Yulian had heard such news. For instance, it was fairly likely that Kiril's daughter, Irina, was in fact his. But Irina's mother was married, and so matters could be managed fairly straightforwardly. And Liliya, when she had realized, had quickly married young Makar, so that had worked out. But that wasn't going to be an option in this case. Izabella was of the lower nobility and her father wasn't a reasonable man.

"What do you want to do, Izabella? Don't wonder what is possible for the moment. Imagine that everything is possible, and tell me what you want. We will work from there."

"I'm not sure. I don't think I can separate what I want from what's possible. I want to not be pregnant, I guess."

"That is possible, but dangerous," Yulian said. He was reasonably well educated, having spent a couple of years at a monastery before he took up his duties here. He could read, write, and figure. He even had a fairly decent little library with no fewer than eleven books, including the Bible, of course. And for the past few years he had been reading every technical pamphlet that came out of the Gorchakov Dacha. There were pamphlets on medicine. "Some of the pamphlets discuss pregnancy and both what you need to do if you want to keep the child and what to do if you want to lose it. None of the options to lose the child are safe, not done here on our own. The techniques that are discussed in the pamphlets might work, but if something went wrong, you could bleed to death."

Izabella shook her head. "It's not that I am afraid, but as much as I wish I wasn't pregnant, the idea of killing it . . . No, I don't want to do that." She thought for a minute. "I don't know what is going to happen when I start to show, though. Father is going to want to know who the father is."

Yulian looked at the girl. She was vain and self-centered, but beneath that, of good heart he thought. More importantly, she was smart. Surprisingly smarter than either her mother or her father. And, in a way, her situation was just as perilous as a serf's, if rather more comfortable. Bringing her into the conspiracy was a risk, but it might well be the least risky option. Besides, if she was on their side, there were opportunities there. He wasn't sure what those opportunities were yet, but he could smell them. "There might be another option. I will need your oath that what we discuss will not be shared with anyone. Lives are at stake."

She nodded and he explained about the plans to escape.

"But why?" she asked.

And, for a moment, Father Yulian really wanted to hit her. "You know about the factory and that many of the men were sent to work in it over the winter. You know that it decreased the cloth that the village could make."

At each statement she nodded, but still looked uncomprehending.

"You know that the excess cloth the village produced was traded for things like food and boots, for tools, and vegetables that the children, especially, need to grow up healthy."

The nod came more slowly.

"Because of that factory, half the children in the village are sick or have been. And the whole village is malnourished, often hungry. We are running because your father is treating us worse than animals—like tools to be used up and thrown away."

"I didn't realize."

"You chose not to."

As she walked through the village on the way back to the house, Izabella noticed the thinness of the villagers and the slowness of their movements. She had seen the same thing yesterday, but now she noticed it and—combined with her own troubles—it started a change in the way Izabella looked at the world.

Stefan, as instructed, thought of something. "Father Yulian, can we talk?" Sunday services had just let out and for a moment Stefan thought the priest would put him off. The colonel's daughter, Izabella, was hanging back, probably hoping for some "private instruction."

But Yulian must have seen something in his face. "Give me just a minute, Stefan."

He went over and said a few words to Izabella, then to the colonel's wife, and they headed back to the big house.

"What can I do for you, Stefan?" Father Yulian waved Stefan into the priest's cottage.

"Vera wants me to make sure there are enough

wagons for the village, but if I make the parts for a bunch of wagons it will quickly become obvious..."

"I understand. But how can I help you?"

"The factory we worked in last summer used a stamp press. That's basically a big hammer that was cranked up and then let fall. It was very efficient, and much more flexible than it might seem. What it made depended on the shape of the dies on the hammer and the anvil. In Poltz, the dies made shaped iron plates, which could then be used to make the shells for *oreshki*, which were sold as far away as Moscow. But the same techniques could be used to make clamps and bearings and a variety of other metal parts needed to make a wagon."

"Excellent, Stefan. But, again, what do you need me for?"

"I'm getting there, Father, but you need to understand how this works for it to make any sense."

Father Yulian scratched his beard, then nodded for Stefan to continue.

"If I made the parts themselves it would make our plans obvious, especially if I made several sets of bearings, say. On the other hand, having the stamp forge and the dies wouldn't, because the dies could be used as needed over the course of years."

Stefan continued before Father Yulian could interrupt again. "I need some reason to make the dies, Father. I need an order for the parts for a wagon, preferably two or three wagons. A farm cart, a *troika*, something else. I don't know. Just enough bearings and hasps, brake pads, springs... enough so that it's plausible that I would take the extra time to set up the dies for the drop hammer. Then, when we're ready, I can make the parts for the rest of the wagons quickly."

For that matter, if he could manage it, Stefan wanted to take the dies when they left.

"I'll see what I can do," Father Yulian said.

Izabella crept into her father's office and stole his seal. Colonel Utkin was literate, but barely, and he did as much as he could with stamps and seals. Generally, orders and legal documents were written by a clerk, or often Father Yulian, and then the colonel would pull out his stamp to make it official. The colonel's signature was a scrawl that was omitted as often as it was included. What was necessary to make a document or instructions legally binding was the seal, and there was a spare seal in his desk.

"It's a letter from Papa," Izabella said, holding up the letter. "He says you're to build a troika-harnessed carriage that has ball bearings and leaf springs."

Stefan wiped his hands on his trousers, then took the letter. Stefan couldn't read. At least, he wasn't what an up-timer would consider literate. But with effort he could make out words one at a time. And by now he could interpret design drawings of the sort that were published by the Dacha. These designs were particularly clear to him because he had worked with Father Yulian in making them. He wondered how Yulian had gotten the seal, and it didn't occur to him that Izabella might have something to do with it. He made something of a show of examining the sheets.

Then he called Anatoly from the wood shop and discussed the possibility of getting a *troika* made, casually mentioning that he was going to make dies for several of the metal parts.

Anatoly wasn't thrilled, but Izabella stomped her foot. "These are my father's orders. He says we'll be going to Moscow after harvest and we are to have a modern carriage with springs." She turned on Anatoly. "And it's to be double walled for insulation. Like Czar Mikhail's."

They learned a fair amount from making the *troika* carriage. They learned to make two-walled wooden panels that were lightweight and provided excellent insulation. The wagons they had decided on were roofed and walled like a gypsy wagon. They had easier access to wood than cloth this year, but they did use strips of cloth, painted with rosin, to cover gaps. They had never heard of a prairie schooner or a Conestoga wagon. The wagons they knew were freight wagons for carrying grain or gypsy wagons for carrying people. That led to a new set of instructions from Colonel Utkin.

". . . so the modules are to be made a consistent size of four feet by eight feet, double-walled with an air space of four inches. All as shown in the accompanying diagrams."

"Why do we need to build a new barn?" complained Kiril Ivanovich, but not until the colonel's lady was out of earshot.

"I haven't the faintest idea." Stefan shrugged. "But the orders are clear."

Even Stefan didn't know how those instructions had gotten into the pouch. He was fairly sure that they had been written by Father Yulian, but the priest hadn't been anywhere near the packet that the messenger handed to the colonel's daughter.

Ruzuka, Russia
June 1636

It was, Stefan had to admit, a really stupid way to build a barn. On the other hand, with the materials for the barn, it would take only a couple of weeks this fall to build a dozen wagons and run. He watched Anatoly splitting a log to make planks then handed the newly sharpened plane to Petr, Anatoly's ten-year-old.

"Thank you, sir," Petr said, with less than full enthusiasm. The plane blade was case hardened and sharpened on Stefan's grinding wheel, but pushing the plane along the planks wasn't going to be fun. Stefan knew that and sympathized with the boy, but not too much. They were all working hard. He heard a horse and turned to see a rider coming into the village. "That's Konstantin Pavlovich, the post rider from the telegraph."

Anatoly looked up from the log he was splitting. "That horse has been ridden hard."

Stefan began to worry.

Elena held out the papers to Father Yulian with shaking hands and he took them with concern. The document was purportedly from Czar Mikhail, and according to it, Sheremetev was attempting a coup d'etat and had committed treason. That was a disaster for the colonel and their whole family, because the colonel was a client of the Sheremetev family. What she had barely noticed in amongst the papers was the grant of liberty to all serfs who joined the czar in the east. In fact, it—by royal decree—freed all the serfs in Russia. Not that the decree was going to hold sway here. But if they could get to the east...Elena was wringing her hands, wondering what was going to happen to the family.

Father Yulian reached out and pulled her to him, kissing her gently and murmured to her to calm down and be at peace. The world was working out to God's plan, just as it should. It took him several minutes to get her calmed down and send her home. Then he sent for Stefan, Vera, Dominika, Anatoly, and Klara, the ringleaders of the escape plan. He also sent for Izabella.

"This doesn't change anything," Stefan said. "The czar is running for his life and this is just to spread chaos behind him to try and keep Sheremetev occupied while he escapes."

"I think you're right, as far as you go," Anatoly said. "But so what? It will make trouble everywhere and that will make it easier for all of us."

"But we aren't ready, not unless you want to leave half the village behind," Stefan was saying as the door opened and Izabella came in.

Stefan and the rest were all suddenly silent.

"Thank you for coming, my child," Father Yulian said. "Have you read the documents?"

"No, Father Yulian," Izabella said. "Mother started reading, then ran out of the house."

Father Yulian passed them over, then he turned back to the group. "Please continue, Stefan. You were saying something about us not being ready to run?"

Stefan looked at the priest, then at the spoiled daughter of the colonel, then back at the priest, then over at Vera.

"So that's how the instructions for the new barn got into the message pouch," Vera said.

Izabella had been working through the dispatches, making slow going of it. Izabella wasn't a reader by preference. Stefan looked over at her with surprised contemplation. In spite of the realization, he couldn't bring himself to speak about this in front of her. For several seconds it stayed like that, Izabella struggling through the information and Stefan looking back and forth between her and the priest, with the rest of the group looking at Stefan.

"Father said that Sheremetev had taken steps to put the Dacha and Bernie Zeppi under control. I guess they didn't work." Izabella's expression was half-amused, half-disgusted. "The politics have gotten weird since the czar went into seclusion. And from what we've heard, Sheremetev was getting everything organized just as he wanted it. Father and Nikita were both insufferably pleased with themselves, as though it was all their doing."

"What will happen now?" Father Yulian asked.

"That's what I've been trying to figure out, and I'm not sure. A lot of Director-General Sheremetev's power had to do with the fact that he had the czar in reserve. It's likely that there were troubles in the duma when the news hit. I don't know if the director-general has kept control. For all I know, he could have proclaimed himself czar by now. Or he could be out of power and another faction may be in charge. Father is with the Moscow garrison and, from his letter, he doesn't expect to be released anytime soon. There may be fighting in Moscow between the factions. . . ." She stopped, her face going white. "Oh, my God. With the radios, the Poles and the Swedes already know, or they will within days. Invasion!"

The location of their village, as it happened, wasn't quite on the direct line between Smolensk, the Polish border fort, and Moscow. Not quite. But they were considerably too close to that direct line for comfort.

"We can't afford to panic," Stefan said, feeling more than a little panicked just at the moment himself. "We will need wagons. We should wait, just as we planned."

"In a month this place could be garrisoning a Polish army," Anatoly said. "And it will be more than a month before the rye is ready for harvest."

"What would you have us do? Try and pack the whole village on our backs?"

"If we have to," Anatoly said. "Better than still being here, putting the finishing touches on our preparations, when the Poles arrive. Or having the colonel show up with his whip." Anatoly had been severely beaten by the colonel's order on his last visit.

"What about a compromise? We spend the next week getting ready as fast as we can, building wagons and loading them with everything we can carry, especially food . . . what there is of it. Then we go," Father Yulian said.

"I don't think we can build even eight wagons in a week, Father Yulian, even using the drop hammer to make the iron parts."

"We will make what we can."

"What about the ones who don't want to go?" Vera asked. "As soon as we get started, everyone in the village is going to know what we're doing."

"We tell them the Poles are coming. Or that Father thinks the Poles are coming. Or might be coming.

And he wants us to get ready to evacuate if they get too close," suggested Izabella.

"It's worth a try," Stefan said.

"I'll write the instructions, and we will insert them into the package that the colonel sent," said Father Yulian.

For the next five days, the villagers worked like demons. Stefan's drop hammer turned out flanges and bolt blanks and bearing facings and axe heads. The ax heads were to chop the trees to make planks for the bottoms and sides of wagons.

The "new barn" was torn down to the modules, which would be used to make wagons. The six teams of ponies were set to work dragging lumber to make construction easier.

"We don't have enough ponies to pull the wagons," Vera said.

"I know. But I can't forge a pony!"

"What about one of those steam engines?"

Stefan looked at Vera, then shook his head. "I don't know enough. You know that some of them blew up on the river? And those were the ones designed by the big brains in the Dacha." Then he looked at her again and said, "Some of them are simply going to have to pull their wagons themselves."

"Them? We don't own a pony! Stefan, you're a blacksmith, not a farmer."

"We own one now," Stefan said. "I traded some parts of the wagons for it. We only have the one, though, not a team. It's going to be slow going and we will have to share them out when we're going up hills."

❖   ❖   ❖

Kiril Ivanovich watched the preparations with an increasingly troubled heart. He didn't like the idea of leaving, and the fact that the modules from the new barn just happened to be exactly the right length to make the new wagons struck him as highly suspicious. He was slowly becoming convinced that the whole thing wasn't the colonel's instructions at all. That fornicating priest and Stefan—who was an arrogant bastard, well above himself—were behind the whole thing. He considered going to the colonel's lady, but that had done little good in the past. She was wholly under the priest's sway, and Kiril didn't think that it was because she was especially pious.

No. If he were to put a stop to this, he would have to get a message to the colonel. He knew where the radiotelegraph station was, and five days after the meeting in the priest's house, he left the village on foot, intending to warn the colonel of dangerous goings on.

It took Dominika a few hours to realize that Kiril wasn't where he was supposed to be, doing what he was supposed to be doing. Then she rushed to see Father Yulian. It took another hour to confirm that Kiril was nowhere in the village.

"Where do you think he's gone?" Stefan asked.

"Wherever he can do us the most harm," Yulian said. "Kiril is a man always ready with a knife for his neighbor's back. Full of suppressed rages and desires that keep him from God."

Time had run out. Father Yulian, Stefan, and Anatoly went to the big house to inform Elena that they were leaving to join Czar Mikhail at dawn, and she was coming with them. Although initially somewhat startled and unbelieving, thanks to her relationship with Father Yulian, she became very pleased and helpful. Her relations with her husband hadn't been good for several years. She went into the house and brought out silver and a lot of the new paper money, which was apparently what the colonel had received for the work of his serfs at the factory in the neighboring village. Then she and Izabella started packing, as did the rest of the village. They took every wagon in the village, the new ones they had just built, and the older ones that they had used to manage the farming village and bring in the crops. They stripped the village of Ruzuka clean. Every animal that could pull a wagon, and they stripped the big house of every valuable.

They traveled well the next day, with Elena informing the headman of the neighboring village that her husband had told them to evacuate in advance of the approaching Poles. "Yes, he's very close to Prince Sheremetev, my husband is," Elena explained. They tried to buy extra horses, but after hearing about the evacuation, the beasts were not for sale. A bit of bad strategy that Izabella complained about the rest of the day and all that night.

For the next week and a half, they traveled without great difficulty. There was enough confusion that no one had much time to look for them and they had the letters and the colonel's seal. They also had the colonel's lady and daughter to act as cover for them by putting on their airs as a boyar's retainer family. Airs that Elena never actually took off, but the villagers accepted that. She was being useful, and they were used to her acting that way, probably wouldn't have known what to do with her if she had acted human.

Russia wasn't like Europe. It was sparsely populated, even in the more civilized western portion around Moscow. After a few days, village headmen started sounding like they might be interested in holding them there. So, after considerable discussion, they started avoiding the villages. It made travel slower, but kept them out of conflicts. And, for that matter, it kept the colonel from knowing where they were.

Part One

Russia East

CHAPTER 1

𝕿𝖆𝖐𝖎𝖓𝖌 𝖙𝖔 𝖙𝖍𝖊 𝕾𝖐𝖞

Russia House, Grantville
July 1636

Brandy struggled through the Russian documents. Her Russian wasn't great and the Cyrillic letters didn't make things easier. But she needed the practice. When she married Vladimir, she hadn't quite realized the extent she was marrying Russia too. Information flowed, not just from the Ring of Fire to Russia, but from Russia to Grantville. Brandy was now working her way through a two-hundred page report on resource exploitation in Russia, compiled by the staff at the Mining Bureau and forwarded to them by Boris Petrov. Iron production was up significantly, especially in the Kursk Magnetic Anomaly area. There was a new iron mine south of Moscow, and more mines in other places, all as a result of the information provided from the Ring of Fire. Not just the information that there was a massive load of iron there, but the knowledge that the iron was going to be desperately needed all through Europe over the next decades, made the government and the new industrial class realize the investment of resources in mining was worthwhile.

The new Russian industrial class was worrying to Brandy. It was a mix of *Streltzi*—the city guards or foot soldiers, *deti boyars*—the retainers of the great houses, and the *dvoriane*—the service nobility, soldiers and bureaucrats who kept the gears of Russia turning. Finally, there was considerable investment by the great houses and the monasteries. All of that would have been fine, but the laborers in those new mines and factories were mostly serfs, and sometimes outright slaves. It looked to Brandy as though none—or at least very little—of the economic boom that was spreading from the Dacha was reaching the lower classes.

Natasha Gorchakov had paid her serfs for their extra labor, before she fled to Ufa, but a lot of people hadn't—and their number was bound to decline further now that Sheremetev had seized power in Moscow. In any event, most of the Gorchakov profits had come from—and still did—selling or leasing patents on the new products, not from making them themselves.

Things seemed to be getting worse for the Russian peasants, not better.

Vladimir came into her office. "How's it going, love?" he asked, then leaned down and kissed her neck. "Have you drowned in Ivan's statistics yet?"

Ivan was Ivan Petrovich Lebanov, the head of the Mining Bureau. "Not yet, but he's clearly trying. You know who I think is drowning, Vlad? It's the peasants and especially the serfs. And worse, the slaves."

"What makes you so sure of that?"

"It's the costs. I have records here of the costs of the mines, including labor costs. But the labor costs aren't being paid to the worker. They're being paid to their landlords. Aside from your sister, no one seems to be using free people as labor."

Vladimir grimaced. He was almost certain she was right, but when he had left for Grantville back in 1631, he would have seen nothing at all wrong with it. He did now, but that was after years of living surrounded by up-timers. Vladimir was frankly shocked that the Dacha had become as liberal as it had, just from the books and Bernie Zeppi. Tami Simmons and her family had arrived in Moscow, but had gone into seclusion with Czar Mikhail and his family, so had had very little influence on attitudes in the Dacha or the rest of Russia. How had his sister become friends with an escaped slave? He never would have believed that Bernie Zeppi, of all people, could have had such an effect.

"I hate to say it, but you're probably right," Vladimir said, then winced at the look she gave him.

"We have a new baby, Vladimir. I don't want us to have to move to Russia and start a revolution!"

"I don't either," Vladimir said as placatingly as he could. What did she expect him to do about it? Wave a magic wand and make all of Russia's problems vanish? He hadn't even been able to keep Sheremetev from putting his man Shuvalov in control of the Gorchakov Dacha, Vladimir's own property.

"I know. But unless Czar Mikhail wins the civil war and puts the new industrialists in their place, there's going to be a revolution. I haven't gotten a letter from Evdokia in months."

Vladimir couldn't help smiling a little, and Brandy

grimaced. "I know. Little Brandy Bates, hillbilly from West Virginny, is upset that the czarina of Russia hasn't sent her a letter."

Vladimir felt his smile die. "It wasn't that. I was just happy that you were comfortable enough in your relations to the czarina that you would call her by her name without title. But given everything that's happened over the past weeks I'm not surprised she hasn't written to you. For that matter, she may *have* composed a letter— but how would she get it to you? She and the czar can't very well land that great dirigible of theirs in Moscow and drop the letter off to be delivered to the USE." He placed a hand on her shoulder and squeezed. "Don't be upset about it. I know from Natasha that Evdokia holds you as one of her true friends."

Bor, Russia
July 1636

The Nizhny Novgorod militia was definitely a bit ragged. It was strange. General Boris "Tim" Timofeyevich Lebedev should have been scared and, in a way he was. But the effect it had on him was weird. He just noticed things. Every detail became intense and distinct. The stench of the air, not just the acrid smoke of the burned powder, but the smell of the river's muddy bank, combined with the dew on the grass. The patterns the smoke made as it wafted away under the light breeze. And, most of all, the enemy across the field. It was almost as if he could see their faces. Feel the fear that was eating away at the little discipline they had. He was honestly a little amazed that they had held this long.

Then the *Czarina Evdokia* appeared over the roofs of Bor. It was massive and it was flying. It wasn't the first time these men had seen it. It had made several test flights and some of them had gone over Nizhny Novgorod. But in this case, it meant that their last reason for being here was floating away.

"Next rank! Forward five paces!"

The Nizhny Novgorod force scattered. Tim let them. Honestly, he had nothing against those men. They were following the orders they had been given by their lawful lords.

Ivan Maslov came over. "So what now, Tim?"

"We go to Ufa."

"How? The riverboats are full."

"That's an excellent question, Ivan. Why don't you figure it out and tell me?"

Ivan looked at him like he was crazy for a moment, and Tim pointed to the star on his collar.

Ivan looked, swallowed and said, "Yes, sir."

Tim tried not to smile . . . but he failed. He was only nineteen, after all. Czar Mikhail had given him the rank because there wasn't an army to give him. It was silly and he knew it, but Tim still couldn't help enjoying it. He wondered how the real generals, General Shein and General Izmailov, were going to respond. Last Tim had heard, Shein and Izmailov were in Tobolsk, keeping company with Siberian tribesmen. But, looked at pragmatically, Czar Mikhail didn't really have that much of a chance. Tim was fully aware of that, and so was Ivan Maslov.

Marat Davidovich, the new commander of Princess Natasha's guards, came over. "Well, General, what now?"

"I have Ivan Maslov working that out."

"Lord help us, the baker's boy," Marat Davidovich said only half in jest.

Tim looked at him, trying to figure out what to do. Marat Davidovich was a good man and experienced. He was one of Princess Natasha's hand-picked guards, and a skilled man at arms. But, even he was stuck with the notion that Ivan couldn't fight because of the fact that he was the son of a baker.

There must have been something in Tim's expression that he wasn't aware of, because suddenly Marat Davidovich braced and said, "Sorry, General."

It was all Tim could do to keep from letting his eyes widen in shock. "It's all right, Marat Davidovich. But Ivan Maslov is very good at figuring things out."

Ivan Maslov looked at the bodies laid out on the ground and tried to think. Captain Ruslan Andreyivich Shuvalov was cold, having been killed in the fighting last night. Now, he and the other casualties from the night before were joined by *Streltzi* from Nizhny Novgorod, but it wasn't the dead that were the problem. It was the living. The staff of the dirigible works were going to be needed in Ufa and so was a lot of the equipment. The steamboats were already overloaded, and Ivan didn't think that the city fathers of Nizhny Novgorod were going to be in any mood to provide them with extra riverboats. Ivan took inventory of what they were going to need and realized that they weren't going to have room. He pared down his list to things they had to have . . . and it was still way too much. Some of the equipment on the boats would have to come off. By the time Tim and Marat got back to the hangar, Ivan had a plan. He explained it.

"No!" Marat said. "Under no circumstances. Those barges are Princess Natasha's and so is the gear on them. Not Czar Mikhail's."

"Captain!" Tim said.

"No!" Marat said. "I'm sorry, General." And he sounded sorry, Ivan noted. He even sounded like he believed in Tim's new rank. "It's not my choice. Those goods belong to the princess, and I have to make sure that they get to her in Ufa."

"And we will get them there, Captain. Believe me, we will. Even if we have to carry them on our backs."

"I guess we could do that," Ivan offered. "There are wagons. We could take some of it with us overland. And if we go overland, that will free up more space on the boats."

They were in Bor for another day as they rearranged the gear and let everyone make up their mind what they were going to do.

Tim insisted that people be allowed to make up their own minds, saying it was Czar Mikhail's will that joining him be a free choice by free men. Ivan looked at Tim, and Tim explained. "You weren't on the steamboat with us coming down from Murom. We talked a lot about what it would take to make the new Russia work, and a big part is having people have a stake in it. Czar Mikhail is convinced that those who follow him to Ufa must decide freely, not be forced into it. There is some psychological study that the up-timers did about it."

Ivan shrugged. It wasn't up to him. No. It was. It had been his decision in a way, even if he had fallen into it. He couldn't honestly say he had been forced or coerced, not really.

Finally the boats left and the army—such as it was—marched out along the shore of the Volga.

Russia House, Grantville
July 1636

Prince Vladimir Gorchakov sat at the computer and typed out a letter. He then encoded it using the program Pretty Good Privacy and saved the encrypted file to a floppy disk. After pulling the floppy out of the drive, he handed it to Gregorii. "You know what to do."

Gregorii would go to the Higgins Hotel and upload the floppy to the Grantville Wide Web from there, leaving no way to trace where it had come from. In a day or two, one of Francisco Nasi's agents would pick it up and send it to him in Magdeburg, where he would decode it.

"Do you think he will go for it?" Brandy asked.

"I don't know," Vladimir admitted. "We have a lot of wealth. We're just short of cash. So a loan on our interest in the microwave research isn't unreasonable. They are making decent progress, after all."

Three days later, they got a response. It was encrypted and put up on the "Secret Message" news group. All the spies in Grantville—at least all the tech savvy spies in Grantville who had access to a computer—downloaded the full contents of that news group on a regular basis. Vladimir did it daily.

Once the message was unencrypted, it simply read "Have a talk with Ron Stone."

Which was interesting in itself. Vladimir didn't think Ron Stone was any sort of spy. But he went ahead and made the appointment.

Tried to, rather. He'd forgotten that Ron Stone and his wife Missy had moved to Hesse-Kassel in the spring, in order to expand the Stone pharmaceutical enterprises.

There was as yet no regular airship run from Grantville to Kassel, but Vladimir was able to get a ride within a couple of days on an airship headed for the Netherlands. The vessel's captain agreed to make a slight detour in order to drop Vladimir off at his destination—for a fee that fell short of outrageous, but only barely.

Kassel, capital of the province of Hesse-Kassel

"Have a seat, Prince Vladimir. What can I do for you today?"

Ron Stone rose politely from behind his desk and gestured toward a chair against the side of the wall nearby. The chair he indicated looked quite comfortable—quite a bit more so, in fact, than the very utilitarian chair Stone himself was using.

Ron Stone looked much like his chair. On the new side—he was still a very young man—and well-made in a plain, undecorated, functional sort of way. His eyes were hazel and his hair was straight, a sort of dark blond in color.

Stone was of medium height, for an American. His physique was perhaps a bit stocky but there was little fat on him. Like his older brother Frank, he had been something of an athlete in school.

(Soccer, though, not one of the Culturally Sanctioned Up-time sports like football or basketball. As Brandy had explained the matter, in up-time high school—at least of pre-Ring of Fire vintage—this placed Ron Stone on the nerd side of the dark and bitter chasm between nerds and jocks. Americans could be peculiar, sometimes.)

"Are you aware of what's going on in Russia?" Vladimir asked, after he sat down.

Stone resumed his own seat. "I think so, at least in broad outlines. A powerful nobleman named Sheremetev tried to supplant Czar Mikhail by placing the czar under what amounted to house arrest. But he escaped, with the aid of the American Bernie Zeppi and Russian associates of his, and is now setting up what he claims to be the legitimate government of Russia in a place called Ufa that's far to the east. I think it's close to the Urals although it's not in Siberia. And... that's where things stand at the moment. So far there hasn't been much military action but that's bound to change before too long."

He shrugged apologetically. "I'm afraid I haven't delved into any more detail than that. We just don't have that much business with Russia and I'm constantly preoccupied with more immediate matters."

Vladimir had no trouble believing that. Ron Stone was the middle one of the three sons of Tom Stone, the man who had founded *Lothlorien Farbenwerke*. But Tom was not well-suited by temperament to be a businessman and preferred devoting his time to teaching. So, initially by nothing more complex than a process of elimination, his son Ron had wound up running the business instead. His older brother Frank was off being a revolutionary in Italy and the younger brother Gerry had devoted himself to becoming a Lutheran pastor.

It soon became evident, however, that Ron had a natural aptitude for the work he was doing. Brandy had told Vladimir that she thought it was because Ron had been raised a hippie and still pretty much had that mindset. For him, making money was a purely practical affair with no emotional baggage that got his ego tangled up in the process. Whether she was right or not, the one thing that was now clear was that Ron Stone—a man who had just turned twenty-one years of age—was the very capable chief executive officer of the world's largest and most profitable chemical and pharmaceutical company.

"What it all comes down to is this," said Vladimir. "For the moment I am cut off from a large part of my family's wealth. I don't expect to be permanently cut off from it, but it could happen. Meanwhile, I'm not going to be receiving the goods I have promised to deliver, giving me a serious cash flow problem and I am considerably overextended. A mutual friend suggested I have a talk with you about it."

"Yes. He wrote me about it." Ron said. "I think I can help, and because our friend gives you good references, I'm inclined to. But I'm not running a charity."

Vladimir opened his briefcase and pulled out documents detailing his level of ownership in various projects. Vladimir wasn't a great businessman. In fact, he wasn't even a very good businessman. But he had had three things going for him over the last few years. He started out rich, Grantville was a boom town, and Vladimir had a spy network. It was focused on political and technological intelligence, but business intelligence fell right between political and technological. So he had acquired a fair amount of financially useful information over the years. There was also the Dacha, which had until very recently been sending him regular updates of what they were doing and what they had learned. Between those advantages, the disadvantage of not having an abundance of business acumen had been swamped. So Vladimir's portfolio was both large and diverse.

In exchange for a carefully selected quarter of that portfolio, and agreements in regard to the data that they both hoped would be available from the Dacha, Ron Stone provided the cash that Vladimir needed to make good his debts.

CHAPTER 2

Outpost

Ufa, Russia
July 1636

Olga Petrovichna went into the tax warehouse with her slate and her charcoal stick. Her worthless husband was supposed to be doing this, but Stanislav Ivanovich Polzin was drunk again. He was usually drunk by noon and it was late afternoon now. Olga sighed. She had long since regretted marrying him, even if he did have a secure post and the family connections to keep it.

"Look up there!"

Olga looked around, even before she identified the voice. It was Sergei Sergeevich, one of the *Streltzi*. It took her only a moment to recall that he would be on guard in the west tower.

She went out the door again, and looked up to see Sergei Sergeevich gesturing at the sky, still yelling. She followed his pointing arm and saw a whale flying through the sky. For a moment she was sure it was a whale. Not that she had ever seen a whale, but her grandpa—who had been a sailor—told her about them. Then, as she watched it, her memory caught up with her. There were stories from back west about great flying machines. And the whale had markings. In fact, it had the imperial crest clearly visible on the bottom of the thing. And it was coming right at them.

Olga wondered how Sergei had failed to see it till it got this close. Maybe because it was silent. Then she heard a faint noise. The thing wasn't silent, not quite, but it was quiet.

Olga turned back to the tax warehouse and yelled, "Someone go to the tavern and get my idiot husband! Mother Russia has remembered we're here."

Bernie looked down at the scurrying people in the town of Ufa. "I wondered when they'd notice us." Bernie felt like he had wandered into a western movie. *Fort Apache*, maybe. But in any case, it looked like one of the movies that had the wooden stockade surrounding the buildings. A high budget technicolor movie, the sort where the camera zoomed in from on high. He was looking down at a western fort with a town next to it, with just enough Russian bits to make him feel off about it all. The fort was vaguely rectangular, with four watch towers, a bunch of one- and two-story log cabins, and one stone church. Just to the east of the fort was a ramshackle bunch of log cabins, all single story and not overly well made. To the south about three hundred yards were the docks on the Belaya River. The Belaya River was about three hundred yards wide at this point and twisty as all get out. Fort Ufa was on the south end of a loop of river. From looking at the land and where the forest ended, Bernie figured that, come the spring floods, the river was going to come almost up to the fort. It was located as near the docks as they could get without flooding every spring.

"It's not their fault," Czar Mikhail said. "Who looks up from a tower? You watch the horizon, or the woods."

"Prepare to drop anchor," shouted Colonel Nikita "Nick" Ivanovich Slavenitsky. He was the commander of the Russian Air Force by personal appointment of Czar Mikhail. The crew made preparations, then a weighted spear with a line attached was dropped from the bow of the dirigible. It fell a hundred yards and landed in the mud next to the river, sinking several feet with the force of its fall. It was a stopgap measure to use if you didn't have proper dirigible docking facilities.

A few minutes later, the dirigible was tied down, at least marginally, and lowered enough so that the passengers could debark by means of a rope ladder. For children—of which there seemed to be many—and cargo, they would use nets.

"The first thing we need is firewood," Bernie Zeppi said.

"Why?" asked the woman who was apparently the wife of the commander of the garrison, such as it was: thirty *Streltzi*, who spent their time taxing the fur trade.

"The steam engines on the dirigible. A dirigible is a lot safer in the air under power than it is tied down in the open. And you don't have a hangar for it."

"Besides, we will want to use it," Czarina Evdokia explained. They had discussed this on the trip from Bor. One of the very nice things about traveling by dirigible was the comfortable ride. There was plenty of room to move around and the ride was mostly smooth. You could talk and pace. You could spread maps out on tables and plan campaigns. You could talk about propaganda and medicine and all manner of things. And they had. They had even had breakfast, lunch, and dinner on the dirigible.

"How much wood?"

"A lot, but we have steamboats coming with people and equipment. We are probably going to end up deforesting a good part of the surrounding territory, both because we need the wood and because we need clear sight lines."

"For now," Evdokia explained, "Ufa is the capital of Russia."

Bernie looked over at Natasha and smiled. There had been time to talk on the trip here, if not a lot of privacy. They were going to be forging a new Russia here. A Russia where a commoner like Bernie could marry a princess like Natasha. There had been time to talk, but no room to be alone. That was going to change now that they were here. No matter what Evdokia said. In fact, she hadn't said they couldn't be married, just that Bernie's rank was still an issue.

In the air over Russia

Nikita Ivanovich Slavenitsky—Nick, according to Bernie Zeppi—looked out into the night sky. It was dark, really dark, and cloudy at nine hundred feet. He couldn't see a thing. The *Czarina* was cruising along at half speed, and Nick was guessing about the wind so they, by this time, might be as much as a hundred miles off course in any direction. Unlike the *Testbed*, the *Czarina* was a real dirigible, with a large carrying capacity for an airship and a large crew. He had spent a couple of days after arriving in Ufa restocking the *Czarina* with wood for her boilers, then Czar Mikhail sent them to the Swedish fortress, Nyenskans, on the Baltic coast with letters to everyone from Gustav Adolf to Brandy Bates.

The *Czarina*, assuming they weren't headed for the north pole by this time, should reach Nyen sometime around noon tomorrow, having left Ufa early this morning. They were running light with the extra weight taken up by extra wood and water to extend their range because the condensers were not exactly perfect.

Petr Nickovich, his executive officer, came up to him with a cup of tea. "How does it look, Skipper?"

"We might as well be on our way to Mars for all I can see," complained Nick.

"I don't think they have fog in space, Captain," said Petr, who had been a braincase at the Dacha before transferring to Bor to take over the construction of the dirigibles. He had calmed down a lot and had volunteered to be part of the crew of the *Czarina*. Pete knew more about the *Czarina* than anyone alive, but he didn't have a command mind. On the other hand, he had proven excellent with managing the details of shipboard operations. The *Czarina* had a crew of twenty-six. Nick was the captain, Petr his executive officer, and the chief engineer. Directly in Nick's chain were his rudder men and the second and third watch pilots. Under Petr were the engineers, electricians, and riggers. The engineers ran the boilers, the engines and condensers. The electricians ran the generators, the radio, the electric lights and phone system. The riggers did just about everything else. There were also a cook and cook's assistant, and four maids.

"Go to bed, Skipper. Let the midwatch handle things."

"I think we ought to go up another five hundred feet," Nick said.

Petr looked over at the barometer. "I don't know, Captain. We don't actually know how high we really are. All we have is the barometer. It's not like we have a radar range finder. We might be higher than we think."

"Or lower."

"I doubt it, not at these temperatures. But if you want, we can pump some more hot air into the balance balloons." The *Czarina* got most of her lift from hydrogen-filled lift chambers, but it had two large hot-air lift chambers, so that it could adjust lift without dumping either ballast or hydrogen. Adding more hot air to the hot-air lift chambers would increase their lift, and as they went up the hydrogen chambers would expand, increasing their lift more. It was a positive feedback loop that, if handled wrong, could lift them high enough so that the hydrogen chambers would start to vent. That was dangerous. What they would have to do was increase the heat in the hot-air chambers; then, once they gained altitude and the hydrogen chambers expanded, they would vent from the hot-air chambers to compensate for the increased lift of the expanded hydrogen chambers.

"Call Valeriya and get a read first," Nick said.

Petr went over to a wall of the gondola and closed an electric switch.

❖   ❖   ❖

Valeriya Zakharovna was climbing a ladder next to the left central lift chamber when she heard the bell ringing. She climbed down the ladder, wondering what it was about officers that they wouldn't let a woman work. It took her a minute and a half to climb down to the phone. "Able Airwoman Zakharovna here," Valeriya yelled into the mouthpiece. The phones on the *Czarina* were about on a par with the phones of Alexander Graham Bell's day.

Then she stuck her ear against the earpiece and heard a very tinny voice say, "Have a look at the cells and tell us their level of expansion."

"Aye aye." Valeriya racked the mouthpiece and went back to the central lift chamber. When they had been moored, the chambers had been about three-quarters full. As the ship got higher and the outside air got thinner, the gas in the hydrogen chamber expanded, filling the chamber the rest of the way. Now they were about eighty-five percent full. She could tell because there were markings on a pole, and she could look across from where she was standing and see the marks. The highest mark she could see was the eighty-five percent mark. She went back to the phone and pushed the switch that would make it ring on the bridge.

"Eighty-five percent, sir," she yelled into the phone. The bridge acknowledged and she got back to work.

* * *

"I don't know. We go up another five hundred feet and it's going to be at ninety-five percent and we'll need to vent hydrogen to come down, even if we kill all the heat to the hot air chambers," Petr said.

"Take us up till the hydrogen chambers are around ninety percent," Nick said, "then set the hot air chambers

at minimum heat. That should put us on a gentle glide
down from around fifteen hundred feet. It ought to be
light before we get back down to this height. And don't
forget the engines and the vanes. We can use power to
force ourselves down if we have to." The *Testbed* had
taught them all a lot about how to build airships, but
this was still the first ship of this size and they were
finding major differences in performance. The *Czarina*
was much slower to respond than the *Testbed* had been,
and Nick hadn't thought that was possible.

"Right, Skipper. We will do that and I'll have
Valeriya call us to keep us up to date on the hydrogen chambers."

Nick held up his hand. "Right, Pete. I'll go to bed."

They came out of the fog around ten the next morning and could see the southern shore of Lake Onega
in the distance. They were a good three hundred fifty
miles east of where they were supposed to be and well
north of where they expected to be at this point in
the trip. Nick had the *Czarina* turned just south of
due east, and they sighted Nyen just before sunset.

Along with its electrical system, the *Czarina* had a
spark gap radio, with the spark kept well away from
the hydrogen. Once the fort was in sight, and while
staying well out of firing range, Nick gave the pre-
prepared messages to the radio operator. "Send this
one first," he said.

"Aye aye, sir." The operator started tapping in the
Morse Code taught at the Dacha.

GREETINGS FROM MIKHAIL CZAR OF
RUSSIA STOP REQUEST PERMISSION

TO LAND AND DELIVER MAIL FOR
GRANTVILLE AND BEYOND STOP

The response was:

CZAR ON BOARD QUESTION STOP

NO STOP CZAR SENDS GREETINGS
STOP A LOAD OF MAIL FOR USE AND
GUSTAV OF SWEDEN STOP

There was a considerable delay before they got any response. But, eventually came:

YOU CAN LAND STOP PUT DOWN TO
THE EAST OF NYEN STOP WE WILL
SEND A TROOP TO MEET YOU STOP

They found a place to drop the anchor, and reeled themselves down to where they could use the winches to lower the mail bags. They lowered the ladder and Gerry Simmons climbed down.

Gerry looked around and saw a Swede with a captain's bars on his collar sitting on a horse about thirty yards away. Apparently the captain didn't want to put himself under the dirigible. Gerry walked across the pasture to an easy speaking distance, then pulled out his documents. "I'm Gerry Simmons, ambassador at large from the Empire of Holy Rus, appointed by Czar Mikhail day before yesterday." He held out the papers with a flourish and a grin. "What have you folks heard?"

The captain looked at Gerry and at the dirigible, then got off his horse and walked over to meet Gerry. "Director-General Sheremetev is saying that the evil wizard, Bernie Zeppi, has cast a spell on Czar Mikhail, and you and Nurse Tami are in on the spell." The guy said it as though he wanted to sound like he was joking, but wasn't really sure that it wasn't true.

"Nope. Bernie couldn't do that. Neither could my wife. What happened was Sheremetev put Czar Mikhail up in a hunting lodge out in the back of beyond, while he took over the government. Then Bernie and Princess Natasha showed up in Bernie's Dodge." Gerry stopped at the man's apparent incomprehension. "Car? APC?"

The captain nodded at APC and Gerry went on. "Anyway, it became apparent that some of the *oprichniki* had orders to kill Czar Mikhail if it looked like he was going to get loose. That sort of pissed Mikhail off."

The captain snorted a laugh. "It would piss me off too. On the other hand, wasn't it sort of to be expected?"

"Maybe. But since Sheremetev was going to kill him anyway, Czar Mikhail went ahead and called Sheremetev a traitor and started the revolution . . . or counter-revolution, or whatever it is. My wife and I, and two of our sons, were at the hunting lodge where they were keeping Czar Mikhail and his family, and we didn't want to be there when Sheremetev showed up to find Czar Mikhail missing. So we went along too."

"Do you want to go back to the USE?" the captain asked.

"Honestly, it's tempting. Or it would be if my wife and boys were along on this trip, but she's in Ufa playing doctor. Not just to the czar, but to the whole town."

"Ufa? Where is that?"

"Way the hell off east of here. Nick—that's Colonel Slavenitsky, the captain of the *Czarina Evdokia*—" Garry hooked a thumb at the dirigible hanging over them "—says it's sixteen hundred and fifty miles in a straight line, but we caught a crosswind last night, so we traveled closer to seventeen hundred."

"When did you leave Ufa?"

"Yesterday morning. It took us a little more than a day and a half. On the other hand, we're getting pretty low on fuel. You guys have any firewood or coal?"

They delivered the mail and bought some firewood. The garrison didn't have any coal. Gerry climbed back up the ladder and they headed back.

On the road out of Bor

"Well, General, what happens next?" Ivan Maslov asked. They were still in sight of Nizhny Novgorod and had picked up some *Streltzi* to swell their ranks. They also had quite a few techs from the dirigible works at Bor.

"We go to Ufa. I told you that."

"Not what I mean," Ivan said. Then, quietly, "Tim, we're going to be fighting a war. We have the AKs and so do the boyars back in Moscow. The army we are facing will have a better rate of fire than the USE troops. Even the AK3 will give them that. Maybe not as good as the French Cardinal rifles, but better than the German SRGs. When you add in the new clips of the point sevens, we'll be as fast or faster than the Cardinals. Also, these are almost universally rifled guns. They have accurate range out to three or four hundred yards." Ivan pointed at the AK4 Long, strapped diagonally across his back. It was a fifty caliber heavy chamber with a long barrel. "With a mount and scope, I can hit a man at six hundred yards most of the time."

"Most people won't be able to . . ."

"I know. But most people *will* be able to hit a man-size target at three hundred yards. Two hundred, even with the carbines. That's four times the range and you know the lectures we got on the American Civil War and World War I. It's going to be a slaughter."

"I know. But unless you have a tank in your ruck-sack, I'm not at all sure what to do about it."

"Dig the Maginot Line across Russia," Ivan said, but there wasn't much conviction in his voice.

Tim shook his head. "There aren't enough people, much less soldiers, in Russia to man a line even as long as the Maginot was, much less the sort of line we would need for Russia. A trench from the Arctic to the Black Sea. If we did nothing else, it would take years."

"I know. But we have to think of something. You and me, we have to figure out the doctrine for the new war. Not the older and wiser heads. You and—"

"Wait a minute. General Izmailov is good and so—"

"What really happened at Rzhev, Tim?"

Tim stopped. It was a deep, dark secret. Or it had been. But maybe now was the time to tell it. "I usurped General Izmailov's authority to move the volley guns. There was no advanced planning or approval from the general, just me acting on my own."

"Well, why not just say so?" Ivan asked.

"Because it wasn't long after that asshole Ivan Khilkov led our cavalry into a prepared pike formation and got them slaughtered. He'd been able to do it because he had a greater *mestnichestvo*. And I do too. If it had come out that I acted without orders, it would have been used as an excuse for any noble asshole to ignore the orders of his superior officer any time he wanted to."

"With all respect, Tim, you guys never needed an excuse." Ivan stopped. "Oh, I get it. Khilkov used his *mestnichestvo* to make General Izmailov let him loose, then screwed up by the numbers. The general didn't want your actions to provide a counterexample."

"Yes. He and Czar Mikhail, General Shein . . . they all wanted it kept very quiet. My uncle knows, but he agrees with the czar, at least on this."

"It also goes to why Czar Mikhail made you the general."

"No. It was just that he didn't have anyone else handy," Tim said. "Don't make too much of it. He had to leave, we had to fight a rearguard action to get him loose, and no one he had handy at the time had much in the way of real world experience. It's not like General Shein was available."

"All I have to say, Tim, is maybe he was lucky Shein was up in Tobolsk," Ivan said. "But it still means we have to figure out how to fight a modern war."

"Not necessarily. It's six hundred miles to Ufa. We'll probably be safely dead before anyone asks us what to do."

"General," a voice from back in the line yelled. "There's a steamboat coming up the river. What should we do?"

Ivan started laughing.

CHAPTER 3

On the Road

Goritsky Monastery
July 1636

Sofia Gorchakovna got off the steamboat and looked around. *Sister Sofia, that is*, she thought. And she was in the company of *Sister Elena*, Dimitri Cherakasky's widow. Elena was dealing not just with the prospect of being forced to take holy orders, but also the death of her husband.

They were escorted by a small contingent of *oprichniki* under the command of a seventeen-year-old lieutenant, Vasilii Golitsyn. The boy had been polite enough. Sofia looked at the stiff little snot with the wisps of beard and the silver dog head collar tab and said, "Remember. Tell your grandfather I said he is being foolish."

The boy didn't sigh, not quite. Instead, he waved Elena and Sofia to the carriage that would take them to the monastery. Convent, as the westerners would call it. Goritsky Monastery was halfway to Archangelsk from Moscow as the crow or dirigible flew, and considerably more than halfway as the steam boat floated. It was in the hinterlands and a good place to put inconvenient upper-class women of all sorts.

Sofia looked over at Elena. The woman had been taken from her home the day after her husband's death, shipped to the Dacha where Sofia had been picked up, then shipped by steamboat downriver to the Volga and then upriver to the monastery. Over a thousand miles and twelve days. The shock had worn off and all that was left was the fury. Fury at Dimitri for getting his fool self killed, fury at Sheremetev for killing him, fury at Mikhail Romanov for not staying in the hunting lodge, fury at just about everyone.

Vasilii Golitsyn had caught the brunt of that fury. There had been times that Sofia suspected that he was going to react with violence, but he hadn't.

Now Elena sniffed at him as she climbed into the carriage. It wasn't a long ride. They could see the walls of the monastery from the docks. Sofia wondered as she climbed into the carriage, *What is going to happen to me now?*

She looked at the monastery and next to it saw a wooden framework she recognized. It was a radio tower. Sofia remembered the chain of radio stations that stretched up to the Swedish territory in the Baltic had a link here. It was also a link in the chain of radio stations that went to the port of Archangelsk.

Several hours later, Sofia was seated in a private room. This was a prison in all but name, but it was a prison for the daughters of great houses, not for peasants. And there was always the possibility that the political winds would change and this year's prisoner would be next year's boss, so you didn't want them pissed at you.

Sofia and Elena had been treated with respect. And gotten the latest news. Czar Mikhail was in Ufa and had sent a message to the king of Sweden. They got that from the radio station in Swedish territory. Aside from that, the news was still very confused. Sofia decided that the rest could wait. She was tired.

Ufa
July 1636

The steamboats arrived late. Aside from a very small amount of gear on the *Czarina Evdokia*, Czar Mikhail's party had been having to work with whatever the locals had on hand. Five years after Bernie had brought plans for the Fresno scraper to Russia, they hadn't reached Ufa. There were no roads in Ufa. There were trails, gaps between buildings. And aside from Filip Pavlovich Tupikov, Bernie, and a couple of others who had arrived by way of airship, there was no one who knew how to make a scraper or even how to use one. Worse, Ufa had proven to have even less privacy than the dirigible. People had seen the *Czarina Evdokia* in the sky and headed for Ufa to see what was going on. Hunters and trappers, farmers and delegations, crowded every building in the town. And Bernie and Natasha were just too busy to go riding off in the country. Not that Natasha's guards would allow her to go off alone, even if there was time. *She might get et by a bar or somthin'*, Bernie told Filip. And then had to explain the reference.

"What took so long?" Bernie asked with frustration in his voice.

"We had a breakdown. And besides, with your damn Dodge we were overloaded," complained Maxim Andreevich. "It overstressed the engine."

"Oh, bull crap. Even I know more about steam than that. What broke?" For the next few minutes, as the two steamboats were tied up and the unloading began, Bernie and Maxim Andreevich argued companionably about steam engines and torque versus horsepower. Filip Pavlovich came down from the Ufa kremlin and started asking about equipment and personnel.

"General Tim insisted that he and the troops could march," Maxim Andreevich explained. "The techies at Bor had to have their hydrogen generators and their—" He stopped and waved his hands. "They wanted to bring the frigging curtains on their windows."

Bernie wasn't as upset by that as the steamship captain. They needed that gear.

Olga reached the docks in time to hear Bernie and Filip talking with this new man and tried to understand what she was seeing. There were bales and boxes, and iron and steel parts, copper tubes and even glass. It was a fortune in goods that simply could not be had here. Stanislav Ivanovich, her husband, was drinking less. He was still drinking, but it was more beer and less vodka, at least. And now there were all these new people with all this equipment and she didn't know where she was going to put them or all these things.

She looked over what was coming off the boats, and she started to notice something. She walked over to where the three men were still talking. "Did you bring anything useful?"

The three men looked at her.

"What do you mean?"

"Axes, saws, hammers, hand drills, looms, spindles, needles, pins? Platters, cups? *Food*?"

She got blank looks. "Crazy people!" she shouted. Then she turned and stalked away. She had to find Anya, someone with some sense.

Anya was in the tax warehouse, going over the records. On Czarina Evdokia's instructions—and against her better judgment—Olga had explained her methods of recording the furs and their quality to Anya and Anya had been translating the records into writing for the last several days.

"They didn't bring anything useful."

"What? Who?" Then Olga saw realization on Anya's face. "You mean on the steamboats?"

Olga nodded.

"It's all useful, but you may have a point about immediate utility. What do you need?"

"Everything. Axes, ham—"

Anya held up her hands. "Wait a minute." She turned to the table she had been working at, and gathered up a notebook, a pen, and a bottle of ink. "Come sit down and we will make a list."

Before Olga had gotten more than started Anya was asking, "Why do you need that? What's this for?" and Olga found herself explaining, "We're going to need food and housing for all these new people."

For the rest of the day Olga and Anya talked.

"We're going to have to send the riverboats after supplies," Anya told Princess Natasha and Czarina Evdokia.

"Is that safe?" asked the czarina.

"I don't know, but it's necessary. I have been worrying about it since I started on the books here and talking with Olga clarified things for me. There's not enough reserve, not nearly enough for the sort of influx of people we are expecting, much less hoping for. If we don't get more food and basic equipment, we are going to freeze to death this winter...if we don't starve first.

"And we especially don't have enough to rebuild Ufa as a modern city, the way the czar and Bernie want to."

On the road northwest of Moscow
July 1636

Elena Utkin was in need of some religious comfort, so she headed for Father Yulian's wagon. Only to notice that it was rocking. Just a bit, in that certain way. Furious, she pulled open the door. Only to find Izabella astride the priest and in such a state of undress that the pregnancy was visible, if barely. She gasped. "Izabella!"

"We're busy, Mama. Wait your turn," Izabella said.

With a shout of rage, Elena reached for her daughter, pulled her away from Yulian, and shoved her to the floor, slapping her face as she fell. Then she turned toward Yulian and slapped him as well. "You rotten bastard!"

"Now, Elena, you need to control yourself. This isn't the way a mother should treat her daughter. You're distraught. You need to calm down." Yulian reached for her.

Elena slapped him again. "Keep your hands off

me, you faithless peasant! And keep them off my daughter too!"

"You don't control me!" Izabella hollered, her hand holding her face where her mother had slapped her. "And you're the last one to be calling anyone faithless."

By now, the shouting had called the rest of the wagon train to the priest's wagon and there was a crowd displaying a mixture of emotions. Quite a bit of amusement, because Father Yulian's habits were more something not discussed than something not known. Especially in regard to his relationship with Elena and her daughter. There was even some jealousy showing on the part of some of the women. And there was a tiny bit of worry on Stefan's part.

Stefan was riding a borrowed horse, scouting the route through the lightly wooded plains to the north of Moscow. Once this had been forests, but now it was a mix of field, pasture, and woodland, much of it abandoned as the land wore out or the peasants to farm it became unavailable. Stefan didn't know this; he just saw the results. Peasant villages left to weather, fields left unplowed, feral goats, pigs, even sheep. The land had been overfarmed, worn out, then abandoned, and then slowly recovered as nature took it back. There were forests and fields interspersed and abandoned paths, where a village's produce had flowed to market before the village was abandoned. Stefan was on one of those. It was about six feet wide and twisty, but he thought they could run a wagon along it, if they were careful. Right up to here, where a four-inch-wide, twenty-foot-tall tree had decided that the middle of the road was the perfect place to grow. Stefan got down and examined the tree.

It was going to have to be chopped down but that was the least of it. Once it was chopped down, it was going to have to be chopped up, because the limbs were interwoven with the limbs of trees on either side of the road.

He remounted and rode around the tree and continued on. There might be more such blockages. As it happened, there weren't, and he eventually turned his horse back the way he had come.

"I need four men with axes to cut down a tree about three miles up the road, but after that it's clear to a crossroads and an abandoned village about five miles further."

"That would be old Geonsk," Yulian guessed.

Stefan shrugged. "Maybe. But no one has lived there in a long time and probably no one will see us." One good thing about the amount of forest they were passing through—unless someone was right on top of them, they were safe from observation. On the downside, things like the tree they were going to have to chop down to make the road passable and fresh wagon ruts meant that they would be easy to track.

Balakhna, a town on the Volga

Lieutenant Nikita Ivanovich Utkin sat at the table with the other lieutenants of his unit. He slapped down a broadsheet. "All the peasants in Russia are running mad."

"Not all of them," corrected Alexander Nikolayevich Volkov judiciously, examining the broadsheet. "No more than a third, I would guess."

"You can laugh. You have that new farming equipment. You don't need serfs."

"That's not entirely true. My family doesn't need *as many* serfs to farm a given amount of land, but we still need serfs."

"So you don't care if half your serfs run off? It's just fewer mouths to feed."

"Not at all, my friend. I am just of a more philosophical bent. We'll get them back, at least most of them. That's what we're here for, after all. To catch the runaways before they get to—" Alexander paused, then continued, leaving off "czar." "—Mikhail." It was a touchy subject, whether Mikhail was actually still the czar.

"Maybe. But I'm worried about Ruzuka. Mother and Izabella are there all alone. And you know that the Poles and the Swedes are going to take advantage of this."

"Maybe not. They seem fully occupied with killing each other for the moment," Pavel put in.

"And since when has a magnate of Lithuania cared about the rest of the PLC? Ruzuka is only two hundred thirty miles from Smolensk," Nikita said.

"That's a long way through Russian forests. Don't get yourself in an uproar," Pavel said.

"And what about the runaways? You know they turn into Cossacks the moment they get out of sight of the village they are tied to. Bandits and murderers, that's all a peasant is. Only restrained by the whip and the noose," Nikita said.

"That's what we're here for," Alexander repeated. He didn't mind twitting Nikita Ivanovich, but he didn't want to say anything that would get him or his family in trouble with the Sheremetev faction. Not since it had become clear that they were coming out on top in the power struggle that had happened after Czar Mikhail had sent his radio message. They were in enough trouble for being what Bernie Zeppi called "early adopters." They had two family members actually at the Dacha and they had been there for the last three years.

It had only been ten days since the czar had captured the airship, and no one knew which side most of the service nobility were going to come down on. In the meantime, the Sheremetev faction—which included the regiment's colonel and Nikita Ivanovich—had been ordered to turn back the escaping serfs.

So far it was mostly individuals or ad hoc groups. A single serf or a family would run. There was no practical way to drag them individually back to the farms they were supposed to be working. If they were to try, the regiment would be turned into individual soldiers, each escorting an individual serf back home. Instead, they were to terrorize them and run them back.

Alexander wasn't sure it would work. He wasn't even totally sure he wanted it to, because Alexander wasn't yet sure where *he* was going to come down.

On the road northeast of Moscow
July 1636

"She's not going to cooperate," Vera said flatly, some days after the incident at Father Yulian's wagon.

Stefan lifted an eyebrow. "Did you expect her to?"

"Everyone knows what Father Yulian is," Vera said. "Expecting him to keep it in his cassock is like expecting sunshine at midnight." She sighed. "Granted, the fact that Elena caught him with Izabella rather than one of the village women was probably upsetting, but really...after all, Izabella was willing enough to share."

Stefan just shook his head. The whole situation was both funny and tragic. But mostly, it was dangerous for the villagers. "We need her. We need her to stand out in front and tell people that we are where we're supposed to be."

"We can use Izabella," Vera insisted, but Stefan heard the doubt in her voice.

"Perhaps. But you know it would be better with Elena. Talk to her again, would you?"

"I told you, she's not going to cooperate." But at his look, she nodded. "It won't work, but I'll talk to her again."

Three days later, they arrived at a small village that had gotten considerably smaller since the stories about Czar Mikhail. "It's been horrible, miss," the village headman said, wringing his hat. "Half the farmers have run off and I don't know how we are going to get the harvest in."

It probably won't matter, Izabella thought. The village, Rogozhi, was part of the pay of the Slavenitsky family, who were *deti boyars*, clients of the Gorchakovs. So there was a good chance there wasn't going to be anyone to collect the rents for a while. Then she had second thoughts. If this was happening all over, there were going to be a lot of crops not harvested. And that meant famine. So far, they had done all right, between hunting, gathering, and trading. They had enough to eat, but she didn't have any idea what was going to happen when they got to the east. She commiserated with the headman and got permission for them to camp next to the village for the night. Her mother was in their wagon, with Vera watching her. Rogozhi was a little village that had moved a couple of times and merged with another village called Bogorodsk, and then separated again. Now there was argument about which village got which name. Nothing unusual. There were a lot of villages, and they lived and died and were reborn and renamed all the time.

They left early the next morning, and reached the Klyazma River that evening. Across the river was the village of Vokhna.

Leaving the wagons and most of the people in the forest, Stefan and Father Yulian rode up to the river to find out about the availability of boats, because it would do them no good to decide to use them if they couldn't find any. They rode up to the edge of the river and waved to get attention. It wasn't much of a river, more a creek, and looking over it, there were clumps of grass in the creek. After looking around a bit, they pulled up their feet and rode across the creek, which came almost to the bellies of the little Russian steppe ponies they were riding.

"What brings you here?" asked a man in a cassock, as they rode up the opposite bank.

"We're looking for boats to travel downriver," Father Yulian said forthrightly.

"We don't have any for sale, I'm afraid. We do a little fishing and a shallow draft boat can get you to the next village sometimes, but you're going to have to go downriver a good distance before you can travel on it."

They had dinner in the village and got the news, then went back across the river and rejoined the wagon train.

✧   ✧   ✧

"Good morning." Stefan snuggled closer to Vera and moved a hand around to cup a breast. She snuggled closer.

"Hello in the wagons," came a voice that Stefan didn't recognize.

"You'd better find out what that's about," Vera told him and Stefan groaned.

Stefan tried to snuggle up again and Vera elbowed him in the ribs. It didn't hurt. Stefan was a big man and Vera was not a big woman, but it did make it clear that the opportunity was gone.

Still complaining, Stefan crawled out of the bed built into the wagon, and went to see what was going on. There was, about twenty yards from their camp, a farm wagon piled with boxes and barrels and two men, four women, and five children.

Father Yulian was out of his wagon too, and Elena Utkin was peeking out the curtained window of the wagon she shared with her daughter.

"What can we do for you?" Father Yulian asked as more people came out to look at the strangers. "Don't I recognize you from Rogozhi?"

One of the men nodded. "I'm Maxim Ivanovich, and this is my wife, Anna. We want to come with you."

"Is that legal?" Father Yulian asked, not sounding condemning, just curious.

"Czar Mikhail's proclamation says it is. Besides, our village is *pomestie* for the Slavenitsky family and Colonel Nikita Slavenitsky is the commander of the airship. So we are almost obligated to go."

Stefan almost wanted to smile, even if these people had ruined his morning.

"You should be ashamed!" Elena Utkin came storming out of her wagon. "You are tied to the land, not to Nikita Slavenitsky, and you know it. You get back to your village before I have you whipped."

Their guests were starting to look frightened.

"Oh, Mother, shut up!" Izabella came into the center of the camp, and Stefan didn't see which wagon she was coming from. By now, Vera was out of the wagon and the children were peeking out of the windows. In fact, just about everyone in camp was watching. "You know perfectly well that Papa will kill you if he catches us. We're all heading for Ufa and it's pretty clear that— Ah, what was your name again?"

"Maxim, lady," said the man differentially. Running or not, they weren't prepared to beard a noble in her lair.

"Maxim and his family and, who are you?" She looked at the others.

"I'm Oleg." He pointed at one of the women. "This is my wife, Eva, and her sisters, Klara and Kseniya."

"Maxim, Oleg and their families want to go with us. And I for one think that if they can pull their own wagon they should be allowed to."

That set the pattern. They were joined by at least one or two people at every village they had contact with. People who hadn't been willing to run on their own, but wanted to go if they had some sort of protection.

The wagon train followed the river down a few miles before crossing it and heading east again. None of them knew the way to Ufa in any detail, so it was a case of scouting each day and looking for paths that could take the wagons.

Goritsky Monastery
July 1636

Sofia Gorchakovna waved at Marta. Marta had been
her maid for years and was—or had been—a serf of
the Gorchakov family. Between Natasha and Czar
Mikhail, she was now free. But she was in her fifties
and was comfortable with Sofia. She made her own
way to the monastery to take up her duties, and she
was now being paid. Marta came over with the tea
service.

"What does Lev tell you?"

Marta looked over at Sister Elena and hesitated,
but at Sofia's nod she spoke quietly, giving Sofia a
rundown of the recent events in Russia. Lev was a
Dacha-trained radioman, and he had strong sympathies
for the Gorchakov clan. That wasn't at all uncommon.
Almost all of the radiotelegraph operators had been
trained at the Dacha and most of them had sympathies for the clan. That had come as something of
a boon to the ladies of Goritsky Monastery. It gave
them better access to the radio.

Sofia listened to the reports and watched Elena
nodding at the interesting bits.

After dinner, Elena went back to her room. She
then sent a note to Ludmila, who had ended up
here after a rather torrid affair with a groundskeeper
offended her husband. The groundskeeper, with her
help, had escaped execution and run off to be a Cossack. Ludmila was a smart woman with a good grasp

of the politics of Russia and little respect for them. A network was developing here in the monastery, not exactly secret, but certainly private. Women who knew Russian politics analyzing the events of the day, and trying to make predictions about what it all meant.

CHAPTER 4

𝕽𝖆𝖎𝖉

On the road again

Pavel trudged along next to his big sister Irina. Pavel was four and a half and very proud to be trusted to help pull the two-wheeled cart with Irina, who was seven. They pulled the cart every day for an hour or so at a time, then Mama would take over while they rested. Then they would pull some more. This was their third time pulling the wagon today. And though Pavel was proud to be helping, it was boring.

Suddenly Czar barked. Pavel looked around and tried to see what had the big dog upset.

"Pavel!" Irina complained. "Watch what you're doing."

Pavel turned his attention back to the cart, but answered, "What's wrong with Czar Mikhail? He's pulling a cart too."

"Not as big as ours is." The cart he and Irina were pulling was just under three feet wide at the wheels and by now, twenty days after they left Ruzuka, they were quite good at pulling it. It was heavy, though. There were just over three hundred pounds of household goods on the cart. "How should I know what has the stupid dog up—" Irina stopped speaking as screaming men came out of the woods.

Pavel looked around, trying to figure out what was going on. Had the colonel's men caught them? No. These men didn't look like the soldiers. They were scruffy and though they had knives, and some of them had guns, they weren't the new guns that the colonel was so proud of. Pavel stopped to look and Irina kept walking and that jerked Pavel off balance. He fell, and that made Irina fall.

The men came running out and got up to the wagons.

Irina screamed, "Mommie!" and tried to get up. Pavel was too busy trying to get himself straightened out to scream, but he was whimpering a little. He couldn't help it, even if he was four.

One of the men came up to the cart and started pulling stuff out.

Irina started yelling at him. The man was in trouble now, and he backed away.

Then one of the other men laughed at him. "What's the matter? You afraid of a kid?"

The first man got all red. Then he raised his knife and stabbed Irina. She screamed and fell.

That pulled Pavel down again. Irina was bleeding all over him and screaming.

The other man stepped back and the one with the bloody knife waved it at him and said something, but Pavel was never sure what it was.

Then everyone was running around. Pavel didn't know what else to do, so he cried.

✧   ✧   ✧

Dominika tried to get out of the wagon, but it was hard and she was scared. Then the knife moved. She scrambled out of the wagon and ran to the little cart that the children pulled...and was just in time to watch her little girl die. Dominika wanted to scream. She wanted to run away, she wanted to kill the arrogant little snot who had stabbed her baby girl for no other reason than to prove he could. But she had a little boy who was still alive. She struggled with the harness and tried to get little Pavel loose from the cart. As she did, disjointed thoughts raced through her mind.

The village of Ruzuka had not been large. It had had eight families of an average of eight people per family. The smith, Stefan, who had planned to run and been so vital to the preparations, along with his wife, Vera and their two children were a small family, generally. Vera's widowed sister lived with them. That wasn't unusual. Other families often had additional family members doing the same. The total when they started out was sixty-seven people, including Elena, Izabella, and their servants. Since Rogozhi, they had picked up a few more people every couple of days. Which made this all make even less sense. This was a really big target for a group of mostly poorly armed raiders to take on.

Unfortunately, several of the men were out scouting for routes that would let them travel through Russia without running into the boyars' sons and service nobility who were more of a threat. Maybe the few men in the train had made them think it would be easy meat. That would fit with the sort who would stab a little girl who was just trying to protect her family's goods.

She pulled Pavel up in her arms and looked around.

Now the remaining men and the women were on the attack. They might not be good fighters, her neighbors, but Irina had been murdered. Clearly, rage had washed their fear away.

Dominika saw the arrow fly into the back of the little bastard who had stabbed Irina, and then she saw Vera running by with a hammer of some sort.

Vera, two wagons back from them, saw the whole thing. She squirmed into her wagon, looking for something to fight with. The guns were all out with the scouts, but she found Stefan's hammers. She grabbed one of the smaller ones and one that had something of a point on the back side. Stefan used it to split wood into boards. She grabbed it up and went out the back of the wagon, then she turned and ran toward the murdering bastard who had killed little Irina.

She was a little late. One of the men from a wagon ahead had a bow. He had gotten it and strung it. The boy was dead when she got there, and the rest of the raiders were running. They had grabbed some stuff and several of the small person-pulled carts, injured two more people, killed Czar Mikhail, the dog that was pulling a small wagon, and a pony. Then they ran back into the woods.

Camped off the road that night

"We'll never find them," Stefan said looking into the fire. "We don't know this forest. They do."

"How could this have happened?" Dominika asked. She was sitting on a trunk, holding Pavel in her lap.

"We worried about the nobles and soldiers, not about being attacked by our own people," Stefan said.

"We knew better," Father Yulian added, ". . . or we should have."

"We should have kept a watch," Stefan said, "and the next place we stop, we need to make some sort of weapons. We have those three chamber-loading AKs that the colonel bought, and I can probably make extra chambers for them."

"That will take time," Father Yulian said. "We need to keep moving while the confusion lasts. You know that Sheremetev will try to stop us. He has to. All the land in the world is worthless without people to work it."

"Well, we have to do *something* about making sure this doesn't happen again. So what do you suggest?"

"I don't know. Perhaps we can find an abandoned village and stop for a few days. What can you do in a few days?"

"Not much. I have some dies that might be useful, but the drop hammer itself was way too big to carry. It would take a couple of weeks to build a new one and that means I'm back to doing it the old-fashioned way. Which I *can* do, but it takes a lot of time to make each item. Worse, I don't have any iron and I don't know where to find ore around here." There was a place near the village where Stefan had been able to gather bog iron for his smithy and that had worked well enough for most of his needs for the village. For the factory, the factory owner had provided the iron, apparently buying it and having it carted in from the river. Here, even if they found a village with a semi-intact smithy in it, he had no way of knowing where the local smith had gotten his ore to make iron. "We would have to buy iron and, in that case, why not just buy guns?"

Father Yulian considered. "Find us a village and I'll talk to the priest, see if we can buy some guns or at least some swords."

Stefan snorted a laugh. "Swords! What use would we have for a sword? Find us axes if you can't find us guns. At least we know how to handle them."

Finding a village didn't prove particularly difficult. Gorki was on the Klyazma River, which was just a creek at this point, but it helped with the gardens. The village had a dozen households, not including the village priest and a summer house of the local nobility who were, at the moment, in Moscow. Or perhaps . . . nowhere. They had been associated with the Cherakasky family, who had come out on the bottom in the recent power struggle, so they might well be dead. If so, the village was at least potentially in a great deal of trouble, because they were likely to end up owned by the Sheremetev family. And the Sheremetev family was not known for the gentleness with which they treated their serfs.

"We were attacked by some raiders yesterday, and madame has decided we need guns," Father Yulian said, once they were seated with tea.

"You won't find them here, I'm afraid. We've had over a dozen young men and two families run off, and the only thing keeping the young women here is knowing how dangerous it is for a woman alone in the forest."

"What does that have to do with guns?"

"What we have, we need. And it's not like we had many to begin with."

"What's the news?"

"Sheremetev has announced that Czar Mikhail has been enspelled by Bernie Zeppi, who is a demon, and the new patriarch has confirmed it. But the new patriarch is in Sheremetev's pocket and everyone knows it. Most of the monasteries have refused to acknowledge him. There are rumors that the Poles or the Swedes are getting ready to attack, but I don't believe them."

Father Yulian sighed at the inequities of the world and got back to business. "We have a good blacksmith. If we could get some iron...?"

"What do you have to trade?"

And they were off. The wagon train wasn't overly well-supplied, but they had done some hunting enroute, so they had some meat. And there was the pony that the raiders had killed. On the other hand, they were in the market for a new pony.

Which, after some serious bargaining, they managed to buy. The local village would send a message to Moscow telling of a pony dying in a raid on the village. Elena's jewelry box would be a bit lighter. The villagers were in no hurry to take the paper rubles. The Sheremetev faction was using them to pay its debts off, but not taking them when they sold something. In the days since the czar's flight, the paper rubles were losing value all over Russia.

Izabella looked at her mother, who was sitting in the wagon staring off into space. At Gorki she hadn't actually done anything to cause a problem, but she hadn't been very helpful, either. And she was sitting there, with her hair undone, and not wearing any makeup. Izabella didn't think she had ever seen her mother without makeup in the middle of the day before she had caught Izabella and Yulian in the wagon. She shook her head. "Mama, you have to snap out of this. You were no help in Gorki and if you keep this up, they are going to dump you on the side of the road and let the bandits have you."

"What difference does it make? They could do no more to me than you have already done, you little strumpet."

Izabella was tempted to leave her mother on the side of the road herself. Not that the others had actually threatened that, though there had been some grumbling. Everyone worked, even Izabella. And Mama's job was to provide them with a reason for being on the road. She wasn't doing it. "Did you ever listen to what Father Yulian said?"

"He said he loved me!"

"He said he loved us all. That it was our duty to love one another, and that the way to reach God was not to suppress our desires, but to sate them so that they wouldn't interfere. Don't try to pray when you're hungry or when you're horny. It gets in the way of caring for God and your fellow men. That's what he said."

That at least got Elena's attention, in the form of a disgusted look.

"I know. I know. Yulian probably adopted that doctrine because that's where his dick was leading him. But he never lied about what he was doing. And he never told you you were the only one, I bet."

"He implied it."

"You wanted to hear it." Izabella shook her head. "Never mind. It doesn't matter now, anyway. These people are desperate, Mama. We've lost a child to bandits, and we're all risking our lives. And you have no right to endanger the rest, just because you're upset."

"After your betrayal, you think I owe you?"

"Yes! But never mind that. What about the rest? Stefan and Vera, Makar and Liliya, and the others? Especially the ones who have joined us on the road."

"They're serfs!"

"So what? If that means anything, it means you owe them more, not less."

Nothing was really settled, but Elena did start taking a little better care of herself.

On the Volga, approaching Kazan
July 1636

General Boris Timofeyevich Lebedev, known to his friends as Tim, looked out at his army and concluded that an army did not in fact march on its stomach. It slithered on its stomach like a snake. A particularly lazy snake. Not that what Tim commanded could within reason be called an army. Mob was closer. Aside from the core of troops that were Gorchakov retainers, Tim and Ivan Maslov had been picking up odds and sods since they left Bor after Czar Mikhail escaped.

"They aren't that bad," Ivan, the baker's son, said.

"Yes," Tim said, "they are, Captain."

Ivan scratched his scraggly red beard in clear consideration. "Yes," he conceded, "they are. But they aren't as bad as they were."

Tim nodded. It was true. The Gorchakov retainers were good troops, well trained, well supplied, and disciplined. To an extent that was rubbing off on the odds and sods. Especially the small contingent from Bor that had come with Ivan. They were soldiers, at least, though a large number of them were more technician than soldier. They were the people who had built the dirigible, *Czarina Evdokia*, some of them, anyway. Those who had declared for Czar Mikhail.

"We should have burned the dirigible works at Bor," Marat Davidovich said again.

"We couldn't. We would have lost half the soldiers who declared for Czar Mikhail and most of the techs. They may be loyal to Czar Mikhail, but they love the airships."

Tim and Ivan watched as a family passed them on the road, walking beside a wagon. It was the family of a *Streltzi* from Nizhny Novgorod. After the battle, Tim's force had gained a good chunk of the garrison, partly out of fear of Sheremetev's response to their defeat. The *Streltzi*, a man of about forty, tipped his cap as he went by. Tim nodded encouragement. The *Streltzi* of Nizhny Novgorod had brought their families because it wasn't safe to leave them, and the other groups they had picked up on the road had done the same. The camp followers outnumbered the camp by a considerable margin.

On a good day they would make five miles. On a bad day, two...or none. Tim wondered what was happening with Czar Mikhail.

Ufa
July 1636

Bernie looked down at the mirrored surface of the theodolite. It was made in the Dacha and had come on the first of the steamboats to arrive. It didn't look all that much like an up-time theodolite, but it worked well. Bernie adjusted a knob till the poles became a single pole and looked at the number. Then he waved to the trapper they had recruited to hold the poles for them.

Bernie and Filip Pavlovich were outside the Ufa kremlin, surveying to find the right place to put the dirigible hangar.

"Steamboat coming!"

Bernie and Filip turned as one and looked upriver to see the smoke and steam.

They made their way down toward the docks and were in time to see the steambarge tying up. "Look! That's Ivan Borisovich," Filip said.

They trotted the rest of the way to the docks. "Are any more coming?" Bernie shouted.

"I don't know." Ivan Borisovich shook his head. "Things were still very confused when we left the Dacha and we were attacked by a steamboat out of Murom. Even if others left, I don't know if they will make it."

"Did you lose anyone?" Filip shouted.

"No. We had a couple of wounded, but Vitaly Alexeev managed to save them."

Ufa was crowded, but that was because Ufa was small. There had been steamboats from Murom following their two and, at Olga's insistence, most of them had been sent back to the Volga and south to buy supplies. But they had left their passengers, craftsmen and workers from the factories in Murom. Not all of the people from Murom, not even a very large percentage. But around five hundred, when you included families. There had also been individuals and small groups walking into Ufa, but even with the boats from Murom it had been a trickle, not a flood, so this wasn't good news. They needed workers to build the new Ufa and they, more importantly, needed skilled workers and the sort of experts that only existed in the Dacha. Men and women who knew how to make and use the modern equipment. They had only managed to get two Fresno scrapers built.

"I'm surprised that Sheremetev has managed to get a force in place to try and stop you at Murom," Bernie said as Ivan Borisovich came down the gangplank with several other men and women from the Dacha. Most of them were Natasha's former serfs, but there were a few professionals like Vitaly Alexeev, as well.

"The service nobility were not happy with Czar Mikhail's emancipation of the serfs," Vitaly Alexeev said.

"What about the serfs?" Filip asked.

"We didn't see much, but it's only been a couple of weeks since the radio messages went out," Ivan Borisovich said. "And for most of that time we were on the river, so I don't know what's happening away from that. Besides, I'm not sure it was Sheremetev's people, at least not exactly. They're siding with him, but I think they were acting on their own. I don't know. Maybe they called him on the radio for instructions or maybe he called them. But Murom was pretty much in ashes as we went by. From the radio telegraph traffic we picked up, we figure that there was heavy rioting after you guys left."

"We heard about the riots from the people who followed us," Bernie said.

"I'm guessing the attack on us was at least partly

in response to that. Bor and Nizhny Novgorod paid us no attention. Same with Kazan. We didn't stop and they didn't try to stop us."

"That could be just because they didn't know where we were from," Vitaly Alexeev said. "Or because the river was pretty wide around there."

"So you don't know what's going on?"

"Not really. Where is the dirigible?" Ivan Borisovich asked.

"Scouting east right now." Bernie waved them up the docks. "Until we get a hangar built, it's going to be safer in operation than on the ground. So Nick is looking for a valley that is deep enough to be out of the wind. Then they are going to try and put a hangar there. Mikhail wants to put a hangar here, but that is at least partly because he wants to build more dirigibles."

"Can you afford that?" Ivan asked as they approached the end of the docks. Stevedores were unloading the barge from the Dacha. Anya had shown up and waved at them as she passed with Olga Petrovichna in her wake. Anya would get the craftspeople from the Dacha situated.

"No. But you can tell him that," Bernie said.

"I know we can't afford it," Mikhail said to Stanislav Ivanovich. "But we can afford to make a start on it, and we will eventually be able to pay for it." Then the czar of Russia smiled. It was a friendly, open smile, not nervous or concerned. "Either that or we'll all be dead. And they can't collect from a bunch of corpses."

Stanislav looked at Czar Mikhail and wondered what had happened to the famously timid czar. He wondered if perhaps Bernie Zeppi had truly cast a spell on him. Everyone agreed that the up-timer from the magical city of Grantville was a puissant mage or a witch from the magical town. And who, seeing the mighty dirigible *Czarina Evdokia*, could doubt the magic? Or, having met the real Czarina Evdokia, doubt that the magic had an effect on people? The czarina seemed to embody the power and majesty of the dirigible in her person. Frankly, she scared him. It never occurred to Stanislav even to consider the possibility that the czar and czarina were the way they were because everything they had was already in the pot and any future risks were meaningless. It didn't matter, though. Stanislav was not going to argue with either of them. "Whatever you say, Czar Mikhail."

The czar pointed to a place on the sandtable that would be about a mile from the Ufa kremlin. "We will put it there, and dig a channel up to the entrance so that we can use the steamboats for transshipment."

It was insane. These were projects that would take thousands of people supported by tens of thousands. More even. Hundreds of thousands. Ufa's entire population before the dirigible arrived was eleven hundred forty-three people. Half of them were farmers who worked in nearby fields. There were maybe another thousand hunters or trappers who spent a few weeks a year here, selling their furs and drinking the proceeds. The steamboats had added six hundred more people and Olga wasn't sure how they were going to find the food for even that many extra mouths.

They had set up a radio here in Ufa, but it wasn't close enough to contact any place but a riverboat that had a radio and was pretty close. Stanislav wondered how the rest of the world was responding to this.

CHAPTER 5

News from Home

Russia House, Grantville
July 1636

Fedor Ivanovich Trotsky handed over the bundle. It was from Moscow, and the news from there had been chaotic, at best, for the past week and more.

"Is it as crazy as the rumors?" Vladimir Gorchakov asked.

"The messages to me were, Your Highness." Fedor Ivanovich had been in Magdeburg to meet the message boat. Vladimir had sent him there as soon as the first rumors began filtering over the USE radio-telegraph system. "Boris Ivanovich Petrov had nothing but the first reports when he prepared the messages. He sent one to his son in Magdeburg, one to me, and one to you. I suspect that they all say basically the same thing."

Vladimir doubted that. He was pretty sure that Boris had sent his sons additional information and instructions. But he didn't correct Fedor Ivanovich. Instead, he took the packet of letters to his desk and sat down to read.

Two hours later, he was still confused. But it was now more a question of why than what. He was also cursing himself for ever having sent Cass Lowry to Moscow. He should have sent the car by itself.

He got up and called in his staff, and his wife Brandy. Especially Brandy. He had come to rely on her advice even before he married the up-timer girl. And now that he and all the Russians he brought to the USE were facing their own political Ring of Fire, cutting them off from all they knew and depended on, her advice would be all the more important.

Iosif Borisovich Petrov brought his own letters to the meeting. He was nineteen, a squat, solidly built young man whose placid, even bovine, expression hid a solid and surprisingly creative brain. For the past year and more, he had been coordinating the information from the Dacha and was responsible for several industrial patents based on work done there.

"Father says I should stay here for now," Iosif said placidly. "He doesn't exactly think that this will blow over, but he does want me and Viktor out of the line of fire for now." He placed a sheet of paper face down on the table and passed it over to Vladimir.

Vladimir took a quick look and nodded. The sheet said what Iosif just said, but it also instructed him to change to the third code set and to arrange a new pad to be sent to Moscow. Vladimir put the sheet back on the table, still face down, and passed it back.

"I never should have . . ." That was as far as Vladimir got before Brandy interrupted.

"Don't be silly. It wasn't Cass. It was Sheremetev, and you had no say in putting *him* in Russia. All that bastard Lowry did was bring things to a head, and get shot for it." Brandy paused a moment then continued. "I'll need to tell his dad, and we'll need to write to his brother. There are a couple of the guys who were on the football team with him that we'll need to talk to. I don't want this to turn into a feud, and it's going to get out that he got himself shot while trying to attack your sister."

"I will be willing to pay reparations within reason," Vladimir said, "but we will not take the blame for what happened. Not me, you, or Russia. From what we know so far, his killing was a fully justified act."

"That is, I think, a minor issue compared to the financial situation this puts us in and the political ramifications," Iosif Borisovich said. "Father would prefer it if we were to keep our relations with Moscow as cordial as we can manage."

"In other words we should let Sheremetev screw us with our pants on," Brandy Bates said. Sometimes, in moments of stress, her habits from Club 250 and similar places came out. It was rather less upsetting to the down-timers, who had little difficulty with profanity but were deeply uncomfortable with taking the Lord's name in vain.

"Well, we should at least let him think we will," offered Iosif, placatingly.

"Frankly, at this point I'm more concerned about Ron Stone than I am about Sheremetev. Ron had every expectation that we would be getting supplies from Russia eventually. Now it looks like that's not going to happen. And totally aside from the fact that Sheremetev is in Russia and can't hurt us nearly as much as the Lothlorien Farbenwerke could if they

wanted to, Ron has dealt fairly with us and we have
an obligation to deal fairly with him."

"You're going to have to go have a talk with him,"
Brandy said, "and see what we can work out."

Vladimir sighed. That would mean another trip to
Hesse-Kassel. But there wasn't the same rush, this
time, so he wouldn't need to pay a small fortune to
the airship company. Even on horseback, Kassel could
be reached from Grantville in a few days, at least in
mid-summer.

Iosif left, and Vladimir started reading the personal
letter from Natasha. All the packets of letters had
arrived on the same ship from Nyen. The rumors
had come from the sailors of that ship talking before
the letters could make their way upriver. They had
received Boris' version of events at the same time
they received Natasha's and Czar Mikhail's. Suddenly,
Vladimir stopped reading. *"Bernie Zeppi?"*

"What about Bernie?" Brandy asked. She had been
reading a long letter from Czarina Evdokia.

"Natasha wants to marry him!"

"Bernie?" Brandy shook her head. "Well, from all
reports, he's changed a lot. He's probably not the same
failed football jerk I remember from before the Ring
of Fire. After all, look at me."

"Yes, perhaps. But the political consequences . . .
Bernie's a peasant, even if he is an up-timer."

"You do remember I used to be a barmaid, right?"
Brandy's voice carried a chill.

"That's different. You're a woman."

Brandy blinked. For the moment, her anger was
drowned in confusion. Why on Earth would it be

worse if a princess married a peasant than if a prince did? It made no sense.

That slight pause gave Prince Vladimir time to realize that his foot was lodged in his mouth with the leg poised to follow it down his throat unless he started extracting right now. "I'm just concerned about the political consequences."

"What political consequences? Czar Mikhail is in Ufa, which is so far east that I had never heard of it. And Sheremetev is probably raising an army right now to go fetch him back, dead or alive. And you're worrying over the political consequences of your sister marrying a peasant?"

"It could affect how some of the other great houses respond.... Besides, it's Bernie Zeppi we're talking about. I don't think that I ever remember seeing him when he didn't have at least a light buzz on."

That stopped Brandy again. Because after the Ring of Fire and the battle of the Crapper, Bernie had spent most of the rest of the time before he went off to Moscow drunk.

"I remember. But he changed after he got to Moscow. You know that. Especially after he ran into the annual typhoid outbreak and saw all those people die."

"Maybe, but he'd have to have changed a lot."

"Well, it's not your choice. Or it shouldn't be. It's up to Natasha."

Vladimir wasn't convinced but wisely kept his mouth shut and for now, at least, Brandy let him. "So what happens now? About Russia, I mean."

That was a good question. Within a few months of his arrival in Grantville back in 1631, Vladimir Petrovich Gorchakov had realized that Russia had to change. But he had imagined that change as a gradual thing, a tweak here, and then an adjustment there. He hadn't expected to see the end of serfdom in his lifetime. And at first he had assumed that the up-timer experts were right, that serfdom and a technological society couldn't coexist. That the machines themselves and the skills needed to run them would preclude it.

The problem was, it didn't seem to be working that way. Oh, here in the United States of Europe with the Committees of Correspondence ready to introduce guillotines to the back of the neck of any recidivist noble, the United Mine Workers of America and Europe unionizing—not just mine workers but steel workers and factory workers of all sorts—and the Fourth of July Party and the Rams giving them all political cover, it was working out that way. But not in Russia, or the Ottoman Empire. The same serfs who had been putting in fourteen hour days getting in the crop before the Ring of Fire were now putting in fourteen hours a day all winter in Russian factories. The Ottomans were using slaves in their factories, according to Boris Petrov, and it seemed to be working just fine.

That information had caused him to take a closer look at the assumptions about slavery that the up-timers held, and even in the up-timer history they just didn't hold up. In the up-time USA the antebellum south used slaves in factories and they worked just fine. The Germans used concentration camp inmates to make their V2 rockets. Again, it worked fine. So far as he could determine, anyway.

Vladimir thought he understood slavery and the attitudes that it engendered in a way that no up-timer could, because Vladimir owned, or had owned, hundreds of serfs. He understood the level of codependency, and institutional syndrome, in the serf communities. Masters came to believe that the serfs lacked the capability of living free of bondage because after being born and raised a serf or a slave, a lot of them did lack that ability. And, even more, had grown comfortable with their lot in life. Put to work in factories, they worked in factories. Some were treated well, some treated poorly, but, so far at least, the serfs and slaves in Russia were adapting to factory life as well or better than the free labor. Perhaps because they had no choice but to do so.

It was all quite depressing and had provided both Vladimir and Brandy with many sleepless nights, along with the goal of building an abolitionist movement in Russia. But now Czar Mikhail was in Ufa and trying to build a new structure of government for Russia. That was much of what Vladimir had received in his packet of letters from Ufa. The question was: how do we design the constitution for a constitutional monarchy in Russia ... no ... longer ... how do we evolve one?

"I don't know. I know that Alexander Hamilton showed up at your constitutional convention with a draft constitution already made up, but didn't get most of what he wanted. And I have studied your three branch government system, both the up-time version and the USE constitution. But I don't think that approach will work for Russia. More importantly, I don't think it will garner the support needed to win the civil war that now seems inevitable in Russia."

"Why not?"

"Because we have to have the bureaus with us to

win," Vladimir said. "It wasn't true in Ivan the Terrible's time, but during the Time of Troubles, the bureaus were the only things holding the nation together. They gained a great deal of power, even if it was a sort of under-the-table type of power. The limitations on Czar Mikhail that were imposed when he was crowned made them even stronger. For Mikhail to do much of anything he had to get the approval of the duma and the *Zemsky Sobor*, but the bureaus could implement regulations on their own. They skirted the restriction and that gave them additional clout."

"Well, come on. It's not like we didn't have bureaucrats up-time or like we don't have them in the USE," Brandy said.

They had talked about this before, but Brandy hadn't lived there and didn't really understand. The term *Zemsky Sobor* translated as "assembly of the land." Representatives of Russia's different social classes could be summoned by the Czar's orders to discuss important political and economic issues. It could be considered the first Russian parliament—allowing for very constipated values of "parliament." It didn't really have any independent authority. The duma was a much smaller assembly of high-ranking noblemen, which had a lot more authority than the *Zemsky Sobor* but didn't effectively wield much power on a day-to-day basis. In practice, Russia was run by deals made between the bureaus and the bureaus weren't going to give that up.

"It's different," was all he could come up with. "They have a lot more power than they officially have, and no government that doesn't bring in the bureau men will survive."

Brandy shrugged, not so much in agreement as in acceptance. "So how do we bring them in?"

"I don't know."

"From what we heard before the escape, Sheremetev hadn't been treating the bureaus well. That has to help us, right?"

"Some, yes. But bureaucrats tend to like stability. I suspect that a lot will depend on what he does next."

Petrov House, Moscow

The servant took the sheets of typewritten paper. He didn't read the address because he couldn't read. The address read: "From Mariya Petrova, to Boris Petrov, Moscow."

Some hours later, when Boris Ivanovich Petrov got home, he could read the address. Inside the letter was a section in the family code. After he decoded it, it read:

> Boris, I received this from Sofia Gorchakovna.
>
> Dear Mariya, the ladies of Goritsky Monastery have been following events over the radio. Several messages have been sent and it is the consensus of the sisters that Archangelsk will attempt to revolt if Director-General Sheremetev gives them into the care of his cousin.

There followed a fairly detailed description of the politics of Archangelsk, who was being bribed by whom and who was getting a rake off from what shipments. Most especially, the realization that with the Swedes controlling access to the Baltic, they controlled all the trade from the rest of the world. It wasn't a new situation, but the fractures in Russia were being seen as an opportunity to break free, or at least get a better deal.

> *The consensus is that Sheremetev will be so busy with Mikhail that he will cut any deal he has to with Archangelsk in order to keep it from being a distraction,* the letter finished.

Then Mariya continued.

> *I have sent Sofia a pad for encoding messages to me. I think that it would be best if we use me as the conduit. That way messages from her will be chatty letters from one old woman to another, while the letters from me to you will be chatty letters from a wife to her husband.*

Boris smiled and nodded. The news about Archangelsk was important if it was true, but even more important was the news about the monastery. It would give him a whole section of analysts that no one would know about. Boris considered and wrote several other letters. He would send one off to a friend of his in Nizhny Novgorod and see if it could be put on a steamboat heading for Ufa. Ivan needed to know about this.

Moscow Kremlin
July 1636

Fedor Ivanovich Sheremetev looked up into the sky with rage and hate in his heart. There, above Moscow, very high, though it was impossible for him to tell just how high, was the dirigible *Czarina Evdokia*, floating above Moscow and raining pamphlets. Sheets of paper poison, encouraging rebellion and sedition in the name of the deposed and possessed Czar Mikhail. Safe in Ufa, Mikhail and his traitors were trying to return Russia to the Time of Troubles. For a brief instant, Sheremetev was ready to turn and order it fired upon. He might have done it, except that it would have just underscored his helplessness in the face of the airship.

It was a still day here on the ground, but there must be a light breeze to the southwest at the airship's height. The airship was pointing to the northeast and maintaining a position a bit northeast of Moscow. And the fluttering pamphlets were drifting down as a sparse snowfall covering the city. Finally, after several minutes of glaring, Sheremetev turned and went back into the building. Then he sent for Colonel Leontii Shuvalov.

"Director-General." Colonel Shuvalov bowed.

"Colonel, I want that beast out of the sky." Sheremetev still felt the rage.

The colonel nodded, a thoughtful look on his face. "I remember that Cass Lowry was always saying that balloons were useless for war in the up-time world because they were so easily brought down. Something about a 'fifty cal with tracer rounds and that's all she wrote.' A fifty cal is a type of gun and a tracer round is one that somehow burns on its track. While I can put some people on it at the Dacha, I doubt we can do a tracer round or even a fifty cal. But something that burns and can be flung or shot at it . . . that we should be able to do. Still, unless it comes down close to the ground, it will be a difficult target to hit."

"Fine, Colonel. You put someone on it and tell me who, but you will not be staying to oversee the work." Listening to Leontii's cold analysis had cooled Sheremetev's temper enough to let him start to think again. "I have another mission for you. Mikhail Romanov is the danger. The dirigible too, but from what you said it may be best attacked at its base in Ufa."

Leontii started to shake his head in demurral, but Sheremetev held up a hand. "I understand the politics perfectly well, Leontii." Mikhail had great personal popularity among the people of Russia and Sheremetev knew very well that his hold on the armies of Russia was less firm than his hold on the bureaus. And even that was none too secure. An army sent from Moscow to arrest Mikhail might change sides before it reached Ufa. "That's why I am sending you to contact the khanates in the east. I want you to bribe them to attack Ufa."

"Wouldn't the Cossacks be better? At least more dependable than the Tatar tribes?"

"Perhaps, and I will send trusted men to negotiate with them. But Mikhail Romanov is already in Ufa and I doubt we can get to Kazan before they do. That limits us to the Don Cossacks. I will see who I can recruit, but for the same reasons, it would be difficult to send an army to arrest Mikhail. Having it known that I hired mercenaries to arrest him could have dire consequences."

"What about General Shein?"

Sheremetev, for the first time that day, almost snorted a laugh. "Shein? He would turn his coat the moment he got the order. For all I know, he's already on his way to Ufa."

Leontii considered. "I doubt he's gotten the word yet. Or, if he has, it had to be recently."

Tobolsk, 517 miles northeast of Ufa
July 1636

General Artemi Vasilievich Izmailov stopped the courier rider's babble with a wave. "Not here, Lieutenant." Here was the steps of the main fort of the Tobolsk Kremlin, which was a very large and complex log cabin. "The news has waited at least a week while you rode here, and probably more." He turned and led the lieutenant inside. He had a certain amount of sympathy for the boy, who obviously had ridden hard. But discipline needed to be maintained. If the news was as urgent as the state of the courier rider made it seem, he doubted General Shein would want it bandied about the town without hearing about it first.

They reached his office, and Artemi finally received the pouch of messages. He waved the courier to a chair and started to read. By the time he had read the first sheet, he wanted to jump up and rush the news to General Shein, but the same thing he said to the courier applied to him. So he forced himself to stay seated till he had read through the entire set of messages. Finally, he looked up. "Do you know what's in these?"

"Yes, sir. It was all over the place after the riverboat got to Solikamsk. Governor Saltykov took a day and a half before he sent me."

Artemi snorted. He couldn't help it. Dimitri Mikhailovich Saltykov was, as Bernie Zeppi would say, crooked as a dog's hind leg and had hated Patriarch Filaret with a passion, so wasn't that fond of General Shein. Or Artemi, for that matter. But none of that was the reason for the delay. Dimitri had spent those two days trying to gauge the wind and choose a side. The Saltykov family was at least as corrupt as the Sheremetev family, but that didn't make them allies. Dimitri Saltykov would be trying to figure out who would offer the biggest bribe for his support. Artemi waved the courier to silence and went back to his reading.

By the time he had finished he knew which way the governor had jumped. He was going to support Sheremetev, at least to the extent of not letting General Shein through Solikamsk to join Czar Mikhail. He stared at the last sheets for a few moments, then looked up and said, "Go get yourself some food. I'll need to talk to the general about this."

General Izmailov went over the messages with General Shein. Despite his other accomplishments, Shein was not a good reader. He preferred to have reports read to him. That was one of Artemi's functions. When they had gone through the messages and the governor's orders, Shein looked at him. Then looked at the map. It was a combination map, based in part on maps from Grantville and in part on information collected in this time. Shein had a grand total of one Dacha-trained surveying team, and he had only gotten them on the promise that they would look for gold and silver deposits while doing their surveys.

"I don't think he can do it," General Shein said. "Never mind whether it's a good idea. I just don't see how Czar Mikhail can win."

"So we go to Sheremetev? Crawl on our bellies?" Artemi noted that his voice carried more resignation than defiance.

"I would if I thought it would work," Shein said, with even more resignation in his voice and not a little bitterness mixed in. "But Sheremetev wants my head. He has since I came back from Poland with the patriarch."

"He's afraid of you, General."

"Yes, which is worse," Shein said, looking at the map again. "Mikhail can't win and we can't make peace with Sheremetev. So what do we do?" General Shein's finger was tracing along the Tobol River as it made its way to the Irtysh and the Ob rivers, and finally to Ob Bay on the Arctic Sea. He looked back up and said, "Russia is coming apart. I see no way of keeping it together. And if we are to survive, that leaves us but one option."

"What, General? I don't see any options at all."

"We must take a piece of Rus and make our own nation. The rivers between Tobolsk and the Gulf of Ob . . . and the town of Mangazeya. It can be our gateway to Europe. The rivers go on south and east into northern China. We have the AKs and craftsmen who can make more, and more chambers as well.

Granted, we can't make percussion caps yet, but we might be able to learn."

"That would be trea..." Artemi let his voice trail off.

"You know, there is a story I heard from, of all people, Cass Lowry," General Shein said. "It seems that in the last days of the Ming Dynasty, there was a group of workers on the Great Wall who were walking to work. One of them looked to the others and said, 'Guys, what's the penalty for high treason?'

"Another workman said, 'Execution. You know that.'

"Then the first man asked, 'What's the penalty for being late to work?'

"Again the second man said, 'Execution.'

"The first man looked around at the rest of his work crew and said, 'Fellows, we're late for work.' So started the revolution that brought down the Ming Dynasty. Now, I'm pretty sure that Cass was full of shit in that story, as well as in most of the other things he said. But the ultimate point is still valid. We, Artemi, you and I, as well as many of our friends, face the penalty for treason already... and we aren't even late for work. I think we have a better chance on our own. I think our families will be better off if we declare independence. Not today, mind. First we need to appear good little lapdogs for a while. And we need to get our families, or as many of them as we can, out of Moscow, out of Sheremetev's grasp. But after we have done that, well, consider yourself late for work."

CHAPTER 6

The Noble Conundrum

Kassel, capital of Hesse-Kassel

"I was sorry to hear about the troubles in your country," Ron Stone said, coming around his desk to shake Vladimir's hand.

"Thank you, Herr Stone." Vladimir said. "Unfortunately, it means that it is unlikely I will be able to provide the products that we both hoped would become available again."

"Never mind that. What about your sister?"

"She's in Ufa with Czar Mikhail, Bernie Zeppi, and a court in exile. They have a dirigible, but it has very limited cargo capacity. And while they have a few of the experts from the Dacha, almost the entire industrial base that has been developing in Russia since the Ring of Fire fell into Director-General Sheremetev's hands. As well as most of the population. Not that I believe that many of the serfs want to be there."

"Any of them, surely?"

Vladimir shook his head. He didn't want to disagree with this man to whom he owed so much. But Ron had never dealt with a society that truly had slavery, or even serfdom as it was practiced in Russia or Poland. "There is a term Brandy's mother told me about people who have been incarcerated for long periods of time. 'Institutionalized.' Russian serfs have, for the most part, been serfs their whole lives, and their parents were serfs before them. They know no other life and the notion of freedom, of having to decide for themselves, is terrifying to them. That is not always the case, and is probably less common than I would have imagined before the Ring of Fire. But don't fool yourself. It is much more common than most of you up-timers believe."

Ron nodded, but the nod seemed to be dragged out of him. "Yes, you're probably right. But you do realize that makes the whole institution of serfdom even worse, don't you? If it's evil to put chains on someone's body, how much worse to put chains on their minds?"

"I don't disagree, Ron," Vladimir said, thinking *not after years in Grantville*. At the same time, he understood much better than Ron Stone ever would how good people raised to believe it could see serfdom as the natural order of the world. "And neither, it seems, does Czar Mikhail." Vladimir pulled out a sheet of paper. "This is a proclamation by Czar Mikhail. It's in Russian but it amounts to Russia's emancipation proclamation."

Ron looked at it for just a second and Vladimir passed over another sheet with the proclamation translated into Amideutsch. He didn't have a version in up-timer English. "I've already given copies of the Russian and Amideutsch to the *Daily News* and the *Grantville Times*. It will be all over Germany by tomorrow, and all over Europe in a week."

Ron had been reading the Amideutsch version while Vladimir was talking. "Isn't this a bit self-serving? They have to run away east to get their freedom?"

"Yes, it is," Vladimir acknowledged. "But it's no more self-serving than the up-time Lincoln's 'Emancipation Proclamation.' Probably less. And what about my sister? At least I am no longer faced with Jefferson's quandary, abhorring slavery and serfdom, but still having my own serfs. I no longer have any serfs."

Ron looked at him. "How do you feel about that, Vladimir? Honestly."

Vladimir found himself smiling. "Poorer. But pleased, actually. Our lives, our fortunes, our sacred honor. Natasha's life is certainly in danger, and the better part of our fortune is gone. Almost all of it in Russia, if the truth be told. But our sacred honor? That's doing just fine."

"Yes, Prince Vladimir Petrovich Gorchakov, your honor is intact. So let's see about keeping your sister alive . . . and perhaps even keeping you from ending up begging on the street."

"I don't see how. The Swedes control the Baltic ports, true enough. But Sheremetev controls the surrounding territory and he controls Archangelsk."

"Well, what doesn't he control?"

"You mean ports? I honestly don't know. . . . Wait. There is one. Or at least, there *was* one. Mangazeya. On the northern sea route, it was called. A trading city. It got very rich and trade through there was forbidden in 1619, if I remember properly."

"Any reason why the people of Mangazeya are going to have warm fuzzy feelings for Czar Mikhail?"

"Everyone knows that Mikhail had very little power

back then. His mother's relatives, the Saltykov family, had power until Mikhail's father got back from prison in Poland. Then it was Filaret who had the power. Mikhail is actually fairly popular. Probably everyone in Russia has heard that he cried when told he would be czar. I don't know the details. My father had some dealings with the merchants of Mangazeya, but he also had dealings with the people that wanted them shut down. Mostly because Mangazeya wasn't paying taxes, but also they were cutting into the trade of..."

"So you're saying that there is a route from some place that Czar Mikhail can control to Hamburg by sea?"

"I'm saying there might be. But if there is, it's only going to be good for a couple of months out of the year. And we won't be able to use it this year."

"Do you think your sister and the czar will be able to hold out for a year?"

Vladimir lost the last of his smile. "I want to think so, but I doubt it."

"Let me think about it. Meanwhile, see what you can come up with that we might be able to buy from your people." Ron Stone pointed at the sheet of paper that held the Emancipation Proclamation of Czar Mikhail. "I want to help. I really do. But there needs to be something profitable in it."

Nizhny Novgorod
July 1636

The steamboat *Danilov* was tied up at the dock and its paperwork said it was owned by a merchant from Samara. Which everyone in Nizhny Novgorod knew was nonsense. But it was nonsense that gave them cover, as the men on the boat sold furs and bought grain, cabbage, and beets.

A few hundred feet away, in a bar just off the docks, Petr Viktorovich sat with the first mate of the steamboat and bargained for a copy of the latest dispatches from the radio-telegraph network. Each radio station was equipped with a typewriter, and Petr was using his as a profitable sideline. Petr set down his wooden mug and tapped the leather bag on the table. "That's right. It's transcripts of everything that's gone through the station in the last week. Even the coded commercial stuff. Not that I have the keys for any of that."

"That's fine," said the first mate. "What do you want in exchange?" Then he took a drink of the potato beer.

"Twenty rubles."

The beer spewed across the table, and everyone in the bar looked around. Wiping his mouth on an already dirty sleeve, the first mate glared at the radio man. Who had the grace to look at least a little embarrassed. Twenty rubles was enough to buy out a serf's debt.

"Don't get excited. Make a counteroffer?"

"Two kopecks!"

So it went. The first mate ended up paying three rubles, and the sniveling little thief of a radioman insisted on real silver. No one was taking paper rubles since the czar ran to Ufa and the printing presses were left in Moscow. No one trusted paper money. That in itself was important news. Loaded with news and food, both of which they had paid too much for, the *Danilov* headed back to Ufa.

On the Volga River, between Bor and Cheboksary
July 1636

"Look over there," said the first mate.

"Well, if it isn't General Tim and his army," said the captain.

"Should we stop and say hello?"

"Frankly, I'd just as soon wave as we go by," the captain said. He was a forty-year-old who had been on the river since he was twelve, and didn't have much use for a teenaged general. But he was loyal to Czar Mikhail and to Princess Natasha so, somewhat disgustedly, he pulled over to the shallows close to the riverbank and used the engine to keep station on the small mob while the baker's boy, Ivan Maslov, rode out on a pretty fair horse.

"Is there any place nearby where you can dock, Captain?" asked the redheaded youth.

"What for?"

"We have some injured."

"We don't have room."

"Captain, I can see that you're loaded, but surely you can find a place to put four people so that they can get to Ufa and decent medical care."

The horse was walking along in the river, keeping pace with the slow-moving riverboat.

There was a cough from behind him and the captain looked around at his chief engineer, another of the youngsters who seemed to be taking over the world. But it was a reminder that even if he didn't say anything, Princess Natasha would hear about it. "Oh, very well. Up about half a mile, we can anchor in close and you can bring out your injured."

While they were stopped, Ivan got a chance to read most of the unencoded messages that the captain had bought. The army also managed to get a couple of wagon loads of beets.

After the riverboat was gone, Tim looked over at Ivan and said, "I think Czar Mikhail made a mistake. Four men injured in falls, no supplies worth mentioning, more camp followers than..."

"No, he didn't," Ivan said. "Look, General..."

"Call me Tim, for God's sake," General Boris Timofeyevich Lebedev said.

"No, General, I don't think I will," Ivan said. "I grant that you never learned to be a lieutenant all that well, and you've never been a captain or a colonel. But you were in the Kremlin studying to be a general for over two years, then you were a general's adjutant. It's true that for the last few months before this you were your cousin's keeper in Murom, but even there, with your cousin drunk most of the time, you basically ran the city guard."

Tim started to interrupt, but Ivan pushed on over him. "You don't know as much as Shein, but that's not all bad. A lot of what the old generals know is wrong, or at least outdated by the new weapons. Besides, you have me to advise you and I'm much smarter than you are."

That at least brought a smile to Tim's face.

"All right, Ivan. Let's see about getting this—" Tim looked around. "I have no words."

"Cluster fuck!" Ivan offered. "That's what Bernie Zeppi would call it."

"Fine. Let's get this cluster fuck moving."

Ufa
July 1636

"We have a steamboat in from Saratov," Olga said. "It's loaded with food stuffs, but they want assurances that the money will be good."

"That's an increasing complaint," Natasha added. "We have steamboats on the river and we can use them to access the products of the Volga River system as long as we can hold it, but we have to regularize the money supply."

"We know there is gold and silver in the Ural Mountains. We even have a decent idea where to look. We can give them gold if that's what they want, or at least we will be able to."

"For as long as we control the river," Bernie said, looking at the map.

"Can we hold Kazan?" asked Evdokia.

Mikhail listened as the discussion wound about him. All his life he had been a quiet person who was surrounded by powerful and forceful people. In a way, he still was. His quiet wife, out from under the protocols and threats of life in Moscow, was blooming into a forceful person. So were Natasha, Anya, Bernie, Filip, and even Olga, now that she had gotten a little used to the invasion by the imperial court of Russia.

"I'm not sure we could take it in the first place," said Natasha. "Much less hold it. Besides, it's on the

Volga, and that means Sheremetev would have to take it back."

Mikhail looked down at the map on the table as he continued to listen. Kazan was a city on the Volga, a major trading port about forty-five miles north of the confluence of the Volga and the Kama rivers and just about as far east as the Volga went before that confluence.

"All the more reason to take it and hold it, if we can. If we held it we would control the lower Volga, all the way to the Caspian Sea. If we can hold it through the harvest, we can get enough food up here to make it through the winter."

"I'm not saying it wouldn't be nice," Natasha said with some asperity. "I just don't see any way we can do it."

"Well, I think we should try," Evdokia insisted. "Mikhail, you're always talking about how that baker's boy is such a military genius. Surely he can work out some sort of defense of Kazan that will let us divert enough food to see us through the winter."

That was a serious problem. Mikhail looked out the window and saw a great deal of forest, but not much in the way of plowed fields. And if they were to build a manufacturing and political center here in Ufa, they would need food and raw materials. "Ivan is a bright young man and I am greatly impressed by Tim's decisiveness in difficult situations. Both because of what we saw in Murom and General Shein's private report to my father on the battle of Rzhev." Mikhail was referring to Tim's taking the initiative, even as little more than a military cadet, to order splat guns moved to attack the Poles on the flank. It had been a decisive move and one that had saved the day. But it had not been made public, because to do so would have been detrimental to good order and discipline in the Russian Army. An army that had little enough order and discipline to begin with. That report, along with the fact that he hadn't had anyone else to appoint at the time, had been a big reason that Mikhail had made Tim a general. "But in spite of Tim's decisiveness, there are only so many bricks you can make with no straw and darn little mud. I don't want to lose Tim by asking too much of him."

"Leave it up to Tim," Bernie suggested.

"You think he's up to it?" asked Filip Pavlovich Tupikov.

Bernie looked back at Filip, then turned to look at Mikhail. "Your Majesty, I think that if he's not up to it, we need to find it out now rather than later."

"That's hard, Bernie," said Anya.

"But he's right," Mikhail heard himself say. "I may have made a mistake promoting Tim so high so fast. And I admit that I did it simply because I had nothing else to give the boy we were leaving in Bor while we escaped in the dirigible."

"He knew that, Your Majesty," said Anya. "He understood."

"He also survived. At least, he has so far. And that makes his rank much more real. It's not something we can ignore."

"Why not?" asked Olga. "I mean, if you . . ." She trailed off.

"The illusion of imperial infallibility," Mikhail said with a foul taste in his mouth. This, as much as anything, was why he didn't want to be a ruling monarch. "I can punish Tim for failing to live up to

my expectations, but I can never admit publicly that
the expectations were in error. Especially since, so
far, he has lived up to them. He's alive, the force we
left under his command is still intact and has grown
to over five hundred men, mostly *Streltzi*, but some
minor nobles. So far, in fact, he's doing better than
we had any right to expect."

Filip explained, "If Tim had died at Bor or a day
or two later, fighting the Nizhny Novgorod *Streltzi* or
a force sent by Sheremetev, then everyone would have
understood that Czar Mikhail had known it was a
forlorn hope and given Tim a great honor. Tim would
be remembered much as Ivan Susanin is."

Not that Mikhail wanted that. He already had the
original Ivan Susanin on his conscience and way too
many others like him. People he had never met who
had died for him or because of his decisions.

"But now," Filip was saying, "since Tim won at
Bor and pulled a fair chunk of the Nizhny Novgorod
Streltzi into his army and has been growing it as he
moved south and east along the Volga, it looks like
a real appointment. Like Czar Mikhail truly thought
that a nineteen-year-old boy was the second coming of
Alexander the Great, with the loyalty of Belisarius. If
Tim falls it will be tragic, but just one of those things.
But if Czar Mikhail demotes him or even just sticks
him off in a corner somewhere to age, it will be seen
as Czar Mikhail going back on his word. A betrayal
of Tim and all the others who might be tempted to
come to Czar Mikhail's colors."

Mikhail looked at Olga, expecting to see confusion
or perhaps disgust, but what he saw was dawning
understanding . . . and even approval.

Mikhail still felt like he had when they forced the crown on him when he was seventeen. Like Jesus at the garden of Gethsemane, desperate to have the cup taken from him. Ever since then he had sipped of that dreadful brew as little as possible. Yet here it was, still before him. Over the years since the Ring of Fire and the knowledge of that other history that it brought with it—and especially in the last few weeks as he had run for his life with his wife and children—he had come to accept that the cup could not be taken from him. He would have to drink it to the dregs. Mikhail looked out at the forest again. "Send a message with one of the steamboats. We leave it to General Lebedev's discretion, but if he feels he can—and for as long as he feels he can—we wish him to take and hold Kazan and deny the lower Volga to Sheremetev."

On the Volga, near Kazan
July 1636

Tim's force didn't have to signal to get the steamboats to stop this time. After reading the message from Czar Mikhail, Tim wished the boats had just gone on by. "Look at this, Ivan." He handed the message over.

Ivan read it and said, "Well, he leaves it up to you."

Tim turned in his saddle with all the grace that might be expected in a Russian of aristocratic lineage. "That makes me feel so much better. I get to lead these men into what is probably a hopeless defense, or I get to leave the Volga open to Sheremetev all the way to the Caspian Sea and cut us off from our best source of food to last out the winter."

"Well, that's why you're the general," Ivan said, with a smug smile.

For just a second Tim wanted to hit his friend. Then he had a better idea. "That's right. I am the general, and you are only a captain." Tim smiled, then waved Marat Davidovich, the commander of Princess Natasha's guard, over. "Marat, Czar Mikhail has sent us new orders. It's up to me whether to try and take Kazan and block Sheremetev, but his imperial majesty would really prefer if the food they grow down near the Caspian Sea were to find its way to Ufa to feed all the freed serfs."

It was clear from Marat's expression that he didn't find this a good plan, but he kept his mouth shut.

"I've decided to send Captain Ivan Kuzmanovich Maslov here to look over the situation in Kazan and advise me of the practicality of taking and holding the city. I was wondering if you thought you could keep him out of trouble while he's looking around."

Marat didn't say, "Do I have to?" in the whiny tone of a five-year-old told to clean out the chicken coops, but it was clear that he thought it.

"Pick a couple of men and go with him. And do it quickly, please. We will be reaching Kazan in another couple of days. I was planning on bypassing it, but . . ." Tim let his voice trail off, holding up the message from Czar Mikhail.

Marat turned in his saddle. "Dimitri, Yuri, come over here."

While Ivan and his guards got ready for their trip to Kazan, Tim called the column to a halt. He needed to give them time to scout, so he would stop the army and drill.

CHAPTER 7

Buying Kazan

Kazan
August 1636

Ivan sat in the coffee house and sipped the strong, dark, sweet coffee. It was horrible. Truly horrible. Abdul Azim sat across from him and smiled. Abdul was a business associate of his father's, and though Ivan had never met him before that morning, he knew that Abdul was a secret Muslim. After Ivan the Terrible had taken this city he had killed, run off, or forcibly converted the populace. The forced conversions had not exactly taken, at least not completely. The same thing had been tried two more times in the last eighty years and until a month ago the Muslims in Kazan had made it their practice to keep their heads down. But, this morning, as he and his guards had been riding into town, they heard the mullah calling the faithful to prayer.

None of them had recognized it, but Ivan had an educated guess. While not of the nobility, Ivan's father was a wealthy businessman with connections all over Russia.

Abdul put his glass of coffee down and said, "No one is in control right now. There was a strong initial push to declare independence like we did in the Time of Troubles, but seeing the dirigible going by overhead slowed that down. And everyone knows that Czar Mikhail is in Ufa and to get to Ufa, or to get back from Ufa, the armies are going to come through here. Everyone is scared."

"How do you feel, Abdul? I know Father always respected your judgment."

"I would declare independence right now."

"You think you can hold Kazan against Director-General Sheremetev and Czar Mikhail?"

"If we are lucky, by playing them off against each other."

Ivan tilted his head. He didn't even realize he was doing it till he saw Abdul's bitter smile. "I know it's more likely that we will be ground between you like grain into flour. But it is hard to deny your faith, and it becomes much harder when the hope of freedom is offered."

Ivan hadn't told Abdul which side he was working for, or even that he was working for one of the sides. Abdul had probably known that he was studying in the Kremlin and possibly that he had been assigned to the dirigible works at Bor, but nothing more than that. And Abdul hadn't asked. For the next several hours, Ivan and Abdul talked about the politics of Kazan. That afternoon, Ivan and his guards strolled around the city, noting the placement and height of the walls and by mid afternoon they had watchers of their own. The local *Streltzi*, city guard, were watching them like hawks. Hungry hawks.

That night they rode out of Kazan, thankful that no faction had enough control of the city to order their arrest. And, even more, that none of the factions had decided to act on their own.

Ten miles from Kazan
August 1636

"I'm fairly sure we could take the town by allying with one of the groups," Ivan said as he drew a map on the ground next to the campfire with a charred stick. "Assuming we could get them to trust us, which is by no means certain. All we would need is for one group to hold the gates open, then between us and them. We could almost certainly get control, but it would be control of a powder keg. The arrival of a force of any size and half the population would switch to their side, just to get back at us for backing another faction."

"So it's hopeless?" Tim asked, looking at the map of Kazan that Ivan had drawn on the ground. "Why the map then?"

"Because if we could get the support of most of the population and keep it, it would be a very defensible position. We could hold out for months. That overturned-pot-looking hill that the city is built on is a great place for artillery. With the right guns, we would control the whole of the Volga."

"So what we need is something to bring them together."

"Something to bring them together on our side, anyway," Ivan said. "My father's friend is ready to throw us all out and declare independence."

"Why?"

"He's a Muslim. Which, aside from that horrible coffee they drink, I don't care that much about. My father has always assumed that he was secretly still a Muslim, in spite of the forced conversions after Kazan's rebellion in the Time of Troubles. They never talked about it, but most of their acquaintance was by mail anyway. Now he's openly practicing Islam and he's afraid that whichever side wins there will be a cracking down after it's over."

"We ought to introduce him to Bernie," Tim said, then stopped.

Ivan was still talking. "The only reason his faction didn't manage to get the city to declare independence was the *Czarina* flying over."

"Yes. We ought to introduce him to Bernie and Czar Mikhail, and very much the czarina," Tim said. "Both czarinas. Ivan, what if Czar Mikhail were to grant Kazan the right of freedom of faith? Make a proclamation? Make a law? What would your friend do then?"

Ivan looked at Tim, at first in shock, then thoughtfully. Tim waited while he worked it out. "I don't know. There is a great deal of bitterness there, now that it's out in the open. I don't know if a proclamation would be enough to rein it back in."

"We'll be in sight of the city tomorrow, and we will stop, not try to enter or go around it. I want you to go back, this time officially. Talk to your father's friend, and to the other leaders too. Meanwhile, the next time that steamboat comes by, I have a new message for Czar Mikhail. If he wants us to take and hold Kazan, he needs to come here and talk to the leaders of the city."

Three days later, Kazan

Asad Korikov stood on the wall of the Kazan kremlin and watched the great airship float gently toward the ground. It was bigger than any riverboat he had ever seen, and it looked like you could pour a whole army out of it. Asad had no way of knowing that almost all of that space was taken up by lifting gasses, cells full of hydrogen and cells full of hot air. What he saw was just the massive form of a whale that swam through the air. He crossed himself unconsciously, and muttered an Islamic prayer that his grandmother was fond of. He could hear a sound. He didn't know that it came from the propellers. Then a short, heavy spear was dropped from the front of the behemoth. It fell quickly, pulling a line after it and plunged into the earth.

A rider from Czar Mikhail's little army rode up to it, then used a hammer to whack the dart farther into the ground. Other men rode up to catch other ropes that were dropped. Once the airship was tied to the ground, a rope ladder was lowered and people started climbing down. Several men and then, surprisingly, three women.

By now the walls on the east side of the kremlin were packed with watchers. Horses were brought and the party mounted.

Czar Mikhail glanced around to be sure everyone in the procession was ready. Then, with Tim on his right and Bernie Zeppi on his left, he rode to the gates of Kazan. Not the gates to the Kazan kremlin, which was to the west of where the dirigible landed, but the gates to the city proper to the east. His wife,

Princess Natasha, and Anya were riding behind him, and there were other functionaries, as well as officers and soldiers of his small army behind them. This was a diplomatic mission so the guards were—hopefully— just there for show.

Czar Mikhail waved to the guards as he led his party through the gates of Kazan and up the street toward the seat of the local government.

A few minutes later, he and his party were seated in a large hall in what on other occasions would have been the central market of Kazan. They were offered wine, beer or coffee. Bernie took coffee and Mikhail took beer, the rest made their own choices. Then they got down to business, starting with Mikhail asking everyone to speak their minds freely. "I will take no offense nor hold any liable for anything said here."

They didn't believe him, of course. They talked around their worries. The questions were there in the background, but all in a way that would let the townspeople backtrack and deny that they meant any such thing. Their concerns were many, but two dominated the discussion. Could Mikhail win? And if he did, could they trust him to keep the promises he made while in need of their help?

Mikhail tried to reassure them without lying out-right. But how reassuring he was, he wasn't sure. He could be firm on the issue of keeping his word, but winning was less certain. "At this point no one knows who will win. Not me, or Sheremetev, or any of the other factions. Kazan, however, is not large enough to survive for long as an independent nation."

"We could, if you would refrain from attacking us."

"No. Even if I were to do so, that would only mean

Sheremetev would take Kazan. And that means I can't do it, because it would be giving that advantage to him."

Mikhail could tell from their expressions that they didn't like hearing that last part, but they couldn't deny it. The discussions went on and got around to religion. Bernie argued for religious toleration and Father Kiril, as gentle as the man usually was, argued against it. But, as a pragmatic political matter, it was clear to Mikhail he needed the support of the Muslim factions in Kazan and the surest way to get that support was to give them religious freedom. And Mikhail was insistent that if the Muslims got that freedom, all religions would have the same.

That led to the question of Sharia law. "No. The worst penalty that any church will be empowered to invoke is excommunication. The laws under which our people will live *will* be civil laws. You can throw people out of your church, refuse to talk to them, but you may not imprison them or impose any physical punishment. Those must be imposed by the civil authority." Mikhail's court had worked this out in advance. It was the only way if there were going to be two or more religions coexisting. Anything else led to one part of his people living under one law and another living under another law.

After a long argument with Bernie and Filip on one side—and just about everyone else in Mikhail's court on the other—it had been decided that religious freedom should be given to Kazan and to Ufa, because for now Ufa was the capital and people ought to be able to practice their faith when they came to the capital to participate in their government. However, it would not be a general liberty. If Muslims in the rest of Rus wanted to practice their religion freely, let them move to Kazan.

"Hey, folks," Bernie said about that point. "I argued

on your side, but in political terms they are right.
Czar Mikhail is pushing the politics of this about as
far as he can. He's already facing a backlash from the
service nobility over the serfs and if he were to make
freedom of religion the law throughout Russia, the
Russian Orthodox church would go over to Sheremetev
en masse. As it is now, the great monasteries can look
the other way and say it's only in a couple of places."

There were looks back and forth on the other side
of the table, and then nods. Some reluctant, and some
enthusiastic. Mikhail noted the enthusiastic nods.
Those were the smart ones and the ones to watch.
Those were the ones who had realized that such a
law would be a magnet for Muslims.

They negotiated for two days and Mikhail then made
a series of pronouncements. Meanwhile, Tim had quietly
infiltrated the Kazan kremlin. With some hesitation,
the garrison had come over. The garrison soldiers were
mostly Russian Orthodox, and not thrilled with Czar
Mikhail's proclamations of religious toleration. On the
other hand, Czar Mikhail was right here . . . and the
duma was way off in Moscow. By the time Mikhail and
the rump court he had brought with him climbed back
into the dirigible, Tim was, at least theoretically, in command of the military forces of both city and kremlin.

Moscow
August 1636

"Didn't I tell you?" shouted Patriarch Joseph, waving
the radio message.

Prince Daniil Ivanovich Dolgorukov looked up.

He was a new member of the *boyar duma*, the royal council appointed after Czar Mikhail had gone into seclusion, but before he had escaped. His position was partly because of ability, but partly because he was a compromise between the Sheremetev and the Morozov families. It was obvious that the Duma was going to have an even greater role in governing Russia from the moment that Czar Mikhail had gone into seclusion. The power shift from the Romanov family to the Sheremetev family had been clear.

"Didn't you tell us what?" Boris Ivanovich Morozov asked.

"He's abandoned the faith." Joseph waved the sheet again, "Under the influence of the up-timer demons, he's made Kazan a city without a faith. All manner of heresies are now legal in Kazan."

"No, they aren't," said Director-General Sheremetev. "It has already been determined by the duma that Czar Mikhail is acting under demonic influence and so may not issue valid *ukase*. Whatever proclamations of law Mikhail has issued are invalid."

"Besides, the agreement on Mikhail's ascension to the throne didn't let him issue laws without the support of the duma and the *Zemsky Sobor* ..." Boris Ivanovich Morozov trailed off.

Daniil hid a grin behind a mostly blank face. It wasn't so much that what Boris said was invalid, as that it tended to undermine the later statements about the demonic influence. Boris was a bright guy, but he tended to get focused on one issue and fail to calculate the politics as well as he might.

Daniil looked around. "What do you think the political consequences will be?"

"I think it will help us with the monasteries, don't you?" Ivan Vasilevich Morozov said.

"It depends on the wording," Prince Ivan Ivanovich Odoevskii said. "May I see that?"

Grudgingly, Patriarch Joseph handed it over. Odoevskii read quickly. "Not as useful as it might be. The proclamation makes it clear he is only talking about Kazan as a permanent free city, and Ufa on a temporary basis. Muslims can continue to practice their faith in Ufa, but if they move there permanently, they must accept Russian Orthodoxy. It's also not limited to Muslims. It includes 'all religions.' Some of the radical monasteries might actually like that."

"*What?*" Patriarch Joseph roared.

"Oh, sit down, Joseph, and spare us your piety. The only reason you care is that it threatens your power," Boris Ivanovich Morozov said. That was true enough. The new patriarch had two mistresses, each set up in style in Moscow. And his primary interest was diddling them, demanding ever finer robes, and more jewels for his patriarch's crown.

"It threatens all of us," Joseph bit out.

"It may actually turn to our advantage," Director-General Sheremetev said. "The religious community was tending toward Mikhail before this. But now we may be able to persuade some of them back to our side. Joseph, write up a condemnation of this so-called *ukase*, but I want to see it before it goes out."

"Be careful, Director-General," Prince Odoevskii said. "The stories of Nikon had a lot of the backwoods churches arming to defend their practices from a too-powerful patriarch. Now we have Mikhail saying that in Kazan you can even be a pagan. Some of them are going to figure that they are better off with him than a patriarch trying to impose doctrine that they don't want."

"That's why I want to see it before it goes out." The director-general turned back to the patriarch and continued. "I want you to stress that this is in no way an attempt to restrict the practices of good and faithful members of the Russian Orthodox church, but is instead to protect them from pagan superstition and Muslim heresy."

A radio station on the Oka River

Yuri read the radio message again. He laughed a little, then got up and walked over to the village church. Father Konstantin was very interested. As it happened, the village's tradition was to bless with two fingers not the three that the Greeks used. Personally, Yuri didn't much care, but Father Konstantin was convinced that it was important.

"Well, Patriarch Joseph is condemning Czar Mikhail's *ukase*, sure enough, Father."

"What does it say?"

Yuri started to hand the radio message over, but Father Konstantin waved it away. "You know I don't read well, Yuri. Just tell me."

"'Under the influence of the demonic up-timers, Mikhail Romanov has issued a false *ukase*.'" Yuri stopped reading for a second. "Did you notice he's not calling the czar 'Czar,' any more?"

"Yes, yes. Go on."

Yuri shrugged. "'False *ukase* that would abandon the people of Kazan to the influence of Islam and all manner of heresies and false faiths, even paganism and witchcraft.'"

"Czar Mikhail didn't say anything about witchcraft," Father Konstantin said.

"Well, he did say 'any faith.'"

"Witchcraft isn't a faith."

Yuri shrugged again and went back to the message. "The Patriarchy, the Duma, and the *Zemsky Sobor* reject this false *ukase* and inform all that the practice of heresy is not allowed anywhere in Russia. However, this should not be taken as any condemnation of the minor differences in practice within the Russian Orthodox faith."

"Well, that's something, at least," Father Konstantin said.

Yuri snorted. "For as long as it lasts."

They talked some more, then Yuri went back to the radio station. He had messages to send and he wanted to know what Petr at the next station thought of this.

All over Russia, the conflicting laws were being discussed by the radio heads who were sharing their views over everything with each other. And that made the discussion one that more of the people in Russia were a party to than had ever been the case before.

Goritsky Monastery
August 1636

Ludmila came in, looking a little bemused.

"What is it, dear?" Sofia asked.

"I received a letter from a woman in Nizhny Novgorod. It's very chatty, but I don't know anyone that it's chatting about. Do you know a Polina Ivanova Vershinin?"

"Not that I recall."

"Well, she knows you. Or at least claims to." Ludmila handed over the letter, pointing at the section that referred to Sofia.

Sofia read. And smiled. "Ludmila, of course you know her. Don't you recall? She is a dear friend of our friend Natasha."

"Natasha who..." Ludmila started the phrase looking blank, but by the time she stopped a look of comprehension had come over her face. "Your Natasha," she said, and Sofia nodded.

And thus a link from Goritsky Monastery to the new capital in Ufa was established. It was a tenuous link that involved letters put on steamboats and coded radio messages stepping from radiotelegraph station to radiotelegraph station. And it was an expensive link. Telegraph messages were expensive to begin with and when you added in the smuggling of the letters in the middle of the chain, it was very expensive. But it meant that the women of the monastery had access to the news from Ufa and Ufa, in turn, had access to the analysis of the dozens of women who had lived their lives in the highest halls of the Russian government.

The nuns were not the only people at the monastery. There were servants and, by now, workers. The monastery had sewing machines. They were not Higgins sewing machines. They were Russian-made copies of Higgins sewing machines, made in a factory in old Novgorod. The monastery also had typewriters, Russian-modified copies of typewriters made in the

USE. They had adding machines, Russian-made copies of USE-made adding machines. They had already
had extensive gardening and minor industries such as
pottery and small partnerships with local craftsmen,
wood and leather workers. The radio station had added
batteries and mica-based capacitors, plus a knowledge
of electronics. Using these machines, the nuns of
Goritsky made their living sewing, typing, keeping
accounts, as well as with gardening and managing
several small businesses.

That wasn't unique to the convent. It wasn't even
unusual. Over the past few years, with the paper
money and especially the radio network, trade and
manufacturing had been booming in Russia. Little
centers of industry had popped up all over the place,
like pimples on a teenager. The radios allowed ordering of goods and the safe and secure transfer of funds
from buyer to seller.

The use of the radios for all these things meant
that the radio network had thousands of messages on
it, going from here to there, and there to the other
place, and back again. Far, far too many radio messages for anyone to keep track of.

So the addition of one more business at Goritsky
Monastery, the business of political analysis, went
essentially unnoticed by the powers that were. Most
of them, anyway.

Grantville section, Embassy Bureau, Moscow

Boris Petrov filled out the requisition for additional
funds. Being quite vague. The money was to provide

greater intelligence on the Polish-USE conflict. And, in part, that was what it was going to do. But it would be analysis, not data-gathering, and the ladies at what he was code-naming Bletchley Park would be analyzing more than just the events on the Polish-USE border. It was a good code name because no one but an expert in up-timer history would recognize the reference. And even if someone did, it wouldn't point them to the women at Goritsky.

CHAPTER 8

Fortifying the Volga

Kazan Kremlin
August 1636

"The first thing we have to do is take Kruglaya Mountain," Ivan told Tim. They were in the Kazan kremlin,
a fortress of pale sandstone. The room was large, with
a square table and benches along one wall. It was
occupied by the commander of the Kazan *Streltzi*,
Mikhail Petrovich Kolumb, who was Russian Orthodox,
as were most of his men and all of his officers. He
wasn't smiling. The Kazan kremlin had been taken
without a shot, by virtue of the dirigible *Czarina
Evdokia* and the presence of Mikhail the czar. But
between being placed under the command of General
Tim and Czar Mikhail's pronouncements about religious
toleration, the officers were regretting at leisure the
decision made in haste.

"That is easier said than done," Colonel Kolumb
told them. "I doubt Metropolitan Matthew will give
over all that easily."

"You may be right, Colonel," Tim said. "But so is

Ivan. That's where Ivan the Terrible staged his conquest of Kazan from and it would be just as useful for Sheremetev. On the other hand, if we hold it, we can block the Volga far enough upriver so as to seriously hamper any attack on Kazan."

"What makes you think that he will object, Colonel?" Ivan asked, "Is he disloyal?"

"The Metropolitan has a duty to the faith," Colonel Kolumb insisted.

"General," Ivan said, "should we consider an airborne assault?"

Tim blinked, then saw Ivan's eyes shift to the colonel.

Then Ivan was continuing. "I know it was something that we were holding in reserve, but if we drop a small army in on top of Kruglaya Mountain in the middle of the night..."

"I'll consider it, Captain," Tim said repressively, finally catching on to Ivan's ploy. "But not until we've given the Metropolitan a chance to be reasonable. Besides, at the moment Czar Mikhail is using the dirigible to make a goodwill tour down the Volga to the Caspian." It was an important use of the dirigible. Having Czar Mikhail fly in on his dirigible and assure you that his government in exile was the real government and that he held the Volga all the way to Kazan was really useful in getting food and supplies needed by the new industries in Ufa—and the factories in Kazan, for that matter.

"What's an airborne assault?" asked Colonel Kolumb.

"It's an ability that they used extensively in the twentieth century," Ivan started explaining enthusiastically.

Tim cleared his throat, and Ivan subsided.

Colonel Kolumb looked over at Tim resentfully. "Am I not trusted, General?" It was clear to Tim that Kolumb had to force the title of rank out. And the truth was that Tim didn't trust the forty-year-old, two-hundred-twenty-pound man as far as he could throw him.

"That's not it at all, Colonel. However, the facilities at Bor are still there and the dirigible they have there is three-quarters finished."

"Why on earth didn't you destroy that place?" Colonel Kolumb complained.

"It was a political decision made by Czar Mikhail, and as much as I dislike some of its consequences, as a political statement it was effective," Tim said. "It pointed up the fact that Czar Mikhail is more interested in the long-term welfare of Russia than short-term military advantage. At the same time, it drew a sharp contrast between the way Czar Mikhail and Director-General Sheremetev will treat the skilled artisans and experts that build and maintain our technological base."

Colonel Kolumb's snort was derisive. "Marvelous. While Mikhail makes his noble political statements, Director-General Sheremetev will be dropping bombs on us from the sky ... and apparently troops as well."

"That is *Czar* Mikhail, Colonel." Tim said coldly. Tim, on the inside, didn't know how he sounded when he said it, but suddenly the room got awfully quiet. He held the colonel's gaze, and the colonel looked away. It was a tactical victory, but with strategic costs. The colonel, who had been resentful, was now likely an enemy. They went on with the meeting.

❖   ❖   ❖

"You want to tell me what that crap about airborne assaults was?" Tim asked quietly, once he and Ivan were in Tim's suite in the Kazan kremlin. It was a nice suite, and until their arrival had been used by Colonel Kolumb. Just another reason for the man to hate Tim. But Czar Mikhail had insisted, and Natasha had backed him up. "There are what—three parachutes—in Russia?"

"There are twenty-eight parachutes in Russia, and Valeriya Zakharovna has actually used one. We also did several tests using weights and dummies. By now we know how to pack a parachute and—most of the time—have it deploy. But I will grant that we don't have anything like a force that can be deployed that way."

"So why?"

"Because that colonel is going to tell Metropolitan Matthew that we can drop a battalion of troops on him in the night. Which will probably make him easier to negotiate with. Then he's going to tell someone who will tell Sheremetev, and Sheremetev will spend the next six months or a year trying to produce a battalion of paratroopers because he is convinced we already have one."

"Possible, I guess. But you know Kolumb is now an enemy?"

"Now or tomorrow or next week," Ivan said. "Kolumb was going to hate you sooner or later, even if you rolled over and showed him your belly. Except then he would have hated you *and* despised you."

Tim considered that. Ivan was probably right. "So who do we get to talk to Metropolitan Matthew?"

"Father Kiril," Ivan said. "And probably by steamboat.

The dirigible would be better but it's busy on the good will tour. And, frankly even if it wasn't, I would rather keep the *Czarina* in her hidden valley, except when we really need her."

Ivan was referring to the news they had received two days before, while talking with Nick Slavenitsky. While Czar Mikhail and the big diplomats were making nice to the citizens of Kazan, Ivan had gotten a chance to talk to Nick and learn about the search for, and finding of, a valley that had little wind. The *Czarina* was mostly safe as long as it stayed in Hidden Valley and they had a crew out there building a hangar to keep it even safer—and potentially build more dirigibles in a couple of years. "Fine, then. A steamboat and Father Kiril. How accurate do you think Colonel Kolumb's estimate of the Metropolitan's response is?"

"I think that the colonel was giving his own motives to Metropolitan Matthew, but the monasteries under his authority have land under Sheremetev control."

"A fair chunk of the diocese's lands are in territory that Czar Mikhail controls," Tim said, then snorted at Ivan's look. The truth was that two months after the escape, Czar Mikhail controlled perhaps as much as twenty miles around Ufa, one small valley in the Ural mountains, and whatever piece of ground that Tim's army happened to be standing on at the moment. Which was in Kazan right now, but how long they could hold Kazan was very uncertain.

"Anyway, put out a flag and send the *Dolgorukov* to Ufa after Father Kiril."

Ivan nodded and left. Steamboats could steam right past towns in a way that was difficult for the riverboats that were pulled by *burlaks* and sailed. To get them to stop at a town you needed an indicator. Ivan would go to the docks and raise the Romanov flag and the *Dolgorukov* flag, and that would tell the steamboat that it should stop here on Czar Mikhail's business.

Two days later

Father Kiril arrived in Kazan, and proceeded directly to the Kazan kremlin to talk with Tim and Ivan. After a short conversation, he reboarded the *Dolgorukov* and headed for Sviyazhsk and Holy Dormition monastery atop the Kruglaya Mountain.

Metropolitan Matthew welcomed Father Kiril with all due ceremony, then led the priest into his private offices and waved him to a seat. "How is Czar Mikhail?"

"Very well, actually. But he would still rather be something else. Czarina Evdokia seems to be blooming under the new circumstances, though."

"I'm a bit surprised by that. She always seemed such a self-effacing woman."

"I think it was more circumstances than character, Metropolitan," Father Kiril said. "Still, I am not here to chat about the imperial family. This fort is crucial to our control of the lower Volga."

"Yes, I understand that. At the same time, Mikhail's recent pronouncement of religious freedom in Kazan is, I feel, ill advised."

"I wasn't thrilled by it myself, Metropolitan. But, under the circumstances, he had to give the people of Kazan some reason to support him."

Metropolitan Matthew stood and walked over to

the stove. It was cold and unlit, but finely made of ceramic tiles with icons of the saints painted on the tiles. "I am concerned that the Muslims will attempt to use this to turn back the clock and force a return to Sharia law. Or at least to coerce the converts to Christianity to revert to their previous faith." He turned to face Kiril. "I like Mikhail and I had the greatest respect for Patriarch Filaret's abilities. But I have to be concerned with the spiritual, as well as the practical, realities. You know I have used a light hand in regard to the Muslims and outright pagans in my diocese, focusing on encouraging the converts to be comfortable in their new faith."

"I know, Metropolitan. Even so, a lot of the converts were happy enough to switch back as soon as the threat of exile was removed."

"So I heard."

"Another point is the fact of the Ring of Fire," Father Kiril said. "I've known Bernie for years, since he first came to Russia. He is a good man, even if he isn't of the Russian Orthodox Church. But the fact of the Ring of Fire seems to me to indicate that the particular way you pray may be less important to the Lord God than we had assumed."

"Even to Muslims and pagans?"

"Bernie is not a Christian. He was an agnostic, if not an outright atheist, before the Ring of Fire. In the aftermath of the Ring of Fire, he was very angry with God for putting him here, where the medicines that kept his mother alive were no longer available. Over the years, he has mellowed, even acknowledged that he is of greater use here than he would have been up-time. But he isn't a member of the church. And that doesn't prevent him from being of great use to Russia and all her people."

"Yes, the Ring of Fire. We all must deal with its blessings and confusions."

They talked more about the specifics of the situation, and finally Kiril said, "You know, if you were patriarch of Russia, you could have much greater influence."

"Czar Mikhail appointed Joseph Kurtsevich, the former archbishop of Suzdal as patriarch last year," Metropolitan Matthew said, sounding disgusted.

"No. Actually, Sheremetev appointed Kurtsevich. Czar Mikhail wasn't consulted on the matter."

"And you're offering to buy me with the patriarch's crown?"

"No. But neither is he going to give that crown to someone who will abuse it." *As Sheremetev did* hung in the air between them.

"I'll consider it," Metropolitan Matthew said.

That pretty much ended the meeting. Father Kiril said his goodbyes and walked back down to the river where he boarded the riverboat back to Kazan.

It took a few more days, but Metropolitan Matthew declared for Czar Mikhail and influenced the garrison at Sviyazhsk to accept Czar Mikhail as the true and legitimate czar. This was helped by the fact that there was a picture of Mikhail on the money. It was hard to declare him a false Mikhail, because there were pictures of him on each paper bill in Russia and they had been in circulation for years now. Sheremetev could declare him "under influence" but he couldn't make the notion that Mikhail wasn't the real czar stick.

Moscow
August 1636

Prince Daniil Ivanovich Dolgorukov sat in the duma and listened to Sheremetev make plans. It had been a harrowing two months. Four members of the duma had been executed for treason, and eight forcibly tonsured since Mikhail had escaped. For a body that only had twenty-eight members, that was a massive amount. The executed and tonsured had fallen into two categories: those most personally loyal to Czar Mikhail, and those with the closest ties to the Gorchakov Dacha. Czar Mikhail's uncle, Ivan Nikitich Romanov, had sided with Sheremetev.

Which, Daniil thought, made quite a bit of sense. Ivan Nikitich hadn't received a single post since Mikhail had been elected. Now he was in charge of the Embassy Bureau, which had control of the Dacha and the Grantville section. The army was finally assembled. It had taken a month of purges and another of reorganization, but a cavalry force of twenty thousand was assembled outside of Moscow, with a contingent of *Streltzi* almost as strong, and twenty of the new breech-loading rifled cannon.

Prince Semen Vasilievich Prozorovskii raised a hand. "I'm concerned about the Poles. I know that they are busy with the Swedes, but the opportunity we offer them by taking so many of our soldiers east..."

Director-General Sheremetev waved for attention. "I have an arrangement with the magnates of Lithuania and the Sjem will not vote to go to war with us."

"What did you have to give them to get that

assurance?" Prince Ivan Ivanovich Odoevskii asked angrily. Which, Daniil thought, was quite brave and rather foolish. Director-General Sheremetev didn't go out of his way to encourage free and open debate.

"Not much," Sheremetev said coldly. "They are busy enough dealing with the Swede." Then, apparently relenting a little, he added, "Mostly simply a promise not to invest Smolensk or attack Poland. That will free up their forces to face the Swede to the west and the Cossacks to the south."

Daniil considered. It might work, or it might not. Mostly because the Polish-Lithuanian Commonwealth wasn't one nation, or even two. It was a loose alliance between a dozen or so magnates who were each effectively independent monarchs of their territory. So the director-general's plan would probably work fine for the PLC as a whole. But any magnate he had failed to adequately bribe might decide to take the opportunity to bite off a chunk of Russia . . . and there weren't that many chunks between Smolensk and Moscow. Daniil found himself wondering if perhaps he should have wrangled a post in the army, just to get away.

Army camp, outside Moscow

Ivan Vasilevich Birkin was wondering the same thing, from the other end. He had been at Rzhev. In fact, he had been part of the cavalry that got slaughtered by the damn Poles at Rzhev. He had been lucky enough to have his horse shot out from under him and had ended up in command of what was left of the cavalry after they got decimated. He had a healthy respect for the effects of technology on warfare and was much less confident in the belief that cavalry was king than he once had been. Yet, here he was. In command of an army that was better than fifty percent cavalry. They had riverboats, even steamboats, but just in support to ferry supplies. The army would be marching across Russia. Eight hundred miles from Moscow to Ufa... He would be lucky if he got there before November, and if he didn't he would have to stop and wait for the rivers to freeze. That would delay any attack till January. It would also mean that his army would be in the field in the worst time of the year. That worst time wasn't winter. Russians knew how to deal with winter. The deadly times were the quagmire seasons, the *rasputitsa* in spring and autumn, when the world was made of mud.

"What do you think?" asked Iakov Petrovich Birkin, his cousin and second in command. "Shall we spank little Timmy for his effrontery?"

"Probably. I know that the boy was in trouble with General Izmailov after the battle at Rzhev, but I didn't get the details. On the other hand, he was the general's fair-haired boy up to then."

"Who cares? He's only... nineteen, isn't it... and he has almost no real experience. He spent all his time playing games in the Kremlin."

General Prince Ivan Vasilevich Birkin didn't say anything. He had said similar things and believed them himself. He still believed them. The war games that the up-timers Bernie and Cass had introduced to the generals at the Kremlin were just that, games. They had nothing to do with facing sword and shot in a real battle. They were at best exercises, and at worst the sort of foolishness that made every idiot clerk think he was the equal of a soldier. But General Shein had doted on the things for some reason. And if Shein was under a cloud for his political position, he was still an excellent general. And General Izmailov had been frankly brilliant in his siege of Rzhev and in the final battle where they had taken the place. All in all, it was a lot easier to criticize the antics of people like that when you didn't have an army to command. He tried to shake off the mood. "How are we set for chambers?"

"Well, Cousin, the gun shop has been delivering more since Lowry died. It's certain that he was diverting much of the output to his purse. I had a little talk with Andrei Korisov and made it clear that if we didn't get what we needed, we would be testing our rifles on him."

"What about the cannon?"

"Not so good. He insists that until he gets better steel, he will have to make the breech blocks heavy to compensate for the weakness." Iakov Petrovich grimaced. "He's probably right, anyway."

The army had twelve rifled twelve-pounders. They were breech-loading but the breeches weighed too much for easy, or rapid, reloading. On the other hand, the carriages were excellent, so he didn't expect the cannon to slow him that much. Not in comparison to the *Streltzi* infantry that would be coming with the army. "All right, then. We have our orders from the director-general. We march next week."

Besides, Ivan Vasilevich told himself, Czar Mikhail and his boy general had had to leave their entire industrial base at the Dacha and Murom. He wouldn't be facing breech-loading cannon. Half of Little Timmy's army would be carrying bows and arrows, and the rest mostly muzzle-loading matchlocks.

"Yes, Cousin. What about Andrei Fefilatevich Danilov's riverboat scheme?"

"Let him try it. If he can knock Little Timmy out of Kazan before we get there, so much the better."

CHAPTER 9

The Northern Route

TwinLo Park, outside Grantville
August 1636

"Good afternoon, Your Highness," said Brent Partow. "Let me start by introducing you to Captain John Adams. No relation to the founding father of the USA, at least none that we know of."

"Captain?" Prince Vladimir Gorchakov offered his hand, but looked to Ron Stone to tell him what was going on.

Ron shrugged in shared confusion. "I mentioned your problems to Trent the other day because TwinLo is good at finding solutions. Since I was back in Grantville for a visit, Trent called me yesterday and asked if I could bring you out to see a possible solution."

"Herr Partow?" Vladimir asked.

"Cap, here, is a retired sea captain and a downtime naval architect. But he's spent the last couple of years in Grantville trying to learn about up-time ship design. He wants to build ships and he's actually been to Mangazeya, and not that long before it was shut down. I got to talking with him about an ice breaker and he thinks he may have a solution."

"You have my full attention, Captain Adams," Vladimir said, and Ron nodded his agreement.

"Well, a steel hull is out of the question, of course. I shudder just thinking how much that amount of steel would cost. It's also not really necessary. The Pomors, the Russian settlers up there in the far north, have a two-masted ship called a 'koch' that is fairly good at making its way through the ice. They are small, though. Less than a hundred tons usually. When I looked up 'icebreakers' in the state library, I learned that much of their design is not exactly taken from the koch hulls, but more grew out of them."

Vladimir nodded and the captain, seeing no objections, continued. "The arctic kochs have a rounded design below the waterline, so that if they get caught the ice will push them out without doing too much damage. And if you just added a steam engine to such a design, you would have something that would mostly work...if the ice wasn't too thick. I don't think they would work in hard winter, though. For that I think you will need something to break the ice. And I think I have that thing."

Vladimir looked around and saw Brent Partow grinning like he was about to hear the punch line to a joke, and Vladimir started to get nervous.

"After I got to Grantville and saw a bulldozer, I got interested in tracked vehicles and continuous track vehicles."

Yes, Vladimir thought, *the joke is definitely on me.*

"I was impressed by the paddle wheels on your riverboats, but they are awfully big for the paddles.

That's a lot of extra weight to drag through the water. So I thought about using continuous track rather than wheels to put the paddles on. I researched it and learned that while military tracked vehicles like tanks use treads that are integral to the chain, civilian ones like on bulldozers have removable treads that can be changed out without damage to the chain."

"Excuse me, Captain, but what does—" Vladimir started.

"Give him a minute, Your Highness," Brent Partow interrupted. "It does all fit together and you do need the background. It's a new system and it has more than one application. But until Ron brought me the question about icebreakers, the uncertainties outweighed any potential benefits. One of the drawbacks of tracks is that they tear up the ground . . . and that's precisely what you want in an icebreaker. So hold your questions till the captain has a chance to explain, please."

Vladimir looked over at Ron Stone, who nodded, then shrugged and waved the captain to continue. Captain Adams kept talking, and his ideas did hang together, at least as harebrained schemes went. Vladimir was familiar with kochs, though he didn't know them as well as Captain Adams apparently did.

This might work. Maybe.

After the meeting, when Vladimir talked it over with Ron, they agreed that it was at least worth a try. The ship Captain Adams wanted would be a three-masted koch-style sailing ship with steam engines. It would carry five hundred tons of useful cargo, aside from engines and fuel. Which would make it a lot bigger than any koch yet built, but not bigger than ships already being built by the shipyards in Hamburg.

"With luck we'll be able to find something already under construction, but not so far along that we can't modify the designs," Ron told Vladimir. "I'll telegraph our agent, Kristof Klein, and have him see what he can find."

Brandy was working on the patent application for the chamber-loading rifle when Vladimir got back to Russia House. Part of the agreement that Vlad had made with Czar Mikhail was that the Gorchakov family would get the international patents to anything independently developed by the Dacha. And, depending on how you interpreted the contract, anything developed with Dacha input. Since Sheremetev had become director-general, there had been a number of challenges to those patents. Mostly from people who owed fealty to the Sheremetev clan or one of the clans that supported them. Brandy had ended up in charge of fighting those claims.

"Are Russian lawyers worse than German lawyers?" Brandy asked as Vlad came in.

"Isn't that a bit like asking which lightless cave is darker?"

Brandy grinned and kissed him on the cheek. "More like which avalanche is heavier. And the only honest answer is 'the one I'm under.'"

"Besides, didn't the Russian embassy hire a German law firm?"

"Yes, but never mind that. How did your meeting with Ron and Brent go?"

"John Adams wants to send a tank across the polar ice to Russia."

"John Adams?"

Suddenly Vladimir remembered Brent Partow's comment. "Not that John Adams. A real person from our time. He's an Englishman, a captain and a ship designer. Apparently some friend of Brent Partow's."

"Okay. What was that about a tank?"

So Vladimir told her about his meeting with Ron, Brent and Captain Adams. Then she told him about the ongoing legal wrangling with the embassy in Magdeburg about which of them was the legitimate representative of Russia. It was important, though not quite as important as it might become later, since the up-time notions of diplomatic immunity and diplomatic status in general were still in their infancy and not fully recognized by the USE.

Then they went in to have dinner. By now Brandy was used to being Princess Brandy Gorchakovna, with all that entailed. They went in to see little Mikey. They had named the baby Mikhail Vladimirovich and left it for history to decide whether Vlad named him after Czar Mikhail or Brandy named him after Mike Stearns. He was happily playing with his milk sister, Branya, under the supervision of Branya's mother, Eva Mateevna. They played with little Mikey for a few minutes, while they continued to chat about the situation in Russia.

They were behind the curve, but between Boris' sons and Fedor Ivanovich Trotsky—who was loyal to Vladimir because his family was on the outs with one of the clans on Sheremetev's side—they had a pretty good idea of what was going on. Or at least what had been going on a month or so ago. "By now the army is probably on the march and the last report that the dirigible provides says that there is a steady flow of serfs and a trickle of *Streltzi* and minor nobility to Czar Mikhail's colors," Vladimir said.

"Which won't do much good, unless we can get them arms and the tools to start up an industrial base," Brandy said. "In freaking Siberia, of all places."

It was an old discussion that they had gone over again and again in the last months. Czar Mikhail's loyal people needed tools and they needed something to pull the lower nobility away from Director-General Sheremetev. Vladimir didn't see how Czar Mikhail could hold out with just a bunch of runaway serfs on his side.

CHAPTER 10

On the River

July to September 1636, on the road

By the end of July, the villagers of Ruzuka were on
the north side of the Klyazma River again, approaching
the Volga. The crops, most of which had been planted
before Czar Mikhail's flight, were getting ripe and
the villages were short of people. The radiotelegraph
net had made rumor even faster—if not noticeably
more accurate.

The operators looked out for one another. They also
had a set of skills that made them difficult to replace.
So the network carried the official messages but it also
carried unofficial messages: what radio operators had
seen or heard, private mail that was often encoded.
Also, while it was by no means universal, the radio
operators had what Sheremetev and his faction were
likely to see as a liberal bias. They were almost universally literate, they had mostly been trained at the
Dacha, so had been exposed to the corrupting influence of Bernie Zeppi and the up-timer books.

Which meant that even little villages out in the

middle of nowhere were generally informed on the events of the day. Czar Mikhail had established himself in Ufa. He had sent the dirigible scouting, and even flown over Moscow. No one knew if Mikhail himself had been in the dirigible when it flew over Moscow in mid-July, but that the dirigible had done so was clear. And, according to rumor, it had sent Sheremetev into a rage.

Serfs were running east in droves and every time the dirigible went over, more ran. So at least the headman of Shalaevo, a village thirty miles west of the Volga, complained. Elena listened as politely as she could. She was, somewhat against her will, acting as the face for the village. With Stefan and Anatoly standing over her, there wasn't much she could do except what they told her. She was really afraid now that they would leave her in the forest.

Elena, with Stefan looking over her shoulder, told the headman of Shalaevo, "Stefan, here, will negotiate with you for my serfs' help with your harvest." Then she retreated to the wagon.

The headman knew he needed their help in bringing in the crop, in exchange for which he offered a small part of the seed. But the bandits from Ruzuka had him over a barrel and they clearly knew it. Almost a quarter of the crop was the price they settled on. And, like any bandit would, they insisted that the seed they were taking be threshed first, because the people of Shalaevo would be able to do the rest of the threshing over the winter.

The people of Ruzuka spent two weeks in Shalaevo, then another two weeks in the next village on their

way, and a week and a half in a third. By the time
they were done, they had almost as much grain as
they would have if they had stayed home. Harvest
season was winding down. It was September now, and
the villagers of Ruzuka made their way to the Volga.

September 1636

As Stefan rode up to the shore of the Volga, he heard
the boatmen singing. Born and raised in Russia, still
Stefan had never heard a song more depressing. "Pull,
pull, pull some more," in tones of ultimate despair.
There were now steam barges on the Volga, but they
were still by far the minority. There were big boats
on the Volga, almost ships, and large crews of the
very poor to haul them up the river. Talking to the
burlak, the boatmen who pulled the boats upriver by
means of ropes attached to the boats and tied around
their upper arms and chests, he learned where the
boats put in. It was fall and cold, and the boats were
not doing nearly as well as their owners had expected
because a good number of the *burlak* had run off to
join the czar at Ufa.

Balakhna was one of the stopping points for the
boats. Stefan rode in and found Boris Petrovich, a
factor for the boat owners that one of the *burlak* had
told him about.

"Yes, we can take you downriver," Boris told Stefan. "How many people do you have and how much
equipment? Downriver is better than upriver at this
time of year. It needs fewer pullers."

They talked price and came to an agreement, some in paper money but mostly in silver and jewelry. Then Stefan went out and brought in the wagons. It would take two days to get all the gear loaded onto the ship.

Balakhna

Nikita Ivanovich Utkin shifted in his saddle. His butt hurt, but at least they were back in town. He looked over at Alexander Nikolayevich Volkov and grinned. The other man looked just as tired as he felt. They were followed by a platoon of soldiers, most of whom were still armed with single-shot muzzleloaders or even pikes. Nikita and Alexander each had AK4s, and Nikita wore a bandolier of chambers as a part of his outfit. Alexander insisted that uniform was not the right word when it was unique, and Nikita had to concede that there weren't two outfits in the platoon that were alike.

Nikita looked back at the docks, and saw a crowd of peasants with wagons and ponies. It looked like this group of runaways had stolen their master blind. Well, he and Alexander would harry them back the way they had come. And if some of their goods got left here for him to pick up, so much the better.

Nikita pointed, and Alexander looked. "More game. And right here in Balakhna."

"They are going to have to be disassembled, Father." Stefan was talking to Father Yulian about the stowing of the wagons. "They take up too much room. We will pull off the wheels and take off the sides and roofs..."

"Oh, my God," Izabella said. "It's Nikita."

Stefan looked up and felt his face pale. Nikita was a stuck-up little bastard. Full of himself and convinced that his lordly birth entitled him to pretty much anything he wanted. He had been a pain in the ass and a real danger from the day Stefan had met him ... and he was riding in their direction, armed and with troops behind him.

On the other hand, the villagers of Ruzuka weren't the same people they had been. They hadn't been attacked since Gorki, but that was only because ever since Gorki they had maintained an alert guard. By now, every adult in the wagon train was armed with something and those who were carrying guns at least had a decent idea how to use them.

Stefan wasn't any good with the guns, but he had a large knife in his belt and he could use it. It was hidden by the coat he wore, but he could reach it if he had to. And, knowing Nikita, he was very much afraid that he was about to have to.

As he watched, Nikita's face changed as he recognized them. Nikita kicked his horse, ignoring the rest of the troops that were with him and rode at Stefan and the rest like he was going to ride them down.

He pulled up when he got to them and leapt off the horse, shouting, "What the hell are you doing here? Father has been worried sick ever since he got the message from Kiril Ivanovich." He grabbed Izabella's arm and that opened her coat, making the fact of her pregnancy blatantly apparent.

"Oh, my—Izabella, Father's going to kill you," Nikita said. "How could you betray the family this way? You have disgraced us all. Who did you give yourself to?

One of the peasants? I'll kill him myself." He swung to look at Stefan.

Stefan held up his hands, disclaiming any responsibility... not that he thought it would do any good.

"You brute! You animal! You defiled my family." Nikita reached into his jacket and pulled out a pistol. It was a chamber-loading flintlock pistol, and it used the same chambers as his chamber-loading rifle. Nikita cocked and opened the pan. Standing not more than six feet from Stefan.

No flintlock, chamber-loading or not, is a quick draw weapon. The pan must be charged before the weapon can be fired, and it is impractical to carry the thing around with the pan charged. Generally, the pan is charged just before a fight and with hope that it doesn't have to be fired more than once. Standing next to the target while charging the weapon isn't the best option.

Stefan saw what Nikita was doing, and knew time had run out. As soon as the pan was charged, the little idiot was going to shoot him just to prove he could. Stefan pulled his knife and lunged. The knife went in just under Nikita's breast bone and angled up. It didn't reach the heart, but it ripped the hell out of both lungs. Stefan clamped his left hand over the pistol in Nikita's right, as he pulled the knife out for another thrust.

Izabella screamed and the battle was on.

Alexander was surprised when Nikita rode ahead. He knew Nikita well enough, but didn't know his sister or his serfs. So he had no idea what had gotten into Nikita till he heard the shouting. His first response was amusement. That would take the little prick down a notch or two.

Then he saw Nikita draw his pistol and kicked his horse into a gallop.

The big, burly peasant moved a lot faster than a man that size should, and when the girl screamed, Alexander charged. It wasn't a conscious decision. If he had thought for even a moment, he would have known that when you have rifles and the enemy have knives, you stand off and fire. But he was a member of the service nobility, born and bred to be a warrior. When under attack, you charged. So that's what he did, and the troops charged after him.

Twenty men at arms charged into the fray and Izabella's scream had brought the wagon train into it. Most of the men of the village of Ruzuka—and more than a few of the women—charged in with whatever they had on hand. Five guns and dozens of knives, axes, and the like.

It's said that no organized force is ever outnumbered by a mob. But there was no organized force on the field that day, only two mobs. And the wagon train had more people.

Sword out, Alexander rode up to the big peasant who had just stabbed Nikita, and there was a shot. His horse reared and went over. Alexander tried to get out of the saddle and almost made it. Almost wasn't good enough. The horse landed on his left ankle and he felt agony as it was wrenched. Alexander bit his lip and pulled his ankle from under the horse. He tried to get his gun out. He tried to stand, and there were several more shots. Alexander didn't know whose shot hit him, then or later. It was even possible that it was one of his men's muskets that had fired the shot. All he knew was a sudden pain in his right thigh, just above the knee. He reflexively drew up his right leg, leaving all his weight on the sprained left ankle, and went down again, losing his gun and sword in the process. By the time he knew what was going on again, the battle was essentially over.

Alexander looked around as Leonid Ivanovich bandaged his leg. He cursed himself for a fool. Four of the people from the wagon train were dead and three of his soldiers. Except for Leonid Ivanovich . . . all those who could run had run, and that big peasant was directing the other members of the wagon train in collecting up the guns.

A priest came over with a young girl who Alexander thought was Nikita's sister. "You are the commander of the local *Streltzi*?"

"Her brother and I commanded this unit," Alexander confirmed, looking at the girl. She was pregnant. It was visible, though not yet blatant. "Did that big peasant get you . . ." Alexander stopped. It was a stupid question. At this point, who the hell cared?

"No," the girl said. She hooked her thumb at the priest. "He is the father and no one forced me."

Alexander felt the next question on the tip of his tongue, wondering if she had married the priest, but he bit it back. There were more important things to talk about. He looked around the docks again. The peasants had gathered up the guns and the wounded. They had laid out the dead and a woman was being restrained. "What happens now?"

"We aren't sure," the priest said. "Introductions, I guess. I am Father Yulian Eduardovich. This is Izabella Ivanovna Utkina. And you are?"

"Alexander Nikolayevich Volkov . . . and I'm in almost as much trouble as you people. Whatever possessed you to run like this?" It was a question that Alexander had wanted to ask ever since he had been given this assignment. Why were so many of the peasants so ready to run? It was especially acute in a situation like this, when they were bringing their master—or at least their master's daughter—along with them.

The girl, Izabella Ivanovna, started to speak, then stopped and looked at the priest.

"People can only take so much. And whether you realized it or not, the serfs of Russia have lived a long time right at the edge of too much. Czar Mikhail offers freedom, and the boyars—" The priest gave Alexander a hard look. "—and their minions, offer only the lash."

"Well, it's the rope for you now, not the lash," Alexander said. "I can't see that as much of an improvement." Then he shrugged and added, "Not that I'm likely to fare all that much better."

"Why not?" asked Izabella, sounding curious.

"My family were early adopters, and while not exactly allies of the Gorchakovs, we were strongly involved with the Cherakasky family. So, considering the latest we heard from Moscow, my family is already in trouble. And we live to the southwest of Moscow, so it's not like we can pull up and leave. Meanwhile, you people have blown my command out from under me. I am likely to be sacrificed on the altar of political necessity. Not that my family will want to, but they won't have much choice, not with Dimitri Mamstriukovich Cherakasky dead."

Alexander knew from his family that Sheremetev was seeing traitors under his bed, and the only thing keeping the purges from going wholesale was the threat that the rest of the high houses would band together against him. The Cossacks to the south had taken several towns and even Archangelsk was making independence-minded noises. Shein had taken his forces in Tobolsk and declared an independent state. The rumors were that he had taken the Babinov Road, the best route through the Ural mountains and was threatening Solikamsk. Any excuse Sheremetev could find for purges in Moscow would be acted on. Alexander had been told, in no uncertain terms, to keep his head down and his nose clean.

The woman who was being restrained started screaming, "Murderers! Killers! You murdered my son and corrupted my daughter! False priest, leading me into corruption and betrayal of my vows! It's all your fault. May God curse you and all you damned, cursed serf scum!"

Izabella rolled her eyes. "My mother has gone crazy."

"Well . . . your brother . . ."

"Yes! My brother. And I helped kill him. I didn't mean to, but it's my belly that sent him raving after Stefan and Stefan had nothing to do with it. Stay away from us. We're all crazy." Then she started crying.

Alexander didn't know what to do. And he wasn't sure she was wrong about the crazy, but she wasn't blaming everyone but herself. That, in itself, said something about her.

The big peasant came over and Father Yulian turned

to him. "Stefan, what are we going to do with the prisoners?"

Stefan gave Alexander a hard look, but as Alexander watched it transmuted to a look that was partly made up of disgust, but mostly just tired. "Let them go, I guess. We don't have enough men to guard them day and night."

Izabella looked at Alexander. "You want to come with us?"

Alexander blinked.

Stefan said, "We can't trust him."

"Why not?"

"Because he . . ."

Izabella turned to face Stefan, and he blushed.

Alexander realized what was going on and tried to calm things down. "I don't see how I could go, anyway. My family would be punished if I joined Czar Mikhail."

"See?" said Stefan.

"That wasn't what you . . ." Izabella stopped herself with a visible effort and took a couple of deep breaths. She looked at Alexander then at Stefan. "If the *Streltzi* are going to get organized and come after us again, he's going to be the one to organize them. When Nikita went crazy, no one did anything till *he*—" She pointed at Alexander. "—acted."

Father Yulian held up his right hand in almost a benediction, and said, "Calmly, Stefan. And you too, Izabella. Alexander, can you walk? I think this discussion should be somewhere a little more private."

Alexander's leg and ankle were hurting enough that it was hard to think, and he seriously doubted that he could walk without aid. His man, Leonid Ivanovich, got under one arm and Izabella under the other. Between them, they took most of his weight, but he still almost fainted when his now swollen ankle was bent as his left foot hit the ground.

They half-carried him up onto the boat, and set him in one of the wagons. Then the priest asked, "Who is your friend?" pointing at Leonid.

"This is Leonid Ivanovich. He's been with me since I was a boy." Leonid was a peasant from his family's estates who had been assigned to look after Alexander when he was eight, and had been looking after him ever since. Leonid took care of his clothing and his kit, saw to the horse, and dealt with tavern keepers and the like. There were few people in the world that Alexander trusted more.

"What do you think of Czar Mikhail's proclamation, Leonid Ivanovich?" asked Father Yulian.

Leonid looked at the priest, then at Alexander and hesitated.

"Speak your mind, Leonid Ivanovich," said Stefan. "No one is going to punish you for telling the truth. We won't, and he can't."

Alexander blinked. He was still hurting and this was confusing. What made them think that he would punish Leonid for saying what he thought? Not that Leonid was big on thinking in the first place.

"I would like to go with you," Leonid said.

It took Alexander a minute to realize that Leonid was talking about going with the peasants who were running, not about staying with Alexander. "What? Why?"

"It's nothing against you, sir," Leonid said. "You've mostly been fair with me, but I want my own life.

Your papa wouldn't let me marry Alla and married her off to Petr the baker because I was to look after you."

Alexander barely remembered that. He had been ten or so, and Leonid had been perhaps twenty-five. He remembered being upset that Leonid was paying so much attention to a girl, and he remembered that Leonid had been unhappy after she married the baker. But he hadn't realized that his father had had anything to do with it. "I'm sorry, Leonid. I didn't know."

"Well, if he's going with us, he's no risk to any secrets that might be told," said Stefan. "So what's this all about?"

"We are going to need another public face. Elena will be useless now, even if we force her to continue with us," said Father Yulian. "And Alexander here might just work. However, we would be better off with his cooperation. He seems like he might be willing to help us, but he is afraid of the consequences to his family if he willingly goes with us."

"So?"

"So I think we should kidnap him from here where everyone can see us do it. That will cover his family and then he can act as our public face. We still have the colonel's seal, and I can write up papers for Alexander, once we decide on his role."

"That would be fine, except that I am not of the colonel's family. He would have no authority over me."

"Not under your own name. But you could be Izabella's cousin or something, escorting her."

"My husband." Izabella pointed at her waist. "I am clearly in need of one."

"I . . ." Alexander stopped, with no notion of how to go on. "I don't want to marry a girl already pregnant

with another man's child" was the truth, but probably
not a wise comment to make. On the other hand, he
couldn't think of anything wise to say.

While he was trying to work that out through the
pain, Izabella spoke. "Not a real marriage. It's just
the most believable story. Alexander can be from any
of the minor nobility families, whether *deti boyar* or
service nobility." Both Alexander's family and Izabella's
were *deti boyar* families. Alexander's to the Cherakasky
and Izabella's to the Sheremetev family, so Alexander
would know how to act the part.

"We'll make him Alexander Nikolayevich . . . Orlav.
And Papa married me off to him for a village and
three hogs."

There was, Alexander noted, considerable bitterness
in the girl's voice.

All in all, Alexander wasn't convinced that this was
a good idea. However, the alternatives weren't looking
all that good either.

The *Streltzi* came back a few hours later, to find
the villagers from Ruzuka on the loaded boats, with
charged and ready muskets. Alexander negotiated a
truce between the town's *Streltzi* and the invading
villagers, and for the next day Balakhna was held in
an armed truce while Stefan and Father Yulian negotiated with the *burlak* who pulled the boats up and
down the Volga River when the wind wasn't strong.

There were, by this time, dozens of steam-powered
boats on the Russian river systems. But there were
thousands of boats on the Russian rivers and most of
them were propelled either by the wind or by men and
women harnessed like draft animals. A good number

of the *burlak* had already run east before the wagon train had reached Balakhna, and the owner of the boat they had rented had responded by working the ones that were left still harder. They weren't happy and were looking for a way out.

The battle with the local *Streltzi* had made it clear that the wagon train wasn't legitimate, in spite of their papers, and the owner of the boat was no longer willing to rent his boat to them. The choice was to buy the boat or leave it.

The wagon train didn't have the money to buy the boat, so they really didn't have a lot of choice. They simply stole it.

"Can we rig the lines to teams of ponies?" Stefan asked Afanasy.

"For stretches of up to a couple of miles, you can. But there are places that a team of animals can't negotiate," Afanasy, the foreman of the *burlak* crew said. "That's one reason that they use people. Also, ponies don't react well to the currents on the river," the man, in ragged clothing and an unkempt beard and hair with considerable body odor, explained. "It's mostly easier just to load the livestock on the boat and have us pull it."

Stefan wasn't sure whether that was the truth or whether the *burlak* just wanted a job for the trip down the Volga to the Kama River. They would travel up the Kama to the Belaya River, which they would follow to Ufa.

"Mother's not coming," Izabella said, entering the little shack on the docks where Vera was working on organizing their supplies and equipment. "She refuses and I'm tired of arguing. Well, of being screamed at."

Vera nodded and waved Izabella to a bench next to the window. It was covered with a thin sheet of tanned intestine, but it kept out the cold wind and let in a little light. She had heard the screaming, and the local priest had agreed to look after Elena till someone came to take her off their hands. Father Yulian had arranged that.

"Is everything on the boat?" Izabella asked.

"Pretty much. We pulled the wheels off the wagons once we got them into the boat and arranged. It will take a few days once we get where we're going to get them reassembled," Vera said.

"Why are we taking them anyway? It's all rivers from here."

"Two reasons. First, they are likely to be useful once we get to Ufa. Father Yulian says we will apply to Czar Mikhail for new lands, and we will probably have to travel overland to get to them. But mostly it's because after all the work we put in on them, Stefan isn't willing to just abandon them. Besides a cabin on wheels is still a cabin, and we are going to need places to stay till we get real houses built."

There was shouting from outside and the two women got up and went out, to see Boris Petrovich storming up the dock with a couple of men behind him.

"Stefan," Vera called, "get your gun!"

"You get off my boat! I just rented it and not to go to Ufa!" shouted Boris Petrovich, the factor. He was a fat, florid man with a red face and a short beard.

Several of the men of the village came to the side of the boat, carrying their guns. Stefan and Anatoly had the rifled AK3s, and other men from the villages had older muskets, including a couple of matchlocks.

Suddenly, Boris Petrovich stopped. He looked at the guns and then at the two large men who had come with him carrying cudgels. Those men were now backing away and while they hadn't actually dropped the cudgels, they were no longer holding them in anything like a threatening manner.

Boris Petrovich's head turned this way and that till he saw Vera and Izabella. Then he started toward them.

"Stop!" Stefan shouted.

"Your women are down here," Boris shouted back, still approaching the women.

"And your *Streltzi* commander is up here," Stefan answered back. "You've already lost one. Do you want to explain how you lost two?"

"Besides," Vera said, pulling a long pistol from her dress, "we aren't helpless."

Alexander was helped—or dragged—to the railing, where he struggled to hold himself up. "Ivan, Petr, what are you doing?"

The two toughs looked a bit shamefaced.

Alexander looked at Boris Petrovich. "They have the guns, Boris. I don't see much we can do about it at the moment."

"And there's not going to be anything you can do about it, either. We're taking him with us," Stefan said, pointing at Alexander. "We'll let him go once we get to Ufa, if we don't run into any problems along the way."

"Maybe even before that," added Father Yulian. "We'll see how things go."

"In the meantime, get off this dock and stop threatening our women, or I'll shoot you," said Stefan.

The Ruzukans finished the loading and set out, being pulled by the *burlak*. And as the docks receded, Boris Petrovich took back the dock, and standing on the end of it shouted, "You're murderers and thieves! Kidnappers too!"

As soon as the pirates left, Boris Petrovich sent a runner to the nearest radiotelegraph station, but it would take the boy a while to get there. The boy who was given the message wasn't in any great hurry to deliver it, so once he was out of sight he stopped running and made his way at a "brisk" stroll. Nikita hadn't been popular in the village, and there was something romantic about Czar Mikhail, even to those who didn't go off to Ufa.

The radio man sent the message, but there were a lot of messages these days and he wasn't all that fond of Nikita, having met the young punk. So he managed to send the message to the boy's father in Moscow, rather than to the commanding officer in Bor or Nizhny Novgorod. It took some time for the message to reach the colonel and more time for it to get to Nikita's commanding officer. Meanwhile, the sun was setting and the boat that the pirates had stolen—with the help of a lot of the *burlaks*—was floating down the Volga at about eight knots, mostly by virtue of the river's current.

The sun had set and they pulled the boat over to the side and loaded on the *burlaks*. Then they pushed the boat back out, and raised the sail. There was a breeze, but not much of one and the ship barely had enough way for steerage. It was dark, but not dark enough for comfort, as they sailed down the river, past the mouth of the Moscova River, past Nizhny Novgorod, then a few minutes later past Bor.

Stefan looked over the deck with their wagons disassembled and people sleeping. There was still close to a thousand miles to Ufa by river. But they were on their way and there was no going back.

Perhaps there never had been.

Part Two

Russia, East and West

CHAPTER 11

The Problem with New Lands

Ufa
September 1636

Czar Mikhail rubbed his hands over the fire and considered. The great houses of Muscovy were dividing up, but in new and surprising ways. Before the Ring of Fire and even after it, the politics of Russia had been clan politics, not much affected by agendas like those that had ruled up-time political debate. In the last few years, there had developed several ... call them parties. There were people who wanted to clamp down even harder on the serfs. There were the people who wanted to loosen the restrictions. There were those who wanted to modernize and those opposed to modernization. However, the factions weren't consistent. A lot of the people who were quite happy to adopt new tools and machines still wanted to clamp down on the serfs and peasants. Even wanted to restrict the *Streltzi* or use the new weapons to bring the Cossacks into line. And many of those who were in favor of lightening the leash on the peasants were not happy with the new tools, because they could be used to make the already hard lot of serfs even harder. In fact, that was a fairly major concern among several of the monasteries, and Metropolitan Matthew was fairly strongly in that camp.

What's worse, Matthew had a point. Too many of the nobles thought of serfs as not much different from other livestock. Their response to a tool that decreased the amount of labor to accomplish a task was to put the serfs to more tasks. Matthew was constantly dragging some peasant who had lost a finger, a hand or an eye to one of the machines before Mikhail. "It's not the tools! It's compassion that we need," Matthew would say.

The truth was they needed both. But Mikhail wasn't at all sure how to introduce compassion. It wasn't like Metropolitan Matthew had managed to do so.

"There you are!" Evdokia said. "You can't hide up here brooding all the time, Mikhail."

"Brooding seems to be all I can do."

"That's not true. You are the standard. You are the beacon that calls out to a freer Russia."

Mikhail smiled. He had never seen himself in the role of hero, but it still felt kind of good to have Evdokia see him that way. "How was your talk with the ladies?" The ladies, at the insistence of Princess Natasha and Tami Simmons had placed themselves in charge of sanitation for the rapidly expanding town of Ufa. It was an issue of disease. They recruited Evdokia, Anya, Olga Petrovichna, and several of the other women. All of them had other jobs, but they met every couple of days to discuss waste disposal.

Evdokia lifted a hand and wobbled it back and

forth in a gesture that she had gotten from Tami. "We make progress, but slowly. We have the honey wagons and the urine is being stored for tanning and the collection of saltpeter. Most of the solid waste is being sold to farmers. But the new arrivals have often not heard of the up-time notions of why disease happens and some of the priests are actively opposing our sanitation campaign as an affront to God."

"In other words, nothing new."

"Not in general. There are some new specifics, but Olga is going to take care of them and it would probably be best if you didn't know any more than that." Olga Petrovichna was fond of direct action, and she had a crew of mountain men who were not squeamish in the least. Evdokia continued. "How did your meeting with Bernie and Filip go?"

"Nothing much new there either, I'm afraid. We brought equipment from Murom, but it was only a fraction of what was there. We've gotten some more from the Dacha and from some of the wealthier groups that have joined us, including the two monasteries that have decided to move their factories out here. But it's still barely a fraction of what is available in Russia. We had four years and more of development, and now we're back to the days right after Bernie got here." It wasn't that they couldn't build anything. It was that they couldn't build anything in large amounts. They could make a radio, but not radios—or at least not many. They could convert muzzle loaders to chamber-loaders but they would have to do it one at a time and each one took time. They could hand build steam engines and boilers, but there had been a steam engine factory in Murom. Not a big one, but a factory nevertheless. As bad as losing what they had left behind was, worse was that most of it had fallen into Sheremetev's hands.

"Iakov is arguing that if I don't reinstate serfdom, I at least have to put some sort of restrictions on the peasants. Otherwise, they'll be running out on their debts and generally running amok." Prince Iakov Kudenetovich Cherakasky was a relative of Dimitri Mamstriukovich Cherakasky, who had seen the writing on the wall when his kinsman was murdered. He wasn't in love with Mikhail's reforms, but he did bring, at least potentially, a good size force to Mikhail's side. "But I don't think he really cares all that much. He's giving me grief over it because of Tim." Iakov had some military experience, but it was all before the Ring of Fire and he hadn't been involved in the study of war at the Kremlin. In essence, he could lead a cavalry charge and that was about it. But partly due to age and partly due to rank, he had arrived asking to be placed in command of the army. To avoid a confrontation, Mikhail put him in charge of the Chancellery Bureau. And Iakov was now trying to keep Mikhail from overturning the rights of the upper nobility. There was no one to counterbalance him. So far, he was the highest ranking person to come to Mikhail's colors, at least by the way Russia counted such things.

"We're building a new city here, Mikhail. And, in a way, it's a good thing that Ufa was so small. There is much less in the way of property rights to step on while we do it. Bernie and Filip are building good roads and arranging things so that we'll be able to put in sewers once the brick works gets going. We can build a modern city here in Ufa. The only way to do that in Moscow would be to burn the place to the ground first."

"Even that won't do it," Mikhail said. "Moscow burns regularly, but everyone still owns their little chunk of it and it gets rebuilt the same way it was before. You're right that here we have more opportunity to build a modern city. But I am worried that I may be focusing on that because I can't do much about the rest of it." They had talked about the great building projects of banana republic dictators over the last few months and Mikhail was worried that "modern Ufa" might turn out to be that sort of monument to ineffectuality.

On the Volga

"How did you end up here?" Alexander Nikolayevich Volkov asked.

"How do you mean?" Izabella replied resentfully. Her pregnancy was clearly showing and she was feeling ugly and fat.

"I mean I understand why the serfs ran away, sort of. But what about you? For that matter, we turned back a lot of serfs in the last couple of months. How is it that you people are so well supplied? Your wagons are loaded with threshed grain."

In a sudden mood swing that made no sense even to her, Izabella found herself on the edge of tears. "I don't know," she said, answering Alexander's first question and ignoring the rest. "I saw my mother with Father Yulian and decided that if she could, I could. Then I got pregnant, and I don't want to spend the rest of my life in a convent. And now I'm the size of a dirigible and I have to pee all the time."

She looked over at Alexander and belatedly realized that she was providing more information than he really wanted. She managed to backtrack to the rest of the questions he asked. "Papa . . . my father . . . is evil, I guess. So was my brother. And, I guess, so was I. After I got pregnant and Father Yulian got me to look around and see what my father was doing to the serfs of our home village, I realized how bad things were. And they were bad." She found herself looking at Alexander like it was his fault.

He held up his hands and said, "I'm not doubting you."

"The children were on the edge of starvation because the men in the village had been forced to work in a neighboring factory for nothing. Since I was already pregnant, they brought me into the escape plan. Father Yulian and Stefan and the rest. Well, Father Yulian did. I don't think Stefan knew anything about it till Czar Mikhail escaped. But we were already pretty close to ready. We had been planning to run once the crop was in, but we rushed to get ready and ran for it."

"How have you managed to keep all the serfs with you?" Alexander asked and Izabella wanted to laugh because she understood the question perfectly.

"I didn't. I couldn't possibly have kept them together. Father Yulian, Stefan, and Vera are the ones keeping all of us together."

She saw him try to assimilate that and she had to give him credit for really trying. Last summer she wouldn't have. She simply would have assumed that peasants would scatter like dust in a wind without a noble to keep them working together. It wouldn't have occurred to her to consider any other possibility. She looked out at the river, flowing black beside the boat in the night. She could hear the ripple of waves as the Volga flowed past the stationary boat. "They don't need us, you know. They don't need us at all. Not you or me or Papa or Nikita. None of us. Do you realize how terrifying that is?"

Izabella looked back at Alexander saw him watching her. Considering what she said, but mostly looking at her. She felt herself start to blush.

Then his expression changed. "You really think that the peasants—*serfs*—can get by without the nobility?"

"We still need them," Stefan said. "At least till we get to Ufa."

At the other end of the riverboat from Alexander and Izabella, the council of the runaways was in session. It included Father Yulian, Stefan and Vera, Anatoly and Zoya, Dominika, and Afanasy, the leader of the *burlaks*. The rest of the people who had joined them, either singly or in small groups during the course of their travels, were not represented directly. The council members were seated on the deck, chatting quietly.

"No, we don't," said Anatoly. "We have the boat and we have guns. We snuck past Nizhny Novgorod. Word is that Czar Mikhail is holding much of the Kama River."

"We will still have to get past Kazan," Father Yulian said. The Kama was the main eastern tributary of the Volga. It connected the Belaya River to the Volga river system and so put the town of Ufa on the Volga system. It joined the Volga a few miles southeast of

Kazan. None of them, not even the *burlak*, knew how many miles. The *burlak* knew the river intimately. They were, after all, the people who had to pull the boats off sandbars when they got stuck, which they did with depressing regularity. Something that had already happened to the *Liberty* twice since they had stolen it. "With Alexander and Izabella fronting for us at Kazan, we should be able to get past the town. Perhaps even stop and do some trading. The people we picked up in Balakhna don't have much, even if we give them the *Liberty* once we get to Ufa."

"They also don't have much money," Anatoly said. "I don't see why we should be supporting all these late additions. We were the ones who prepared."

"That 'we' includes Izabella," said Vera.

"And we are working our way. You would still be stuck on that sand bar not five miles past Bor without us," Afanasy said.

"I'm not talking about you," Anatoly said, rather unconvincingly Stefan thought. "I'm talking about all the villagers who joined us in dribs and drabs as we went along. There are more of them now than there are people from Ruzuka, and they all seem to think they are entitled to a share of what we built and brought. As to the colonel's little slut, we got her out—"

"Anatoly, your greed is blinding you!" Father Yulian said, hotly.

"Calmly, all of you," Stefan said, not feeling all that calm himself. "We don't want to draw a crowd."

"In fact, Izabella is a fairly accomplished young woman. She can read some and she understands politics," Father Yulian said, but in a quieter tone. "We are going to have to deal with Czar Mikhail's representatives once we get to Ufa and we don't know what we are going to find there. It may be that we will need her even more once we get to Ufa."

"Czar Mikhail said we would be free, not serfs."

"Fine. If we are free, not serfs, what will we do for land?" Vera said. "The czar is just going to give it to us?"

"That's what his proclamation said."

"No. He said new lands would be granted," Father Yulian pointed out. "He didn't say to whom. It could mean us, or it could mean the service nobility. It could be dependent on service in the army or the paying of taxes. Who knows? And we can work with Izabella. Don't burn our bridges, Anatoly. We may need to cross the river again. We don't know what we will find downriver."

Kruglaya Mountain, Sviyazhsk, confluence of the Volga and Sviyaga Rivers

Major Ivan Maslov looked out the window, then back down at the map. The czar's army didn't have very many cannon and none of them were breech-loaders, so none of them would have great rates of fire, even if he could get new carriages for them. Also, none of them were rifled, so they weren't going to be very accurate. Worst of all, most of them were in Kazan or on their way to Ufa. Here on the mountain, he had just two of them. And he was supposed to interdict the Volga river with that. Since Metropolitan Matthew had persuaded the local garrison to side with Czar Mikhail last month, several river boats had passed in both directions. And all Ivan had been able to do was send out small boats to ask them for news. He needed a new weapon, something that they could make here. He thought of rockets, but those needed venturi. It said so in all the books and Ivan didn't have a way of making venturi. He wasn't even sure what they were or what they did.

The truth was that Ivan was in here working on the problem of interdicting the river mostly because he didn't want to be out there being scowled at by Captain Sergei Viktorovich Lagunov, the commander of the garrison. He was a member of the service nobility who was loyal enough, but not happy with Czar Mikhail's policies in regard to serfs . . . or Ivan himself. Captain Lagunov had objected to Ivan being put in command over him because of birth and experience. He was, or had been, of the same military rank, a captain, and of nobler family, being of the service nobility while Ivan's father was a baker. And he had been a captain longer. So, by all the rules, he should be in command.

Tim had promoted Ivan to major right in front of Captain Lagunov. In essence, telling Sergei to shut up and soldier. It was pretty threadbare, especially considering the issues of *mestnichestvo*, but unless Captain Sergei Viktorovich Lagunov wished to complain to Czar Mikhail, he was stuck with Major Ivan Maslov. And Ivan was stuck with a resentful staff.

There was a knock on the door, and after no appreciable delay the door was opened, and Lieutenant Vadim Viktorovich Lagunov came in. Vadim was twenty-three and owed his position to the fact that his brother commanded the garrison. He, even more than his brother, objected to having to deal with the son of a baker on anything like equal terms. Also, he had never been to the Kremlin or seen the war games played there in the last few years. Like his big brother, he didn't imagine that they could be of any use. He had a thick black beard and beady eyes. "So have you figured out how to interdict the river yet?"

"Not unless you can make venturi."

"I'm not a smith and they wouldn't work anyway. What we need is a galley with a strong force so that we can get out and board ships that pass us."

"Fine," Ivan said. "Do you know how to build a galley full of soldiers?"

"Well, I know how to make the soldiers. It takes girls and about twenty years. The galley? You put the serfs to work on it."

"Right. You go out and find a bunch of blind girls. That way they won't see you and run away. If that works, we'll be fine in about twenty years. Assuming the director-general gives us twenty years. Meanwhile, is there any word from Bernie?"

"No," Lieutenant Lagunov said in a voice that made Ivan realize he should have kept his mouth shut. Then Lagunov continued. "But there is another boat sailing down the Volga. Sergei wants to send out a couple of small boats to ask them for news."

"That's fine. I'll be down directly."

Ivan Maslov thought about standing gallantly in the prow of the little oared boat that was making its way to the riverboat. Then he thought about falling into the river and gave up on the notion. It wasn't a new thought in any particular. Instead he waited in the center of the boat, as they rowed out to meet the riverboat. He looked up and saw Alexander Niko-layevich Volkov on the rail. "Oh, shit."

Alexander wasn't one of his favorite people. He had been at the Kremlin back in '33, and Ivan and Tim had won a fair amount of money off the stuck-up snot. Ivan pulled his fur cap down to cover his face. It wasn't calculated, more the automatic reaction of a nerd when encountering a jock. Having reacted though, he realized it was useless. He was going to have to climb up onto the boat and face Alexander. Still, having pulled the cap down, he wasn't willing to push it back up. So he waited. When the rowboat came alongside and a rope ladder was tossed down, Ivan and his men started boarding. There was a girl Ivan had never seen being introduced as Izabella Utkin. Then Alexander was introduced and Ivan's head came up. Alexander Orlav wasn't Alex's name. Then Alex saw Ivan's face and his went pale.

"Hello, Alexander Nikolayevich," Ivan said, then started to smile.

The smile died as Ivan noticed all the peasants holding weapons. There was a big man with a chamber-loading carbine that looked like it came out of the factory at Murom. In fact, it looked a lot like the one Tim had sent Ivan.

"Everyone calm down," Ivan said, looking around. "You can always shoot us in a minute if you decide to. And whatever you do, it's going to be seen by the people on Kruglaya Mountain. So it probably won't do you a lot of good if what you're after is sneaking by."

"Which side are you on, Ivan?" Alexander asked. "You were always with Boris Timofeyevich, and he's..."

"That's right. General Tim now, appointed *okolnichii* by Czar Mikhail." Ivan said. "Why are you running, Alex?"

"It's complicated."

"Tell me about it. Or better yet, let *me* tell *you* about complicated. Are you trying to reach Czar Mikhail?"

Alexander looked at the girl. She looked at an older priest. The priest looked at the big peasant and the big peasant shrugged. "Yes."

Ivan looked around. There had been peasants coming down the river since he and Tim had left Bor, but always in ones or twos. The largest group Ivan had seen till now was ten. But there were at least two hundred, possibly more, people crowding this boat. "How? Never mind. You're in Czar Mikhail's territory, at least for now." He wished he'd left that last part out. It was true but bandying about that you don't think you'll be able to hold the ground you're standing on isn't a good idea.

Alexander looked at the mountain then back at Ivan. Ivan waited for Alexander to make some comment but, surprisingly, he didn't. Alexander had done well enough in the war college at the Kremlin and Ivan could see that he was following Ivan's logic now. Sviyazhsk was a guard post, little more than a trip wire. Kazan was defense in depth, expected to be lost. All to keep Sheremetev and his forces away from Ufa for as long as they could.

"So, you control the Volga below the Kama?"

"Yes," Ivan said, and could hear the next question before Alexander asked it. *For how long?* But Alexander didn't ask.

Instead he just nodded. "Well, you've been more

successful than I would have expected. We'll go on to Ufa then. What can you tell me about Czar Mikhail's position on the granting of new lands?" He waved his hands at the gathered serfs.

"As I understand it, that's been pretty catch as catch can. Up till now it's only been small groups and they are mostly just expanding the farmland around Ufa. They are mostly villages owned by the villagers, but there has been someone put in charge. You'll have to ask when you get there."

They talked a bit more and then the boat went on. Ivan went back to trying to figure a way of interdicting the river.

CHAPTER 12

Delays on the Volga

Ufa
September 1636

"Where am I going to put you?" Olga Petrovichna complained.

"I don't see that you need to put us anywhere," said Stefan. "Just point us to the land that Czar Mikhail has offered us and we will take care of ourselves."

"Oh, you will, will you? What are you going to use for seed next year? For that matter, what are you going to eat this winter?"

"We brought grain with us!"

"What? How much?"

"However much, it's ours. Not yours."

"Perhaps this conversation might better take place some place other than a public dock," offered Izabella.

That took a while. First they had to decide where everyone was going to stay for the moment, while they worked out the rest. After some argument, the fugitive villagers decided to stay on the boat . . . or at least on the dock. So the Ufa dock was full of running, laughing children. Two hundred people on a river boat the size of theirs were about a hundred too many. Add in several tons of grain, wagons and gear, and they had been living in each others' laps since they loaded on the boat. The children went a little crazy with freedom.

Meanwhile, news of a boatload of people had reached the escaped serfs who had already arrived, and the dock where the boat was docked started drawing peasants like flies to honey.

Ufa kremlin
September 1636

"What's going on?" Mikhail asked, as he looked out the window at the activity on the docks.

"I don't know, but I expect we will be finding out soon," Evdokia said. A knock at her door indicated that she was probably right.

"Come in," Mikhail shouted, and Anya came in, followed by Olga, a big blond man, an older dark-haired man wearing a priest's cassock, and—was that Alexander Volkov? Mikhail thought it was, but wasn't sure. He had seen the young man perhaps half a dozen times on visits to the officer academy at the Kremlin. There were also two smallish women, one of whom was obviously pregnant, but for the moment Mikhail paid them little attention. "Alexander? Has your family come over to my side?"

"Your Majesty," Alexander said, bowing, "I don't know. I was kidnapped." The others stiffened, then Alexander continued. "It was done to keep me and my family out of trouble, but it still kept me out of touch with the family."

"I take it then that these are your kidnapp—ah, rescuers?"

"Yes. This is Stefan Andreevich, the blacksmith from a village called Ruzuka and the leader of a large party of former serfs wishing to take advantage of your proclamation."

"A whole village?"

"More than that. Others have been joining us since we left," said the little pregnant blonde.

"How many?"

"Two hundred twenty-seven, including the children," said the priest.

That was the largest group not led by a noble by a factor of four. "In that case, why don't we gather up some chairs and you can tell me all about it."

For the next hour and more Mikhail listened and asked the occasional question as he learned about the trip across Russia of the villagers of Ruzuka. It was mostly Father Yulian and Vera, the smith's wife, who carried the conversation.

Finally, he said, "You've done a very impressive thing in bringing so many. I can use talent like that. Now, ever since we got here our cartographers, with the aid of the dirigible, have been mapping the area. I think we can find a suitable place for your people to set up your new village. We've set up several villages so far, and to the extent I can, I am trying to keep them fairly close to Ufa so that transport will be easier."

They went over to the map table and found a place. It was about ten miles east of Ufa, in a lightly forested area. To get there, they would be taking the river boat about five miles up the Belaya River, to the mouth of the Ufa River, then follow the Ufa back north. The lands actually included a small stretch on one side of the Ufa River, though Stefan, looking at the map, thought they would want to put the village itself about a mile and a half from the river.

"We would like to know who will own the land," Izabella said.

Mikhail grinned and said, "What we have been doing is providing all the new arrivals with a range of choices they can make. If they wish, they can be settled on a suitable—and suitably large—piece of land owned collectively by their village. Or, if they prefer, we will give each individual refugee a stake that they can use for land or sell to someone who wants land. In the up-time America, they offered forty acres and a mule to the freed slave families, at least according to Bernie."

"What's an acre?" Izabella asked.

"It's an English measure the up-timers used. Forty acres make about fifteen *desiatinas*. We will be offering each adult a grant of five *desiatinas*. That will also be the standard we use to determine the amount of land given a village, if they choose to own the land collectively. So if we can't give you a mule, your families should get something close to the forty acres, depending on how many adults in the family. A single man or woman gets five *desiatinas*, not really enough to farm. On the other hand, a married couple with their parents living with them might get twenty or even thirty *desiatinas*. More than a single man can farm without the new plows and reapers. But not everyone wants to farm. A young man or woman can bank or sell their grant. For the most part, the grants are being combined into village corporations."

"What's a corporation?" Vera asked and Czar Mikhail could hear the suspicion in her voice.

"It's not required, Vera. You and Stefan can set up your own little farm. But even with the improvements we have gotten from the up-timers and the research at the Dacha, it takes a lot of work to manage a farm. And a lot of it is better done in a group. There are the free villages—" The term Mikhail used was *obshchina*, which translated into "commune" and what it meant was a village that was held in common by the villagers themselves. The term had very little in common with the later idealistic communes where everyone owned everything in common, so no one owned anything. "—but one of our scholars studying up-time law suggested corporate farms, where the villagers would pool their grants into one large grant and the land would be owned by the corporation. The people would own shares in the corporation, based on their contribution. As I said, you don't have to do it that way, but it seems to work fairly well."

"We'll look into it," Izabella said before Vera could ask another question. "What about members of the service nobility?"

"There has been some debate about that," Mikhail acknowledged. "In fact, Bernie Zeppi and Tami Simmons suggested that members of the service nobility should be granted the same deal as everyone else. As you can imagine, the service nobility weren't thrilled with that. What we finally came up with was somewhat larger land grants based on the rank your family held back west. But also with military or administrative duties attached. You will want to check with the land office. On the other hand, you won't have any serfs to work your land unless you make some sort of arrangement with them."

"So it will be me putting my land grant in with their land grants and what? Getting a larger share of the corporation?"

"Probably something like that. But it will be between you and them to work out."

Stefan had kept looking at the map. He figured that once they got set up, they could see about cutting a road from the village back to the Ufa River, get some boats and have good transport to Ufa city. The Belaya and Ufa rivers surrounded a spit of land that ranged from a couple of miles across to seven miles across at its widest point, and nine or ten miles long before it widened out again. That was why Ivan the Terrible had chosen to put a fort here. Mikhail was not giving out village-sized plots in that spit. The city that was planned would eventually fill it. That, of course, was many years away.

For the next week, as the Ruzuka villagers made their preparations, sold grain and bought equipment in Ufa, their village doubled yet again. Part of that was due to the fact that many small groups of runaways had tended to be young men. On the other hand, those who had joined the Ruzuka wagon train had been women by a ratio of at least two to one. The women had wanted to go east just as much as the young men, but had been less willing to go alone through a Russia filled with wild animals and wilder men.

Now that they were here and there was the opportunity to start a new life, the young men wanted to go to the future village that had young women in it.

Also Izabella's land grant came in at almost ten times a standard peasant's land, and she put her land in with the villagers to increase the size of their farm even more.

Meanwhile, Alexander had been drafted. That additional clause for the service nobility had come into play. He, like Izabella, got a larger land grant but he also had service obligations.

"The duma and I are jockeying for position, both politically and militarily," Czar Mikhail said as Alexander was still recovering from his bow. The czar waved him to a chair and Alexander sat. "We buy support and punish collaboration with the enemy. When one of the great houses comes over to me, Sheremetev has the duma seize their property in territory he controls and grants it to one of his favorites. In my way, I do the same. So the great houses are splitting up, sending some of their connections to me—or at least allowing some to come—so that if should I win, someone in the family will get to keep the family lands. And they're keeping some with Sheremetev and the duma, so that if he wins they will have someone to speak for them. The courtiers and service nobility are doing the same."

Alexander nodded. Russia in the seventeenth century was a mix of east and west, but whatever the terms, it was all about alliances and backing the right horse. When he had been assigned to watch for peasants in Balakhna, it had looked to the family like Sheremetev was sure to win. Even when Alexander had been "kidnapped," it had still seemed like Sheremetev and the boyars would eventually bring the errant czar back under control. Now that he was here in Ufa, Alexander wasn't so sure.

"In spite of the fact that your family were early adopters of the tech from the Ring of Fire and the Dacha, politically you're more conservative. And, almost all of your family's lands are in Sheremetev-controlled territory. One of the things I am trying to do is make sure that I'm not just passing out benefits to my favorites. As it happens, you're the ranking Cherakasky connection to come over to my side. Do you know why that is?"

"Honestly, Your Majesty, I think it's because they are playing the odds. None of them have seen what's happening in Ufa, and they don't see any way you can hold out. That goes both for my direct family and, I think, for the Cherakasky clan. I know that the political notions coming out of the Dacha made my family nervous and I know that they wanted to avoid a war with Poland, which might be why they sided with Sheremetev when you—" Alexander paused and then continued. "—when you went into seclusion.

"Did Sheremetev actually have your father murdered?"

"I think so. Or, to be more precise, Ivan Borisovich Petrov heard from his father that Sheremetev arranged my father's murder. Some of the things said by the *oprichniki* who were guarding me in my—" Mikhail stopped and gave Alexander a half smile. "—*seclusion*, indicated that he probably did. We may never know for certain. But we have wandered a bit far afield. You're the ranking Cherakasky connection and because I don't want to just take the Cherakasky lands and give them to one of my favorites, I am minded to give them to you."

Alexander felt a mixture of terror and elation. Rather heavy on the terror and light on the elation, as he considered the way his family was going to react to the news of his elevation. Father would not be pleased. Neither would his older brothers. And the Cherakaskys weren't going to be happy at all. "I'm not sure..."

"No. But I am. Not that it will mean much if we don't win." Czar Mikhail stopped. "No. It will mean one thing, at least for now. You will be able to draw on the projected income of those lands at the Land Bank here in Ufa to buy what you need or even make investments. You should check with them and establish your credit limits before you go to Kazan to report to General Lebedev."

"Report to where?"

"I'm sending you to Kazan and assigning you to General Lebedev," Czar Mikhail told him. "I don't have nearly enough officers and even fewer that have any actual training."

"Don't discount experience, Your Majesty," Alexander said. "I know that General Lebedev has done well, and I certainly lost enough money to him and the baker's son. But war is not chess. However skilled they are at the games, it's not the same as real war."

"You may be surprised to hear that General Lebedev has told me the same thing. But in our case, a war is at least a bit like chess. Capture the king and the other side loses. If I die, it doesn't necessarily mean that Sheremetev will ultimately win... but it certainly means that we—all of us—lose."

"Is that true in the other direction, Your Majesty?"

"Not as true, perhaps. But, yes, the loss of Fedor Ivanovich Sheremetev would probably eliminate the Sheremetev faction in the duma. That doesn't necessarily mean that the duma would send emissaries inviting me home and swearing undying loyalty, but it would help our cause a great deal."

Alexander wasn't sure he wanted to leave Ufa. In fact he was almost sure he didn't. He was confused and the image of a blond girl returned to his mind.

Czar Mikhail was watching him. "What's the problem? Is it that little blonde? What's her name? Izabella?"

"No! Of course not. You . . ." Alexander trailed off. Maybe it was Izabella. But if it was, it wasn't only her. He was concerned about the villagers. He wasn't sure how that had happened in just the few days it had taken to get here. But it had. "I'm concerned about the villagers."

"Well, the best thing you can do for them is keep Sheremetev's army away from the village they are trying to build right now."

"Yes, Your Majesty."

"Meanwhile, go have a talk with the girl."

"Anya says that there should be more grain shipped up from the area around the Caspian Sea in the next month or so," Izabella was saying. "She thinks that while there is going to be a market for grain next year, she's not at all sure how good the market will be."

"That assumes that the Volga stays in our hands," Alexander said. "I don't see how Lebedev is going to hold it with the forces he has. Czar Mikhail's proclamation got a lot of serfs to come join him, but not that many soldiers."

"But we have the dirigible and more of the steamboats!"

"We have the dirigible, but they are working on their own. As for the steamboats, we have a few more, but not many. And the steam engine factory is in territory controlled by Sheremetev. So are the gun factories, especially when it comes to cannon. With the new gun carriages, they are going to be able to move the cannon more easily. The cannon will still delay Sheremetev, but not as much as they would have."

Izabella was starting to look frightened. Well, that made sense. Alexander was pretty frightened himself. Their biggest advantage was simply the amount of time it would take Sheremetev to get his forces into position. Moscow to Ufa was seven hundred miles as the dirigible flew. Over a thousand on any reasonable marching route. Even more along the rivers, but with steamboats they could travel fairly fast along the rivers. That was why Sviyazhsk and Kazan were so important. They blocked the river route and would have to be taken before the river could be used to attack Ufa, or even to supply an army marching on Ufa. "Don't worry. It's going to take them a long time to get here, and I think time is on our side." That wasn't true, but it sounded good.

Izabella was giving him a careful look, but she let it pass. Suddenly she quirked a smile. "Then I guess you at least are some use to the former serfs of Ruzuka. Your job is to protect them while they grow the crops and build the machines. Now all I have to do is figure out what use I am."

"It has always been the job of the nobility to protect and govern the common people. It's your job too."

"I don't think I'm going to be leading any gallant charges." She patted her increasingly prominent belly. "And they seem to be able to govern themselves quite handily."

Alexander wasn't at all sure what to say to that. So he just sat there like a lump and she looked at him. Then she leaned forward and kissed him hard. Before he could react at all, she jumped up and ran off. Leaving Alexander—as uncountable young men before him—totally confused.

There was too much on Alexander's mind. There was the money and the new military assignment and that kiss. Alexander had to get on the road to Kazan, but he couldn't take this...whatever it was...with Izabella any longer.

He was tempted to leave and concentrate on his duties, but he had to face it. If he went off to Kazan, what would she do? She was pregnant. She wouldn't have a lot of options, and she was worried about what she was going to do in the village. She might even get desperate enough to marry that damn horny priest.

That thought galvanized Alexander. He didn't want Izabella marrying Father Yulian, his baby or not. He rented a horse and headed for the village of New Ruzuka.

"Izabella...Look, why don't you marry me?" Alexander said. "We're of the same class and I have all this money because Czar Mikhail decided that I now own my family's lands, so you will be a proper member of the nobility. I'll even forgive your dalliance with that randy priest of yours."

"You'll *forgive*?" Izabella felt her face going red and didn't care. "You arrogant ass! I hadn't even met you! What business was it of yours what I did with who? And you're going to *buy* me with your family's money and *lock* me back in the same cage that had my mother running off to Father Yulian in the first place! I never want to see you again!"

She turned and ran into the wagon, slamming the door behind her and not sure whether she wanted him to follow her or not.

As it happened, he didn't. And by the time she had gotten herself together and realized she might have overreacted, just a little bit, he was gone.

Bernie was snuggling up to Natasha on the couch when the door opened. Not even a knock, just flung open with the little blonde from New Ruzuka, Izabella, charging through, followed by Anya. *Every single time*, he thought. *Every damn time*.

"He's run off to Kazan, the cowardly bastard!" Izabella screeched.

"Father Yulian?" Natasha asked, sounding confused.

"No! Alexander! Why would I care where Yulian went?"

Bernie blinked, now totally confused. What did Alexander have to do with anything?

"What did you say to him?" Natasha asked, this time sounding irritated, but not at all confused.

Bernie looked back and forth between the women, trying to figure out what was going on. Suddenly Anya started to giggle.

Natasha and Izabella looked at Anya, Natasha looking curious and Izabella looking betrayed. Anya pointed at Bernie. Both the other women looked at him and clearly saw something funny in his expression. Even the little blonde was starting to smile.

"Why don't you go check on the progress of something," Natasha suggested. "The girls and I are going to be a while."

Since all that giggling had, er, reduced his circumstances, Bernie stood up and left. Muttering about "the female conspiracy" all the way.

"Now," Natasha said, not actually any happier than Bernie to be interrupted again, "what did you say to Alexander to make him run off to Kazan?"

They told her. Izabella, now upset at herself, but still blaming Alexander for his presumption, and "the way he messed up everything and made me so mad!"

"Wait a little while, then send him a radio message and apologize," Natasha suggested.

Izabella immediately bridled.

"Do it, girl," Anya told her.

Natasha said, "Don't blow your chance with him out of pride."

Izabella couldn't bring herself to send that sort of radio message. Partly because she wasn't real good at apologizing in the first place, and doing it where the radio operators could overhear... "Bunch of gossips... the lot of them... would be a public humiliation."

And that was how things stood as the steamboat took Alexander into the front lines of a war.

CHAPTER 13

The River Defense

Kazan
September 1636

"The general is in the radio room."

"Radio?"

"Yes. It's in the tower." The private in the city militia pointed at the Kazan kremlin.

It took Alexander a few minutes to get to the tower located in the kremlin wall. It was a tall tower and above it was a pole reaching even higher. He made his way into the tower and was directed to a room on the bottom floor. Even with the large antenna, this wasn't a powerful radio. They didn't have the amplifiers that up-timers had to make radios that would reach across hundreds of miles. This radio only reached about twenty miles. That meant it could reach Sviyazhsk sitting on top of Kruglaya Mountain and through Sviyazhsk a chain of back country radio outposts that would eventually reach the radio network already established in western Russia. It was also planned to reach Ufa eventually, but for now it was basically a link to Sviyazhsk.

The radio room was also the telephone room. Within Kazan they used telephones connected by copper wires and a switch board. It allowed Tim to talk to just about anywhere in the kremlin and most of the rest of the city, at least within the city walls and bastions. Right now there was a great mass of construction work going on. It was mostly sandbags and using Fresno scrapers to dig trenches and build up mounds. Alexander found himself wondering how effective that sort of wall would prove against a determined cavalry charge. He had heard about the disastrous cavalry charge at Rzhev, but he hadn't been there and he couldn't help but wonder if it was just that it wasn't carried through as it should have been.

General Lebedev was standing behind the radio operator, reading over the man's shoulder as he wrote out the message clicking in.

"Four steamboats loaded with troops and cannon left Moscow by way of Moscova River yesterday."

"How does Sviyazhsk know that?" Alexander asked.

"This isn't from Sviyazhsk. It's from the dirigible." General Lebedev didn't look up as he answered the question. He kept reading. "Estimate a hundred *Streltzi* and two cannon per riverboat. The dirigible is heading for Ufa, but will try to keep us informed as they can." Then he stood and turned to Alexander. "Who are—Alexander Volkov?"

"Yes, General." Alexander decided at the last minute to address Tim as general. "Czar Mikhail has assigned me to your forces."

"Really? I must thank him when I get an opportunity." Then General Tim shook himself. "I'm sorry,

Captain. I should have long since given over schoolboy resentments. I really can use you. What do you know about river combat? Ivan Maslov is out at Sviyazhsk, with not much of anything to stop those boats, and I don't have a lot more."

Alexander was at a loss, then something Cass Lowry had said while drunk in a tavern occurred to him. "'Damn the torpedoes, full speed ahead.'"

"What?"

"I'm not sure. I'm not even entirely sure what a torpedo is. But I think it has something to do with naval warfare. It's something Cass Lowry said when he was drunk. He said it's from river fighting in the up-timer's civil war. Of course, he also said his prick was a torpedo. It didn't make much sense."

The general turned back to the radio man. "Is the *Czarina* still in range?"

"I think so, sir."

"Have him ask Bernie about torpedoes in the American Civil War."

The radio man started clicking. "Well, Captain, I hope Bernie knows about torpedoes. Even if he doesn't, though, it was worth a try. Welcome to Kazan."

As it happened, Bernie didn't know about torpedoes in the Civil War. In fact, the information that Bernie had about torpedoes was useless . . . except to explain Cass Lowry's reference to his prick. However, Ivan Alexandrovich Choglokov was very interested in American history. He had been at the Dacha since '32 and had been on the second steamboat out. His family was prominent at court, but not quite of great family status. And Ivan knew where to find out what

a torpedo was in 1860. He looked it up in the encyclopedia.

And suddenly they had a plan.

Colonel Mikhail Petrovich Kolumb looked at Alexander with a less than fully pleased expression. "Well,
Captain, I take it you're another of the baby general's
favorites."

Alexander listened to the colonel's voice and the bitterness in it. "No. I'm one of the ones who picked on
him in the Kremlin," he said, putting as much regret
and resentment in his voice as he could. He was able
to put *a lot* of regret and resentment that statement. It
was easy. Alexander hadn't realized till just now how
much he resented Boris Timofeyevich's rapid advance-
ment. Little Tim wasn't even the smart one. That was
Ivan Maslov. Tim was just in the right place at the
right time. Alexander had been a full lieutenant when
the Rzhev campaign had happened, but he had missed
it and Tim had come back promoted. Then the little
bastard had been in just the right spot when the czar
needed someone, and now he was a frigging general.

"Can't blame you," the colonel said, his voice much
less resentful or at least a lot more congenial. "I
haven't seen much sign of the military genius that
everyone talks about."

"Tim's not the smart one. That's Ivan Maslov, the
baker's son. Tim was just his cover in the upper
nobility."

"Is the baker's boy really that smart?" Now the
colonel was sounding doubtful but interested.

Alexander considered. "At the time I didn't think so.
It just seemed like he had a knack for the war games

that General Shein was so enamored of." Alexander
saw the colonel's nod and held up his hand. "I'm
beginning to think that Ivan Maslov may actually be
a very smart operator, and I've seen some things that
make me think that the games may be more useful
than I had thought when I was at the Kremlin. I
think that the new rifles really mean a lot when it
comes to tactics."

"Humph! Well, perhaps. But what about all these
sand bags? General Lebedev is starting to be called
Sandbag Timmy, and the price of cloth has gone up
because of all of it he's turning into sandbags." The
man shrugged. "Meanwhile, I'm supposed to fit you
out with underwater mines."

Alexander nodded. Word had come back quickly and
designs, even models, had arrived almost as quickly
by riverboat.

"Well, I've looked at the designs. The craftsmen of
Kazan are quite capable of making the things."

They talked it through and Colonel Kolumb sent
Alexander off to a craftsman's shop. A few days later
Tim had a load of mines and instructions about placing and retrieving them. And the craftsman had a
voucher from the Czar's Bank in Ufa.

On the Volga
September 1636

Andrei Fefilatevich Danilov looked up at the dirigible
and cursed. That monster had been tracking them
since they left Moscow a week and a half—and three
breakdowns—ago.

It was hard enough convincing General Birkin to let him take the steamboats without that skywhale hanging up there marking their location. His was a small force. Partly that was because General Birkin had to deal with Director-General Sheremetev, who didn't trust the steamboats, and at the same time didn't want them wasted in combat. They were too valuable transporting goods, especially food, considering all the serfs that had run off. Reports that Kazan and Sviyazhsk had gone over to Mikhail Romanov had been ignored. Andrei hadn't gotten permission for this expedition till the reports of diverted riverboats started coming in.

Most of the army was slowly slogging along the Klyazma River, not that far from Moscow. And it was starting to look unlikely that they would be able to get to Kazan before the winter freeze started. If that happened, they would have to stop and wait for hard winter, after the rivers froze. Andrei looked forward and smiled. It wasn't all bad news. If his was a tiny force, he still had two of the breech-loading six-pounder cannon mounted on each of his four river boats. That would let him fire on Sviyazhsk as soon as Kruglaya Mountain came in sight. Which, if they didn't have another breakdown, ought to be tomorrow or the next day. He could steam right up to the docks, drop his troops, then stand off to give covering fire with the breech-loaders. Once Sviyazhsk was taken, he would move the cannon to the port side for the assault on Kazan. He might as well. He wasn't going to have surprise in his favor, anyway. Not with that damned skywhale watching.

❖   ❖   ❖

Quietly, eighty feet ahead of Andrei Fefilatevich Danilov's lead boat, eight inches below the surface of the Volga, an iron pot waited. It was upside down, filled with black powder and air, making it light enough to bob to the surface if it weren't for the rope and anchor keeping it below the muddy surface of the Volga. There was no malevolence in the waiting murderer, nor any sense of fair play. No intellect at all. It was a device, nothing more. The pot had had holes cut in it and nails, driven through wax seals. It would only take a tap to drive one of those nails forward to release a catch and allow a wound wheel lock to spin making a shower of sparks to ignite the powder and . . . *Boom!*

It wouldn't be a good day for the steamboat.

On the shore, not two hundred feet from the mines, was a group of sixty men, hiding in the brush that covered the shore. Each man had a chamber-loading rifle—the AK3 flintlocks, not the new AK4 caplocks. The production of caps was also still in that part of Russia that Sheremetev commanded.

Ivan Maslov was using an AK3. Not because he didn't have an AK4, but because he didn't have the caps for it. There was a cap factory setting up in Kazan and another in Ufa, but as yet they had very limited output. For now at least they used what caps they did have just as sparingly as they could. He watched as the lead steamboat approached the mine. *Just about now. . . .*

Nothing happened.

The boat hit the mine. The nail went in. The spring didn't release. The nail was moved, but not quite enough to release the spring.

Meanwhile, a trickle of water started to leak through the disturbed wax around the nail. The mine that had been pushed away by the contact with the hull of the steamboat floated back up and hit it again with a thump. Again, nothing happened. The spring quivered, but didn't release. More drops of water leaked in. The iron pot went down and bounced up again. The spring released. The wheel lock spun and the powder, which was mostly dry, ignited.

Whump!

The explosion was contained by the water surrounding the pot, but it was less constrained where the water was closest to the hull. It ripped a four-by-seven-foot hole in the bottom of the boat. There was no sudden explosion... unless you count bilge water shooting all over the place. But a sixty-by-thirty-foot steamboat with a hole that size in the bottom of its hull amidships is going down. It's just a matter of time. And not much time.

The steam boat behind the leader turned to port to avoid the leader, which took it to the other side of the river from the waiting ambushers. Ivan cursed under his breath. Not only did that increase the range, it meant that the sinking steam boat would act as cover for the follower. The third boat in line, seeing the river blocked ahead and to port, turned to starboard. The fourth, having more time, reversed its engines and tried to back away at least long enough to gauge the situation. The standard conversion from sailing riverboat to steam riverboat was capable of reversing thrust, but it wasn't a quick process and the steamboats had been traveling in line with not that much space between them.

The good news, Ivan didn't know, was that the third boat had blocked the first boat's cannon and, because it was turning, its cannon too were pointed in the wrong direction.

"Fire," Ivan shouted and shot at a man standing on the bow of the third boat with a line and sinker in hand. He missed, but that didn't stop the man from dropping the line and ducking away from the railing.

Another forty odd shots rang out, as well as a few curses as flintlocks failed to fire. There were three hits. Ivan popped the chamber from his carbine, tapped the second chamber over the pan, inserted it into the lock and closed the lock. All the while, he heard Lieutenant Vadim Viktorovich Lagunov crowing.

Vadim hadn't liked the plan. Mostly because it was Ivan Maslov's plan, but also because it didn't quite fit in with his notion of martial glory. He was now starting to reconsider. There were four boats full of troops and cannon being held by sixty men and a bunch of mines. Besides, Vadim had hit his man. The captain, or perhaps a mate, but clearly someone important. He popped the chamber from his AK and started reloading.

On board the third boat, the first mate, now in command, was cursing the pilot for abandoning his post. The Volga here was not particularly deep and it had sand bars. Which was almost certainly why the ambush was placed here. He tried to guess where the sandbars might be, then he found one with the bow. "Stop engines," he shouted. It was the right thing to say. The engineer pulled a lever that disconnected the prop from the engines. Now there was only momentum and current pushing the nose of his boat onto the sand bar. That was enough to push the nose a couple more feet into the sand, but the boat was at an angle to the current and the current pushed from the side. The third steamboat pivoted on its bow and came within a foot of wedging its stern on the sunken first steamboat. But a miss is as good as a mile, and the third steamboat of the expeditionary force pivoted around till it was facing upriver and came loose from the sandbar.

The first mate took that as a sign from God that upriver was the way they should be going. "Full speed ahead!" he shouted. The fact that they had taken seven more casualties in the two minutes it had taken for the boat to pivot might have had something to do with the mate's interpretation of God's will. That and the fact that he couldn't see any slackening of the enemy fire and he couldn't even see the people shooting at them, just the smoke from their guns.

The second boat, which had turned to starboard to avoid the first, got by without a scratch. However, its captain, who was not a boatman but a member of the service nobility, was now looking downriver and seeing in his mind's eye a mine under every square foot of water. There was shooting behind him, but he was an experienced officer and gunfire was something he understood. He looked at the river ahead, then he looked at the battle behind. And he shouted to the boatman, "Turn us around!"

The boatman looked at him like he was crazy and the captain pulled his pistol. It was a six-shot black-powder caplock pistol, copied from an 1851 Colt and made in the gun shop. The boatman turned the boat around. "You're going to take us right back the way we came." The captain pointed. "And we're going to drop ropes to pick up survivors from the lead boat."

They made their way back up the river and didn't take much fire. Most of the ambushers were still shooting at the retreating third boat. Much of the crew of the first boat were picked up, but the expedition commander had gone into the water wearing a steel breastplate.

Ivan looked around at the aftermath. His little force hadn't taken so much as a scratch and there were three riverboats retreating back upriver. On the other hand, Ivan was pretty sure what he would do in this situation. He'd go upriver half a mile or so, till he was out of direct fire from the enemy, then he would unload the soldiers and sweep down the bank. "Sergei, head upriver and keep watch on the boats. If they land, run back and tell us." Ivan turned to Lieutenant Vadim Viktorovich Lagunov. "Well fought, Lieutenant. Signal our steamboat to collect the rest of the mines, and let's see if there's anything on that—" He pointed at the riverboat sunk to its smokestack in the center of the river.

"Right, Major," Vadim said with less resentment than Ivan was expecting.

It took an hour to collect up the five other mines that had been placed and by that time Sergei was back with a report of infantry marching along the riverbank. "The boats are staying back of the infantry," Sergei added, grinning a gap-toothed grin.

"How many?"

"A lot, Captain. Three hundred and more, I make it, and they have the AK4s. They left the cannon on the boats, though."

"Shit. I'd like to try and bring up the guns on that wreck out there, but ... How long before they get here?"

"Maybe a half-hour. I ran after I got a look at 'em."

"We could put out a screen to delay them," offered Vadim.

Ivan shook his head regretfully. "I'd like to, Vadim, but we just don't have enough men. All right. Get everyone on the boat and we'll go to the next spot."

The next spot was seventeen miles downriver, where the Volga split into three channels with visible sandbars between them. Only the rightmost channel was deep enough for a boat, and if they put out the mines in that channel there was a good chance that they would get another boat. Seventeen miles was a couple of hours by steamboat, but a long day's march along a twisting, muddy riverbank.

"Will we set up another ambush?"

"No. Just a couple of scouts, and they will be a half-mile or so downriver from the mines. Then we'll see what they do next. If they have people on both sides of the river, we'll keep retreating before them. But if they put them all on one side, we'll set up an ambush on the other."

"Why?" Vadim asked. The question wasn't derisive, but curious.

"Because a group like that can only go as fast as its slowest unit. Every time the troops on either side of the river run into an obstacle, everyone has to wait till they negotiate it. So we want them split into as many groups as we can manage."

Ivan's force had good news—well, mixed news—when they camped that night. The three remaining boats had stopped at the ambush site to recover the cannon and the lost rifles from the sunken steamboat. They spent two days doing that, then the riverboats went on, while many of the troops marched along the riverbank on the southwest side of the river.

CHAPTER 14

Arsenal of Constitutional Monarchy

Ufa
October 1636

Stefan got off the horse, then went to help Vera down. They had ridden in to Ufa in response to a request from Czar Mikhail, delivered by a messenger rider. They were met by Olga Petrovichna, who led them up to the Ufa kremlin.

"What's this all about?" Vera asked.

"I don't know for sure. You know that Anya had everyone tell her about what they did and put it all in a book?"

Stefan nodded. He remembered. It had taken days and it wasn't just Anya. There had been half a dozen interviewers and they wanted to know everyone's skills.

"Well, they were talking about rockets and Anya was going through that book and came up with Stefan's name. So we sent for the two of you."

Bernie adjusted the down-time-made Coleman lantern and went back to the table. He looked down at the plans for the black powder rockets. They were mostly wood, but they needed metal or ceramic venturi.

Then he looked up at Natasha and couldn't help but smile. She wasn't wearing the white makeup that she had worn the first day they had met, but her natural complexion was pale and she was wearing ruby-red lipstick. Her hair was just as straight and black as ever and her eyes just as blue. She looked up and saw him looking and there was just a hint of blush in her cheeks as she smiled back. Then the door opened and Olga brought in a big man and a little woman who had to be Stefan and his wife, Vera. Natasha turned and the smith and his wife started to bow.

"Don't bother with all that," Natasha said. "How is your new village coming?"

Stefan remained silent, but Vera said, "Slowly, Your Highness. The land is mostly forest and we've been chopping down trees for the last couple of weeks. We'll have plenty of logs to build our houses, but it's a lot of work to clear the land."

"If you have extra lumber, we will want to buy some of it," Bernie said.

"Is that why we're here?" Vera asked.

"No," Natasha said. "It's about Stefan's experience with drop forges. We have people with similar experience, but we also have a lot of jobs for them."

Bernie noticed that Vera didn't seem thrilled at this news, and he remembered that Stefan had been, for all intents and purposes, rented to a neighboring village last winter. Which was where he had gotten the experience. "We pay people to work for us," Bernie said. "And we don't force them to take a job if they don't want it."

Natasha looked over at him, then back at Stefan and Vera. "You do need to understand that this is important. There are steamboats coming up the river right now. They want to take Czar Mikhail, and you and me, all of us, back into captivity. We have a young man with a small force out on the river slowing them down, but he needs better weapons than he has. We don't have the equipment to make cannon, but we can make rockets. At least, we can make most of the parts needed for rockets. But one part is not easy to make, especially by hand. It's called a venturi, and it is vital for making the rocket fly straight and fast." She waved them over to the table and showed them the drawings.

"From what we were told, you built your own drop hammer and stamps for parts for your wagons. Is that right?" Bernie asked.

Stefan nodded.

Bernie was starting to wonder if the guy knew how to talk. "What we need help with is a stamp or a set of stamps that can be used to make venturi."

"Do they need to be made in one piece?" Stefan asked, as he looked at the drawings.

"What do you mean?" Bernie asked.

"Well, this thing is two bowls with a tube between them. It's a pretty short tube too. You can't make it as one piece with a drop hammer. You need to make two pieces at least, and probably three, then fit them together."

From there the discussion went into technical details of how the stamps for each part would be made and how the parts would be assembled, clamped, bolted or welded. Induction welding would be best, but most of their electronic equipment had been left in the Dacha.

Stefan was clearly confused about the notion of induction welding, but also interested. So the discussion digressed a bit at that point, but then got back to the venturi. They finally decided on a sort of heavy wire clamp to lock the two main pieces together.

By that time the ladies had drifted away to talk about costs, and if their discussion was rather sharper, it was collegial in its own way. Olga, Anya, and Vera were all experienced bargainers and Princess Natasha—if she wasn't used to bargaining over a half dozen eggs in a market stall—was quite familiar with the costs of labor and materials.

For two weeks Stefan worked on stamps while another drop hammer was built in Ufa. Then, in two days, they made five hundred venturi. Which was a hundred more than they had rockets to use them.

Izabella was not comfortable. She was living in New Ruzuka and still not at all sure what was going to happen to her. Most of the villagers were willing enough for her to fill a role not that dissimilar to the role that her family had played in old Ruzuka as an arbiter of disputes. But they weren't going to be in any great hurry to give her half the crop to pay for that service. Granted, she owned a good share of the corporation, and if it ever started paying dividends it would help support her. But the way it had worked out was that the corporation was paying the farmers, and that pay came out first, before everyone divided up any profits. So Izabella's net was not going to be the same as the fifty percent of gross that her family had gotten in old Ruzuka.

Izabella's baby was going to be arriving soon and would need things. It wasn't that she was broke. She and her mother had cleaned out the family coffers when they ran off, and she still had most of her mother's old jewelry and most of the cash they had taken. It hadn't occurred to anyone to divide up the stuff when Elena became insane. No. That wasn't true. Izabella had thought of the money and jewels, hidden in a compartment in their wagon, then she'd thought of the fact that she was pregnant and kept her mouth shut.

The Czar's Bank in Ufa had taken that money, even the paper money, at face value, as a deposit, so she had money. But if she didn't figure out what to do with it, she was going to run out in a year or two. Then she and her baby would be living on her share of the village profits. And Izabella had expenses. She had a position to maintain. Her share of the profits of a farming village might not be enough for a proper household.

She heard Vera and Stefan coming up the path to her wagon arguing about something. Actually, Vera was arguing. Stefan was grunting. It wasn't an uncommon phenomenon.

Izabella got up and waddled to the door. "What did they want?"

"They want Stefan to build a factory to make rocket nozzles," Vera said.

"That's interesting..." Izabella didn't know whether it was good or bad. She'd heard Vera arguing with herself while Stefan grunted, but she hadn't heard what Vera was saying.

"The Czar's Bank in Ufa is willing to make us a loan to set up a factory to make the nozzles. But it's going to be expensive and only the government is going to be interested in buying the rocket nozzles and that means..."

Izabella listened as the older woman described the deal and she had a thought. "Wouldn't it be better to have a more general factory so that it could make more than just rocket nozzles?"

"Sure. But that would cost even more and even though the loan is at what Anya assures us is a sweetheart rate, we're going to have to pay it back. And if we ask for more, they are going to up the interest rate."

"I don't like putting the family back in debt," Stefan put in. "It's too much like being a serf again."

That clearly was what the argument had been about, and Izabella understood. She had been living with these people all her life, and on the trip from old Ruzuka they had talked to her. She had learned their fears. To a Russian peasant, debt was a chain. A chain that tied them to the land and made them the property of whoever owned it. That was why everyone in New Ruzuka walked around with their chests puffed out. They owned their own land. They were their own people. They had taxes to pay, but no debt to tie them to the land.

"Czar Mikhail is forcing you to take on debt?"

"No. Anya says that it will be the company that will take on the debt. She says that the worst thing that could happen is that the bank would take the factory if the debt got too big."

"Do you believe her?"

"Yes, I think I do."

Izabella considered. She had money, even a lot of money by the standards of a Russian peasant village. What if she were to own the factory? "Do you think they would give me the loan? I mean, then I could hire Stefan to make the rocket nozzles, add in my money to make some different molds. You're talking about using a drop hammer, right?"

Izabella looked over at them and Vera was shaking her head. "What's wrong?"

"They're offering the loan to Stefan because of his experience with the drop forge in Poltz and because he made a drop hammer in old Ruzuka. Also because they sent a guy out to New Ruzuka to see how he had set up his drop hammer there as part of his shop..." Vera trailed off and Izabella realized that there was something else.

"What's wrong?"

"It's not wrong, Izabella. Not exactly. You were a big help on the trip and even in getting ready. But the truth is, we don't want to work on your land or in your factory."

Vera was trying to be fair, even gentle, but it was like a slap in the face. Izabella turned and ran— waddled—back to her wagon.

"I should go talk to her," Vera said worriedly and started to follow. Stefan reached out and took her arm in his large hand. It was a gentle hold, but it might as well have been an iron cuff, so far as her being able to break free was concerned.

"Give her time," Stefan said, "and talk to Father Yulian."

"Part of the problem is that young Alexander is off at Kruglaya Mountain and nothing is really settled between the two of them," Father Yulian explained. *And part of the problem,* Stefan thought, *is that she has your child in her belly.* Father Yulian often gave excellent advice and his skill at dealing with people was phenomenal. He was also well-, if self-, educated. But he was quick to shift responsibility from himself to almost anyone else. Stefan couldn't help but like the man, but he had little respect for him. On the other hand, Izabella didn't seem any more anxious to marry Father Yulian than he was to marry her, so maybe it wasn't quite as straightforward as it seemed.

"But, in truth, I don't think that is the real issue. She doesn't know her place in the world. She helped us out of bondage, risking her father's wrath and even death. That was a brave and noble act. But in doing so she left behind her place and her certainty. She doesn't know where she fits and when she tried to make a new place on the only terms she knew, you rejected her."

"You think . . ." Vera began hotly, but Yulian held up his hand.

"No, I don't. To an extent we all owe her for our present liberty, but that doesn't mean she has the right to make us serfs again. You were right to reject her offer as it was offered, but she wasn't offering nothing. Correct me if I am wrong, but wasn't she offering to put up her money?"

"Yes, but she was going to own the company," Vera said and Stefan nodded.

Yulian nodded. "That banker in Ufa, the one who studied up-time law in the Dacha and helped us set up the New Ruzuka corporation . . . he said something about ownership being as complicated up-time as in the here and now, just in different ways. Perhaps we could do something like the village corporation, with Izabella and even the rest of the village buying in.

In any case, he is someone we should talk to about
Izabella's proposal. Perhaps we can find a kind of
ownership that will suit us all."

It wasn't till later that Stefan realized that Father
Yulian had managed right then to cut himself in on
the deal. Everyone had gotten their share of land, but
not everyone in the village was going to be a farmer.
Stefan had his smithy, Anatoly had his carpentry shop,
Father Yulian had his church and a school, and there
were several other villagers who wouldn't be farming.
Even the ones who were farmers in farming season
would be spending their winters weaving, assuming that
they could get the thread. Stefan was paid in promissory notes for the tools and parts he built in his smithy.
It was much the same for Anatoly. Father Yulian got a
stipend for the church and the school. Next fall, when
the crop came in, the New Ruzuka Corporation would
make all those promissory notes good before paying
dividends, along with the notes that the farmers would
get for their work plowing and reaping. It had all taken
a great deal of negotiation. It looked like the iron works
was going to be just as confusing.

There were two more trips to Ufa to discuss the
issues of ownership and control. One with just Father
Yulian and Izabella and a second with Stefan, Vera,
Dominika, Anatoly, Klara and Boris. Dominika and
Boris, aside from their own investment, represented
a bunch of the villagers who had scraped together
what they could to add to the pot. Even all together
it was less than Izabella was putting in, and she had
managed to get a message to Alexander and gotten
his authority to bring him into the deal. At the same
time, Stefan's and Anatoly's skills were crucial to the

endeavor. The way it worked out, no one would possess a clear majority of ownership. Izabella and Alexander would together have a plurality with twenty-five percent, but Stefan, Vera, Anatoly, and Father Yulian could match them. The added capital investment meant that they could get a bigger loan from the bank as well.

The new factory in Ufa would make venturi, but even while it was making them they would add in induction heating, steelmaking, and additional dies. Also, a woodworking shop, both to make parts for the factory and to make stuff to sell. They hired consultants from the Dacha immigrants.

They weren't the only ones to hire Dacha immigrants as consultants.

Not every farmer in Russia wanted to be a farmer. That was especially true of former serfs. Farming had very low status in Russia in the seventeenth century. It was the occupation of serfs. There were exceptions to that and gradations, but in general a smith was higher status than a farmer. Almost anyone was of higher status than a farmer. Besides which, farming is heavy and uncertain work. Some of the escaped serfs who poured into Ufa were looking for land of their own, but by no means all. Most wanted some other form of work, work that paid them money with which to buy food. Factory work filled that niche, and the new farming equipment— new plows, new reapers, and so on—meant that they didn't need as many farmers to grow a crop. So the switch from primarily farming to primarily industrial didn't necessarily mean everyone starved.

It was a very good thing that for now at least they held the lower Volga and access to the farms along the lower Volga, and the fish from the Caspian Sea.

CHAPTER 15

Cocktail Hour

Five miles upriver from Sviyazhsk, Volga River

Andrei Fefilatevich Danilov had expected to be in sight of Sviyazhsk in a day and a half. Of course, he hadn't expected to be dead either. Petr Ivanovich Chaplygin was a wiser, or at least more cynical, man. He had been personally less sure of the steamboat as a weapon of war from the beginning. But the Danilov family were the patrons of his family and he had supported his patron.

After the first ambush where Andrei Fefilatevich had been killed, they had put troops out on the southwest side of the river. Then they'd been ambushed from the northeast side. Two more mines had gone off, neither sinking a boat but both doing serious damage that had forced them to stop and make repairs. Almost three weeks to cover sixty miles. Leaving the damn boats in Moscow would have been faster. Petr was just angry and he knew it. The truth was that for most of the trip from Moscow the steamboats had traveled at a speed to put the fastest cavalry to shame. But once they got into enemy territory, the weakness of the steamboats became apparent. They were incredibly vulnerable to ambush, and the underwater explosives were deadly.

Kruglaya Mountain, Sviyazhsk

Lieutenant Vadim Viktorovich Lagunov walked up the hill to the citadel in good spirits, if utterly exhausted. After the first four days, Major Ivan Maslov had left him in charge and he had spent the rest of the time leading his contingent of scouts and his one supporting steamboat back ahead of the attacking force, slowing them. He was quite proud of his accomplishment.

"Sergei!" He waved at his brother.

"Vadim! I have been worried since the red-headed bastard left you out there with just a bunch of Cossacks."

Vadim felt himself stiffen. He remembered calling Major Maslov the red-headed bastard himself. Now it was like something from another life. But his brother hadn't been with them, hadn't seen . . . didn't know. "It wasn't like that, Sergei. The major . . . he knows what he's doing. We delayed four steamboats for almost three weeks, and we only lost four men. They crawled every step of the way, always looking around for us. We bought you the time to get the rockets. Where are they?"

Sergei was clearly not impressed. "He left you out there, outnumbered and on your own, while he got fireworks. He's been playing with them for the last couple of days. Taking ranging shots, he calls it. And they don't even have explosive heads! They have something he's calling Molotov vodka bottles."

"How do they work?"

"They mostly don't. Just land in the river and go to the bottom." Then, apparently trying to be fair, Sergei added, "Well, he got a couple to the far bank and one of them lit the bank on fire for a few minutes."

They continued walking up the hill, then climbed up to the bunkered platform where the rocket stands were set up. Major Maslov was bending over a framework, talking to a craftsman in the uniform of a Gorchakov retainer. The captain looked up. "Welcome back, Lieutenant. You did well. You bought us more time than I expected. I'd show you the results, but if we fire a rocket now they will be able to see its arc. And I want them to come as a surprise for our guests."

Vadim looked at the stands and then at the rockets. There seemed a lot of rockets. "Do we need so many?"

"I'm afraid we won't have enough. They aren't all that accurate and the Molotovs don't always ignite. I'm afraid they will get past us."

"Should I take the men back out and continue the harassment?"

Major Maslov shook his head. "No. If we can savage them, so much the better. But General Lebedev has cannon at the Kazan kremlin. They aren't great cannon, but he does have cannon. And they are making more rockets even as we speak. Also, the general now has over a thousand men under his command. Those four boats aren't going to take Kazan. Besides, have you noticed the Volga is freezing at night? The ice is thin and it breaks up when the sun comes out, but steamboats are going to stop being an issue in another month or so. The best we can do is the best we can do. Now we wait for the battle."

Sviyazhsk
October 1636

Ivan looked through the telescope at a stake pounded into the far bank of the Volga and waited. Impatiently. He looked up from the telescope, and saw the riverboats. Eye back at the telescope, he waited some more. Finally the bowsprit of the first converted riverboat came into sight through the telescope and Ivan yelled, "Fire."

It took a few seconds. The rockets had fuses and the fuses had to be lit and burn down. That had all been taken into account, the calculations made. In theory, the salvo of rockets—twenty of them—would arrive at a point in the river at precisely the same time as the lead riverboat got to the same place.

The fuses burned down and the rockets flew and Ivan enjoyed the consternation of the crew as they saw the lines of white smoke tracing the rockets' route across the sky.

They flew mostly straight, but at almost two miles "mostly" isn't nearly good enough. Of those twenty rockets, only one hit the lead steamer. And all it seemed to do was crash through the rear decking and disappear into the ship. The ship didn't slow and there was no visible fire.

Ivan was disappointed, but not dismayed. He had hoped for better, but it wasn't like he had expected every missile to hit. "Ready the next salvo."

Petr Ivanovich Chaplygin was on the second ship again. He had decided early on that the place for the commander of the expedition wasn't on the first ship. Also, he had spread the ships out so that they would have more time to respond in case of mines. It was, he decided, a very good thing he had. Because one of the rockets landed in the water not thirty feet ahead of his boat. And that meant that he would be in the shot pattern of the next set of rockets. Petr was a quick-thinking man, and the first thing he thought of was keeping Petr alive. This wasn't cowardice, just pragmatism. He couldn't do his job if he was dead. Going into that shot pattern would do no good. He could try getting away, either turning around or making for the far bank. But he didn't know what might be waiting on the far bank and putting his tail between his legs wasn't going to win him any points with the director-general. "Hard to port," he shouted. "Make for Kruglaya Mountain and have the other boats do the same. Let's take the fort." His ship was the first to turn and it took a bit of time to signal the leader and get it turned. A bit too much time as it happened.

The lead ship was still in its turn as two rockets from the second salvo hit amidships and in the stern. Blind chance had the second hit strike the edge of the hole that the first rocket had made. It ripped the Molotov cocktail warhead wide open, spreading burning alcohol and fish oil throughout the aft hold. That hold already had quite a bit of flammable liquid in it from the first hit, and that ignited as well. There was a gusher of flame from the stern of the steam boat, then a delay. The crew was busy fighting the fire at the bow, and they failed to notice the fire igniting the fuel for the steam engine. The flames spread and the engine crew were forced to retreat from the engine room. The boiler explosion almost managed to save the day by driving the oxygen out of the compartments, but it didn't quite put the fire out. Once the steam escaped, the fire came back.

All this took time, and by the time steamboat one was abandoned, no one else had time to notice.

The last thing that Ivan Maslov was expecting was that the steamboats would turn and attack. In part that was because it was, in Ivan's opinion, incredibly stupid. The enemy would be attacking uphill and Ivan had almost a hundred men at arms, not counting the monks, who would probably fight on his side.

Even if all three boats got here, there wouldn't be more than three hundred men attacking. Three to one up against defensive positions was not good odds. Ivan looked around to see if there were any more troops coming from another angle. From his position atop the small mountain, he had an excellent field of view. But nothing seemed to be coming this way. There were some troops ashore, but they were on the other side of the Volga.

Ivan looked back at the boats. The tactic looked like it would work, at least to throw off the aim of his rockets. He would have to raise the rocket troughs and that would increase the flight time while the targets were moving straight at them, so it would be hard to gauge their speed. Ivan calculated in his head and gave instructions. Then another salvo was launched. It flew up and up and seemed to hang there at the top of its arc forever. Then the rockets slowly started back down. By the time they hit the water, they were all well behind the steamboats heading for the docks.

Ivan considered taking the troughs out of the bunker

and pointing the rockets directly at the approaching boats, but that would take five minutes at least. More likely ten. By then the steamboats would be at the docks. He calculated again, adjusted the aim once more, and sent another salvo. But he didn't watch this one. Instead, he turned to Captain Sergei Lagunov. "Captain, gather the men and head for the docks. It looks like we are going to have company. I'll try to support you with indirect fire." It wasn't an order that Ivan liked giving, but at this point he knew more about firing the new rockets than anyone. Besides, he was going to have to be the one to decide whether the risk to his own people . . .

"Got one," shouted one of the rocketeers.

Ivan looked over. A second of the steamboats was on fire and turning away. That left one untouched, and coming up on the docks.

As he watched that single ship coming on, Ivan noted the fundamental difference between land armies and waterborne armies. On land the army would have broken by now, as hundreds of individual soldiers decided for themselves whether to stand or run. Each man who ran made it easier for the next to run and harder for the others to stand. But the boat that was steaming for the docks was doing so because the ship's captain decided to. The soldiers on the rails, and even more the sailors manning the engines, had very little idea what was going on in the rest of the battle and no choice at all where the boat went. Not unless they wanted to mutiny, which was a whole different question than just turning and running in the confusion of battle.

Sergei looked at the steamboat and considered his options. The dock was a long stonework dock that went along the bank, so once the enemy debarked they would be spread out. On the other hand, if he charged now he could take the boat. He started up and a hand grabbed his arm. "Sergei, no!"

Sergei swung around and almost hit his little brother. Vadim shouted. "No! If we go out there Major Maslov can't support us with the rockets."

"He can't anyway, not at this range. He'd be shooting almost straight up. They would go wherever the wind took them."

"There is also cover. We have it here and we won't on the docks."

By the time he and his idiot little brother had finished arguing, it was too late. The troops on the boat weren't on the boat anymore. They were on the dock. On the other hand, Sergei's men were in place with their AK3s loaded and ready.

"Fire!" shouted Vadim. "Reload. Quickly now, boys, but don't forget to prime your pans."

The smoke was clearing from the first volley. It had been effective. At least five men were down down there, and the return fire from the dock had not hit anyone. It was the difference between standing in the open and crouched behind cover.

The commander down there was shouting to his men too. "Reload! Cock and aim. Fire!"

The enemy were firing their second round while Sergei's men were still reloading. That was the difference between flintlocks and caplocks. A bullet flashed by and Sergei felt a stinging in his right arm. He reached across with his left hand and felt wetness. Then it really started to hurt.

"Fire!" Vadim shouted again, and the battlefield was

wreathed in smoke. Between them and the attackers, they were firing too fast for the smoke to fully clear before the next volley blinded them all again. And that, Sergei realized, was to the enemy's advantage. So far Sergei himself was the only one of his people wounded and that was because he was standing up arguing with Vadim, not crouched behind cover. He crouched and shouted. "Wait for the smoke to clear!"

He looked around and turned back to Vadim. "They are going to charge soon."

Vadim nodded, then pointed up the hill. "We need to get some people up there to cover our retreat."

Sergei looked down at the docks and up the hill, then nodded. "You do that. Take the men you had out on the march and get up there."

Vadim nodded again and started shouting names. He shouted some orders and Sergei didn't pay much attention. He was watching the gun smoke slowly drift away. He could see the enemy again, shadows in the acrid gray fog. "Wait a little longer," he shouted.

Suddenly the enemy were running up the hill toward his men. "Fire!"

The bayonets were an adaptation that had gained rapid acceptance from Russian troops. Everyone wanted one. And by now, with the stamp presses, just about everyone who had a gun of any sort had a bayonet. They were not great steel. Anyone from Damascus would spit when they passed by. But they were sharp and hard enough to cut. And there were scores of them charging his command. Sergei drew his sword with his right hand. His arm hurt, but it seemed to be working. Sergei didn't have time to worry about it.

❖   ❖   ❖

Vadim got his men in place just in time to see the enemy charge strike home. Now there weren't two forces, just a milling mob. Well, not entirely. His brother was holding—being pushed back, but slowly. "Aim for the rear ranks, men. And only aimed fire now."

His men started shooting. Not a volley this time, but the crackle of individual fire. Sergei was holding them in place while Vadim's boys were sniping them. Vadim looked at the battle and saw a man in the fanciest coat that he had ever seen. The man had a tall fur hat as well. Vadim took careful aim and fired. And missed. Apparently not by much, though. That man was looking right at Vadim. He turned and pointed his pistol up the hill, aiming at Vadim, and started shooting. Vadim was under cover, only his head sticking out, and he was at least forty yards away, so it wasn't surprising that the man missed with all five shots.

What was surprising was that one of the shots was close enough for Vadim to see the wood chips from where it hit a log. Ducking behind his cover, Vadim reloaded quickly and then laid his AK3 on the log and took careful aim. The fancy coat had managed to reload his pistol faster than he'd been able to reload his AK3 and there was another fusillade of shots. Then Vadim fired again, and the man went down.

That caused consternation in the enemy's ranks, and they started peeling away and running back toward the boat.

Ivan Maslov watched the battle from the hilltop till the enemy broke, then he realized he hadn't given any instructions for what to do if they won. Ivan ran for a horse, any horse he could find. He needed to get down there now and avoid a blood bath. Besides, he wanted that boat. He wanted those guns. Especially the cannon.

As it happened, he needn't have worried. Sergei and Vadim had been happy enough to take the enemy's surrender, even patching up Petr Ivanovich Chaplygin, who apparently Vadim had shot in the left leg. Vadim insisted that it was intentional, but Ivan didn't believe it. He also didn't publicly question it. In fact, he was fulsome in his praise for everyone from Alexis who had been in charge of placing the mines through Sergei and Vadim and the troops. The first battle of Ivan's first command had been a victory, and nothing breeds esprit de corps like victory.

Now if they could only survive long enough to get some sort of armaments.

The next evening

The cannon from the steamboat were still being hauled up Kruglaya Mountain. They were good guns, if light. Rifled breech-loaders that would reach across the river. And once they got the ones from the sunken steamboats they would have eight.

Petr Ivanovich Chaplygin was drinking copious amounts of vodka as anesthetic for his leg. The bullet had apparently chipped his thigh bone and the surgeon had been busy for a couple of hours, cutting him up and sewing him back together.

"General Birkin has an army of fifty thousand men," Chaplygin said, sounding both belligerent and aggrieved to Ivan. "You won't stop him with your fancy tricks."

"I don't expect to stop him," Ivan offered calmly. Chaplygin had been one of those officers who despised the academy and the baker's boy. Ivan knew him and didn't like him at all, but the more important issue was getting some intelligence. Ivan needed to know what the enemy had in mind. To do that he needed to engage Chaplygin in conversation.

"Even so, Ivan, I wonder if we have enough men," Alexander Volkov said. "Sure, this is a great position. I know that, you know that. Ivan the Terrible knew it when he put the fort here. But the best fort has to have people manning it."

"'At's right," Chaplygin slurred. "And peasants won't do it, not like Vadim here. I put a dozen shots into the tree he was behind and he kept calm and shot me in the leg. Lazy peasant wouldn't do that. Buggers would run as soon as the wood chips started flying!"

Ivan hastily waved Alexander down before he could correct Chaplygin on the courage of peasants when they were armed and defending their own.

Alexander raised an eyebrow, but subsided and sipped at his vodka. Luckily, Chaplygin had been too absorbed in his declaration to notice.

"Perhaps. But we are getting more warriors coming to our side every day." He waved at Alexander.

"What got into you, Alexander? I thought you had better sense than to go over to the revolutionaries."

"It's the czar, Petr," Alexander said. "How can it be treason to serve the czar?" Alexander, Ivan knew, was a friend of Petr Chaplygin. They had lived in Moscow, serving together, the young men of the royal court.

"Hah! Mikhail is a nothing. Weather vane turning with the lightest breeze. It's the boyars and the great families that matter. And us, the *deti boyars* and the *dvorianes* who run the empire. That's what you are. A traitor to your class."

"And how is Sheremetev treating the *deti boyars* and the *dvorianes*? Like we are peasants, that's how," Alexander shot back.

"Gentlemen, let it pass," Ivan said, and Petr Chaplygin sneered at the upstart baker's boy promoted above his station. Ivan found it hard to let that pass, harder than it had been when he was back in the Moscow Kremlin. But he kept his mouth shut, by remembering that his side had won. "As to your comment about General Birkin, we have more men every day and the differences in range and rate of fire of the new weapons means that the balance of force has shifted in the direction of the defender."

"You and your war games." Chaplygin snorted. "Little cardboard cutouts aren't men, and calculations aren't battles. Battles are won by courage and willingness to get in close and rip out your enemy's guts. Birkin will go right around you. And what will you do then? I'll tell you what you'll do. You'll sit on your hill and lose, or you'll come out of your fort and be slaughtered by real men."

"And how will General Birkin supply his army with us sitting on his supply route?" Ivan asked, letting some of his irritation show.

"He'll draft peasants and have them carry the supplies. It's all they're good for."

Ivan couldn't help it. He snorted a laugh of his own. "So he's going to stop his boats upriver of us and carry his supplies by land three hundred miles. That's going to take a lot of peasants and a lot of horses. And where is he going to get the wagons, carry them on the riverboats?"

"Maybe," Chaplygin insisted, sounding belligerently uncertain.

"He might even be able to do it," Alexander cut in. "But the time, Petr, the time."

Ivan Maslov listened with half an ear as the conversation continued. It was a race now. They had to get enough troops into Kazan and the top of Kruglaya Mountain to hold them and block the river. As long as they held the river, any progress that Birkin's army made after that would be at a snail's pace. They weren't ready to do that yet, but if Birkin gave them a couple of months they would be. They would have a thousand men and more guarding the mountain, and ten times that in Kazan.

General Ivan Vasilevich Birkin's army was refitting in Nizhny Novgorod when they got the news of the loss of the steamboat flotilla. He didn't curse, at least not much. He hadn't had great hopes that the steamboats would take Kazan, but it had been a chance and it would have made his life easier. He looked at his cousin. "Well, that decides it. Unless we get orders to the contrary, we'll wait here till hard winter, then proceed to Kazan. In the meantime, I want to turn Nizhny Novgorod into a supply base. I want all the food, shot and sundries needed to support an army of fifty thousand for four months in place here."

The war and the rest of the world were just going to have to wait.

Goritsky Monastery
October 1636

"I don't believe it. The riverboats didn't even get to Kazan. They were stopped at Kruglaya Mountain," Elena said.

Several of the new arrivals chimed in. When husbands had been shot or even tonsured, their wives had been sent off to the nunnery. Goritsky Monastery probably held more women who had been married to boyars than any place outside Moscow. Some were widowed, some forcibly divorced, some had taken their divorce well. In two cases, even thankfully, but many were highly resentful of the Sheremetev government. And many if not all of them were political animals.

The conversation quickly turned into an analysis of which great house was going to switch sides now that Czar Mikhail had proven much harder to handle than predicted.

Sofia listened with half an ear. She was preoccupied with the mica industry just now. A great deal of the Gorchakov family wealth was tied into the delivery of Muscovy mica capacitors to the USE. And here she was, not very far at all from major mica mines. She looked over at Tatyana Dolmatov-Karpov. She was the widow of Lev Dolmatov-Karpov, who was an ally of Sofia's family on the duma, and been executed in the weeks after Czar Mikhail escaped. Tatyana was the low end of the great houses, but her family was deeply involved in the mica mines.

Hamburg, Germany
October 1636

The hammer hit with a dull thud. It was a weighted wooden mallet and it drove the rod holding the paddle in place four inches. Two more blows knocked the paddle out and it landed on the floor. Guy Sayyeau grunted as he lifted the replacement paddle up to the tread and the hammer worked again, this time pounding the new paddle into place on the caterpillar tread. It was a big paddle, a yard tall and two yards wide. It took two men to manhandle it into place and a third to drive in the oak stays. Or to knock them loose. The chain and the sprocket wheels were working well.

Captain John Adams had just about given up on his original design. The main issue was weight distribution. The Russian *kochi* were built more for ice traversing than ice breaking. They had a false keel to protect the ship during portage over ice floes. John had wanted to run his caterpillar tracks in front of the ship to break up the ice, but testing had shown that the weight-forward design was going to cause a series of problems. On the other hand, if the caterpillar tracks were placed back—but not quite all the way back—then they would lift the bow. The bow, as it pushed up on the ice, would raise the front of the tracks so that they would be able to bite into the ice and push the boat still farther.

"You really think we are going to have to do this much?" asked the man with the hammer, wiping sweat from his brow.

"I don't know. I know that we are going to have to make adjustments as we shift from in the water to on the ice."

"We always had to do that." Which was true enough. The *kochi* were constantly dragged up out of the water, then across an ice floe into the next stretch of water. In fact, the steam winches would make that easier. Which was essential, because this ship would be more than twice the size of the largest *kochi* John had ever seen.

Meanwhile the hull of the "fluyt and a half," Brent Partow's nickname for the oversized fluyt-style sailing ships, had been modified so that below the waterline it was much more like an uptime icebreaker's hull shape. And reinforced with heavy oak. The ship was coming along fine and the steam engine was being custom built by a shop in Magdeburg, while the chains were being built here in Hamburg. The chains were modified heavy roller chains, the sort used on motorcycles up-time, only much larger. There were two sets of chains, the drive chain that would transmit the power from the drive shaft down to the caterpillar tracks, and the caterpillar tracks themselves, which were actually only triple-wide roller chains with attachments on which a variety of treads could be placed. The treads could be spikes for a grip on ice, or even to rip up ice if it was weak enough, or paddles to push the boat through the water like a paddle wheel, but considerably lighter for the thrust delivered.

In testing, the system had worked moderately well and caused some modification in how the paddle-treads were made, and also a decrease in the number of paddles on the treads. It turned out that extra paddles gave diminishing returns once they got too close together. The other thing that had changed was the shape of the paddles. They had started out as simple flat panels. Now they were T-shaped with supports, so that the water pressure didn't push them flat or break them off.

Still, John had no illusions about how well those paddles would stand up to mud or ice, which was why they were detachable and why they would be taking lots of extras in the cargo.

Different parts of this ship were being built by different companies, even in different towns, so that they didn't have to wait on one part to be finished before starting on the next. It was going to save them time, but it was still not likely that the whole ship would be ready before January at the earliest.

CHAPTER 16
𝕿𝖍𝖊 𝕭𝖔𝖞𝖆𝖗𝖘 𝖔𝖋 𝖀𝖋𝖆

Ufa
October 1636

Timofei Fedorovich Buturlin looked out at the sprawl
that was Ufa and wondered why he had spent the last
week on a horse to get here. And he wondered, especially, why he had brought his frigging army with him.
He was the *pismenny golova* for Saratov and actually ran
the *Streltzi*. When Czar Mikhail escaped and the news
reached them, Timofei dithered till he got word from a
cousin that Director-General Sheremetev had purged
several boyars. Two killed and four sent to monasteries.

Then he decided that he preferred Mikhail Romanov
to Fedor Sheremetev. So he arranged a mass defection
and even hired a thousand Cossacks to accompany
them, and set out marching to Ufa. Now he was
wondering if he had made a mistake.

Three days later

Bernie and Natasha sat down to a private dinner.
Bernie smiled and showed her a rare bottle of wine

shipped—actually, smuggled—from France through western Russia.

Natasha smiled at Bernie's antics in showing her the label.

"Does Her Highness wish to try the..."

The door burst open and Timofei Fedorovich Buturlin stormed in. "You have to talk to Czar Mikhail!"

Natasha felt her face congeal. *Every time. Every single time.* She turned a cold eye to the latest addition to Czar Mikhail's court in exile. "I will certainly speak to His Majesty. I do so regularly. I am not at all sure you will like what I have to say."

"You have to get him to issue directives on taxing the Volga trade." Buturlin had apparently not listened. "The regulations are—"

He continued, but Natasha listened with only half an ear. As it happened, she agreed with him for the most part. The regulations did indeed need reforming to decrease the opportunities for graft from the local administrators. Back before Sheremetev had taken over, Mikhail would have simply issued the imperial decree and the law would be changed. Of course, he would have had to get the permission of the duma and the *Zemsky Sobor* before issuing it because of the agreement he had signed when they made him czar. The new law would have then been administered, or not, by one of the bureaus.

"No. We need a legislature," Bernie said. "Rule by decree will end up with a mishmash of laws that..."

Bernie was quoting Filip Pavlovich Tupikov. What Bernie had known of democratic government before he got to Russia could have been written on a postage stamp. Natasha wasn't convinced that Filip and Bernie were right on this one. Sure, in the long run, that was the sort of government that they wanted to set up. But they were in no position to elect a chamber of legislators to enact laws. It seemed the wrong approach in the middle of a civil war. Natasha looked at the wine that Bernie had set unceremoniously on the table when he started arguing with Timofei Buturlin and sighed. Then she went back to work as a diplomat, smoothing ruffled feathers.

Timofei had been made commander of the Ufa garrison because of the troops he had brought. Then the Cossacks had been detached from his command and sent to support General Tim in Kazan. The *Streltzi* were busy setting up businesses in Ufa and adding to its industrial base. Russia was coming apart, but not totally. The serfs were running, yes. But while there had been some atrocities as they ran, most of them were too busy running to stop for retribution. Cossack clans were breaking away and choosing sides. General Shein in Siberia had declared independence, along with Archangelsk. The situation was, at best, fluid. Natasha wished Colonel Nikita would get back.

"They have the second dirigible up," Nick told Czar Mikhail. "We saw it making a test flight."

Nick carefully didn't call the dirigible by name, but Mikhail grimaced anyway. It was already all over Russia that the new dirigible was named *Czar Alexis* not *Prince Alexis*. *Czar Alexis* ... It was a subtle move, declaring loyalty to the royal house, but at the same time declaring Czar Mikhail deposed. All without ever actually saying any of it in so many words.

"What do we do about it?"

"I talked with Tim and he wants to put rockets in every major city we control."

"How do you feel about that?"

"I hate it, Your Majesty," Nick admitted with a grimace. He looked out the window to the uncompleted hangar where the *Czarina Evdokia* was tied down. "Mostly because the idea of what those rockets would do to our hydrogen cells terrifies me."

"I don't like it either, Colonel, but we can't let them control our skies. What about the *Czarina Evdokia*, though? If we use rockets, they can do the same."

"Yes. I will be staying higher. It's not perfect, but it's the best we can do."

Moscow
November 1636

Director-General Sheremetev looked up at the sky and smiled. The *Czar Alexis* was circling Moscow to demonstrate that the government of Russia had its own dirigible. They didn't need Bernie Zeppi to fly. "Get my horse."

Colonel Vasily Chaadaev helped the director-general into the airship's gondola. It was fifteen feet above the ground and the older man was looking a little pale, no doubt from the climb.

Fedor Sheremetev looked around, then turned to Colonel Chaadaev and asked, "How quickly can we get to Bor?"

"Four hours, give or take, Director-General."

"Take us there, then."

"Yes, sir."

❖   ❖   ❖

Ten minutes into the flight, Fedor Sheremetev was regretting his impulsive order. The airship was so high that the land below looked like a detailed map. But Fedor knew it wasn't. He knew perfectly well that were he to fall out one of the gondola windows, he would fall for a long time before he hit the ground. And nothing was holding them up but sacks full of gas. Yet he couldn't retract his order. That would be too obvious. Fedor Ivanovich Sheremetev was a strong-willed man. He had faced armies and he knew how to hide his feelings. In a voice that was firm—if not as firm as he would have preferred—he said, "Colonel, I have some work to do. Please find me a room, some paper and a pen."

For the next four hours, Fedor Ivanovich Sheremetev endured constant gut-wrenching terror in a small, plain room with a table, chair, a steel-nibbed fountain pen and several sheets of blank paper. When, after an eternity, they reached Bor, Sheremetev rolled up the blank sheets and put them in his tunic. He stood and left the room, walked down the passage, and since the dirigible was docked in its hangar, he could walk down a ramp to a staircase.

The inspection of the facilities was thorough, as Sheremetev put off the trip back to Moscow. But when there was nothing more to inspect, he still could not face climbing those stairs and getting back in the dirigible. It was the knowledge that nothing would be beneath him, just thousands of feet of empty space. He couldn't admit to the fear, though, not when all the world knew that Czarina Evdokia loved to fly, and Mikhail enjoyed it as well.

"Colonel, I was impressed with the *Czar Alexis*'s

speed. So I want you to fly over Ufa. Circle the
city at low altitude and let them know we're here.
I would like to accompany you, but I have business
that needs my attention. I will be taking a steamboat
back to Moscow." As excuses went, this wasn't great.
It would take him longer to get back to Moscow by
river than it would take the *Czar Alexis* to go to Ufa,
come back to Bor, pick him up, and take him back
to Moscow. But he was the director-general and no
one questioned him.

Ufa
November 1636

Bernie and Natasha walked hand in hand down the
hall toward Natasha's apartments, talking about car-
toons and the printing of flip books in Ufa and looking forward to a little privacy. A commodity in short
supply in Ufa in this year of 1636. The lack was bad
enough in the seventeenth century in Europe, but Ufa
had about three times the people it had room for,
even including all the new buildings that were going
up at an amazing rate. They reached the door to the
room Natasha shared with Anya, confident that Anya
was down at the docks with Olga. Natasha reached
for the door handle and a shout rang out. "Dirigible!"

Bernie shook his head, took another step, and
started pounding his head against the door frame.
"Every time. Every single time. I think I'm going to
kill Nick."

"They wouldn't be shouting like that over Nikita.
He's in here every week or so."

Bernie was suddenly all business. "You're right. We'd better go see."

"Not that there's anything we will be able to do about it."

When they got outside, they saw the *Prince Alexis* sailing overhead at no more than eight hundred feet. The name painted on the side of the dirigible was *Czar Alexis*, but Bernie had been in the room when Czar Mikhail had explained to his son, "You're not czar yet, and it will be a while before you become czar."

Alexis was jumping up and down on the battlements and imperiously ordering his dirigible to land and take him for a ride. The thing was low enough that he could see people in the windows and moving along the catwalks. One guy actually waved to Alexis, or perhaps it was to the czarina, who was next to her son on the wall.

Bernie turned to Natasha. "Do you know where Nick is supposed to be right now?"

"He's supposed to be in Dirigible Valley doing maintenance and resupply." Dirigible Valley was a box canyon in the Ural mountains—or at least their foothills—that was almost impossible to reach by land. Also its precise location was a fairly carefully guarded secret. In that box canyon, they had built tie downs and were in the process of building hangars and repair facilities that were to eventually become a construction facility for future dirigibles. Now, three months after they had found the valley, it was a thriving—if small—community with a couple of hundred people who, when not busy building stuff, hunted and fished to supplement the supplies brought in by the dirigible. They chopped wood and made charcoal for fuel for the dirigible and were building the sheds in which new gas bags would be made as materials became available. It was going to be at least another year before they could start on new construction, but even now they had enough of a structure in place so that the *Czarina Evdokia* was safe while they worked on it in its hangar.

"It would take him at least an hour to get here, then, even if they don't have the *Czarina Evdokia* opened up for repairs."

"So you don't think we should send him a radio message?" Dirigible Valley was out of direct radio range, but they had put together two repeater stations which gave them a three radio chain to Dirigible Valley. They could get messages to and from the valley in minutes.

"Not unless it looks like they are going to camp here," Bernie said, pointing at the dirigible in the sky.

The *Prince Alexis* made another couple of circuits of the city then flew away to the west. By the time it was leaving, Bernie and Natasha had been called to Czar Mikhail's council chamber.

The discussion was short and sharp. The consensus amongst the boyars of Ufa was that the dirigible *Prince Alexis* must be captured or destroyed.

Once that was decided, all appearance of consensus disappeared. Bernie and Natasha were pulled into an argument between the Embassy Bureau, Ufa Branch and the Streltzi Bureau, Ufa Branch. Young Ivan Borisovich was in charge of the Grantville section, just like his father was in Moscow. He and the other desks at the Embassy Bureau were upset at the complete dependence on the *Czarina Evdokia* for communications with all western powers. They wanted a secure route. Meanwhile, the Streltzi Bureau wanted more resources spent on upgrading the armament of the *Streltzi* and the new peasant levies that were being formed with volunteers from the escaped serfs.

By the time that was done, Anya was back in the room she and Natasha shared. Bernie, who had two roommates, had even less possibility of a private place.

"Bernie, I have a letter from my father," Ivan Borisovich said as they were finally leaving the meeting.

"Why didn't you show it to Czar Mikhail?"

"Perhaps I should have, but I don't want it spread around and some of the boyars talk."

Bernie stopped and looked at the teenager. They were in a whitewashed hallway with closed shutters and Coleman lanterns placed far enough apart so that Bernie got the impression of street lights. Islands of light in a dim hallway. He and Ivan were between islands. "What's so secret?"

"Sheremetev has been cracking down on the service nobility and Father says Georgii Petrovich Chaplygin has had enough." Ivan kept walking, and Bernie turned to walk with him. "He's running this way and would like a guide. He has three villages as *pomesti* and he lost about half his serfs when Czar Mikhail declared the end of serfdom. So he wasn't thrilled with Czar Mikhail but... well, Father didn't say, but something must have happened."

"How are we supposed to make contact with some guy on the road?"

"I know where his villages are. And he moved all the serfs into one village. He intends to bring them with him."

"Does he realize that they will be free once they get here?"

"I'm not sure," Ivan said. "He's not a bad man, Bernie. He cares for his family and he's loyal. It's..."

Bernie shook his head, half in disgust, half in resignation. The attitudes that were common among the service nobility, and not all that uncommon among the serfs, made no sense to him. "So what, exactly, does he want?"

"Like I said, a guide."

"And just how are we supposed to...? You're not planning on going, are you?"

"No. But I could show Nick on a map and then he could drop a guide."

"Just fly over and toss a guide out at five thousand feet?"

"I thought that the dirigible could land..."

"On the basis of a letter from your dad, who got it from some guy he knows, you want us to *land* the single most expensive and irreplaceable piece of equipment we have in enemy territory, at a predetermined location. What if your dad's friend is lying? What if he lets his plans slip to his cousin, who turns him in? Look, Ivan. I trust your dad's judgment, but he's asking a lot. Let me talk with Nick and see what he thinks."

On board the Czarina Evdokia

"So what do you think, Nick?"

"I think Able Airwoman Valeriya Zakharovna is going to get to play with her toy again," Nick said. Then, after a short pause, "No. She's going to have to teach someone else to do it. I don't want her wandering around in the woods where Sheremetev can get hold of her. Besides, she shows up in a village in Russia claiming to represent Czar Mikhail, no one is going to believe it. But we can map out a route for them to take, and then drop them a pathfinder with maps who has over flown the route."

"How long?" Bernie asked.

"At least a month."

"Why so long?"

"First we have to find someone. Then we have to teach them how to land. Val almost broke her ankle the first time she did it. We've since learned about the landing roll and the five points of contact." Nick pointed out the window and down to a stand of trees near the city. "Tim's going to have to fortify that, or cut it down."

Bernie followed the pointing finger. They were overflying Kazan to help with the mapping of the defenses. The Volga was starting to freeze up now. Once the rivers froze, they became paved and graded highways for troop movement. By January at the latest, General Birkin would reach Kazan with an army. Bernie made a note, then went back to the previous discussion. "Who do you figure to send?"

"We'll ask for volunteers," Nick said. "We won't tell them what they are volunteering for. Just that it will be dangerous and involves jumping out of a dirigible. I doubt we'll have any trouble finding people willing to try."

Bernie laughed. "As long as you don't expect me to do it!"

❖   ❖   ❖

They didn't have any trouble. Young men are young men and the urge to prove themselves is universal. The month of November passed and the rivers froze. Sheremetev's main army began to move. Meanwhile, more and more people were arriving in Eastern Russia. And the constant search for places to put them only got harder.

As well, controlling the members of the great houses who had defected from Sheremetev was getting harder and harder.

"This isn't working," Czarina Evdokia said. "The bureaus are too busy squabbling to get anything done." The government of Russia was—in theory—a totalitarian system. The czar told the bureaus what he wanted and the bureaus did it. That had probably been pretty much how it had worked in Ivan the Terrible's day. But Ivan had been a homicidal maniac who had ruled Russia through terror as much as anything. Boris Godunov hadn't been a lot better. Then the Time of Troubles had been anarchy. Mikhail had been chosen as czar because he was young and weak, and the government had become a literal bureaucracy—rule by the bureaus, with first Mikhail's mother, then his father, exerting more control than Mikhail had ever tried to exert. With Mikhail's escape and setting up in Ufa, they had entered a new phase. Mikhail had promised a constitutional monarchy, where the people of Russia would elect their own government. The problem was that, aside from some theoretical knowledge held by people like Filip Tupikov, no one knew how to do it. By now, even Filip was ready to admit that theory didn't match reality.

Bernie wasn't much help, because up-time he had paid no attention to politics and down-time he had mostly been drunk after the Battle of the Crapper. He hadn't paid any real attention to how they were trying to form a new nation. Besides, he had left for Russia before the Germans and up-timers voted on the New US constitution, much less formed the CPE or the USE. All Bernie could add to Filip's theory was that "politics are corrupt" and "political promises are always lies."

But how they were corrupt, he didn't know. Though Bernie was starting to suspect that the problems they were having with politics had something in common with the problems he had explaining plumbing right after he got to Moscow. It wasn't that they didn't understand how to work the system, just that they used different terms. "I agree that it's not working, Your Majesty. But unless we can ship in Mike Stearns, I don't know who we're going to get to explain it to us."

"Brandy!" Natasha said. "She wasn't that interested in politics at first, but starting in late '32, after Gustav and Stearns formed the CPE, she started talking about it in her letters. Also, Vlad said he used her to explain to him how the politics of the CPE and the USE worked."

"Vladimir's letters have discussed the structure and politics of the German government quite a bit," said Czar Mikhail. "Mostly in terms of what it meant in regard to the likelihood of the CPE or the USE invading Poland. Father was pushing hard for us to invade Poland after Gustav finally went to war with Poland in 1635. That's probably a big part of what pushed Sheremetev into actually having him assassinated. Anyway, Vladimir seemed to have a good understanding of the politics of the USE, and for that matter, the State of Thuringia-Franconia. He would be the one—" Mikhail paused at a look from his wife. "—in consultation with Brandy, of course, to help us figure out how to make politics work."

"Let's send them some letters. The dirigible can drop off letters at Nyenskans in the Swedish Ingria," Natasha offered. "The USE is recognizing both our government and Sheremetev's, at least to the extent of extending ambassadorial status to both Vladimir and Iurii Petrovich Buinosov-Rostovskii." The USE wasn't extending ambassadorial status to General Shein's Siberian state. From what they had heard, some of the English merchants were assuring Shein that England would recognize Siberia as an independent state next summer, in return for concessions.

There had been ongoing moderately cordial relations with Shein since he had taken Solikamsk in August. Aside from declaring Northern Siberia as independent from Russia and making sure that he had a route to the Volga, though, Shein had taken no action, declaring his neutrality in the conflict between Czar Mikhail and Director-General Sheremetev. It wasn't what they would have preferred, and after discussing it with Natasha and the rest, Bernie figured that Shein's position was unwise at best. If Sheremetev won, he would waste no time in crushing Shein, and if Mikhail won . . . well, he was less likely to crush Shein, but the general would not have much credit with the new government of Russia.

"Speaking of letters, how are negotiations going with Siberia?" Bernie asked.

"Shein says he will let us move goods through Siberia if we will take letters from him to the Swedish

Ingria on the Baltic for transmittal to England and the Netherlands. We're still negotiating the tariffs."

On the Czarina Evdokia, *over western Russia*

Fedor Yurevich looked out at black nothingness and wondered if this was a good idea. The dirigible was five thousand feet up and Fedor couldn't see a thing.

He looked over at Jump Mistress Valeriya Zakharovna, and she smiled. "Just remember your five points of contact. We're dropping you about a mile upwind of the village. You ready?"

Fedor managed to jerk a nod, even though he wasn't ready at all. She slapped his shoulder and he jumped. The harness jerked him up. It always came as a surprise. At least, it had in the two training jumps he had made before this. But once he was out, there was a feeling of freedom and peace that was like nothing he had ever felt before. He pulled on the wooden dowel attached to a cord that went up the risers to one of the two gaps in his chute, and his chute started a slow turn. He looked around, checking for landmarks and seeing vague shapes. The landscape looked different at night. He'd known that, but it looked more different than he expected, and he couldn't make out where he was or where he was going. He saw a light in the distance and steered for it.

Two minutes later, he landed on a trail and started gathering up his chute. Parachutes were expensive.

Fedor reached the village of Adelino about midmorning the next day. He had gotten turned around and ended up three miles west of the place. Georgii Petrovich Chaplygin was a well organized man. He had his villagers set up and prepared for a winter trek. He was also arrogant and supercilious, and Fedor didn't like him at all. They were forced together, however, and over the trip developed at least a grudging respect for each other.

Fedor wasn't the only pathfinder sent out to support defections. Some had better relations with the people they were sent to guide, others had worse. Some few were captured by the dogboys or turned in by the people they were there to guide. Over all, though, they did a good job of weakening Sheremetev and strengthening Czar Mikhail.

Russia House, Grantville
December 1636

"We have another request from Czar Mikhail and a letter from my Aunt Sofia," Vlad told Brandy as he plopped down on the couch in their private sitting room. It was a bit baroque for Brandy's taste, but much of its furnishings were made by the Russians here in Grantville. Gifts they couldn't refuse.

"What does Czar Mikhail want?"

"He wants us to write up a report about how to create a constitutional monarchy."

"We can probably do that. I mean, we have all the theory and we've been right here while the CPE and the USE were formed. Tell you what, though. You should talk to Ed Piazza and Helene Gundelfinger. Also Karl Schmidt..." Brandy went through a fairly long list of people who were involved in local and national politics that they knew and could call on, ending with "... about how to actually get things done in a constitutional government."

"Then I'll try to translate that to a form that will make sense to my friends back in Russia's bureaucracy."

"What about Aunt Sofia?"

"That's good news. She thinks she might be able to get us a shipment of mica. All she really has to do is get it into the Swedish territory on the Baltic."

"That is good news, but I worry about her. If Sheremetev catches her..."

"There is nothing we can do about that," Vladimir said. "We might as well do what we can. So, the report?"

It took them a while, but they managed to put together long letters on *how it's done in the real world*, which is a lot more messy than theory would suggest and had quite a bit in common with the ways the bureaus interacted. The real world techniques included things like trading your vote on this issue for someone else's vote on that issue.

Meanwhile, the *Catherine the Great* was mostly built. It was the talk of Hamburg. The *Catherine* was the new icebreaker. They were following the new Russian tradition of naming ships after royals, but they had decided to go with up-timer Russian royals. It was a compromise. Vlad had wanted to call it the *Brandy* and have "Brandy (You're a Fine Girl)" as its theme song. That was when Brandy threatened princeocide.

Vlad had several meetings with Ron Stone on what to take. Latest word was that they could make primers, even in Ufa. They considered sending rifles, but copper was the issue. There was now some copper production in Russia, but it wasn't enough for a brass cartridge industry. Besides, most of the copper production was in territory controlled by Shein, not Czar Mikhail. That meant that for now at least, Russia was going to be staying with the reloadable iron chambers of the AK series. Instead, Vladimir would be sending breechblocks for cannon, the new vacuum tubes that were just starting to be produced, litmus strips, catalysts, tube boilers, plus a host of other bits and pieces that could be the core of war production and industrialization.

In Russia, the rivers had frozen into roads. General Birkin and the army of western Russia were on the march from Nizhny Novgorod to Kazan.

CHAPTER 17

Kazan

December 1636

Nick looked out the window at the other dirigible. There wasn't much he could do about it. The *Czarina* wasn't armed except for the crew's personal small arms, and he doubted that the *Alexis* was either.

Nick was headed for Kazan to scout the position of Birkin's army and he figured that the *Alexis* was heading for Ufa to sneer at Czar Mikhail.

Ufa
December 1636

"It's back," Mama said.

Alexis looked at his mother, then at his father, and fought back tears. They had talked about this. And, in fact, it was his begging that had kept his papa from shooting at the *Prince Alexis* the last time it had come over Ufa. "Do we have to?" he asked.

Papa nodded. "Every time it comes here, it makes Director-General Sheremetev stronger."

"*I'll* do it then," Alexis said fiercely.

Papa looked at him for a long minute, then nodded. Slowly, Mama, Papa, and Alexis left their apartment in the Ufa kremlin and walked out to where the rocket men were manning the rockets.

Alexis looked up at the dirigible that bore his name and warned it one last time. "Land!" he shouted in his seven-year-old soprano.

The dirigible didn't land.

Alexis turned to Petr Fedorovich, who commanded the rocket men. "Shoot it down!"

Petr Fedorovich barely even looked at Papa before turning to the men. "Fire."

Several dozen rockets flew into the sky. Whoever was in command of the *Prince Alexis* was being over-confident. They hadn't considered that more effective antiairship weapons might exist than rifles and cannons. Even good land-based antiaircraft weapons could be negated by simply flying high enough. In the world the up-timers came from, German dirigibles bombing England had been quite safe as long as they stayed ten thousand feet above the ground. It was only after the English developed airplanes with machine guns capable of firing incendiary rounds that the German airships started suffering serious casualties.

Czar Mikhail and his forces didn't have any airplanes, much less ones capable of firing incendiary bullets. Even the USE didn't have any yet. But they had developed weapons which—with a bit of luck and some recklessness on the part of the enemy—had a chance of shooting down airships at low altitude.

The rockets had no guidance mechanisms whatsoever. Nor did they have contact fuses. Their fuses were as primitive as it gets—basically, the warhead was ignited when the fuel burned through to it. They were really best suited for area bombardment against land-based enemies.

Even with as big a target as an airship flying less than two hundred meters above the ground all but seven of the forty-one rockets missed the *Prince Alexis* entirely. Of the rockets which did strike, four simply bounced off the taut fabric skin, barely leaving a scorch mark. The other three managed to puncture it, but one of them uselessly over one of the hot air bags and one of them whose warhead went off too soon, after it had just penetrated the fabric. It tore a rent in the skin but did no more damage than that.

The last rocket, however, punched through the skin and into the forward hydrogen cell. The hole let hydrogen and oxygen mix and the rocket's warhead went off at the right time. The front of the dirigible jetted flame. With three cells, two hot air and one hydrogen, losing their lift, the *Alexis* nosed down. The engines couldn't compensate and the dirigible fell to earth in a slow-motion crash.

If the reporter who exclaimed "Oh, the humanity!" at the crash of the *Hindenburg* had been there to see it, he might have said something sounding shocked. But the seventeenth century was a hard-bitten century. And Russia was a hard country. So, aside from some cheers at their good shooting, no one in Ufa was particularly upset.

Not even seven-year-old Prince Alexis, not really. Yes, it was his dirigible, named after him and everything. But it had failed to land when he told it to. So it had gotten what it deserved.

✧   ✧   ✧

Across the river, the herd of goats that had to run for their lives as the crippled *Czar Alexis* crashed into their field were less sanguine about the matter. But no one was asking their opinion.

Nor were they asking the opinion of the men on board. The *Czar Alexis* carried a crew of twenty-three and could have carried twice that number. Instead it carried extra fuel, charcoal soaked in plant oils and alcohol which, by good fortune and good design, didn't catch fire. Most of the crew survived. A dirigible crash can be a slow thing, and people had time to brace themselves. Only seven members of the crew died in the crash and two more died of damaged lungs because they had been working next to the front hydrogen bag. A hydrogen fire is a hot fire. And inhaling burning hydrogen is deadly.

Lev Ivanovich survived the crash with only a broken arm. He was in the left engine car of the *Czar Alexis*. The body of the airship had absorbed the blow and it wasn't till the left engine car broke off the dirigible's main body that it was dropped. But that drop flung him into the radiator, which was how he broke his arm and burned it too. Broken arm or not, he knew the danger if the boiler blew so he was screaming at Lyubim Borisovich before they had stopped moving. "Open the release valves! Open the release valves!"

Lyubim looked at him in confusion for a moment then seemed to come to himself. He tried to stand on the tilted floor and managed to reach up and pull the lever that released steam from the tube boiler. That was in addition to the automatic pressure release valve which would, in theory, release the pressure if it got too great. The automatic pressure release valve had been working fine this morning, but Lev was in no mood to take chances.

Lev would learn later that the other engine car had ended up under the body of the airship and all the crew in it had died. It hadn't blown up either. The crash had smothered the fire as well as the crew and the steam in the boiler had never reached a pressure to cause an explosion.

Ufa kremlin, three days later

"In one way it's a total loss," Petr Nickovich said, looking around the room. Czar Mikhail, Czarina Evdokia, Princess Natasha, and Bernie Zeppi—not to mention Yuri Alekseyevich Dolgorukov, who had just been made the head of the Air Bureau—were in the meeting. Also present were Crown Prince Alexis, his older sister Irina, and little sister Anna. "At the least it will never fly again. On the other hand, with the knowledge of the *Hindenburg*, the skin of both the *Czarina Evdokia* and the *Prince Alexis* were treated with fire retardant chemicals and it appears to have paid off. Not so much stopping the airship from burning, but at least keeping it from going up like Bernie said the *Hindenburg* did. Still, the front hydrogen bag is gone and the front hot air bag is too. The middle forward hydrogen bag is badly scorched and I'm honestly surprised that it didn't go up. The aft portion of the airship is in better shape, if not good shape. All the bags were ripped in the crash and at first it seemed likely that fire would spread. But, probably because of the locations of the rips, the escaping hydrogen failed to find a spark." Petr was amazed at that. The *Alexis* could have just as easily gone up entirely. "Aside from the tears in all the gas bags which, except for the ones that burned, should be repairable, there is the damage to the superstructure. Airships are not designed to withstand hard landings. There isn't a ring that isn't broken in at least two places. The gondola and both motor cars are badly damaged."

"What about the engines themselves?" Bernie Zeppi asked.

Petr had to smile at the amount of up-time science the up-timer had learned since he had come to down-time Russia. "They came off surprisingly well. Some fittings will have to be replaced, but they can be repaired."

"So you can fix my dirigible?" asked Prince Alexis and Petr smiled again.

"Not exactly, but there are enough parts to help us build a new one."

"The *Princess Irina*," declared Princess Irina, "which is what it should have been in the first place."

Seven-year-old Crown Prince Alexis started to cloud up, and Petr lost all thought of smiling. Getting caught in the middle of a fight between royal siblings wasn't something to warm the heart of the wise bureaucrat. "We can use the *Czarina* to take the parts to Dirigible Valley and they ought to cut six months to a year off the time it will take us to build the next one."

"The *Princess*—."

Crown Prince Alexis kicked his older sister.

"Alexis!" Czarina Evdokia said sharply.

"Papa, he kicked me!" Princess Irina complained.

"Quiet!" Czarina Evdokia said, and there was quiet, even if it was leavened by baleful looks from the older children. "If you don't behave, it will be the *Princess Anna.*"

"Yay! I get a dirgabul!" proclaimed six-year-old Anna.

Bor
December 1636

Arkady, the radio operator in Bor, had the newest high speed recorder on his radio set, but it was only good with synced messages from other stations with the new system. What he was getting from the *Czarina Evdokia* was Boris Ivanovich clicking keys. The message came through clear enough. The *Czar Alexis* was down and Boris sent a list of dead, injured and captured. Arkady jotted it down as it came in and was yelling for little Petr before the message was finished.

As might be expected, the radio was attached to the dirigible works, so the casualties were friends and acquaintances of the radio operator. So was Boris Ivanovich, who was clicking out the message. Arkady acknowledged receipt, caught between anger over the deaths of his friends and sympathy for Boris. Boris Ivanovich had been friends with many of the crew of the *Czar Alexis* too.

Petr was there by the time he signed off and Arkady turned to his typewriter with the written note. He flipped the switch that engaged the transmission to the next station and started typing out the message. Two things happened as he typed. One was that a coded signal was sent to the next station and the other was a typed copy was made. The moment he was finished, he pulled the typed copy from the writer and handed the message to Petr.

Grigory Mikhailovich Anichkov, the new manager of the dirigible works at Bor, had been appointed after half the staff had run off to Ufa, and much of his job had been to make sure that that sort of defection didn't happen again. The other half of his job was to make sure that the dirigible works continued to turn out dirigibles. It wasn't easy and he didn't much like the job. The intellectuals—what Bernie Zeppi and Cass Lowry had called geeks—were all under a degree of suspicion after large numbers of them had followed Czar Mikhail into exile. Grigory wasn't a geek; he was a cavalry officer. He didn't particularly like the dirigibles or the radios or any of the other new innovations that led to the chaos that they were all facing. But Grigory wasn't a fool either. He realized how vital the *Czar Alexis* was to scouting the route of General Birkin's army on its way to Kazan.

He talked to the geeks and then ordered them to get something the size of the *Testbed* built as quickly as possible. It was a major change in priorities. Up till then, they had focused on making ever larger dirigibles because of what the intellectuals called "economy of scale." A larger dirigible could lift more for the amount of time and effort it took to make it. Now they would focus on making several smaller dirigibles, tiny by dirigible standards, with a lifting capacity measured in hundreds of pounds, not in tons. Work on the as yet unnamed third Czar-class dirigible was stopped and the D'iak class was introduced. They wouldn't carry nearly as much or have nearly the range, but they would be quicker to build and faster in the air. They would also be smaller targets and they could make three of them for the materials in one Czar-class dirigible. All of this took time and it would be months before the first D'iak came out of the hanger, but the decision was made that day.

Moscow
December 1636

News of the downing of the *Czar Alexis* was delivered to Bor by radio from the *Czarina Evdokia*. The *Czarina* was equipped with a spark gap transmitter. It wasn't all that powerful, but it did have a long antenna, so anytime it got close enough to a land-based radio it could share the news, so to speak. From Bor, it took less than two hours for the news to reach Moscow. Sheremetev wasn't grateful for the news, and he was even less pleased that the radio network had spread it all over Russia before he could do anything about it. In the days just following Mikhail's defection, the director-general had tried to get a handle on the gossip of the radio operators by making some of them examples. Within days he had lost dozens of radio stations. The operators had taken themselves and their radios off to join Mikhail.

In this case, the news was made even juicier because someone had leaked the argument between Crown Prince Alexis and Princess Irina as well as the czarina's decree that Anna would be the new name. It was just the sort of story that no radio man or parent could keep from sharing. It also put Sheremetev in the category of a an erring child.

In spite of knowing it wouldn't do any good, Director-General Sheremetev was tempted to make a few more examples. He didn't, though. Radios, even when they weren't transportable, were easy to break. And radio operators had a set of highly valuable skills that made it dangerous to mistreat them.

Instead he sent off radio messages of his own.

En route to Kazan
December 1636

General Birkin took the message from the exhausted post rider and handed it to his cousin. He could read, but it wasn't something he was all that good at and he didn't do it if he didn't have to.

    GO DIRECTLY TO UFA STOP
    BYPASS KAZAN STOP

He could do it. He was already marching along the frozen Volga. He could take his army south off the Volga, head directly for the confluence of the Volga and Belya River, and avoid Kazan altogether. But if he did, he would be stuck between Tim's forces in Kazan and Czar Mikhail's in Ufa. That would let Tim pull his army out of Kazan and shadow him all the way to Ufa, where Birkin's army would be trapped between the walls of Ufa and Tim's army. The *Czarina Evdokia* would keep Tim informed of his movements as well, so there would be little chance of turning and catching Tim in the open. Also, going cross country would be slower.

Additionally, General Birkin didn't have just a few malcontents in his army anymore. In the time he had spent waiting for the rivers to freeze, Czar Mikhail's forces had increased a great deal due to the "good will missions" that he and his wife had made on board their dirigible, stopping in any town or city where Sheremetev wasn't in firm control and promising a constitutional convention where all the peoples of Russia would have a say in the structure of the government. It was an effective ploy, and it had produced a lot of defections to Czar Mikhail's side.

Well, he didn't have to decide yet. The best place to leave the Volga highway wouldn't be for another three days.

General Birkin sent off his own dispatch. It went to Bor, insisting he needed an eye in the sky as soon as possible. That was true in any case, but especially true if he was supposed to march all the way to Ufa leaving the force in Kazan in his rear.

Well before that time, General Birkin got another dispatch canceling the order. Apparently cooler heads had prevailed. Or at least the director-general had had a chance to cool off a little.

Goritsky Monastery

"Bernie always said that the dirigibles were fragile in combat," Sofia said, a bit complacently.

"Sheremetev must be spitting nails," said Elena.

There was general laughter.

"Tatyana, have you written..." Sofia trailed off because Tatyana was shaking her head.

"I wrote my brother about them, but it's not so easy. Sheremetev has his cousin, Ivan Petrovich, overseeing the mica production. And he's skimming off so much of it that there's barely enough to satisfy the Moscow contracts."

Russia was still selling Muscovy glass or Muscovy mica to the USE, but it was not going through Vladimir. Instead, it was going to support the Sheremetev-appointed ambassador to the USE—and apparently to line the pockets of Ivan Petrovich Sheremetev, who was widely considered to be the most corrupt man in Russia.

That was bad news, but Tatyana continued. "He's doing what he can, but it will be months before he can find enough to make a shipment."

"Thank you for your efforts," Sofia said. "They will not be forgotten when Czar Mikhail wins."

Tatyana looked at Sofia, and she wasn't the only one. "Do you really think that can happen?"

"Yes, I think I do," Sofia said. "I wouldn't have believed it in June when Czar Mikhail ran off to Ufa, but now...I think he can win. It's not a sure thing by any means, but it's certainly a possibility."

New Ruzuka

Father Yulian went for a walk around the town of New Ruzuka. The buildings were mostly built by now, but it was way too late to do any planting. They had gotten most of the tree stumps out before the ground froze. Well, over half anyway. Barely over half, but over half, and that lumber had been put to good use. There was a lumber mill in Ufa that could cut logs into boards and the villagers, with the help of the riverboat they had stolen, had been shipping logs to Ufa and boards back to New Ruzuka from the beginning of October to the middle of November and then using those boards to make the double-walled wood panels that they had developed back in old Ruzuka from Dacha designs. Now those double-walled wood panels were being used as walls for the town buildings. The weaving shop and the carding house, smithy and the carpenter shop, the church and the barn, and the mill building were up, though they didn't have the millstones yet. A bunch of the young men were trying to build a freeze-drying facility. The cooper from Konevo had set up a cooperage.

Most of the houses were finished as well, and it was starting to look like New Ruzuka was going to be a nice town.

"Father Yulian!"

Yulian winced at the voice of Petr Petrovich, one of the young men who had joined them in Ufa. Petr Petrovich had delusions of martial prowess. "Yes, Petr?"

"When are we going to get the new chambers?"

"When Stefan gets around to it, Petr," Yulian said for what must be the hundredth time. Well, tenth, but Petr was so irritating about it that each repetition counted for ten. "First, we don't have the caps for the new chambers. Second, we don't have the need. An AK3 is fine for hunting and we have no great need of anything more. We're only a few miles from Ufa and any attack will come from the west through Ufa."

"They'll encircle Ufa, Father Yulian. I explained that.

And when they do that, they are going to start searching for villages to raid for supplies. Our being close to Ufa is a bad thing then, because we'll be first in their path."

"By then, assuming that Birkin gets this far, we'll all be in Ufa."

"Ufa doesn't have walls, either. And what if they surprise us?"

"That's not entirely true. The walls may not be complete, but there are bastions and several of the buildings are quite solid. As to them catching us out, don't be ridiculous. The *Czarina Evdokia* is keeping good track of General Birkin's forces."

The conversation went on from there. Petr being irritating and utterly convinced that the sky was about to fall on New Ruzuka. Yulian couldn't ignore the young man. He was a leader among the new additions to the town who had joined them in Ufa and used their land allotments to add to the size of the town's land and bank account in Ufa.

After a few minutes, Father Yulian lost patience. "What do you want me to do? Go into Ufa and demand that instead of sending caps to Kazan or Sviyazhsk they should instead send them to us?"

"They're making their own caps in Kazan," Petr said belligerently and Father Yulian threw up his hands in frustration.

Sviyazhsk kremlin, Kruglaya Mountain

"Alexander, do we have the caps?" Major Ivan Maslov asked.

Alexander Nikolayevich Volkov shook his head,

wishing he were back on the steamboat, laying mines. That had been his job after General Lebedev had assigned him here. Or better yet, he wished he was back in Ufa, with Izabella. Alexander could now admit without too much rancor that the baker's son was a truly clever young man, and even that his plans and plots had been the main factor that had stopped the riverboats. But the red-headed major was a horrible worry wart. The new caps for the caplock chambers weren't even expected for another two days, but Major Ivan had been harping on them for the last week.

It wasn't as though Alexander didn't understand the importance of the caps. A flintlock, or even a wheel lock, AK misfired fairly often. They also took longer to load. A caplock AK with loaded chambers could be reloaded almost as fast as an up-time single-shot weapon and almost never misfired, even in a pouring rain.

General Lebedev and the craftsmen in Kazan had promised them fifty thousand caps. Which wasn't a lot, but the main army was in Kazan, not here.

Major Ivan started to say something else, then managed to stop himself. "Sorry, Alex. I know it's not your fault, but the *Czarina* reports that Birkin and his men are less than forty miles from here. I really don't want them to invest us before we get those caps."

Alex nodded this time. It wasn't all that hard to convert a flintlock AK3 to a caplock AK4. There were kits to do it and they had plenty. The AK4 also took a different chamber, but they had a good number of the caplock chambers too. The holdup was the caps themselves. Ivan didn't want to change the AKs over till he knew he would have the caps for them.

The garrison on the mountain had grown with the addition of *Streltzi* and freed peasants. It was three thousand men now, and they were well dug in with some six-pound cannon and a lot of rockets. It would be a hard nut for General Birkin to crack when he got here, and he would be subject to attack from Kazan while he was trying.

Alexander remembered the war games he had played right here in this room over the last weeks. He had been Birkin, then Ivan had been Birkin, then Captain Lagunov. In fact, every officer in the fort had gotten to play Birkin several times. Scenario after scenario, trying to figure out what they would try. Alexander smiled. Captain Lagunov's frontal assault had been a disaster for the attackers, even though they had taken the mountaintop finally, because Lagunov had lost half his army doing it and General Lebedev, played by Ivan, had attacked his rear after he had committed to the attack. Almost, Alexander hoped that Birkin would try it. Not that Alexander wanted to be Davy Crockett at the Alamo, whoever that was and wherever that was. But from a strategic viewpoint, that would be the best outcome.

They went on talking about supplies and fortification. Alexander had become Major Ivan's logistics officer. He was the only other officer on the mountain with Moscow Kremlin training.

General Birkin looked up at the fortified mountain top and decided. A frontal assault was out of the question. His twelve-pounders could knock down the stone walls sure enough, but they couldn't knock down the mountain they were standing on. His troops would spend hours climbing that hill under fire. General Birkin had never heard of Pickett or Pickett's Charge, but even Pickett with Lee's spurs in his backside wouldn't have charged that hill.

"What do you think, Cousin?" asked Iakov.

"Well, we could sit out here till they starve," General Birkin said. "That shouldn't take more than a year."

Iakov laughed, but there was little joy in the sound.

"No. We'll do what we discussed. Leave a blocking force to invest it and move on to Kazan."

"How many?"

"It will have to be ten thousand. Five thousand might do it, but they might not either. So, without firing a shot, those people up on the hill have taken a fifth of my army out of the fight."

It took a week to invest the fort, during which Ivan, Alexander and the others manning the fort were caught between glee and chagrin.

What did you do in the war, Daddy?

Well, I sat on my ass on a mountain top while everyone else fought.

In the meantime, thanks to the view from the top of Kruglaya Mountain, Ivan was able to give Tim in Kazan clear and detailed reports on every move the enemy made, without any need for the *Czarina Evdokia* to stay around.

Kazan kremlin

General Boris Timofeyevich Lebedev looked out at the advancing armies with an assurance that wasn't exactly feigned. He believed his show of confidence was justified, at least intellectually. Kazan was a city on a hill. While some of the suburbs spiraled down the hillsides, the main city was an uphill slog for any sort of attacking army. But he only had six thousand men here. And in spite of the people who had been shipped to Ufa and old Kazan to get them out of the line of fire, he still had almost twenty thousand civilians in the city. Most of them busily working in the shops, making everything from extra chambers for the AKs to sandbags to reinforce the walls. That was a lot of lives depending on book learning from up-time books and Ivan Maslov's analysis.

Besides, Tim had just turned twenty and it didn't feel right to be confident facing generals with twice his age and much more than twice his field experience. In spite of which, he turned to the man standing next to him, who wasn't looking very happy at all. "We'll do fine," he said. From the expression on Abdul Azim's face, he was sounding a little too confident.

He looked over at Colonel Mikhail Petrovich Kolumb, who was scowling at him. "Relax, Colonel. Either we win or you get to crow over my defeat. You can't lose."

Colonel Kolumb's face started to turn red, but he was interrupted before he could speak.

"We are outnumbered, General," Abdul said.

"Yes. But they are attacking uphill against walls reinforced by sandbags with . . ."

Abdul held up a hand. They had gone over this before. The changes in war fighting technology had an effect on tactics. And they could see that General Birkin was following Ivan the Terrible's play book from eighty years ago.

"The longer he takes getting ready, the better off we are," Tim continued.

"I wish Czar Mikhail hadn't sent the dirigible off to Germany," Abdul said.

Tim wished the same thing, but it was an emotional wish. Between their location and Ivan Maslov's forces atop Kruglaya Mountain, they had most of the enemy under observation. Still, whatever the political advantage to fetching Prince Vladimir back from Grantville, Tim would have liked to see the *Czarina Evdokia* in the—

There was a roar of cannon. The attack had started. Birkin's cannon weren't very big. They were rifled twelve-pounders, but the twelve-pound projectiles were enough—if just barely—to knock down the walls that had been built to defend Kazan because those walls were curtain walls.

It would take them a while, but the cannons would blow a breach. It didn't surprise Tim, but it wasn't good news.

"They will be at it for days," Tim said, "perhaps weeks, before they get a breach big enough for an assault." He looked back up at the clear blue winter sky and wished the *Czarina* was in it.

CHAPTER 18

Death of a Czarina

Czarina Evdokia, *over Poland*

The sky over Poland was anything but clear. And the *Czarina Evdokia* wasn't a pressurized-cockpit jet that could fly over the weather. Instead when they didn't expect danger from below they flew at less than a thousand feet. Over Poland, they were flying at two thousand feet because they weren't sure how the Poles would respond to them. They had left Nyen five hours earlier, with a full load of fuel. For the first four hours, things went swimmingly, but for the last hour they had been getting deeper and deeper into cloudy skies. By now they were sailing under a bank of clouds and Nick seriously considered turning back.

An hour later, Nick wished he had. The clouds had closed in behind them and at this point he wasn't sure that he could get back, even if he tried. They moved on through a day that was as dark as night. Nick haunted the bridge, worrying. The winds were pushing them south from the coastal route they had been trying for.

Nick had some more of the hot bitter tea as he looked out at a night black sky and saw the first snowflakes illuminated in the airship's lights. "Shit," he muttered under his breath. "All right. We need to try and get above this, even if it means we have to vent hydrogen to get back down. Let's increase the hot air to the front cell and angle the motors down."

The *Czarina* climbed up into the clouds, but she did so slowly. There was a light dusting of snow on the massive airship, but even a light dusting on that large an area is a lot of weight and the *Czarina* struggled under the extra blanket. Slowly, they made their way through Poland to the USE. Unfortunately, to do it they were using fuel at a prodigious rate, and all the while the weather was getting worse.

By the time they reached the area of Berlin, they were struggling under a thin coating of sleet and the winds were picking up. They passed fifty miles north of Berlin, but by then even if they had passed directly over the city, they wouldn't have seen a thing.

The wind shifted and buffeted the huge airship. It jerked and jerked again. The tea set was tied down and so was most of the rest of the gear, but you can't get everything tied down. Pins came loose and rolled across the airship deck. Petr, who was trying to get a fix on their altitude, slipped and fell, then slid across the floor of the pilot house. Nick reached for him, but he was strapped in by a seat belt. Before he could get loose, the shaking had settled and Petr was trying to get back up. Reports of things coming loose and people injured came in as the wind jerked them again.

"Emergency!" came over the phone. "The hydrogen cell is leaking! I can see the fucking rip from here."

It took Nick a moment to identify Airman Lev Olegovich, a rigger assigned to section three. "Cut power to section three."

The chief electrician of the dirigible opened a knife switch and Nick prayed it wasn't too late. He looked out at the snow-filled night and at the edge of the ship's lights. He saw shadows. They were losing altitude.

For the next fifteen minutes, hydrogen cell five in section three vented hydrogen into the main body of the dirigible. They didn't lose lift because the hydrogen wasn't leaving the dirigible. The ice had frozen the vents closed, but no one had noticed in the dark.

Nick could now see trees drifting by just below the gondola. He took a deep breath. "Everyone to 'abandon stations.'" There were places on the dirigible where you could jump if they weren't too high and have a good chance of surviving. There were also places like up near the top of the airship where you had no chance at all. "Abandon stations" got the crew and—if there were any—passengers to places where they had at least some chance of surviving if the *Czarina* were to crash. But sending the crew to "abandon stations" meant that he wouldn't have crew in the rigging to try to fight the leak. It was a tacit admission that the *Czarina* was going down. The crew started making their way to places where they would have a shot at living if the airship crashed. But Nick stayed and so did the bridge crew. Partly that was because the pilot house was already a good location to abandon from, but mostly it was because a lot could still be done. Or at least Nick hoped that they could limit the damage.

The hydrogen escaped into the body of the dirigible where it mixed with oxygen as the *Czarina* sank closer to the ground. There was no spark in section three. But the wind was still whipping the sinking airship around and at fifty-three feet the stresses broke a circuit in section one...and there was a spark.

When a balloon filled with hydrogen is ignited, it burns. But slowly, relatively speaking, as the oxygen and hydrogen mix. But if the oxygen and hydrogen are pre-mixed, as was the case here, it doesn't burn. It explodes. Of course, even an explosion over the volume of an airship the size of *Czarina Evdokia* is not instant. Over the course of twenty-three seconds, the hydrogen and oxygen in the dirigible burned at a temperature half that of the surface of the sun. Hot gasses expand. The skin and the thin coating of ice on the skin contained the explosive force of the combustion, forcing it down. People in abandon stations were literally blown out of the dirigible, as though fired from a cannon. The force ripped loose the engine cars. There were no survivors in the engine cars.

Able Airwoman Valeriya Zakharovna was wearing her parachute, more because it was the easiest way to carry it than because she thought it would be any help. However, it did save her life. When she was blown out of the dirigible, she hit a tree, parachute first, so only her arm and not her back was broken.

In the command car, Yuri Danovic was thrown through one of the windows, leaving his legs behind. Petr was talking to the right engine car on the phone when the blast front hit. He was protected by the heavy circuit board and though he was shaken and bruised, he suffered nothing worse than that.

Colonel Nikita Ivanovich Slavenitsky was thrown clear of the wreck, but landed badly. He broke one arm and cracked his skull. He was unconscious and there was swelling of the brain. He would never regain consciousness. Of the crew, there were seven survivors. Petr Nickovich, Valeriya Zakharovna, and five others.

Petr found himself in command of the small contingent of Russian aeronauts, none of whom spoke German. Petr had some up-timer English from his time at the Gorchakov Dacha, and he could read a bit of German, but he couldn't speak it. He couldn't understand the version of German spoken by the local farmers who came out to see the fire and take him and his fellows into custody for burning down their firewood grove.

Three hours after the crash, when Colonel Nikita died, Petr was wondering if he would ever get back to Russia.

Sviyazhsk kremlin, Kruglaya Mountain
December 1636

"We have a message from a Father Yulian for you, Alexander," said Lieutenant Vadim Lagunov. "Did you get some peasant girl pregnant?"

Alexander took the radio message and read. Then, not even beginning to understand why, headed for Ivan Maslov's office. "She's not a peasant," he explained as he walked away. "And I'm not the father."

Once he got to the major's office, he held out the radio telegram. "Sir, I need to get to Ufa."

"And according to this, fairly soon if you're not going to miss the blessed event. Is this the girl who was with you on the boat?"

"Yes."

"Then you're not the father. Or at least I don't see how you could be. So why is it any concern of yours?"

Alexander didn't know what to say and Ivan waited. Finally, Alexander said, "I don't know. But, somehow, it is."

"If you say so," Ivan said, for once sounding his age—which was a couple of years younger than Alexander. Then the military officer was back. "Wait till this evening. I have some papers I want to send with you if you're going to Ufa. Meanwhile I'll send a radio message and see if I can get you some transport."

"What sort of transport? Isn't the *Czarina Evdokia* in Germany by now?"

"I have no idea but we might as well ask." Ivan Maslov shrugged. "The siege lines around us are hardly tight. And it looks like Birkin is getting set to launch an assault on Kazan. Everyone will be looking that way, so you should be able to get through. Take the Sulitsa River to get past Kazan, then head for the next radio link."

Kazan

After a week of shelling, there were two partial breaches in the curtain wall that surrounded Kazan. "General, there are troops massing across the Kazanka River."

Tim took his telescope and examined the area that the watcher had pointed to. It was true, if early. The breach wasn't big enough.

Tim issued a set of orders.

❖   ❖   ❖

"All right, men. They're going to be coming through here. Get into position," Captain Ustinov commanded. The *Streltzi* moved up to crouch behind the wall of sandbags they had built just inside the breach in the curtain wall.

The breach was thirty feet wide and choked with the rubble of the wall. Once the men were in place, Captain Ustinov moved up to the left edge of the breach and looked around to see what was coming. The ground was covered in snow and ice and the river was solid as rock. Across the river, two hundred yards away from the wall, a troop of cavalry were forming up and Captain Ustinov suddenly remembered something that the general had said. "Don't wait till you can see the whites of their eyes. Don't even wait till you can see their eyes. Shoot the sons of bitches as soon as you can see their bodies. If they're cavalry, shoot their fucking horses." *Well, they are cavalry.* He turned to his men and leaned back against the curtain wall. "Yuri, bring your boys up here. Hide in the rubble."

Yuri looked at him, then shrugged. He waved to the men and then picked up a sandbag and came forward with it over his shoulder. The rest of the *Streltzi* did the same. By the time they were in place and used their sandbags to close up the gaps in the rubble, the cavalry was mostly formed up.

"Is everyone ready now?" Captain Ustinov asked sarcastically. "Anyone want to put up a parasol, perhaps?"

No one said anything, but a couple of the *Streltzi* grinned. One looked around like he was considering it.

"Load your clips!" Ustinov shouted. The AK4.7 had a clip of five chambers. It was inserted from the right side and a sliding grip both cocked the hammer and shifted the chamber. Bernie Zeppi had said it worked like a pump action shotgun. But these were rifled, with chambers holding a hundred grains of black powder and a heavy bullet. They were deadly accurate at well over two hundred yards.

He waited while they loaded the clipped together chambers into their AK4.7s, watching the horsemen who were advancing at the walk and still a hundred and fifty yards off.

"Cock!"

"Take aim!"

"All right, fire!"

"Cock!" Captain Ustinov yelled then he started to say "Aim!" but didn't. The space in front of the men was smoke shrouded and they would be firing blind. He waited for the smoke to clear. As it cleared he saw the results of the first volley. Not great. A few hits, but not many. "Didn't any of you idiots hear me say 'aim'?"

He looked down the line and saw that everyone had shifted the clip to the next chamber except Gorgi Davidovich who had somehow gotten his AK4.7 lock in half-cock position. "Yuri, see to Gorgi. The rest of you . . . aim this time. Ready, Aim, Squee—"

Crack! Crack! Crackle!

The guns started going off before he finished saying "squeeze," and it wasn't a very solid volley. However, it appeared that more of his people were aiming . . . or at least keeping their eyes open when they fired. When Captain Ustinov peeked around the wall there were considerably more of the enemy horses down.

That was disrupting their charge. Some of the enemy

were getting impatient and putting their horses into a gallop. Others weren't. They were still too far away to be charging their horses. But they weren't used to taking fire at this distance. He looked back at his people, crouched behind fallen stones and sandbags in a ragged line, long-barreled AK4.7s sticking out through the cracks in the ruined wall.

"Cock!"

"Captain, we only have one more preloaded clip each," Yuri called out.

Captain Ustinov started to snap back that he knew that, but in the heat he had forgotten. They had two clips for each man in the unit. Some of the men had more but, for the most part, when those were fired they would have to stop shooting and reload the chambers. It looked like two preloaded clips weren't going to be enough.

"Everyone, make sure your used clips are stowed." Some of the men had bandoleers, but mostly they just had pouches.

Ustinov looked around the wall again and smiled. The enemy who had gotten into a gallop were coming up the steep part of the hill now. But they were spread out and he could see the horses puffing in the cold air.

"Yuri, have them fire by the right." That was a maneuver that had each of the men wait till the man on their right had fired, then aim and fire himself. It wasn't the sort of thing that you wanted to do against a massed charge, but with the cavalry struggling up the hill in ones and twos, it would mean a lot fewer misses.

Captain Ustinov looked back around the wall and watched the result. It was a little better than the volleys had been, but not much. "All right, boys. Do it again!"

They did it again and there wasn't much left of the enemy leaders, but the rest weren't giving up. The Kazan defenders kept on firing, and the thousand and more men on horses kept feeding themselves to the fire. There were piles of them on the ground in front of the breach, enough so that the horses behind were having to pick their way over and around the bodies of fallen horses and men. Meanwhile, the less than a hundred men manning the breach had used up their first clip and half their second. "Cease fire! Cock! Everybody ready? One more volley, then we'll fall back!"

Captain Ustinov wondered what was going on in the rest of the battle. "Fire!"

Tim looked out from the Kazan kremlin tower. For communications within the city, they had run telegraph wires. And that meant that Tim couldn't be down at the front. He had to stand here and watch the battle unfold so that he could see what the enemy was doing and send orders to counter it. It wasn't like the battles at Rezhv or Bor. There, he had been with his men, giving his orders while standing in the line with them. Here, even the sound was muffled by the distance. Here, it was like watching the attack on Rezhv from the dirigible *Testbed*. All those men down there on both sides, like so many counters on a gaming table.

Tim had fought battles. He had heard shots pass by his ear. He hated the fact that he liked it better this way. He could see what was going on, and he had the telegraph to send his orders quickly to the commanders. This position let him do his job much better, but it also left him a great deal safer. And Tim couldn't be sure which part of that equation made him feel better about being here.

But he didn't have time to worry about it. Birkin was attacking from three points. He was hitting the lower city from one and the kremlin from two. Tim shook his head. The attacks up the hill to the kremlin were feints, most likely. Even if they weren't feints, they had little chance of success. It was the attack on the lower city across the frozen river that might have a chance. It was uphill too, but not as much. Tim ordered more troops to reinforce that breach.

The reserves behind Captain Ustinov's company on the east wall of the kremlin seemed to be sufficient.

Captain Ustinov waved his men back and followed them. They had shot their wad, two clips each from a ninety-three men, nine hundred thirty rounds in less than five minutes. It had blunted the charge, and the enemy was reforming. But while that was happening, Ustinov and his men were falling back to be replaced by Achmed's company. His men would reload while Achmed's boys held the cavalry at bay.

The day continued like that. The Muscovites would charge and the range and rate of fire would rip them up. They would retreat and reform while the defenders got their chambers reloaded by teams of reloaders just behind the lines with reload kits that reloaded a clip at a time. Twice, it looked like the enemy would break through. Twice, the other defending company was ordered up before they were fully reloaded to add their fire. They took losses, but their losses were small. Gorgi Davidovich had stood up in the middle of an enemy charge, trying to change clips, and been shot. Yuri had a sword cut on his right arm from a time when two horsemen had made it all the way up the hill to the wall. There were three more dead, but casualties had been incredibly light.

Ivan Ivanovich Ustinov had been a Russian soldier since he was sixteen. He had been in border skirmishes against the Tatars and the Cossacks. He had lost men. But in all that time, he had never seen a battle that had produced nearly so many enemy casualties. There had to be a thousand men lying dead or badly injured out there. They were overwhelmingly the enemy . . . but they were fellow Russians for all of that. What shocked him was just how much more deadly the new weapons made war. And, as he thought about it, just how much they shifted the advantage to the dug-in defender.

In his camp outside Kazan, General Birkin had yet to reach the same conclusion. His intellect was arguing for it, but his gut—years of experience in war, every story from the time he was a boy, every bit of his knowledge of how wars were fought—was arguing against it. He knew that what he was seeing was an aberration. He knew that the enemy's casualties had to be almost as bad as his had been. It couldn't have been any other way. His men had poured even more fire into the enemy than the enemy had poured out on his men. He had to have killed thousands of them. He had to have! Besides, there was no possible way that a nineteen-year-old political general could possibly do this to him.

In fact, the whole day's attack—cannon and rifle together—had only killed fifty-three of the defenders and almost half of them had been civilians working on the walls. Or, in one case, five women in a market stall when a shot aimed at a section of wall had overshot and gone into the city. The difference between charging in the open and firing from cover and concealment was, quite literally, the difference between life and death. Only half a dozen times in the whole day's battle had soldiers gotten close enough for bayonet or sword to come into play.

But General Birkin didn't know any of that—and wouldn't have believed it if he had. So the next day he tried it again. And the day after that. By the fourth day, he had lost too many men to ignore. His army of forty thousand was now an army of thirty eight thousand. He still had the ten thousand investing Kruglaya Mountain, but he couldn't pull them out without the enemy on that mountain becoming a serious threat.

Still convinced that somehow Boris Timovich Lebedev had cheated, General Birkin settled down for a winter siege.

It took Alexander and Leonid Ivanovich three days to reach the next radio station past Kazan. It was in a little village just far enough off the river to be mostly out of sight.

Leonid was grinning at him the whole way. Surprisingly enough, Leonid had stayed with him after they got to Ufa. Leonid had never been much of a farmer and he was a very good batman. Alexander had given him a raise and promised not to interfere with any romances that might arise. And a romance

of sorts had arisen with the older of Izabella's maids.
More of a friendly thing, Alexander thought, but it
was the maid who had gotten Leonid over his silent
anger. Alexander noticed that Leonid, now that he
had the option of quitting and wasn't under threat
of whipping, was a lot more open with his opinions.

"Yep, very clever of you, young master, to swoop
in after that priest did all the work. She ought to be
well trained up by now."

Alexander noted that the lack of a whipping post
might not be altogether advantageous. Civilized maybe,
but not without its disadvantages. "We're here," he said,
pointing at the antenna sticking up out of the trees.

It was only a few more minutes before they reached
the small village compound. The village only had five
families, a couple of trappers and a couple of shops.
There were no crops. They traded for food and the
radio and radio operators were a great boon to the
small community of Laishevo.

As they entered the clearing where the houses were,
they saw the Dodge sitting there. It had a trailer
attached behind it, a two-wheeled trailer, piled high
with gear including a dozen Russian-made jerry cans
that probably held fuel.

"Wow, you must be important!" Leonid said. Then,
clearly reconsidering, said, "No. Must be the girl. They
don't want the baby to be illegitimate."

"Why am I paying you?" Alexander muttered.

"For my sage advice. Why else?"

They had dinner that night with Bernie Zeppi and
Leonid Ivanov, one of Princess Natasha's personal
armsmen.

"Welcome, Alexander," Bernie said.

"Welcome, Leonid," Leonid said. "Has the boy been giving you trouble?"

"Not too bad, Leonid. Is Bernie still making cow eyes at the princess?"

"Sure enough. He gets above himself, Bernie does."

Bernie looked at Alexander and sighed. "It's going to be a long trip."

"Speaking of which, *Gospodin* Zeppi, why the Dodge?"

"Anya has something going with your Izabella and that factory," Bernie said. "And I don't know why beyond that. It's part of the female conspiracy, I guess. It's not like that factory is the only one in Ufa."

"Izabella has been keeping in touch over the radio. Between the village and the factory and the land grant that Czar Mikhail gave me when he drafted me, she had quite a nest egg of capital in the bank, so she has been investing in businesses in Ufa. I think Olga's involved too."

Bernie was nodding. "It makes sense. Even before you guys got there, Ufa had two or three steamboats a day, in and out. Things have slowed down now, but there is still a lot of sleigh traffic and ice boats."

That fit in with what Izabella had been telling Alexander in her radio messages.

They finished dinner and the Leonid "twins" continued to comment on the care and feeding of their charges. Then they headed out the next morning, Bernie and Leonid Ivanov taking turns at the controls of the Dodge.

Ufa
December 1636

They were too late by four hours. The baby had been born at 11:15 AM on December twentieth, and they didn't arrive till almost four. It didn't matter. Alexander took one look at the little girl and was in love. It didn't make him forgive Father Yulian, but he wouldn't have traded baby Anya for anything.

Alexander and Izabella were married two days later in a ceremony performed by Father Kiril. Father Yulian offered to give the bride away, but the offer was refused.

Czar Mikhail waved Alexander to a seat. "I see no need to send you back to Sviyazhsk. They are besieged and unless Birkin proves to be an utter idiot, nothing much is going to happen there. Do you agree?"

"Yes, Your Majesty," Alexander said. "Things might get a bit dicey in Kazan, but there is no way that the force Birkin has at Sviyazhsk is getting up the mountain."

"There was bad news about the dirigible, *Czarina Evdokia*. It crashed near Berlin with great loss of life. Nick Slavenitsky was killed in the crash. The head of our air force and the first Russian to fly has died. Russia has lost one of her greatest heroes, and I have lost a friend."

"I heard, Your Majesty," Alexander said, not knowing what else to say.

"What that means is that the good will tours the czarina and I had been making . . . we can't do any more. Not because of the risk, but because of the time it will take to travel. The most amazing thing about the *Czarina Evdokia* was the speed. We could go from Ufa to the Caspian Sea in a day, well, almost. It meant that we could visit personally the local heads of government and it allowed us to make much greater headway in negotiating with the various factions.

"I don't want to lose that progress, so I need to send someone on a goodwill mission down the Volga to the Caspian Sea. To facilitate that, I am making you a roving ambassador to the states along the Volga and appointing you *dumnye dvoriane*."

Alexander's mouth opened. Then closed. Then opened again . . . and nothing came out. There were several reasons for this. First was he was a newlywed man with a baby girl, and had not yet had an opportunity to sleep with his wife. And this mission almost certainly meant that he wouldn't be here when she was ready to resume conjugal activities. Second, because this was one hell of a promotion. *Dumnye dvoriane* was just one rank below *okolnichii* and his family was just barely of a rank to receive such an appointment. It would normally go to someone much higher in the family hierarchy than a scapegrace third son of a second son. And finally, because Alexander wasn't at all sure that he was qualified. No. That wasn't nearly strong enough. He was utterly certain that he wasn't qualified. This was a job for someone far more experienced. "Your Majesty, this is a job for a master diplomat. Not a . . ."

Czar Mikhail held up a hand. "No, for two reasons. I don't have nearly enough experienced people for all the jobs I need done. But also because I need someone who actually served in the fall campaign and is a member of one of the great families. I need someone who can tell them, from personal experience, that Tim knows what he's doing, that his holding Kazan is not a fluke."

Izabella wasn't happy about it, but three days later Alexander and Leonid were off on an ice boat. It was a hybrid of up- and down-time designs. Three blades, widely spaced, allowed for a large sail, but it had a nice cabin and was marginally comfortable. Given the right wind conditions, it could go quite fast.

Part Three

The Way East

CHAPTER 19

𝔖urvivors

Outside Berlin
December 1636

Petr Nickovich held out a shaking hand and heated small beer was poured into the mug it held. The local farmers had taken them in and fed them after the crash of the *Czarina Evdokia*. The snowstorm had simply gotten worse, and for the last week they had been stuck here. The farmers weren't overtly unfriendly. More cautious than anything. They had treated their wounds and given them a place to stay, but had also taken any weapons and other valuable gear. It was dark. There were windows but they were shuttered against the cold and the lamps didn't even have glass chimneys, much less the Coleman pressurized fuel system. All that was bad enough, but worse—so far as Petr was concerned— was the fact that they hadn't been allowed near the *Czarina Evdokia* since they had been rescued. There was a fortune in gear out there. Steam engines, radios, goldbeater's skin, treated fabric, struts and more. And the locals seemed to think that it belonged to them.

Petr sipped the small beer and moped while Valeriya Zakharovna managed the other survivors. Valeriya was strong for a woman, probably because she'd been raised on a farm. The "wrong side of the blanket" daughter of a minor nobleman, she had gotten her posting in the Dacha and later the crew of the *Czarina Evdokia* through her father's influence and had proved hardworking and capable. She was only a couple of inches short of six feet tall, rangy and well muscled. But she had gotten her father's looks, unfortunately. She was a hatchet-faced woman with brown hair, and in her uniform overalls she looked more like a man than a woman.

But she was a forceful person. While, normally, Petr was well organized, the death of his captain and friend Nick had left him too bereft to think straight. He felt guilty about that, but didn't seem to be able to pull himself out of it.

There was a pounding on the door of the peasant's cottage they were staying in and no appreciable wait for an answer. The door opened and a young man in a waist-length cape and vest combination that had never occurred in the almost four hundred years between 1631 and 2000 in that other timeline, came through the door. He was also wearing a fur-lined hunting cap, and black calf-length boots that had clearly been polished to a high gloss before he put them on to ride through a blizzard to get here.

The young man pulled off his fur-lined gloves and slapped them against his creased—and very tight— pants. The local authorities had arrived. "Who's in charge here?"

"I am Lieutenant Colonel Petr Nickovich, executive officer and chief engineer of the *Czarina Evdokia*."

The young man sniffed. "I take it that the burned wreckage cluttering up my father's lands is the *Czarina Evdokia*?"

"Yes. We are a diplomatic mission from Czar Mikhail of Russia."

"Do you have any proof of that?"

As it happened, they did. The *Czarina* had a very nice fireproof safe on board and the official documents had been in that. The furs that they were bringing hadn't fared so well.

The young man, who turned out to be Adolph Grossmann von Rheinsberg, became rather more congenial after seeing the papers, which were copied in Swedish, Russian, and Amideutsch. But he did point out that damage had been done to his family lands by the crash of the dirigible and they were due some compensation. He also wanted to keep the engines and well, pretty much everything from the crash until that debt was settled.

Still, he did agree to radio Prince Vladimir Gorchakov, who then arranged transport for them to Grantville.

Grantville
January 1637

"Welcome." Princess Brandy Bates greeted them in Russian with a pronounced accent. It was the same accent that Bernie Zeppi had, and she sounded a lot like Bernie had back in 1632. By now, there wasn't much of what Petr thought of as the up-timer accent in Bernie's Russian, but the up-timer twang was still pretty clear in Princess Brandy's voice. One look at Princess Brandy and Petr knew where Czarina Evdokia and Princess Natasha—not to mention a large number of court ladies in Russia—had gotten the inspiration for their attire.

She was dressed in a calf-length split skirt, tucked into a pair of fancy pointed-toe boots with about a two-inch heel, and a ruffled, embroidered blouse, with a fur-lined vest over all of it.

They were ushered into a small not-quite-palace, with electric lights, and Petr got to see an actual television—a working one. For the first day or so, just the amazement of Grantville and the Ring of Fire were enough to distract him from Nick's death and the urgency of the mission. He knew that Prince Vladimir and his wife were discussing it, but they left him alone.

"This is crazy, Vlad. Why do they want us in Russia? We're much more valuable here. Who else can work with Ron Stone to get the funding for the *Catherine the Great* and its cargo?"

"You—" Vladimir started, but Brandy interrupted.

"Forget it, Vlad. If you go, I go."

"Brandy, the *Catherine the Great* is an experimental ship. I won't risk—"

"Forget it, I said. If it's too dangerous for me, it's too dangerous for you. For that matter, I'm gonna raise the stakes. If you insist on this particular bit of idiocy, you're going to be bringing little Mikey with you too."

Vladimir, who had been about to continue the argument, stopped. "You're not serious?"

"Mom's dead and Dad's a cold fish. I wouldn't want

him raising our son. I don't have any brothers and sisters or even any close cousins, except Jabe McDougal. So just who should we leave little Mikey with?"

"We leave him with Kseniya and Father Gavril. We are going to have to leave a presence here anyway."

Brandy shook her head. "Kseniya is good people, but I'm not leaving *my* son with anyone. I am not going to miss his growing up while I go gallivanting off to Russia or wherever. And Mikey isn't going to grow up without a father, either. So you either figure a way out of this or you arrange suitable quarters for us all on that experimental boat of yours."

It was, Vladimir thought, a totally unreasonable attitude. But he knew Brandy quite well by now. The woman had a whim of steel. Most of the time, she was perfectly reasonable. Even moderately pliant. But on some things, she would dig in her heels and when that happened, nothing would move her. For a moment right then, Vladimir considered sneaking out one night and leaving her here. But he knew it wouldn't work. She would figure out a way to follow him. Besides, as much as he knew it was a bad idea and as frightened for her and little Mikey as he was, he didn't want to leave her behind.

That just left the question of whether to go or not. Unfortunately, that was even less a question. Czar Mikhail hadn't sent a request or advice. He had sent an imperial command, cosigned by the rump duma in Ufa. If Vladimir refused it, he would discredit Czar Mikhail—and there was no way at all that Vladimir could do that.

So, wise or not, Brandy and little Mikey were going to travel the Arctic Circle. Since that was the case,

Vladimir was going to make sure that there would be a warm comfortable place for them on the ship.

Hamburg
January 1637

The Hamburg shipyard was a blend of down-time and up-time, with rather more of the down-time than the Magdeburg yards. That, however, didn't mean that the shipwrights of Hamburg had turned up their collective noses at up-time tech. Certainly not after Admiral Simpson had used that up-time tech to forcibly open the gate to the North Sea. If Magdeburg was the Chicago of the USE, Hamburg was the port of New York, and the port of Los Angeles, as well. This was the place where the goods produced in Magdeburg, Grantville, all the factories and shops along the golden corridor were transshipped from riverboats to seagoing ships that would take them to the rest of the world.

To facilitate that, the shipyards of Hamburg, both naval and privately held, were if not the largest in the world, close to it.

It was a dirty, busy place filled with sailors and longshoremen, with knocking shops and bars, but also with coffee houses and business offices. And it had the fine hotels that went with all the wealth pouring through it.

The offices of the Kruger shipyards were surprisingly modest for the fourth largest shipbuilder in Hamburg. They were also located closer to the docks than some.

"I was surprised that you decided to visit, Your Highness," said Paul Kruger. "Captain Adams has done an excellent job working with our shipwrights and the ship is progressing quite well. But we are still at least a couple of months from launching it."

"I guess you hadn't heard," Vladimir said. "The airship *Czarina Evdokia* crashed a few miles north of Berlin. It brought urgent orders for me to return to Russia as quickly as possible. If it hadn't been caught by the storm, I would be flying back to Russia on board it right now. We need to put a rush on the completion of the *Catherine the Great*. When it sails, I will be aboard. Also my wife and son will be accompanying me, so a level of comfort that might not be necessary if it were just me will be required."

"Those are somewhat contradictory goals, Your Highness. There is an up-timer saying, 'You can have it fast, good, or cheap. Pick any two.'"

"This wasn't cheap to begin with, Herr Kruger."

"With all due respect, Your Highness, for what you want, it *is* cheap. This is a ship that was never built even in that other history. We are combining up-time and down-time techniques in a way that is producing a thing never before seen in the world. The tread chains may be based on motorcycle chains, but they are five wide links across and every tenth link along the line there is a tie on that will hold either a paddle or a shoe depending on the use the tread is to be put to."

Vladimir nodded. He had seen the specifications and he knew that wasn't the only point involved. The whole tread assembly could be cranked lower or higher, though that would be a job in itself. "I understand. What I'm talking about, though, are almost cosmetic changes. It was suggested that we could use foamed panels to provide extra insulation with little extra weight. I want to add an aft cabin that will hold myself and my family, and a few others who will be returning with us to Russia."

The discussion continued and Captain Adams was brought in, as well as Petr Nickovich, who had years of experience with Russian-made steam engines. It couldn't be honestly said that Captain Adams and Petr Nickovich got along like the Kilkenny cats. They didn't come to blows, after all. But it was still early in the conversation when Captain Adams mentioned that Petr's ship had crashed after less than a year of service. Petr had responded that Captain Adams' design had yet to touch the medium in which it was meant to travel.

In spite of the possibility of homicide, Vladimir had to leave them here and go back to Grantville to raise even more money. Partly, that was to pay off the extortion of Baron von Rheinsberg, who was unwilling to release the engines and, well, everything from the *Czarina Evdokia* till the exorbitant price he was claiming for the small grove of wood ignited by the crash was paid in full. If there were going to be more dirigibles, Russia needed those engines and boilers and so on.

Her Highness Brandy Bates Gorchakov sat down across from Her Serene Highness Millicent Anne Barnes and asked her for a loan. "Gee, Millicent, can you spare me a little cash? I'll pay you back just as soon as I can."

Millicent giggled. "My mother warned me about you! How much?"

"Just a million reichsmarks or so. Come on. It's not like I'm asking you to let me borrow your last up-time lipstick."

"Maybe not, but it's still pretty risky to loan money to a government involved in a revolution. I doubt that loans made to the last Romanov czar got paid back in the original timeline."

"I know, but Czar Mikhail is trying to set up a constitutional monarchy. And Sheremetev is a bit too much like Stalin for my peace of mind."

"Maybe, but I'm not a politician." Millicent paused. "Look, Brandy. I know that you're trying to do something good. But it's still a pretty big risk for the reichsbank to take. I thought you were getting funding from Ron Stone."

"We are. But it's not just the one trip we're dealing with. We have to keep the investments in the USE going and we are going to need more of everything. Tubes, guns, engines, factories, latex. And there is tremendous wealth in Russia, if we can just exploit it effectively. Besides, Vladimir's aunt is trying to smuggle out a load of mica capacitors."

Brandy didn't get a million reichsmarks, but she did get enough that some of the immediate pressure was relieved. But the *Catherine the Great* was going to have to come back loaded to the gills in furs and gold to keep them from losing their property in the USE. Even more importantly, to keep the credit line open. That, or Sofia would have to get considerably more than a single shipload of mica.

A letter carrying a coded message was sent to the station in the Swedish Ingria on the Russian Baltic.

From there, it flowed along the radio network to Nizhny Novgorod, where an agent took it to a station on the Ufa net. It took three days for the message to cross the gap and then Czar Mikhail learned of Vladimir's plans to come to Ufa by way of Mangazeya on the Northern Sea Route. Unfortunately, the Northern Sea Route had been made illegal on pain of death, in 1619—the year his father, Patriarch Filaret, returned from exile. Czar Mikhail repealed that edict after he escaped from Sheremetev, but that was seen as something of a desperation move. Besides, General Shein's Siberian state controlled the route between Ufa and the North Sea. Before anything could reach them by that route, they needed something approaching an alliance with Shein.

"We're going to need more than neutrality on General Shein's part," Czar Mikhail said. "He was a great friend of my father, but I doubt he ever held me in very much respect." He looked at Evdokia and she nodded.

"General Shein hates the Poles and he knows that Sheremetev was one of those pushing for his execution in that other history. There is no love lost between him and the usurper. The only reason I can see for his not coming out for us is that he doesn't have any faith in Mikhail."

"Besides," Natasha added, "Shein has been acting as an alternative destination for Russians who don't like Sheremetev. He has attracted a lot of the *Streltzi* and lesser nobility. Shein is no more enamored of Czar Mikhail's emancipation of the serfs than Sheremetev, and some of the defectors who have gone to him have taken their serfs with them."

"Not that all of them have gotten there. We've had runaways from the north showing up here in dribs and drabs for a couple of months now," Anya said.

Mikhail looked around the room. This was his inner council, not the Ufa duma, but his true advisers. "We need to send a representative to Shein now that we have lost the dirigible. Word from Dirigible Valley is that even with what they got from the wreck of the *Alexis*, it will be at least a year before they will have another one."

"That's too long," Bernie said. "We don't need a big one like the *Alexis* or the *Evdokia*. But we need something to carry the mail. Something with enough range to reach Shein in Tobolsk or Nyen. Maybe something the size of the *Testbed*."

"It's a thousand miles from here to Nyen!" Natasha said. "That's a long way for anything small."

"So we find places to refuel along the way. But the point is, even if it can't carry more than a couple of people and a hundred pounds of mail, we need something to keep the messages flowing. Even if it can't go all the way to the USE, we at least have to get mail to the Baltic."

Filip nodded. "They might be able to do something along those lines in a couple of months. I wish Petr Nickovich was here."

"I wish Nick was here," Bernie said sadly.

"A smaller airship is an excellent idea. But we still need to send an embassy to Siberia," Evdokia said. "Who can we send?"

"I always got along with General Shein well enough," Bernie said hesitantly, looking at Natasha. It was clear he didn't want to leave her here while he went off to be the ambassador.

"You're not of the upper nobility, Bernie," said Filip. "General Shein is less rank obsessed than many of the great families, but sending a peasant—even an up-timer peasant—to represent Czar Mikhail would likely be seen as an insult."

Evdokia smiled a subtle smile and said, "Natasha will have to go along."

Natasha, who had been looking quite downcast, suddenly brightened.

"That still leaves the question of how we get you there," Filip said. "We don't have enough gas for the Dodge."

"And we left the sleighs back at the Dacha," Bernie complained.

"We'll find something," Evdokia said.

Goritsky Monastery

The "sisters" watched and reported, but they had at best limited influence. Partly that was because they were not on the scene and radio messages don't have the same immediacy as your wife, sister, aunt or cousin ragging on you in person. But also because though the radio network that had grown up in Russia was extensive, it was much more extensive to the east than to the west. There was a radio link to the Swedish Baltic, to the Polish Baltic, to Archangelsk, to the Polish border, and the border forts to the south. But it didn't go west into the territory controlled by General Shein, and the radio network around Ufa was only intermittently connected to the main Russian network. So letters to General Shein were still letters, and radio messages to Ufa had to be transcribed by someone and sent part of the way by boat. Still, the ladies learned of the loss of the *Czarina Evdokia* almost before anyone else in Russia. It was discussed and considered in the monastery, and the conclusion was that if it had happened in July or even August or September, it might have been a fatal blow to the czar's prestige. But now—especially since it happened in far off Germany—it was less important. It would damage Czar Mikhail's position, but not fatally.

Hamburg
February 1637

The room was small, but surprisingly modern and cozy warm. It had steam heat. The designers had integrated the condensers with the heating system. That was going to be important where they were going, and it was nice even here in Hamburg. The walls were six-inch-thick panels filled with foamed rosin. The windows were double-paned which, combined with the less-than-perfect flatness, meant that they were fine for letting light in, but mostly useless for looking out of. Mikey was holding his stuffed Brillo. Brandy smiled, thinking of the book of stories about the fictional ram, Brillo, and his constant hunt for freedom. She even knew the real Brillo and his owner Flo. But little Mikey loved the stories and loved his stuffed toy.

His crib was locked into the corner and their bed was in the other corner. Brandy could see right now that there wasn't going to be a lot of privacy. It was a ten-by-twelve-foot room with a low ceiling, and the bed folded up into a couch. There was a table that at the moment was folded up next to the wall. The ceiling was low enough that Brandy was afraid that she would bump her head, and Valeriya Zakharovna was in real danger of it.

Mikey dropped Brillo and wobbled over to the tie downs for the table. Brandy rushed over to keep him from hurting himself in his explorations. As she was scooping him up, Vlad came in, wearing a fur coat.

"Brrr," he stuttered. "Say, it's warm in here."

"Steam heat." Brandy pointed. Vlad went over and put his hands out. "Careful. It'll burn your hands if you touch it."

"They aren't running the engines, are they?"

"Charging the batteries, maybe?"

"Maybe," Vlad agreed.

"In the meantime, I want some sort of a screen over the radiator there. The burned hand may teach best, but I don't want Mikey learning that way."

Vladimir nodded. "I'll talk to John about it. Meanwhile, let's you, me, and Mikey adjourn to the wardroom."

In the wardroom, Captain John Adams and Petr Nickovich were arguing about the winches for the sails. The *Catherine the Great* was intended to spend most of her time as a sailing ship, with her treads raised up out of the water. That had proven to be one of the most difficult aspects of the whole tread concept, and one of the less necessary ones, in Vladimir's opinion. A combination sail and paddle wheel ship would leave the wheels in the water while it was under sail and they had apparently worked well enough. But John had insisted that the whole tread assembly had to be adjustable. He did have a point. The paddle wheel sailing ships had not been icebreakers. A North Sea ice floe would turn a paddle wheel into so much scrap lumber in a trice. The treads were designed to take rough handling and the paddles on them were removable.

"It's going to freeze!" John Adams roared and Vladimir's wandering thoughts were dragged back to the discussion. Vladimir had seen portraits of the founding father, and based on that he suspected that Captain John Adams of Portsmouth, England was related in some way to President John Adams, USA. A great granduncle several times removed or the like. Because Captain Adams looked rather like the president. At forty he was a short, florid-faced man with graying hair and a hairline that wasn't just retreating but in full rout. And he had a voice that cut through the surrounding noise like a cleaver.

"What's going to freeze?" Brandy asked. "And please, John, we are not in the midst of a sea battle. You don't need to make yourself heard over the roar of cannon."

"Cannon." John paused and visibly took a deep breath.

Petr Nickovich started to interrupt but Vladimir gave him a cautioning look and the Russian scientist subsided. That was precisely what Petr Nickovich was, a true scientist. You might need both hands to count the number of people on Earth who knew more of airships and the principles they worked on than Petr Nickovich, but Vladimir doubted it.

"The electric motor! He wants to use it for the mainsail winch," John explained in a voice that carried fewer decibels but no less intensity.

"It can be insulated and the chain drive that Captain Adams wants to use instead will freeze even more readily. It will also represent a danger for everyone on deck."

Ah. It was the chain versus electricity argument that Petr and John had been having almost since Petr had arrived. John wanted to use direct, or at least reasonably direct, mechanical linkages for everything. Or at least as much of everything as he could manage. Petr noted that the steam engines were going to run generators anyway to power lights and radio. He wanted to make the generators bigger and basically run everything off electrical power. They both had fairly good points, but in Vladimir's opinion John had the better one. You lost energy in converting mechanical power into electrical, then again in converting it back. There was a reason that the *Catharine the Great* had sails. The less of its cargo space that was loaded with fuel, the more could be filled with goods. Spending extra fuel to convert the mechanical energy of the steam engines into electricity and then back into mechanical energy was just wasteful.

Petr had given up on using electric motors to power the treads only after the chain gears had actually been installed.

"Captain, what about the risk from the chains?" Brandy asked calmly.

"There is some, but it shouldn't be too bad. We can put a railing around the chains."

"And the freezing?"

"The chains are a robust system. They will freeze, but the engine will break the ice."

"So would—" Petr started, but Vladimir held up a hand and he quieted, sullenly.

"Surely we could install a powerful electric motor at the winch location and that would eliminate the need for the long chain drive along the deck," Brandy said.

The main steam engine was located aft, and the sail in question was the foresail. A chain drive from the engines to a winch at the foresail would travel close to fifty feet. That would be a heck of a long chain and plenty of opportunity for accidents and failure.

"How much energy are you going to lose in chain friction over that distance?" Vladimir asked.

"Some," Captain Adams conceded grudgingly. "But the chain drive is a system all my people are familiar with by now. We know how to fix them when they break. Electric motors are fragile things, and expensive. Only Karl Weber is really comfortable around electrical systems at all, and he's the radio man."

"Electric motors are basically simple devices," Petr Nickovich said. "I know how to deal with them and I can train the crew."

It took another hour of discussion, but Petr Nickovich got his electric winch for the foresail.

The *Catherine* was almost completed, and they were still doing design modifications. That was because a ship was not a log, or even just a floating hull. It was a complex of systems that had to interact with each other, and all of which had to be hardened against stresses that no land-based building would have to deal with except in the middle of an earthquake.

"What's the situation in regard to the cargo?" John asked, after he grudgingly conceded that *in this case* an electric winch might be the better choice.

"We're ready when you are, John. It's all in a warehouse right here in Hamburg. Including two hundred pounds of powdered red and yellow dye from the fabworks." Considering that a one ounce packet of the dye was enough to color four shirts or fifty sheets of paper, a hundred pounds was a lot. There was also a set of plates for the printing of money, two hundred of the new radio tubes, lathe heads, instruction books, and wagon-portable metal detectors, as well as a host of other stuff.

"Prince Vladimir, let me again ask that I be allowed to take the *Catherine* on a shakedown cruise out to the North Sea ice packs to see how it operates. *Before* we attempt the North Sea route."

Vladimir shook his head. "You're right, Captain, and I know you're right. But it would be at least another month to make that cruise and we need to get to Russia soon. In fact, we should already have been there."

Pechora Sea

"Ice ho!" the lookout called.

Vladimir headed for the bridge. It had clear glass windows, the still very expensive sort. The *Catherine the Great* was under full sail and approaching the Pechora Sea. Until now, things had been going quite well. Ten days had taken them from Hamburg around the Scandinavian peninsula and most of the way across the Barents Sea. Thanks to a judicious combination of sail and engines, they had averaged about two hundred miles a day. They had maneuvered around icebergs before, but so far the icebreaking aspect of the *Catherine the Great*'s design hadn't come into play. Those thoughts were enough to take Vladimir from the wardroom to the bridge, and as he looked out over the wide white expanse of ice he realized that was about to change. The ice floe was at least two kilometers across.

Captain Adams started giving orders and men in heavy coats moved out onto the deck. They had drilled for this, but never done it for real till now. The sails were reefed and the treads engaged. Each tread was like a large tractor tread, save that it had a series of paddles attached. As the tread moved, the paddle pushed against the water. A propeller gets its force by pushing a little bit of water very fast. A paddle, whether it's in the hands of a kayaker, on a paddle wheel, or attached to a continuous track, gets its force by pushing against much more water at a much lower speed. The difference was somewhat analogous to the difference between an internal combustion engine and a steam engine. The internal combustion engine needs speed to work well. The steam engine can have much lower horsepower, but still have greater torque. Eight paddles, four on each tread, were in the water at once. They were two and a half feet deep and five feet wide. That's a hundred square feet of ocean to push against. Even at very low velocity, they pushed the *Catherine the Great* forward with tremendous force.

Captain Adams flipped a switch and ordered, "Stations, report." He got reports back in order, a lookout at the bow, the engine room and boilers, the port and starboard tread watch, and others.

"Slow ahead," he ordered the engine room.

The bow touched the ice floe, and kept right on going, pushing up onto the ice and applying increasing weight to the ice. The false keel concentrated

that weight on a small area, and the ice broke. The
shape of the hull pushed the ice down and to the
side, stressing the sheet of ice as the bow moved on
into the ice. Thus breaking up more ice, which got
pushed to the side and under the surrounding ice.

Captain Adams ordered more speed and the bow
of the *Catherine* slid higher on the ice. Then they got
a report from the treads. "Churning water."

Churning water was the paddle equivalent of cavi-
tation on a propeller. It was almost a constant on a
paddle wheel, where the paddles were constantly going
into and out of the water. But for a paddle track where
the paddles went into the water and stayed in the
water for the length of the track assembly, churning
water meant a loss of efficiency—less of the power
of the engines used to push the ship and more of it
wasted, churning the water. Not surprisingly, as they
broke ice they faced greater resistance. The paddles
started churning at a lower speed.

Captain Adams ordered them back to slow ahead
and the churning decreased. They were lucky to make
a couple of knots. But, for almost an hour, everything
went according to plan.

Then a chunk of ice, five feet long, six feet wide,
and three feet thick, popped up where the starboard
tread was dragging a paddle into the water.

Each paddle had support wedges, three on each
side. They rested against the tread and kept the paddle
close to perpendicular to the tread. The paddle was
not weak. It was two-inch-thick oak, plus the supports
and backing. It broke the chunk of ice quite nicely,
but that wasn't the first piece of ice that paddle had
faced. It had been ripping up chunks of ice for over

an hour and every chunk of ice it hit, hit it back with equal force. This was one whack too many and the outboard support wedge broke. That added a diagonal stress to the paddle and the middle support wedge cracked. More importantly, the stress on the lock bar on the outboard section was suddenly a twisting stress. The tread kept moving and the paddle made most of its transit before it ripped loose.

As the tread pulled the paddle up out of the water, the damage became apparent and the call to stop the treads was given.

Captain Adams picked up his Grantville-made galalith plastic phone handset and pushed the button that connected him to the starboard tread watch. "What's wrong?"

"We have a paddle loose and dragging, Captain," said Engineer's Mate Guy Sayyeau. "It's ripped loose and is halfway to hitting the next paddle."

Captain Adams looked out at the ice floe. They were perhaps a hundred yards from open water. "Can you knock it loose?"

"Should be able to, Skipper," Guy said in Dutch-accented Amideutsch. "Take maybe five minutes."

"Do it then. We'll see about full repairs when we're out of the ice."

Guy climbed out of the small compartment that was his duty station when the paddle treads were operating. He used a harness and rope on pulleys as a safety measure, but he climbed down a ladder to the continuous track. It was five feet wide and twenty long, with a front power wheel, ten road wheels, and five return rollers. It was also freezing even as he watched.

Franz Heuber handed him a ten-pound sledge hammer once he was standing on the track. Guy walked along the track, climbing over paddles to get to the broken one. The paddle was attached to the tread by three one-inch diameter oak dowels that attached at the ends and the middle. The outboard dowel had been shredded by the force of the ice impacting the paddle. That wasn't the problem, as it turned out. The problem was the middle dowel. It was still there, but it was wedged in and there wasn't enough of it showing that he could reach it to pound the damn thing loose. "Hand me down a punch. No. Franz, you're gonna have to come down here and hold it."

"Wait a moment," said another voice, the husky raspy voice of Valeriya Zakharovna. "I'll bring it."

Guy looked up at Franz and shrugged. Valeriya had been working with the crew of the *Cath* since before the icebreaker sailed out of Hamburg. She was big and strong, and no one wanted to argue with her. Franz called her the Aristotelian ideal of bosons, but Franz was proud of his flowery language. Guy . . . he just liked a woman he could look up to. Guy was a strong man, but not tall. He stood only five feet six inches. He had curly, sandy brown hair that was never in place and often matted. He had survived smallpox as a boy and it had left its mark on his face. But he had come to understand steam and the chain drives on the *Cath* and had been working on it from the beginning.

Franz stepped out of the way. Valeriya reached up to the grab bar and pulled herself up and through the porthole, then lowered herself onto the tread. Guy noticed the way she moved and was distracted. But once she was down, he looked away and focused on the broken paddle.

Guy whacked at the paddle with the sledge, trying to get it loose. He busted it up some, but couldn't get it free.

"Hold up, Guy!" Valeriya shouted. "Let me set the punch."

Guy stepped back and Valeriya set the three-quarter-inch punch in place, then held it while Guy hammered. It took only a couple of minutes to pound it loose. That stressed the inboard dowel, so they had to use the punch again and they ran into a design flaw.

"This should be farther outboard," Valeriya complained.

"Or it should be designed to punch out the other way," Guy agreed.

The placement wasn't a problem if you were using an ordinary hammer, but a ten-pound sledge needs swinging room. Unfortunately, the inboard portion of the tread was less than a foot from the side of the hull. They should have either had the dowel more offset from the side of the track or made it so that it could be punched out in either direction. By the time they were done, the whole continuous track assemblage was glued together with a thin layer of ice. It took ten minutes of pounding and two buckets of boiling water to get it loose.

By that time there was a thin layer of ice surrounding the ship. It was very thin, a sixteenth of an inch or so, and in and of itself didn't represent much of a problem. However, it indicated that if they had to stop for any appreciable time to make repairs, they could find themselves frozen in place. The placement of the paddles was based on tests using models to measure force. Losing one meant less force, so the starboard tread had to run faster to compensate. They also had to back up a bit and get a running start. All in all, they lost close to an hour. Not too bad, considering that even in open water with sail and tread they rarely topped ten knots.

By the time they were through the ice floe and back in relatively clear water, they all had a much better idea of the sort of trouble they were going to face on the trip.

For the next seven days, *Catherine the Great* traveled much more slowly. They rarely used the sails. It seemed to Vladimir that they would exit one ice floe then run into another.

Yesterday they had spent the whole day and night breaking ice. The *Catherine* was a good size ship for the seventeenth century, and very solidly built. She had broken through the ice quite well, actually better than expected. There had only been a few times when they had to back up and ram a floe repeatedly to break through. The hull and false keel were both holding up well but they had broken more paddles than they had expected.

And now this...

They were looking at ice too thick for their ship to penetrate.

Ice so thick that the bow had ridden up onto the ice without breaking it. They had backed off and tried again three times, but it looked like they were going to have to try what John Adams called "the snowmobile feature."

They carried two ice boats, as was standard on a *koch*, but their ice boats were of mostly up-time design. Three skates and a sail, with a good cargo capacity. They used the winch to set one of them on the ice and had it pull a heavy line out a hundred meters ahead of the *Catherine*, then anchor the cable to the ice. That took hours, while the *Catherine* moved back and forth to keep from getting frozen in.

Finally they got the thick cable anchored in the ice. They attached it to the electric winch with a block and tackle and pulled the *Catherine* up onto the ice.

But that was just the first step.

Once the *Catherine* was on the ice, it was tilted over on its side, but not all that far. The hull was rounded, but on the ice the *Catherine* wasn't at more than about a fifteen degree angle. It made going from port to starboard an uphill climb and made working more difficult, but that was about all.

Guy tossed a line to Valeriya and she pulled it over to a spot about thirty feet off the port side and tied it to a piton driven into the ice. Guy pulled the line over to a set of pulleys connected to the foresail lifting motor and tied it off. Then he called down to the engine room and asked for power to the motor. The line tightened and slowly the *Cath* righted herself. Just before she was fully upright, Guy had them stop the motor. She was balanced on her keel, held in place by lines.

It took them days to remove the paddles and replace them with the hardwood treads that they hoped would power the *Cath* over the ice.

First they disconnected the power chain, then they

cranked the treads down using a set of winches. Then they reattached the power chain with the tensioning wheel adjusted to the new configuration.

Halfway through the process, the storm hit. For two days, everyone who could huddled inside. Guy and Valeriya spent the time talking about the engineering systems on the *Cath* and the difference between sailing in a ship and flying in a dirigible. It was during the snowstorm that Valeriya decided they should huddle together for warmth. Her argument would have made more sense if it was actually that cold in the ship, but the designers had done quite an effective job of getting all the use out of the steam they could. The interior of the ship wasn't toasty by any means, but it was hardly freezing either. Guy didn't argue, though. Partly because one didn't argue with Valeriya, but mostly because he rather liked the idea.

Once the storm passed, they continued with the work, but now had to do it under the cover of a coating of ice and snow that the storm had left behind. Three days later, the continuous tracks were on the ice.

Altogether, it took over a week. There were four cases of frostbite, and these were men who had experience working and living in these conditions. Vladimir, Brandy, and little Mikey stayed inside. So did most of the surviving crew of the *Czarina Evdokia*.

They finished the reconfiguration, and fed power to the treads. Nothing happened. The treads were frozen up. Literally. Boiling water and steam were used to weaken the ice enough to let the treads start to move. And now they were in what amounted to a huge snowmobile. Huge, but incredibly underpowered for its weight. And also fragile as hell for its size.

There were massive timbers holding everything in place, but they almost might have been toothpicks. Still, once it got going, it could make a steady three miles an hour across the ice.

"We're going through the coal fast," John Adams said.

"How fast?" Vladimir asked.

"Faster than we prepared for. Besides, we ran into thick ice sooner than I expected, and it has lasted longer."

"So what you're saying is we're going to run out of fuel before we reach Mangazeya?"

"Yes." John nodded. "Unless we run into much weaker ice, weak enough for us to get back in the water and use the sails."

"How likely is that?" Vladimir asked.

"Not very."

"So what do you recommend?"

"We could use the ice boats to get the crew to safety, but that would mean abandoning the *Catherine*. By the time we got back to her, who knows what would have happened to her and her cargo?"

"What about sending the ice boats to gather wood?"

"That's a long trip," John Adams said. "And it would be easy to get lost."

"Where are we, Captain?"

"Assuming the inertial compass is right, we should be right about here." John pointed at a spot on the chart.

Vladimir examined the map. "Where are the nearest trees?" He ran a finger along the chart where the shore was marked.

"There should be some forest there." John pointed. It was almost due south of their position and they needed to be traveling northeast from here.

"Turn us south, Captain. Get us as close to those trees as you can," Vladimir said. "Then we will send out crews to cut us firewood, and bring it back to the ship, get a full load of firewood and go on."

It was another delay in a trip that had already been delayed overlong, but Vladimir wasn't going to put Brandy and little Mikey to any greater risk than he could avoid. Czar Mikhail and the constitution would just have to wait a while longer.

Part Four

The Wild, Wild East

CHAPTER 20

North to Mangazeya

The sleigh didn't have bells, but it did have a team of four horses and the bone-shod runner cut through the frosting of snow that had settled on the frozen river. The sleighs were surprisingly fast on the iceways of Russian winters. It helped too that their party was relatively small, three sleighs and a dozen riders. The other two sleighs held goods. One had the tents and camping gear for the party, and the other had bribes for Shein. Officially, the goods were gifts. But what they were, were bribes.

The very good news, so far as Bernie was concerned, was that while he and Natasha weren't alone in their sleigh, they were under a thick layer of fur blankets. They couldn't do much, but at least they could snuggle. They had been on the road for almost a month, and in a way the trip was reminding them both of the trip they had made to pick up Bernie's Dodge back in 1632. The bad news was this time they wouldn't be picking up anything as valuable as the Dodge had proven to be. The good news was that they wouldn't be picking up Cass Lowry.

"Riders ahead," shouted Marat Davidovich, the commander of the guard detachment.

Bernie reached over and opened the panel. It was a wooden frame with two sheets of goat intestine stretched over it, with a one-inch gap between them. It let only a little light through, but it was a good insulator when closed. Now Bernie opened it and shivered at the cold air. "What have we got, Marat?"

"I'm not sure yet, sir." As Bernie's relationship with Natasha had become more public knowledge, the people around them—especially those in Natasha's service—had become less and less comfortable using Bernie's first name. There had also been some resentment directed at Bernie. Apparently they felt he was getting above himself. Marat was not the worst about it, but he wasn't happy with the situation. Czar Mikhail had considered the possibility of ennobling Bernie, but there were issues of family status involved and more than a little resentment of Bernie—and up-timers in general—among the nobility of Russia.

Besides, Bernie was uncomfortable with the idea. Bernie wasn't overly enamored of the idea of nobility in general. In fact he didn't like it at all. Up-time, before the Ring of Fire, when Bernie had thought about nobility—not often—he had thought about the princess and the pea or Snow White, or maybe Charles and Diana, or Elizabeth II. Maybe Grace Kelly. But his attitude had been basically neutral. Down-time, on the other hand, he had run into the real thing, seventeenth-century Russian style. He had come to despise the whole structure. He was fond of certain members of the nobility. More than fond, in the case of Natasha. But he despised the system itself. However much he would like to have gotten rid of the whole thing, his discussions with Czar Mikhail, Filip Pavlovich, even Anya—and most of all the reaction of the service nobility to Czar Mikhail's emancipation proclamation—had convinced him they couldn't. That the people with the guns wouldn't stand for it.

Bernie stuck his head out of the small window and saw a troop of perhaps twenty men at arms riding up. He slipped back in and pulled out his Dacha-made Colt. It was a caplock and he had a spare cylinder for it. He left his up-time rifle in its case. He only had seven rounds left for it. "Stay—" Bernie started, then seeing the expression on Natasha's face, he shook his head and said, "Never mind."

When the sleigh stopped, he opened the door and stepped down, then held out a hand for Princess Natasha to alight from the sleigh.

The riders looked like Cossacks, but they were carrying AK3s and wore bandoliers of chambers.

"What are you doing here?" asked one with ice on his thick black beard.

"I am Princess Natalia Petrovna Gorchakovna, Ambassadress from Czar Mikhail to General Shein. This is the up-timer, Bernie Zeppi."

"What an amazing thing," the big man said with a grin wide enough to be clearly seen through his beard. "You don't look a thing like the Bernie Zeppi who came through here in August, selling magic up-timer beans."

"It's worse than that. I don't have any magic beans."

"Neither did he." The smile was gone from the big

man's face, and the AK3 was tilting ominously in their direction. It wasn't aimed at them yet. In fact, it was still pointing at the sky. But it was getting close to pointing at them and Marat was shifting his AK4 too.

"Everyone, calm down," Bernie said. "We have a bunch of documents for General Shein and he, at least, will recognize both Natasha and me."

The big man tilted his head at Bernie. "What about General Izmailov? Will he recognize you?"

"He should. I've met him a few times. I wish we had Tim with us, but he's busy holding off Sheremetev's army in Kazan."

"So we heard," the man with the icy beard said. He waved over another man. "Ivan, here, will guide you in."

Solikamsk

General Izmailov bowed gracefully to Princess Natasha, then gestured them to chairs in a large room that Bernie took to be some sort of reception hall. It had glass windows, though they were the small diamond-shaped panes. Russia was still very short of large panes of glass. The chairs were padded, and the room was painted a sort of ivory white. "Welcome to Siberia."

Natasha grinned and Bernie felt his own lips twitch. Izmailov wasn't giving any ground at all. His greeting established that he felt that this was a different country than Russia.

"Thank you, General," Natasha said. "Czar Mikhail is pleased that General Shein has not thrown his support to the usurper."

Here we go, Bernie thought. *Shein is looking for recognition of Siberia as a separate nation and Czar Mikhail wants Shein to acknowledge his authority as czar over all of this territory.*

Over the course of the afternoon those two positions went from implicit to explicit, but were not resolved. Then they got down to practical business. Shein, though personally loyal to Patriarch Filaret, didn't feel nearly as much personal loyalty to Czar Mikhail. Mikhail was already doing what Shein wanted from him, because as long as he survived, he would be the primary focus of Sheremetev's ire. And his armies . . . which was buying Shein time to build his Siberian realm. And Czar Mikhail was going to keep right on doing it, because his alternative was to be imprisoned or executed.

"So what can Mikhail do for General Shein that he isn't doing already?" General Izmailov asked, and Bernie noted that even now it was "General" Shein, not "Czar" Shein. There were many political reasons for that, both in Siberia and in the rest of Russia. But the most important of the reasons was that until Shein took the title he could change his mind and become the loyal general again. Once the title attached to his name, there would be no going back. Bernie wasn't surprised. Shein was a good general but he was, at his core, a cautious man. He was more comfortable on the defensive, especially now that he didn't have Patriarch Filaret pushing him.

Bernie and Natasha spent two days in Solikamsk, then took the Babinov Road to Tobolsk, where they met with General Shein and learned that he actually controlled less territory than they thought. He controlled most of the Ob River, and had a more limited control over the land around it, but he didn't control Mangazeya.

Mangazeya was effectively an independent city-state and it—not Shein—controlled access to the Kara Sea.

Russia was even more fragmented than they thought back in Ufa. Relations between Shein's Siberian state and the Mangazeya city-state were cordially tense, if that wasn't too much of a contradiction in terms. And it wasn't. Both Shein and the city council of Mangazeya wanted stable and friendly relations, but Shein wanted an open route to the rest of the world through the Arctic Ocean, and Mangazeya wanted to control that trade. Shein could take Mangazeya and both he and they knew it, but he didn't want to. It would cost him and it would mean moving his troops away from the Babinov Road, which would open the way for an attack by Sheremetev...or even Mikhail.

"We need to go to Mangazeya!" Natasha said. They had been in Tobolsk for three days, and had a read of the political situation that was much improved. But if Vladimir's strange contraption was going to be coming this way, they needed to arrange passage for it. Besides, Tobolsk had proved just as crowded and interruption-prone as Ufa.

Bernie was afraid that he and Natasha would have to go all the way to Alaska before they got a chance to go all the way.

The trip to Mangazeya was going to take upwards of forty days if it went well, so it would likely be sometime in April before they got there. And there

was a real chance that Vladimir would get there
before them.

Ufa kremlin

"It's a petition from the villagers of New Ruzuka
asking for—no, demanding—a seat in the Ufa duma.
Not the *Zemsky Sobor*. The duma," Czarina Evdokia
said as she read the document.

"That makes a certain amount of sense," Czar
Mikhail told his wife. "We haven't called a *Zemsky
Sobor* since we got here."

"I know," Evdokia said. "We need a constitutional
convention, not a series of pronouncements made by
the *Zemsky Sobor* and duma under the influence of
the bureaus."

This wasn't a new argument.

When Mikhail had been given the throne, his
"absolute" power had been diluted by a series of
things that he couldn't do without the consent of the
Zemsky Sobor and the duma. That had necessitated
the calling of the *Zemsky Sobor* every year to officially approve the actions taken in his name by the
government. But when Sheremetev sent Mikhail into
seclusion—for his own safety, of course—the role of
the *Zemsky Sobor* had been usurped by the newly
formed Director-General's office. The *Zemsky Sobor*,
under Sheremetev's eye—and under his guns—had
signed off on the change in authority. It could be
argued that everything that Sheremetev did was legal.
In fact, he had—again under his guns—had Mikhail
sign off on the change as well. The issue then became

whether Sheremetev's proxy for Mikhail's authority was revocable by Mikhail. Mikhail held that it was, Sheremetev held that it wasn't. Neither Sheremetev nor Mikhail had called a *Zemsky Sobor* to confirm their position.

Mikhail had wanted to call a *Zemsky Sobor*, but Evdokia had argued against it. At a minimum, the *Zemsky Sobor* would insist on veto power, and Evdokia pointed out that it was unlikely to willingly replace itself with an elected body. Mikhail guessed that Sheremetev's reason for not calling it back was similar to his own. Mikhail being on the loose meant the *Zemsky Sobor* would be in a much stronger position and would demand concessions that Sheremetev was unwilling to grant.

All of which meant that petitions like this one were becoming much more common. The manufacturers of Ufa and Kazan were each asking for a representative in the duma. So were monasteries, other villages and towns, riverboat owners and riverboat crews. It was all Bernie's fault. Mikhail had made Bernie a member of the duma, a *dumnyi diak*, the lowest rank on the duma. Which, while a high office, wasn't at all the same thing as a noble title like prince. More like appointing him secretary of agriculture than knighting him. Bernie had been made one because Mikhail wanted the up-timer perspective in his councils, but the official reason was as representative of the Dacha and technology. So now everyone wanted a seat in Mikhail's duma for their group.

Then, of course, Bernie was sent off to Tobolsk so he could be alone with Natasha. And from the latest letter, they were probably halfway to Mangazeya by now.

En route to Mangazeya
February 1637

They were pulling up again. Bernie opened up the shutter on the sleigh window to see a group of riders in heavy cloaks and furs. They looked somewhere between Native American and Asian, but some of them were redheaded. One of them spoke accented Russian and the rest spoke a language that Bernie had never heard but would later learn was called Khanty. However, one of the guides Shein had provided them with spoke the language, and it quickly became apparent that Bernie was invited to visit. Even here they had heard of up-timers and since there was apparently one handy, they were going to bring it back to be looked over by their tribal elders.

"Right now, it's an invitation. But if we don't go along, it's going to turn into an order."

"In that case, tell them we'll be happy to visit." Bernie waved at the Mongols and climbed back in the sleigh. But before he got the door closed, there was a shout. More discussion followed, in which it was determined that one of the Mongols would be riding in the sleigh with them. Again, no choice was really offered unless they wanted a fight. Bernie almost went with the fight option, but decided against it.

The man got in and pulled off his peaked cap. It was fur-lined, and he was bald under it except for a red scalp lock.

The guy also took off his outer fur, and in the warmth of the enclosed sleigh, he was quite aromatic. Rancid reindeer grease, at a guess.

Unfortunately, their guest wasn't the one who spoke Russian, and neither Bernie nor Natasha spoke Mongol. Assuming that was the language the guy spoke. By the time they got to the village, Bernie was ready to ride on the roof of the sleigh.

He opened the door and looked out at the village. "Hey, teepees?" And they were. Not all of them. There were a variety of structures in the village, but several of them were, for all intents and purposes, teepees. Except for the feathered headdress of movies and TV, these guys might almost be American Indians. Bows, horses, the works. But, no. There was also steel—or at least iron—armor and swords.

They spent two days with the Tangu, and in the course of their talks with the tribal elders they mentioned that they were going to Mangazeya to meet Natasha's brother and his up-timer wife, who were coming to Russia to discuss with Czar Mikhail how to produce a constitution that would give all the people of Russia a say in their own government.

At that point, the Tangu elders got very interested and they ended up with a Tangu elder and an interpreter coming along. From what their translator said, the local tribe was going to be sending messages to its associated clans. By the time they got back on the road, it sounded to Bernie like the Mongol equivalent of Sitting Bull or Crazy Horse would be sitting in on the constitutional convention. At least, that was how it was going to work if there was still a czar in Ufa when they got back. General Shein hadn't had much faith that Tim could hold out in Kazan.

Kazan
February 1637

"It's trench warfare," Ivan told Tim. He had slipped out of Sviyazhsk without much trouble. The lines were formed and it was easy enough for an individual to sneak through the lines.

"It's not," Tim disagreed. "I mean, it's not like we have lines twenty miles long. We have trenches and bastions around Kazan. You have them at Sviyazhsk." Tim pointed out the window at the small fortified city across the frozen river. "And General Birkin has them around his camp."

A grin twitched Ivan's face. "It was fun watching them chop their defensive lines out of the frozen earth."

"What's the word from Moscow?" Tim asked. Over the course of the winter, new radio stations had been installed between Sviyazhsk on the Kruglaya Mountain and Nizhny Novgorod, and exchanges of information had begun. There were now radio operators running their own network, and left alone by both sides because of their utility.

"Not much," Ivan said. "Sheremetev is raising a bigger army and putting together siege engines. I don't think he is going to be able to get them here before the spring thaw."

There were two military campaign seasons in Russia, summer and winter. And two seasons you couldn't campaign in, spring and fall. In spring, the melting snow and ice turned Russia into a muddy swamp. And in fall, the rains did the same thing. But in summer or winter, the rivers made excellent transportation conduits. They were nearing the end of the winter combat season, and that brought them back to Ivan's point about World War I. The machine guns they and Sheremetev had were more analogous to the Gatling guns of the American Civil War than the machine guns of World War I. They were an outgrowth of the AK4.7, also created by Andrei Korisov. To give the devil his due, Korisov was a brilliant innovator in the field of firearms. And from what Tim had heard, devil was an altogether too apt a description of the man. That had one great advantage to Czar Mikhail. Almost every serf or slave employed in the gun shop, and better than half the *Streltzi* who had worked in the gun shop, had run east, and a lot of them had made their escape good. Most of those people were in Ufa and Kazan now, making AK4.7 Korisov guns and the tools to make breech-loading cannon. It would be a while before they got breech-loading cannon, but they were already making Korisov guns.

The Korisov gun used a large clip of caplock chambers and a crank to move the chambers and cock the hammer. They worked, but being black powder weapons, they tended to foul quickly and had to be taken out of action for cleaning or risk a jam and an exploding gun. And, having a single barrel, couldn't be fired as fast. A Korisov gun couldn't put more than a hundred and fifty rounds a minute down range without severe danger to the gunners. The new artillery was much superior to anything the seventeenth century had known before the Ring of Fire, but wasn't up to the standards of World War I artillery. Besides, Birkin only had a few of the new guns and Tim didn't yet have any cannon made since the Ring of Fire. But that didn't matter, because they had rifles that combined long range with a good rate of fire.

The mass charge was over, and if Sheremetev hadn't learned that, Birkin had. For the past two months they had been doing nothing but maintaining their lines. And it looked like it was going to stay that way till after the spring run off dried.

"Are you sure, Ivan? There is still almost a month for Sheremetev to bring up his new army."

"I almost hope he does, General. It would be a repeat of what happened to Ivan the Terrible in 1548, when the ice melted under his army and his siege engines sank."

"Unless we get a cold spell," Tim said, then waved a hand in negation. "Pay no attention. It's being stuck here all winter with nothing to do but fortify and fortify some more."

"And dodge the enticements of every marriageable girl in Kazan," Ivan said with a grin. "They are a greater danger than Birkin's army."

CHAPTER 21

Federation?

Moscow
February 1637

Fedor Ivanovich Sheremetev watched the army leaving from the Kremlin wall. It had been a hard winter for him as well. He had spent it trying to keep his nation from dissolving as Mikhail sucked the workers from farms and towns all over Russia, and Cossacks on the Don River were talking about declaring independence from Russia and Poland. Archangelsk declared independence, as well, and his only link to the up-timer knowledge was now through Polish back channels or whatever access the Swedes allowed.

The good news was out of the gun shop. They had improved steel for the breeches and breech-locks and improved cartridges. His intent as he had raised this army was to send it to reinforce Birkin and finally take Kazan, opening the way to Ufa. But now that was going to have to be put off, possibly for another year. He had to take Archangelsk back. He had to have his own port. Independent access to the rest

of the world, especially the USE and its books. So
the army that should be marching east was going to
march north instead.

The one thing that Patriarch Filaret had been right
about was that Russia could no longer be a nation in
seclusion, walled off from the rest of the world.

Fedor turned back into the Kremlin and to the
always increasing round of paperwork that filled his
days. The bureau men pretended to be cowed, but
they constantly threw up roadblocks of paper. Every
sheet was a list of excuses, whining about why they
couldn't do their jobs. And the purges he had used
over the fall to force them to obedience had cost
him too many of the bureau men. It turned out that
the files still had to be filed, even if you killed the
uppity clerks.

Grantville section, Embassy Bureau, Moscow

Boris Ivanovich Petrov decoded the latest message
from his son in Ufa. It was a fairly clear description
of who had gone over to Czar Mikhail. It was also
encoded using the family pad. A set of five number
groups that designated, book, page line and word.
The fifth number indicated length of phrase, So 3,
15, 6, 2, 2 indicated the fifteenth page of the boyar
book, the sixth line, the second and third words on
that line. Which were "Yuri Mikhailovich." The next
group G, 125, 32, 5, 1 was the G volume of the Dacha
encyclopedia, the one hundred and twenty-fifth page,
the thirty-second line, and the fifth word. Which, as
it happened, was Tupikov. Yuri Mikhailovich Tupikov

was now in Ufa. That was interesting. Yuri was a fairly
staid sort in the Roads Bureau, not the sort that Boris
would have thought of as ... No, wait. Ivan Petrovich
Sheremetev, the director-general's cousin, had been
playing with the roads budget again. Yuri might have
had to run for his life.

The next code group started them on a new subject.
The craftsmen of Ufa, who were mostly the refugees
from the Dacha and Murom with a leavening of the
refugees from Kazan, were using induction to melt iron
and make steel. It was still very small scale, but one
of the advantages of doing it that way was that they
didn't have to build a whole factory to make a few
pounds of steel. It was more suitable to the making
of small quantities of good steel. That was something
that they had picked up on at the Dacha in 1634.
The important thing, as far as Boris was concerned,
was that it was still more evidence that an industrial
base was developing in the east faster than it had in
the Dacha. That surprised Boris, but as he thought
about it, it made sense. They had been teaching people
how to use chemistry and electricity for the past five
years and more. There were a lot of people who had
the basics by now.

Each of Director-General Sheremetev's purges had
pushed more of the skilled craftsmen, whether *Streltzi*
or minor nobility, to defect to Czar Mikhail. In fact,
given other circumstances, Boris might have taken his
wife and run for it. But he was in a crucial position.
He got information from the USE, and through his
son Ivan, he got word of the happenings in the east.
That let him provide private information to a number of bureau men who were worried about family

members who had gone missing. The bureaus were a world of traded favors, and Boris was in a position to trade a number of them. It was dangerous to live and work in Moscow these days, but Boris had been a field agent for most of his life and the danger made him feel at home.

"Yuri, see if Ivan Alexovich Tupikov is free sometime today. And see what's happening in the Dacha with induction forging," Boris hollered out the door of his office. "Let's see if we can send something to Iosef to patent in the USE."

"*Da!*" Yuri called back. "Did you hear they will be launching the new dirigible soon?"

"How soon?"

"A week, maybe less."

The Grantville section had agents in the dirigible works. It was new tech, after all, and there had been several innovations in the field of making dirigibles developed at Bor. Boris had been able to follow the redesign of the dirigibles at Bor and the development of the D'iak-class dirigible. He also managed, through the Goritsky Monastery, to send copies of the new design to Ufa. It was a good design. The D'iak had almost neutral buoyancy at take off, and got some of their lift aerodynamically. It was a new design and Boris didn't know if anyone had tried anything like it up-time. That new design offered a lot of possible patents in the USE.

That too was part of Boris' job, getting foreign credit for Russia. Russia was perennially broke and now that it was in five or more bleeding pieces, it was more broke than ever. Boris really wished that Czar Mikhail had stayed in that damned hunting lodge.

He wished that Bernie and Natasha were still in the Dacha making stuff, rather than wherever they were.

Goritsky Monastery

The ladies of the monastery watched the army marching by in something close to shock. What had possessed the man? Sheremetev had sent his army in the wrong direction. To attack Archangelsk made no sense at all. Mikhail was the threat. The consensus was almost total. "Sheremetev is insane."

Ludmila was not convinced. She knew Sheremetev. Stuffed shirt, he might be. Egomaniac, yes, definitely. But maniac? No.

That left her with the question, what did Sheremetev know that she didn't?

Even before the army had passed out of sight of the monastery, she was closeted with Sofia and several of the other sisters, trying to figure out what they had missed. It was hard, and took them weeks to figure out because it wasn't a single thing, but several factors. First, from Sofia, she got the prices of mica capacitors in Grantville. They were higher than she had thought. Then, from Tatyana Dolmatov-Karpov, she got the prices that the Polish merchants were paying for mica and it was lower. Rather a lot lower than it should be.

The difference in prices wasn't just because the Sheremetev family was raking off a fortune. The Polish merchants were ripping them off too. And so were the Lithuanian magnates they were having to ship the stuff through, to keep from shipping it through the Swedish enclave. Which they had to do to keep it out of the lawsuits that Vladimir Gorchakov had introduced in the USE.

From Elena Cherakasky, Tatyana learned that some of the information that the Poles had provided was falsified or distorted. When that was all put together, it meant that Sheremetev needed a route into the USE and its libraries that was not controlled by Sweden or Poland.

By the time they had gone through the books and papers and put it all together, Archangelsk was besieged. The local government of Archangelsk had made the same erroneous calculation the ladies of the monastery made. They had started with assuming that Sheremetev would be too busy with Mikhail to trouble them, and the price for that miscalculation was going to be high.

And that was the other piece of information they had missed. It was entirely possible, even probable, that even that second army would have failed to get to Ufa this year. That would have left Sheremetev with all his forces tied up in an indecisive campaign in the southeast while the whole Russian empire fragmented around him, with each apparently successful revolt encouraging the next.

Archangelsk would make an excellent example of the cost of rebellion.

Mangazeya
March 1637

The Gateway to the World! Bernie thought. Then, *Yeah, right.* He was feeling just a bit testy. Over two freaking thousand miles of travel and he and Natasha

still couldn't get together. The frustration was about
to kill him.

Mangazeya was two hundred plus miles up the Taz
estuary from the Gulf of Ob. And Bernie couldn't
quite figure out why anyone would put a town here.
Yes, he could. It was far enough off the direct route
so that it was inconvenient to the customs agents, but
close enough so that the smugglers didn't need to go
too far out of their way to get here.

And, in Mangazeya, there was Sir William Blake.
A stocky, bearded man who dressed like a Russian
and spoke Shakespearean English, he was a fur trader
and he was quite illegally shipping Russian furs and
pearls and other things out of Siberia to England
every summer. About the only thing that war in Russia meant to Billy Boy was the possibility of grabbing
a chunk of Russia to turn into the arctic version of
twentieth-century Hong Kong. A British territory in
Russia. Of which he would be the viceroy.

Fortunately, Billy Boy wasn't the only voice in
Mangazeya, just the most obnoxious. There was a
faction that wanted to stay in Russia and a faction
that wanted to start their own country. There were
the natives, who were the core of the separatists. The
Pomors were the core of the "stay in Russia" group.
The "join England" faction were the smallest group but
the richest, and mostly consisted of English merchants
and their families. They were still arguing about it
when the *Catherine the Great* arrived.

"More teepees," Brandy told little Mikey, who was
bundled up in heavy furs, but still not happy to be
out in the cold.

The *Catherine* had been collecting wood enroute for some time and everyone was tired and looking forward to a rest. Also, the *Catherine* wasn't breaking the ice at this point. It was traveling on the ice, using its false keel as a skid and the continuous track and engines to get where it was going.

They would stop here and do repairs before any further travel. The *Catherine* pulled up beside a frozen dock and they ran out the gangplank.

Brandy looked at the town of Mangazeya and felt like she'd been transported to yet another time. Which was helped along, when—of all people—Bernie Zeppi, wrapped in a fur robe, walked up to her, held up his right hand and said, "How."

Brandy started laughing and Vladimir looked confused. The woman next to Bernie, who must be Vlad's sister Natasha, rolled her eyes. Apparently she had heard about the joke beforehand. Then Vladimir hugged the woman and swung her to meet Brandy.

"Come on, everyone. Let's get in out of the cold," Bernie said. "I would have used a feather, but all they have up here is penguin feathers."

"Aren't penguins from the south pole?" Brandy asked.

"Never let the facts stand in the way of a good line," Bernie told her. "I have no idea, but I haven't seen any of them. Now, let's get inside before I freeze my feathers off."

The got inside and John Adams renewed his acquaintance with Billy Boy. The discussion went back to who would own Mangazeya and the rest of Siberia, especially points farther east. The *Catherine* was capable of making the trip, but she was just one ship and with the amount of fuel and effort involved, even considering what they had learned, there was some question of whether she could make the return trip before the summer thaw. More crucially, there simply wasn't enough population density this far north to mount any serious defense against any invader, whether from the south or the sea.

Vladimir called his sister aside. "Is this what you've been dealing with?"

"Yes, and not just here. In Tobolsk too. And the Don Cossacks are making noises about forming their own nation, as well. I understand Archangelsk has declared independence."

"I wasn't convinced till we got here, but perhaps Brandy and President Piazza are right."

"Right about what?"

"Perhaps what we need is a federal system." It wasn't the first time this had come up, but especially among the bureaus there was a great deal of resistance to the notion. They were afraid of having their bureaucratic regulations challenged by local governments, which was hardly something unheard of.

"Czar Mikhail is opposed to that because he's certain that some of the states will insist on continuing serfdom," Natasha told him. "He can see a civil war over serfdom if it's allowed to stand."

"Yes, you're right. But . . ." Vladimir looked over at Bernie and Sir William Blake, arguing over the fate of Mangazeya. "Where are the Mangazeyans in this?"

John Adams insisted that they couldn't go back to Hamburg until extensive repairs were made. And after reading the list of repairs, Vladimir agreed that they would leave the _Catherine_ in Mangazeya till the summer melt, and take the ice boats down the river to Tobolsk, then a caravan on the Babinov road to Solikamsk, then sleighs to Ufa. That was necessary because the false keel that had acted as skid for the last part of the trip was worn down and would have to be replaced. So would several other parts of the ship that had suffered excessive wear or damage in the course of the trip. They weren't going to have to rebuild the ship, but they would be all of April and probably most of May repairing it. In the meantime, they would collect furs, pearls, diamonds, and whatever else they could manage as high value cargoes to go back to the USE to pay for the goods they had bought on Ron Stone's credit.

The *Cath* had a shipload of gear, including radio tubes that would extend the range of the radio stations considerably, and designs for directional antenna that would extend them more. That was especially important in Eastern Russia, where the population was small and distances were great.

They spent a week in Mangazeya setting up a radio station with a rotateable directional antenna, then got on the road, taking much of the cargo of the *Catherine the Great* as well as representatives of the Khanty and Mansi peoples. And as they made their way back south, Bernie was thinking about the Napoleonic quote. Not the one about eggs, the one that went "You may ask me for anything you like, except time." It was going to take time to get back to Ufa and there was nothing they could do about that. In the meantime, they were out of touch.

CHAPTER 22

Preparing for War

Ufa
March 1637

"The lines are stable," Evdokia read the radiotelegraph message aloud. "Birkin has backed off a bit and we still hold Kazan. Once you can get steamboats back on the river, we will be in good position to hold the Volga from the Caspian Sea to Kazan. However, I do not have the forces to push Birkin back. With the new weapons, the defense is much stronger than it was in the past. Not three to one, but ten to one, or a hundred to one."

Evdokia looked over at Mikhail. "Stable, he says. We have Don Cossacks in the courtyard, Mongols in the halls, boyars in the conference rooms, and peasants in the streets. And all of them demanding that the constitution give them everything they want. Dictatorship is starting to look good, Mikhail."

"It's not . . ." Mikhail trailed off. The truth was that things were that bad. Last fall, Mikhail had promised a constitutional monarchy. Over the winter, word had gone out that Czar Mikhail was going to be holding a constitutional convention. And, aside from the people invited, there were whole groups that had just shown up. Increasingly, the former serfs were pushing for a voice in the deliberations. Mostly under the leadership of Vera Sergeevna, Izabella Ivanovna Utkin, and—much to Father Kiril's annoyance—Father Yulian Eduardovich who, it turned out, was a very effective public speaker. Father Yulian, aside from his speaking ability, was moderately well read and becoming more so with each passing day. When he wasn't screwing around with the local women, he was reading translations of up-time political texts or giving speeches and sermons. And the point he kept harping on was that up-time, it was "the people," not the nobility, who ran things. As though nobles were actually not people, but some lesser breed that had, by some horrible accident, gotten control.

Every time the man started talking, Mikhail felt the guillotine at the back of his neck. And if he made Mikhail nervous, he made most of the nobility—both the great houses and the lesser nobility—positively livid. If Mikhail hadn't acted to prevent it, Father Yulian would have already been dead in a ditch somewhere. Followed by riots. Followed by that guillotine again. Sometimes, Mikhail wished he could deal with a nice simple war rather than all this politics.

Two hundred fifty miles southeast of Ufa

Salqam-Jangir Khan was young, Colonel Leontii Shuvalov thought. He was also weak and in need of allies. Leontii was willing to use that, and he had spent the last three months working his way into a position to convince the young khan to attack Ufa. To do so, he had promised the khan ten thousand AK3 rifles and one hundred thousand chambers. Then he explained his inability to deliver the rifles, by virtue of Czar Mikhail's forces holding the lower Volga so they couldn't ship the rifles to them. It had not been an easy sell, and his influence was still far from certain. Leontii had had to bribe, and promise bribes, to half the khan's court to get their support.

But it had worked. He had a force of almost thirty thousand Kazakh warriors with bows and steppe ponies ready to go. It wasn't going to do little Tim Lebedev much good to hold Kazan if Ufa was hit from the southeast. He bowed, the full, forehead to the floor bow, and backed out of the boy's presence.

Turning away from the tent, he saw Togym eyeing him and hid a grimace. That damned little bastard was trying to get the boy to change his mind again. He had been pushing the young khan toward stronger ties with the Turks from the beginning. Leontii forced a smile and Togym snorted. Worst of all, Leontii hadn't had a beer in three months.

He kept walking, heading for his horse and his small company of guards. They weren't any happier to be here than Leontii was, but at least they were civilized.

Togym watched the outlander go and then went in to see Jangir. "Great Khan."

"Don't say it, Cousin. Honestly, I don't trust him much more than you do. But the Ring of Fire happened. He is not our only source for that. And in that other history, we were subjugated by the Russians and Islam was outlawed by the Soviets."

"Whatever Soviets are," Togym answered.

The khan picked up his coffee and sipped. "We need those guns. We are beset, my Cousin, and we need the strength."

"Then why not deal with their Czar Mikhail?"

"Because Director-General Sheremetev is in Moscow looking west and Mikhail is in Ufa looking south and east. Who is more likely to try and gobble us up, do you think?"

"Czar Mikhail has offered freedom of faith to Muslims in Kazan."

"And we should trust a man who will not defend his own faith to defend ours?"

The boy had a point, Togym had to admit. He wasn't stupid, just young and probably scared. He had only been khan for a few years, and he had been a child when the crown had fallen to him. Togym just wished he'd managed to get an ambassador from Czar Mikhail's court to counter Colonel Leontii Shuvalov. Well, it was too late now. They were in the field, on their way to Ufa.

Dirigible Valley

"It flies," Dimitry Ivanov said, gratuitously. It was pretty obvious that the new dirigible flew. It had four hydrogen cells, not the twelve of the big ones, and the cells were smaller, as well. But it would lift four tons of usable cargo, in addition to engines, boiler water, and fuel. It didn't have the range of the *Czarina*, but it was probably going to be a little faster.

"That's very good. Because we're almost out of grain, and I don't want to walk out of the valley," Gregorii said. The box canyon had an exit, but it was down a hill that was almost a cliff. It could be gotten into or out of, but not easily. When they had had the *Czarina* to ship in supplies that had seemed a great idea. Since they got the radio message that the *Czarina* crashed in Germany, the security had seemed less important than some way of getting in fresh supplies. The dirigible team turned all their effort into getting something into the air as soon as possible and they had done it, even if it was an almost reversion to the *Testbed* that Colonel Nick had first flown in 1633.

"We still need to finish the shell and we will need a detachable gondola for shipping supplies."

"Then don't you think you should get to that?" Gregorii asked. "Or do you plan on eating grass this summer?"

Dimitry got back to it. It was a hacked together thing made of cut down parts, but in its way, it was a work of art. The unavailability of aluminum had encouraged experimentation in alternate structural materials and the knowledge that composites were cutting edge science up-time had encouraged experimentation into composites as structural members. The *Testbed* had used bamboo shipped up from China and to a great extent so had the *Czarina Evdokia*, but she was starting to use shaped composites as structural members. The *Prince Alexis* had gone even farther in that direction. It still used bamboo where they couldn't spread the load, but mostly it used shaped composites that were lighter for their overall strength, but weaker at any given point than bamboo. The shaped composites had another flaw. They had to be designed and made for a specific size of airship. The shaped composite components of the *Prince*

Alexis's shell couldn't be cut down or reshaped to make a smaller dirigible. But Dimitry had come up with an alternative. The skin and skeleton of the *Prince Alexis* was mostly made of a series of curved triangles. The triangles were made of fabric impregnated with stiffener then stamped into shape and cured. Once formed, they were quite strong for their weight and they had stamped-in attachments that let them be tied together to form a cylinder of a predetermined circumference.

But the new dirigible needed a smaller circumference. Dimity's solution was to use the pre-made panels from the *Prince Alexis* and add in special new panels that curved quite sharply. It gave the *Princess Anna* a boxy, flattish appearance and increased the stress on the new panels to a level that worried Dimitry. But it let them use the *Alexis*'s panels for two-thirds of the exoskeletal skin.

Dimitry figured another week to finish the skin and put together a cargo gondola and they would be ready to fly for real.

Bor
March 1637

The *D'iak 1*, first of the D'iak-class airships, sailed down out of the sky. It was tiny compared to the Czar class and it had a useful lift of just over a thousand pounds. It made its way into the hangar and there was room for the almost completed *D'iak 2*. Dimitry Alekseev Dolgorukov climbed out, cursing. "The damned radio failed again." He waved back at the airship. "When are your techs going to get it right?"

The radio miniaturization was less than fully effective, and the little ones were more prone to breakdowns. Grigory Mikhailovich Anichkov was fully aware of that fact, and the radios had been giving them trouble from the beginning. "They're working on it. In the meantime, what's your report?"

"There is a huge delegation heading for Ufa. If I'd had a radio I could have told General Birkin about..." Dimitry trailed off at Grigory's look, "Anyway there is a huge train of sleighs packed with goods and people heading down the Kama river..." Dimitry gave a description of what the caravan on the Kama had looked like yesterday afternoon.

On the road from Solikamsk

Bernie leaned over to kiss Natasha and the sleigh stopped again. *Every freaking time, dammit.* "I'm going to kill them. I don't care which tribal leader or minor Mongol potentate it is this time, I'm going to kill them."

Natasha laughed, but she didn't quite carry it off. "Maybe you should let General Izmailov deal with it." They had been picking up representatives to the Russian constitutional convention since they left Mangazeya. Shein had sent orders for General Izmailov to accompany them as Shein's representative to the convention. No one was committed to joining by sending delegates, but having delegates from all the different groups—or as many of them as they could get—would give the convention additional credence.

This time it was a group of *deti boyar* sons on

their way to join Shein. After some discussion, most
of them headed on for Shein's Siberian state. But Petr
Vasilievich Yazykov, who was near the upper end of
the lower nobility, decided to go to Ufa and see what
was what.

Ufa
March 1637

Stefan Andreevich waved the man with the wheelbar-
row over to the corner. It was a load of iron ore. Not
great iron ore, but not bad, and the wheelbarrows had
been bringing it in for most of the morning.

"Excuse me. Are you Stefan Andreevich?"

Stefan looked over at a short, pudgy man, with a
neatly trimmed beard. Peter the Great would never
be born to force the nobles of Russia to shave, but
Czar Mikhail, leading by example, had introduced the
short, well-trimmed beard. And this fellow was clearly
a follower of fashion, and not just where beards were
concerned. He was well-dressed. Very well-dressed.

"Yes. What can I do for you?"

"I need a stainless steel bowl."

Stefan blinked. "A what?"

"A stainless steel bowl. Actually, I need a dozen of
them, in several sizes, for the czar's kitchen."

"We don't do small orders here. You need Yuri
Petrovich's shop on Anna Lane, the other side of
Hangar Road. He's very..."

But the chubby little man was shaking his head.
"He says that he doesn't have an induction furnace
and copper won't do."

Stefan blinked again. Then, giving it up as a bad job, called out, "Lady Izabella, can you help this gentleman?"

A moment later, Izabella's head popped out of the office. "What's the problem?"

"He wants stainless steel pots."

"Bowls," the man said. "For the Czar's Kitchen." Stefan could hear the capital letters on "Czar's Kitchen."

"Oh, that's marvelous." Izabella beamed. "That means you have a source of chromium."

The little man looked confused. "What? No. What's cromanaman?"

Stefan turned back to his work as Izabella guided the man to the office. Yes, this was his factory, or at least partly his. But the truth was, Stefan would always be a shop floor owner, not an office owner.

"And what is your name, sir?" Izabella asked. She could already tell what he was. He was a courtier to the czar's court in exile. It was a safe bet that he had just received some posting.

"Artemi Fedorovich Polibin," the little man said.

Izabella recognized the name. They were successful courtiers, not really aligned. "I am Izabella Ivanovna Utkin, part owner of this factory. Why don't you tell me about it?"

He did. In rather boring detail. With emphasis. He was the New Master of the Kitchens at the Czar's Court. He had consulted with the cooks and discussed the issue with the staff of the New Dacha Complex and come to the conclusion that what the kitchens needed were induction cook tops and induction ovens. "Several of the staff at the electrical center thought it was an excellent idea. And it would have the advantage of keeping things like charcoal dust and soot away from the food."

Izabella had seen the induction furnaces that they used on the factory floor. There were several of them, powered by a steam-powered alternator. It had proved a moderately expensive, but very efficient, way of heating steel to the point of plasticity and of melting iron to a liquid state so that the amount of carbon in the steel could be controlled with a good degree of precision. It also concentrated the heat in the metal, which meant that the containers didn't have to be quite as heat-resistant. But cooking with it? It seemed to Izabella that it would melt the pots in minutes and burn the food in seconds.

She knew that you could control the heat by controlling the power of the alternating magnetic field, but the coolest she had ever seen from one of them was red-hot iron. Not as hot as yellow-hot or white-hot, but way too hot for cooking.

"Why do you want stainless steel?"

"Why, because it must be stainless steel to work with an induction heating element."

"No, it doesn't," Izabella said.

"Well, of course it does. I have it on the highest authority."

"Come with me."

She led Artemi out to the shop floor and, being careful to make sure that she didn't interrupt anything in progress, looked for a worker at one of the induction coils. She found one quickly. "Petr, can you show Sir Artemi how your induction forge works?" Petr was one of the slaves who had been working in the gun shop when Czar Mikhail issued the emancipation proclamation. Petr had good skills in metal working, but not so good when it came to finding his way in the wilderness. He had wandered into Ufa in November of last year, half-frozen, and Stefan hired him on the spot.

"Sure," Petr said. "Come over here." He pulled a lever and a heavy weighted stamp lifted. "First, we raise the hammer using the electric motor here." He disconnected the switch when the hammer was at the top of its arc. "Then we grab the part. You can see that these parts have already gone through some shaping and they have had the fringe knocked off, so they are ready for the next step." He held up a pair of tongs and pointed. "We use a bronze mouth on the tongs, so that the coil won't heat it. It still gets pretty hot from the part heating, but not as hot as if it was iron." He used the tongs with skill to pick up a part and move it into the empty center of a heavy copper coil and pushed a button. In just a few seconds the part went from black through red to orange. He released the button and pulled the part from the coil, then set it in the hollow in the drop hammer base plate. Then he pulled a lever and the hammer fell on the part. He used the electric motor to lift the hammer a bit and reached in with the tongs to grab the part and drop it into a cart.

Izabella looked over at Artemi. "See? That's not stainless steel. It's high-carbon steel, but not stainless." She looked over at Petr. "Isn't that right?"

Petr wiggled his hand. "Medium-high carbon steel. About point seven percent. But no chromium or anything else that would prevent rust."

It wasn't cool on the shop floor by any means, not even at this time of year. But it wasn't like standing at the gates of hell, either. That was another advantage of induction heating. It helped keep the heat where it was needed.

"But the up-time books said that you had to have stainless steel for induction cooking. That copper and even aluminum won't work."

"Really?" Petr asked. "Myself, I can't read. At least not much. Never had a chance to learn. But it makes sense that copper and bronze won't work. Hey, maybe the chromium in stainless makes the induction not work as well, so the pot doesn't melt."

"Perhaps." Izabella shrugged. "On the other hand, there might be better, cheaper ways to cook without ash getting in the food. I don't object to the expense of induction heating, not for what we do here. This place is dangerous enough as it is. Having a bunch of open flames hot enough to melt steel would make it a disaster waiting to happen. But I don't think kitchens are quite so deadly." She saw the looks that she was getting from Petr and Artemi. "What? Did I say something stupid?"

"Well, let's just say I doubt you ever spent much time working in a kitchen," said Artemi. "Honestly, I hadn't either, not till I got here and received this posting. For the first two weeks, I sat in a corner and watched. A kitchen is a dangerous place, and no two ways about it."

It was probably true. Izabella had never been all that interested in kitchens, except for what came out of them. And she had never needed to work in one, not even while they were on the road.

❖   ❖   ❖

Across Zeppi Road from the factory was the chem shop run by Alexis Khristianovich Patrikeev, who had studied chemistry at the Dacha and was making the caps for caplocks. It took him months to get into production, but now they were taking sheets of refined copper and turning them into nipples, then loading them with a carefully measured compound. It wasn't fulminate of mercury. It was the other stuff. Alexis had told Izabella what it was several times, but for some reason the name of the new process never stuck in her mind. Perhaps because people didn't die nearly as often using it as they did making fulminate of mercury caps.

Izabella knocked on the door of Alexis's office and then went in. Alexis was a skinny man with a short cropped beard and thick bushy hair. He wore glasses because he was nearsighted and always had been. It meant that the world away from him had been a blur for most of his life and encouraged him to read while making more manly arts like shooting out of the question. "What is it this time, Izabella?" He sounded irritated.

"What has you so upset?"

"The generator is out again," Alexis told her. The new process used electrical current in brine to make some chemical. Izabella didn't know what chemical and didn't care. Alexis didn't get along with electricity. His generators were always getting broken and one of the guys from the New Dacha had pointed out that making a generator was on the order of a thousand hours of labor and it wasn't labor that was easily divisible since most of it consisted of winding coils. There was a coil winding machine in Murom but it hadn't made the trip. They had made a new one here but it kept breaking down. So a lot of the coils for generators, alternators, induction devices, transformers, and the like, were hand wound.

"I heard they had the coil winder up and running again."

"It's not the coils this time. It's the brushes."

That was good news, sort of. The stamp forges could be used to make graphite brushes and mostly the factory made its own. But the process wasn't simple. It involved the right mix of carbon and copper and heat treating in an non-oxygen atmosphere. It was a complicated process, and expensive in its own right. Also the ones they could make here didn't last nearly as long as the ones she was told they made up-time. They didn't even last as long as the ones that they made at the Dacha or in Murom.

"We might be able to get you some new brushes. We still have a few from the last brush run."

The look Alexis gave her at that news was neither relieved or grateful. It was more like she had offered to let him stick his head in a wolf's mouth. "What do you want in exchange?"

"They need caps out at New Ruzuka."

"Forget it," Alexis said automatically. "The army needs those caps. They need them in Kazan and they need them at . . ."

"And you can't get them there. Besides, Kazan has its own cap factory."

"We'll get them there as soon as the ice melts."

"If we can build mines, so can they."

"You know that the guys at the New Dacha are working on a mine sweeper."

"Fine. Maybe it will even work. In the meantime, the villagers out at New Ruzuka have AK4.7s and they can't use them because they don't have caps." No one had come up with an automatic method of charging the pan for a flint or wheel lock, so the slide-action AK4.7 had to use a cap chamber.

"And how many rounds does it take those people out at New Ruzuka to shoot a rabbit?"

Suddenly, Izabella's mind was back on the road on the way here watching that stupid idiot murdering Irina because no one in the wagon train had a gun. It was just for a second, but any thought of smiling at Alexis's quip was gone. "Alexis, you came here straight from the Dacha on a steamboat. It took you, what? Three days? We were on the road for three months. I watched as a little girl died because a boy wanted to prove how bad he was. Fine, so the duma's army is on the other side of Ufa from New Ruzuka. But what about bandits? What about drunken idiots trying to prove they're real Cossacks? Those are my friends out there. I want them armed."

She got her caps. Not as many as she wanted, and Stefan spent the next week complaining about having to stop the chamber line so they could make another load of green brushes and bake them. He complained, but not too much. He remembered Irina too.

CHAPTER 23

Blueprint

Ufa
March 28, 1637

"Welcome back!" Czar Mikhail grabbed Bernie in a Russian bear hug. "Did you and Natasha get any alone time?"

"Oh, shut up," Bernie said, then—clearly as an afterthought—added, "Your Imperial Majesty."

The czar of Russia—at least this part of it—laughed. Then he looked over the rest of the new arrivals. It was a sunny day in Ufa, and there was a wagon train of sleighs stretched out from the gates of the Ufa kremlin. Natasha wasn't looking a lot more pleased than Bernie, but Vladimir was displaying a truly sinister smile. Beside Prince Vladimir was a young woman holding a baby and so wrapped up in furs that it was hard to tell much else. Behind her was General Izmailov with aides. And a gaggle of others. "Where did all these people come from?" Mikhail whispered.

Bernie gave a slight grimace, then said quickly and quietly, "These are representatives from tribes and towns from here to Mangazeya and Vlad thinks you should spend some effort in showing them respect. It's part of his plan."

Czar Mikhail was a bit surprised by that comment, but went along and spent the next hour greeting each delegation and ensuring that they be quartered. Not easy. Ufa was by now pulling in people considerably faster than it was producing room for them.

An hour later, in Czar Mikhail's office, it was just Bernie, Natasha, Vladimir and his wife, Brandy. And, of course, Evdokia. "So, no firm agreements, not even from General Shein?"

"Especially not from General Shein," Brandy Bates said. "We had to give him fifteen of the tubes just to get him to send Izmailov."

"Tubes?"

"Vladimir brought amplifier tubes," Bernie said. "And designs for making them. With the tubes, we can extend the range of the radios."

"And you had to give them to General Shein?"

"Not all of them," Natasha said. "Only fifteen. And there are another ten that we will be using to produce a chain of radiotelegraph stations between the Gulf of Ob and Tobolsk. Shein will be using the ones we gave him to set up a link from Tobolsk to Solikamsk along the Babinov Road, across the Ural Mountains."

"That's fine for General Shein, but what does it do for us?" Evdokia asked.

"It gets us a link," Vladimir started, then corrected himself. "Well, it *will* get us a link, once the radios are actually built from Solikamsk to Mangazeya. And we have arranged the construction of other radio stations, so that we will have communications from here to Mangazeya in a few hours, once all the stations are up and running. Solikamsk to Dobryanka, a touch over eighty miles. Then to Yagoshikha, which at thirty miles is almost close enough to make it without tubes. From Yagoshikha to Osinskaya Nikolskaya, just under sixty miles straight line distance, if twice that by the River Kama. From Nikolskaya to Voznesenskoye was around eighty miles.

"That gets us almost to here. We put in a station at a little place with four farmhouses and a church that is called *Letyaga*, apparently named after the Flying Squirrel pamphlets. That one, once it gets built, will reach us here in Ufa and from what Bernie tells me, will also link into the chain that goes to that hidden valley you have the dirigible hangars in."

"Also from Voznesenskoye," Bernie said. "We sent a mission to Mamadysh, on a tributary of the Kama River. They're going to build a radio station there and smuggle tubes to Kazan. And, if they can, to Kruglaya Mountain. Given the right weather conditions, an amplified station on Kruglaya Mountain has a good chance of sending to, or receiving from, Bor."

"So the radio network will connect a very large chunk of Russia, at least in terms of communications." Mikhail nodded. "That's good. And we have a stock of some of the components that we can send back the way you came to hurry things along. Batteries, generators, that sort of thing."

"So Natasha told me," Vladimir said.

Mikhail turned to Vladimir. "I guess that brings us to your plan, young man."

"Yes, I guess it does." Vladimir picked up a cardboard

tube and removed one end, then pulled two large sheets from it and unrolled them. He laid them out on the desk and then had to use the pen stand, an ink well, and a couple of books to hold the corners down.

"This is the plan that Brandy and I, with the help of Ed Piazza and several of the teachers at Grantville High came up with. We're not sure how much of it we're going to be able to get. And, for that matter, it's all subject to Your Majesty's approval. The basic structure is based on the up-time federal model. Two houses, an upper and a lower, a judiciary, and— especially—a tiered government system, so that some laws are made locally, some by the states, and some by the federal government. It all comes together in you, Your Majesty. You are the last court of appeal, administratively, legislatively and judicially, but not the head of any single branch. The administrative head of government will be a president, who I want to be elected by popular vote. But we may not get that. The bureaus will be part of the administrative branch of government and will want some input in selecting the president. We expect them to insist on some say in the legislative branch as well. The judiciary will be a supreme court that is only superseded by you. And lower courts that the legislative branch shall determine are necessary will be established. Judges will be proposed by the administrative branch, but approved by the congress and will require your consent."

"Why so complicated?"

"Partly to keep any one branch from gaining too much power," Brandy said, "but also so that there will be offices to give to people."

"This is the most important part," Vladimir said.

"The grant of rights. This is a set of restrictions on what the government can do."

"Can anything this confused ever work?"

"Something very like it worked in the up-time United States for over two hundred years. And was still going strong when the Ring of Fire happened," Brandy said. "But we are going to have some problems getting all of it accepted. See this section? 'All people in Russia shall be held equal before the law.' The boyars aren't going to like that. And it could be interpreted to include you. And everyone having the right to vote may cause problems as well. I've talked to General Izmailov some on the trip here, and a big part of the reason that General Shein isn't on your side is the emancipation proclamation. But it's also a big part of the reason that we got support from Ron Stone and a loan from Millicent Anne Barnes."

"Who?"

"Ron Stone is a major industrialist, and may be one of the richest individuals in the USE. Or maybe not. It's hard to tell. Her Serene Highness Millicent Anne Barnes is a member of the Barbie Consortium and runs the branch of the Royal Bank of Austria-Hungary in Grantville. Between them, but mostly Ron Stone, they backed the construction of the icebreaker *Catharine the Great*, and paid for the further supplies that will be coming once the ice in the Arctic gets a bit thinner."

They discussed the proposed constitution and the international politics of Mikhail's emancipation proclamation well into the night. The next day, they called the constitutional convention.

CHAPTER 24

Convention

Ufa
March 30, 1637

"The convention will come to order!" proclaimed Patriarch Matthew in a deep ringing voice.

That had taken arrangement. The president of the convention had yet to be selected and they had already been through a heavy round of squabbling. The Muslims didn't like Patriarch Matthew taking the lead role. Czar Mikhail had been considered, but the truth was that Mikhail wasn't a great speaker—which wasn't something they wanted to advertise. Letting Matthew do it was a concession to the Russian Orthodox church that was necessary after Czar Mikhail had declared Islam legal in Kazan and Ufa. And it was even more so, now that the convention had collected a bunch of tribal representatives who were Buddhists, Taoists, Zoroastrians, or sometimes even out-and-out pagans.

The Convention Hall, a new building in the expanded Ufa kremlin, was a big log cabin. More a long house than anything else, and it was warm inside. Almost hot, because of all the bodies crowded in.

Wham! Patriarch Matthew banged the gavel on the desk. *Wham!* Slowly, the conversation started to yield. Then he opened the floor to nominations for president of the convention. And for the next hour, people were nominated.

Everyone was nominated. Bernie was almost sure someone nominated Sheremetev. Natasha, Bernie, Brandy, Vladimir, Czarina Evdokia . . . they were all nominated.

When Vladimir was nominated, he stood up and asked that his name be removed from the nomination, because he had a proposal for the convention and didn't want anyone to feel that he had used the position of president to force through his agenda.

His nomination was removed with a flowery speech of regret by Vera Sergeevna, who had nominated him. Vera had never actually met Vladimir, but she had agreed to put his name up in talks with Anya. In return, Anya had arranged for a representative from Kazan to nominate Vera. A lot of what was going on here was political theater that had been carefully arranged in advance by Czarina Evdokia, Anya, and Natasha.

General Izmailov was proposed by a Don Cossack from near the Caspian Sea, so it was clear that the ladies weren't the only ones playing at political theater. General Izmailov thanked the man, but also declined the honor on the basis of his doubts about whether Siberia would be able to sign on. "I would feel obligated to support the final document if I were the president of the convention, and since I don't know what the convention will come up with, I don't feel I can accept the honor."

Which was a pretty clear statement that General Shein wasn't committed to Czar Mikhail, even if he had sent a representative to the convention. It went on like that. All the major players stepped aside, including Patriarch Matthew and a mullah from Kazan.

That got them down to the second tier candidates and Vera Sergeevna made a surprisingly good showing, getting support from the manufacturers of Ufa and the village leaders from seven of the twenty-three villages that had sent representatives. It finally came down to Alexander Nikolayevich Volkov, Georgii Petrovich Chaplygin, Petr Vasilievich Yazykov and a tribal leader from Siberia, who bowed out because he was unfamiliar with the rules of order for the convention.

After two more ballots, the president of the convention was Alexander.

"Thank you for your trust," Alexander said. "Now I will open the room to proposals."

Vladimir and half a dozen others raised their hands.

"Prince Vladimir, you said when you removed your name from contention that you had a proposal for the constitution, and I know that Czar Mikhail was waiting to convene this convention till you were here, because of what you have learned of the up-time governmental systems. So what knowledge of governance have you brought us from the future?"

Vladimir stood, opened his up-time style briefcase and removed a document. "When Czar Mikhail informed me of his desires, I consulted with the up-time experts and I have been working on an outline of what might work for Russia on the trip from there to here. This document is the result. The up-time constitution of the United States of America set up two houses, the House of Representatives and the Senate. By the time of the Ring of Fire, the senators were elected by popular vote, but Ed Piazza explained to me that it had not always been that way. Originally, the senators had been appointed by the state governments. And, for now at least, I believe that the governments of places like Siberia and the Don Cossacks will be more willing to accept the laws of their new federation of Russian states if each state is allowed to select their representative to the Senate in its own way..."

Vladimir went through the whole document that way, explaining not just what was in it, but why it was that way. And then the council was opened for debate and debate happened. Serfdom was the first major issue. Even with the new tools and techniques that had come with the up-timers, the labor shortage in Russia was acute. That being the case, the people with the guns— that is, the upper and lower nobility and the gentry, otherwise known as the *Streltzi*—were not happy with a peasantry that was free to quit. Especially when it could quit or threaten to quit just when everyone was most needed like, say, harvest time. On the other hand, the former serfs who had run east to escape their ties to the land and their debts weren't at all happy with the power that the nobles had had over them since the time of Ivan the Terrible and how much that power had grown over the ensuing years.

The Cossacks, who held strong views on freedom— which, in that other timeline, would be beaten out of them over the next couple of centuries—sided with the peasants. Yermak Fedov and Patriarch Matthew led the charge for a free Russia.

For the first week or so, Czar Mikhail and Vladimir were convinced that they could bring the northern and western states around. Then General Izmailov made an effective speech and almost a third of the delegates walked out of the convention.

They didn't leave Ufa, but the message was clear. Serfdom would be legal and binding, and so would slavery, at least in some of the states of the New Russia . . . or there would be no New Russia.

"We're going to have to give it to them," Vladimir said to Czar Mikhail.

"No," said Father Kiril. "Children yet unborn will curse our names if we give in and leave them chained to the land. Will you come before the Lord God with the enslavement of millions on your conscience?"

"The Bible doesn't forbid slavery. The Old Testament endorses it and Christ was silent on the matter," said Patriarch Matthew. Then he quickly held a hand up as Kiril started to object. "I don't disagree with you as a matter of personal conscience, Father Kiril. But politics is the art of the possible."

"It's a blot on all our consciences," said Brandy. "If we let the down-time Russian version of the 'peculiar institution' take root in the Russian constitution, it's going to be a blood debt through the generations."

"Maybe so," Anya said, "but we'll be long dead and won't hear a thing. You get what you can get in this world, and no more. What we can get is a mixed nation with free states and . . ."

"And have a civil war in four score and seven years," Bernie added.

"That works for me," Vladimir said. "Remember,

we have a war to win right now. And if we don't win, none of the rest of it matters. We need General Shein and the Siberian Corridor. We need support in the west. If we don't get those, Director-General Sheremetev and his *oprichniki* are going to march right over us. If not this year, then next. What happens to the serfs then?"

So they met with General Izmailov for the pro-slavery faction and Yermak Fedov for the anti-slavery faction, and managed to get the issue delayed.

They went on to the next issue. At the insistence of the northwestern groups, they had to limit the upper house to nobles. States would have the right to appoint two lords to the house of lords. Bureaus would have the right to appoint one per bureau. No one could sit in the house of lords unless they were a lord. On the upside, it would be up to the czar to make any new lord. So unless the person a state or bureau appointed to the lords was already a member of one of the great houses, the czar would have what amounted to a pocket veto. He could prevent any commoner from joining the house of lords simply by declining to make them a lord. He couldn't, for instance, keep Vladimir or even Brandy out of the house of lords, but he could keep Anya out of it by declining to make her a court princess.

They were busy arguing over which house the prime minister/president would come from, when the attack came.

"What is that?" Boris looked out at the horses. He was supposed to be working, but was pretty good at finding other places to be than work. And he had snuck away from the weaver's shop where he was supposed to be working. What he was looking at was the lead element of the Kazakh army. Not that there was any way for him to know that. What he could see was a bunch of men in chain mail armor, with pointed helmets and swords and carrying bows. To Boris it looked like another delegation to the congress, except that they just kept on coming. There had to be hundreds of them.

"Hey, Olga! What is that?" Olga was a forty-something woman who made a little money washing clothing in the river. Most of that money was spent on vodka the same night she made it. She looked up from her washboard and scowled at him. Then she looked the way he was pointing and went pale.

Olga wasn't stupid or even lazy. She was just beaten down by circumstances. She recognized what was coming, at least in general, and she took perhaps five seconds to take it all in. Then she turned around and started running for the town screaming, *"Attack! Attack!"*

Ivan, the guard in the east tower of the Ufa kremlin, was drinking his small beer and eating a cheese sandwich as he stood his post. He didn't hear Olga screaming, but dutifully looked around. He scanned the sky even, though the dirigibles were all gone. Then he looked out at the tree line and followed it around to the river, and saw the troops. He had never actually seen an army before. He was an escaped serf who had hired onto the city guard once he got to Ufa. He had dreams of someday being a great captain, but it took him some time to figure out what was going on. And even after he determined that the armored men on horseback might be an army, he didn't realize that they might be an *attacking* army.

But finally he called down to the sergeant of the guard. "Hey, Sergeant! Are we expecting a bunch of Mongols coming to the convention?"

"What are you talking about?"

"There are a bunch of Mongols in armor with bows, riding out of the woods next to the river."

"Why do you think they're Mongols?"

"They're dressed like Mongols. Pointy helmets, bows, and stuff."

The sergeant shook his head. "How many?"

Ivan looked out and tried to figure that out, but he lost count quickly. "A whole lot. Hundreds, maybe."

The sergeant wasn't the sharpest tool in Czar Mikhail's tool box. The sharp ones were out with General Tim or Colonel Ivan. But he had seen an army before and this didn't sound good. So he climbed the stairs to get a look at what was going on. It took him almost a minute because the sergeant liked his sausage.

By the time he got to the lookout, there were five hundred plus Mongols filling the fields between the forest and the outskirts of expanded Ufa. One quick look was all it took and he was screaming the alarm and causing the bells to be rung.

Stefan Andreevich was in the large forging factory on the east side of Ufa when he heard the noise.

He wasn't using the stamp press. He was supervising the workers using it. Stefan had gotten the contract to make chambers for the AK4. He and partners, including Izabella Ivanovna Utkin, who had put up much of the original capital—her mother's jewels and her father's money that they had taken from the original Ruzuka. Father Yulian and Alexander Nikolayevich Volkov were also partners. It provided Stefan with a large enough nest egg to build a factory and hire workers, so he was turning out interchangeable chambers at a rate of hundreds a day, and had been for the last three months. Almost all of those had been sold to Czar Mikhail for credit in the Czar's Bank in Ufa, but some had gone to making sure that the village of New Ruzuka and the staff for his factory were all equipped with AK4s, and even the AK4.7s, and had at least ten chambers for each rifle, extra caps, and reloading kits. The memory of coming back to the wagon train to find the dead child Irina still haunted Stefan's dreams.

He went to the door and out into the crowded, dirty street. On the street he heard lots of people shouting. The words "attack" and "Mongol" were common, but so were words like "bullshit" and "ridiculous." Then he heard the bells from the kremlin. Stefan stepped back into the factory and shouted, "Everyone, stop work and get your guns."

"What?" "Are you nuts?" "You're still paying me," came from various people but as the noise of the stamp presses, drills and other equipment quieted, they began to hear the bells. And the responses shifted to "what's going on?" In a surprisingly short time, Stefan's work crew were armed and ready. Which left only the question of what to do with them.

❖   ❖   ❖

President of the Constitutional Convention Alexander Nikolayevich Volkov heard the bells. He motioned to the clerk of the convention. "Would you go see what's happening? I don't want to interrupt Sir William unless we have to." He didn't add, "because if I do, he'll just start over at the beginning."

It took a few minutes for the clerk to find out and by then the first arrows of the Kazakh army had been fired. There was no longer any room for doubt about their intent.

The clerk, who had left sedately, returned at a dead run, screaming, "We're under attack!"

Stefan and his workers headed for the edge of town and the dirigible hangar. Seeing armed men moving in that direction acted like a lodestone. Other men, and more than a few women, made quick trips to their homes or workplaces, grabbed up a weapon, and rushed out to join the defense. Others, more cautious and perhaps wiser, headed for the kremlin walls and the safety they might provide.

By the time Stefan got to the edge of the city, he had almost two hundred armed people with him, along with two other men who thought they should be in command.

There wasn't actually an edge to Ufa, not in the sense of a wall around the outer city. There was a preferred area between Hangar Road and the shore and between the kremlin and the hangar canal. Hangar Road was a mile long road that went east from the south gate of the Ufa kremlin to the dirigible hangar. It was a good road, raised bed macadam construction, and thirty feet wide with deep ditches on either side for drainage. Naturally enough, people who could afford it lived on Hangar Road. The most expensive properties were between Hangar Road and the river.

The buildings were more dense in close to the kremlin and old city, and thinned out as they spread east along Hangar Road. The hangar canal was, at this point, a half-finished ditch that didn't even have ice in it, much less water. It was muddy from melted snow, though, so acted as a barrier for attacking troops. Not a barrier that couldn't be bypassed, but one that they would have to slog through under the guns of the defenders. There were also partially completed bastions farther out, but they were mostly just the preparations that would allow some basic defenses to be put in place if they had a few days' notice of an attack.

Stefan's factory was on the north side of Hangar Road, about four blocks north and three-quarters of the way to the hangar. His trip to the hangar had left him on Irina Way, which was one block north of Hangar Road. They got to the vicinity of Hangar Road and Irina Way, went between two buildings—one of them a half-built warehouse where goods were stored in the open. Stefan saw the goods and started ordering his people to grab them and make a barricade between the two buildings. Someone quipped that Princess Irina was too young to let the Mongols in this way. Some people laughed, but Stefan paid no attention. He could see the troops out there, moving around. He didn't know what the movement meant, but it looked like they were getting organized.

"This is the wrong place!" shouted a man Stefan didn't know, but had seen around.

Stefan shouted, "Then go somewhere else!" He turned to two of his foremen. "Yuri, Petr, grab the barrels."

The man grabbed Stefan's shoulder and tried to force him around.

Stefan was terrified and busy. He was having flashbacks from the fights en route here, and he had never been comfortable with being manhandled. Stefan was a big man who had worked in a blacksmith shop from the time he was a boy. He always hated being handled, but put up with it most of his life. He risked his life and, more importantly, his family's lives to ensure that he wouldn't have to put up with it any more. He didn't move with the first jerk and the man jerked him again.

That was it. Stefan turned and with all the strength of rage combined with the muscles of a wielder of heavy hammers, he punched the man in the chest, right over his heart. The man flew back and hit the wall of one of the warehouses, and then sank down to the earth. He seemed to be unconscious.

Stefan didn't have time for him. Not for regret or help or curses or anything. He turned away from the man. "Move those barrels!"

They moved the barrels, and Stefan gave other orders. Those too were obeyed without hesitation.

Colonel Leontii Shuvalov stayed on his horse with difficulty. He stayed up with the lead element of the army during the hellride of the last three days. So had three of his four aides. The khan was back with the main army, but with luck they would have taken Ufa and Czar Alexis before Salqam-Jangir Khan caught up with him. It would be best if Czar Mikhail were to die in the fighting.

Togym, the khan's cousin, waved a sword and a signal flag flew. The army pulled up and launched a flight of arrows at the small group of people who were trying to fortify a section of street between a couple of warehouses. It was stupid. The smart thing to do would be to bypass them, perhaps leaving a small force to pin them here and head for the kremlin. Either that, or just ride over them.

Leontii muttered a curse under his breath and rode to Togym. "You're wasting time. Ride them down. We need to get to the kremlin."

"They are armed."

"They're peasants."

"You're a fool!" Togym turned away and waved his sword again.

Another flight of arrows came in and people were hit, but a bunch of warehouse workers joined in. Grain sacks were added to the barrels blocking the street. It wasn't a great wall. It was about four feet tall with gaps where the fat part of the barrels kept the skinny parts apart, or just where the barrels had been placed sloppily. It was topped in places with sacks of grain. In spite of its flimsiness, a man behind it was safer from the flights of arrows than he would be standing in the open.

Stefan started sorting his people into a line behind the barrels. And a third flight of arrows came in. One of them scored Stefan's tunic and left a red line across his chest till it stuck in his bandolier. He looked back and forth. Mostly people were in line behind the barrels and it looked like the whoever-they-were were getting ready to charge. "Load your guns, boys!"

Stefan was almost sure that there was some official way you were supposed to say that, but he didn't know what it was—or at least couldn't think of it right now. It didn't seem to matter though. The guys from the factory were sticking clips of chambers in their AK4.7s. Not everyone in town was equipped with the AK4.7s. Quite a few had AK4.5s, AK4.2s, or even the many variations of the AK3s.

"Is everyone loaded?" Stefan looked back and forth again and everyone seemed to be ready. "Then shoot those fuckers!"

They shot, most of them. But at least two of his guys actually managed to hit the warehouses they were between, and one shot came uncomfortably close to Stefan. "Ivan, if you point that rifle at me again, I'm gonna shove it up your ass and pull the trigger."

Every one of Stefan's factory workers equipped with the AK4.7s were firing as fast as they could. *Clickity bang, clickity bang.* The rest were taking longer, but in seconds they were firing into a dense cloud of gray-white smoke. That's what happens when two hundred men shoot black powder rifles and fifty or more of them fire at a high rate.

That's *part* of what happens. The other part of what happens is that in the space of less than a minute close to a thousand rounds go down range. A thousand rounds against massed cavalry is murderous fire.

The firing slowed as the slide-action AK4.7s finished their clips and had to be reloaded. But by then Stefan couldn't see a thing beyond the smoke. "Stop shooting! Reload!"

Everyone got reloaded and Stefan waited while the smoke cleared. Then he looked out at the Mongols. They weren't just sitting out there shooting arrows anymore. The letup in fire seemed to have let them get organized. Even as Stefan watched they started a charge.

The thing Stefan wanted to do more than anything was run away. But he couldn't. Vera was back there in the kremlin. He looked around in desperation and saw Petr Yurievich starting to edge back from the barrels. "Get back in line, Petr!" he roared. "Now! And this time, aim, damn it! Everyone aim at one of those suckers!"

Stefan looked back out at the charging Mongols and they were getting way too damn close. It looked like they would be riding his people down in another couple of seconds. "Fire!"

They fired. And even if their aim wasn't great, this was the next best thing to point blank range, and most of his people were pointing their guns at the larger targets, the horses. A dozen horses along a fifty-foot front went down, and the horses behind them got tangled up and went down. The ones that managed to jump the tangle landed right at the barricade and didn't have room to jump it. They knocked quite a few of the barrels over, but in the process they made the tangle worse.

The Mongols were stopped and though they were out of sword range, they weren't out of rifle range. Not even the range of poorly aimed rifles fired by terrified factory workers who would have already run away except for the ogre standing with them. The ogre who had killed a man with his bare hands and was standing there with an arrow sticking out of his chest, screaming at them to shoot. Then shoot again. And again.

Shoot they did. The AK4.7s had a rate of fire that

was frankly miraculous, even to the men using them. Even the AK3s had rates of fire that the invaders found hard to credit.

It was hardly what even the worst professional soldier would consider a well-planned defense. And for organization, it lacked even more ... from a purely military point of view. But there was a mass of dead and wounded horses and Kazakh warriors crushed under those horses, or dead from gunshot wounds that could testify to the effectiveness of that defense.

Even so, it wouldn't have held for long. But the initial rush was blunted and the Kazakh warriors pulled back. They would circle around, but other defenders were taking up positions between the buildings of expanded Ufa.

Togym saw the collapse of the charge. More importantly, he heard the shooting. There was no way anyone should be able to shoot that quickly. Once someone with a muzzle-loading matchlock fired, they were done for half a minute. These people were firing constantly, a continuous crackle of fire that increased or faded like waves on the ocean, but never ceased. He looked for gaps, for ways around, and what he saw were more barricades.

No, this was not the time to waste men in a mad rush. When the rest of the army got here, there would be time to plan and time to organize.

Colonel Shuvalov wasn't pleased by the decision, but he couldn't do anything about it.

General Izmailov climbed to the kremlin watchtower in time to see the charge bog down and was amazed at how lucky they had been to hold. It made a sort of sense intellectually, but it went against all his experience of warfare. No... that wasn't entirely true. It fit all together too well with what he had seen and done at Rzhev, both what had happened to his cavalry when they attacked massed infantry, and what had happened to the enemy infantry when they had faced modern guns.

But still, it felt wrong. Those men at the barrels should have broken and run. Even *Streltzi* should have broken under that attack, much less peasants. He looked out over the mishmash of buildings that was Ufa and knew they couldn't hold that much territory. They would have to pull back. They would have to build lines closer in, nearer the kremlin.

General Izmailov started giving orders. He didn't have any authority to give orders, not here. But looks were exchanged. First Bernie Zeppi, then Vladimir Gorchakov, and finally Czar Mikhail nodded, and General Izmailov was in command of the defense of Ufa.

CHAPTER 25

General Izmailov, for the Defense

Ufa
April 1, 1637

In a room in the Ufa kremlin, there was a sand table map of Ufa. It had been used by Bernie and the Dacha city planners to plan the sewers and streets. They had even managed, mostly, to get people to build their buildings where they were told. That placement had had a lot to do with efficiency of trade and manufacturing, and not much at all to do with defensive works. Even when they had looked at defense, they had focused on attacks from the west, not the southeast.

Now Artemi Vasilievich Izmailov used that sand table to plan the emergency fortification of Ufa. That they would lose half the city was a given. At least as far as Izmailov was concerned. The people who owned those buildings weren't so easily convinced. On the other hand, the army that was building up just east of the city was a convincing argument.

Stefan picked up a ceramic pot full of iron that must have weighed a hundred pounds and set it on the wagon. His chamber factory was in a building that they couldn't hold, but everything that they could move to a protected location would be something they didn't lose and something that the Kazakh wouldn't have to use. Stefan's factory had a steam engine, an alternator, and induction furnaces. The knowledge, and more than a few of the tools that had been developed in the Dacha and Murom over the last few years, had found their way to Ufa. Now much of it was being stacked up against the wooden kremlin wall in the hopes that it might be used again in the days that followed.

The same process was going on all over Ufa as people pulled back and jerry-rigged defensive works.

General Izmailov had made Stefan a captain. Once he got the stuff from the factory into storage, he would be in charge of a hundred-yard section of wall.

"Wall" was actually much too grand a word for what they had, but they were well armed. Not everyone in Ufa had an AK. Not even AK3s. But a lot of them did. And they had plenty of chambers for all the AKs. They were short on cannon, but they had a decent supply of rockets. Stefan loaded a barrel of iron ore onto the wagon, and he and his men went around front to grab the wagon tongue and pull. They had wagons, but not enough horses.

New Ruzuka

The villagers heard the fighting at Ufa. It was only ten miles away and there were a lot of guns shooting. They sent a runner and the runner saw the army outside Ufa.

"Is there any way of sneaking into Ufa?" asked Dominika.

The scout, one of the young men who had joined the village at Ufa, shook his head. "A few might. But with children and old folks, not a chance we would get there without being caught by the Tatars."

They had spent the winter building buildings, and New Ruzuka was full of peasants who had every reason to fortify their position against raids by bandits. The issue was that they didn't have thousands of people. They had about eight hundred, only two hundred fifty of whom were young men. They had eight-foot palisades with firing steps around the village, but they didn't have enough men to fully man the palisades.

Father Yulian took command. They would stand watches and have weapons ready, and everyone would know what to do if the enemy attacked. Then they would pray that the Tatars didn't notice them. That wasn't unreasonable. While the fields had been denuded of trees, they were not so much as plowed yet. There were no crops to steal.

Ufa
April 2, 1637

"The convention will come to order," Alexander called. He pounded on the table with the gavel. "Sit down, everyone. The defense of Ufa is being arranged and we can't go anywhere, anyway. So we might as well get some work done. The committee, the *Rukovoditel Prikaz* committee, has a report to make."

A direct translation of *Rukovoditel Prikaz* would

be something like "head orderer," but it could also be translated as "head minister." Closer to the real meaning would be "chief executive" or "head of government." It was a part of the constitution that defined the executive branch of government and also would convert the bureaucracy of the United States of Russia into a single cohesive system...or at least something that resembled one a bit more than the mishmash of bureaus that had grown up since the time of Ivan the Terrible.

It took some more banging, but eventually Alexander got the delegates to come to something vaguely resembling order. And the committee on *Rukovoditel Prikaz* made its report. There would, in the nature of things, be more members in the house of commons than in the house of lords. If both houses voted on the head minister, then the lower house would consistently elect one of its own. The head minister would usually be a commoner, and the lords would not consent to being put under the command of a commoner. Not a majority of the time, not even occasionally. *Mestnichestvo*, the Russian system of social ranks, still held sway.

The committee had two proposals. One that the *Rukovoditel Prikaz*, head minister, would be elected by the house of commons, and the second that he must be a member of the house of lords. Yermak Fedov was on the side of the nobles in this one. Even though his Cossacks were strongly anti-slavery, they had their own form of nobility and Yermak was a member of it.

The convention had more commoners than nobles. It passed the first and voted down the second. At that point it was a good thing that the town was surrounded, else a bunch of the nobles would have walked out. In fact, several of the nobility did leave the chamber, and not without justification. The *Rukovoditel Prikaz* had proposed the two rules as a compromise, and when the nobles had voted for the first one it was in the expectation that the commoners would vote for the second one. The nobles felt like they had been cheated.

General Izmailov walked along the lines talking to people, trying to get a feel for this place and the people who occupied it. Partly, that was because he had command of the city's forces under the authority of Czar Mikhail. It wasn't like he could surrender, but as long as he limited himself to military matters, he mostly had a free hand. He stopped at the section of the wall where Stefan Andreevich was in command and found Vera Sergeevna talking with him. He learned that Vera, the delegate from the village of New Ruzuka and representative of the manufacturers of Ufa, was also Stefan's wife. They talked politics for a few minutes and defensive works for a few more. General Izmailov left, wondering how long an independent Siberian state would survive if it had this on its southern border.

General Shein was considering joining the United Russian States, but he was also considering declining to join. And if Ufa was any example, that last might be a very bad idea.

Salqam-Jangir Khan wasn't happy with Togym, but wasn't going to admit that in front of Colonel Shuvalov. This might have been over if Togym had just had the guts to carry through. Now that Ufa had had time to fortify, taking it was going to be a lot more costly. But he needed those guns Shuvalov promised. The reports for the first day's battle had made that plain. Salqam-Jangir hated the guns, and the effect he could see them having on war and warriors. But hate them or love them, they were here. If a bunch of peasants could hold off warriors with the rifles, what was to become of the warrior's training and creed? What mattered the strength and valor of a man of war if any beggar off the street who had a gun could bring him low?

"We will have to make a coordinated attack," he said. "Togym, you will take a third of the army and..."

Czar Mikhail looked out at the crowd. He didn't have time for this. There were Kazakh khanate soldiers investing his city at this very moment. Ivan Alexandrovich Choglokov was there, with his cousin's wife. And this trial was to determine if her dead husband, Ivan Petrovich Choglokov, had been murdered. It was clear that she had been crying, but she wasn't any more. Her eyes were too full of hate directed at the well-dressed former serf, Stefan Andreevich of New Ruzuka, the accused murderer. Mikhail looked over at Timofei Fedorovich Buturlin and said, "Let's get started."

Buturlin called up the first witness and questioned him. It was one of the men who had been at the improvised barricade.

"I don't know how it got started," the man said. "I saw a bunch of people with guns heading up Irina Way. And they said that the Mongols were attacking. I wasn't going to let my shop get burned, so I grabbed my gun and joined them." The story went on from there till he got to the argument about where to set up the barricade. "Well, we were starting to move barrels and stuff to keep the Mongols out of Irina Way, and this guy says we're in the wrong place. He grabs the captain by the arm."

"One moment," Buturlin said. "You said he grabbed the captain. What captain?"

The man pointed at Stefan Andreevich. "Him."

"What made you think he was the captain?"

"Well, look at him. Besides, a bunch of the men were asking him stuff as we were going along the road and he's the one who started people making the barricade. And I sure wasn't going to argue with him."

Mikhail looked over at Stefan Andreevich. The man stood over six feet tall and probably weighed two hundred fifty pounds, all of it muscle. He didn't look all that much like a captain to Mikhail, but he didn't look like a serf either. Mikhail could understand why the man didn't want to argue with someone that size.

Buturlin looked at the big man and nodded. "Go on."

"The captain tells him to go somewhere else if he don't like it here and turns back to giving orders. Then the guy grabs him again and the captain, he turns like a cat and punches the guy. The guy goes flying back and bounces off a wall. The punch must have been hard enough to stop his heart. But the captain had gone back to giving orders. We hopped to it too, I'll tell you."

There was more testimony. Mostly repeating the story the first man had told. None of the witnesses had paid much attention to the man who died. They had been in the middle of a battle.

There was also discussion of how long it had taken for them to get the barricade set up and how quickly the Kazakh warriors attacked after the barricade was finished.

Buturlin asked the room in general, "Does anyone know where Ivan Petrovich Choglokov wanted them to move?"

There were a lot of head shakes. Someone offered, "I think his leather works was a couple of blocks north."

"Which way was he pointing?"

"North, I think."

"It doesn't matter," said General Izmailov. "The issue was time, not location. If they had moved anywhere, it would have delayed the construction of the barricade and the Kazakh warriors would have overrun them before the barricade was ready." Then General Izmailov looked at Czar Mikhail. "Your Majesty, the decision of whether to move or stay where they were isn't the issue. The question is who had the authority to make it. An army needs discipline above all else."

Mikhail knew what he was talking about. The first attack on Rzhev had been a cavalry charge led by an idiot of high social rank, who had gotten his command slaughtered. He'd been able to do it by using his status to co-opt military command of part of the army. Later, an aide of Izmailov, also with high social rank, had usurped command authority, and in doing so saved the battle. For political reasons, the second incident had been kept quiet. And that aide was now General Boris Timofeyevich Lebedev, commander of the defense of Kazan.

But that wasn't what Izmailov was talking about. Even if Stefan was perfectly right in what he did, there was still the question of whether he had the right to do it. The issue was command authority within the army versus social status. If social status controlled, Stefan should have obeyed the commands of the higher-ranked Ivan Petrovich Choglokov. If it was military rank that had precedence, then it got a lot murkier.

"I understand, General. However, in this case, neither man was in legal authority over the other."

Buturlin was looking back and forth between them, not knowing what they were talking about. Well, there were only a few people who did know what had happened at Rzhev. Most people thought Boris Timofeyevich had been acting under General Izmailov's orders when he moved the guns.

Izmailov shrugged. "I'm among the last to support the notion that social rank should trump military rank and discipline, Your Majesty. But there was no military rank involved here."

"I disagree, General," Buturlin said.

"Oh?"

"The core of the defenders of Irina Way were workers in Stefan Andreevich's factory. That gave him de facto command of the largest contingent of the defenders. While Ivan Petrovich Choglokov clearly had the higher social rank, it seems to me that Stefan Andreevich had the military rank. None of Ivan Petrovich Choglokov's workers were there."

Sofia Choglokov broke then. "I don't care about your battle. My husband is dead and that serf killed him!" She pointed at Stefan Andreevich.

Back in Novgorod, that was all that would have mattered. Here and now, what mattered was that Stefan's actions had held that street and stopped the attack.

Ivan Alexandrovich Choglokov turned to her. "Sofie,

there are Kazakh warriors surrounding the city. They will have no respect at all for your rank or little Petr Ivanovich's. This man didn't try to kill Cousin Ivan. He was just trying to protect the city."

Czar Mikhail reentered the hall, waved, and a gun butt crashed against the floor.

The crowd quieted and Mikhail stepped up to the throne and took his seat. "We are here gathered to judge not one man, but the laws under which he would be judged. We are in a time of flux, when the laws of Russia are being reformed, and the first act of that change was the emancipation proclamation I issued when I was freed from my own captivity. It was under that promise that Stefan and his family—his whole village—came east to the frontier, risking life and limb. And it is that promise to him that must govern his *mestnichestvo*.

"But *mestnichestvo* is not all that is involved. In fact, Stefan Andreevich was in military command of the scratch force that assembled around him to guard the entrance to Irina Way. And, as must always be the case in the heat of battle, that rank—not social rank—must control. The confusion was the fault of the circumstances, not Stefan Andreevich or Ivan Petrovich Choglokov. The death was not murder, but an accident of war.

"In order to prevent future accidents, I make Stefan Andreevich now a captain in the Ufa militia, and a *dvoriane* with the family name of Ruzukov. But be aware, Stefan Andreevich Ruzukov, of all that this means. You are now under the orders of your lawful superiors in the defense of Ufa, and failure to obey those orders quickly and to the last, will be met with harsh punishment."

CHAPTER 26

Word of Ufa

April 3, 1637

In Kazan, the report of the attack on Ufa came as a shock, but there was very little they could do about it. Ivan and Tim talked about this a lot, both before and after Czar Mikhail had escaped from captivity. The question was: how did the new guns change warfare? The answer was complicated by the fact that there was no direct corollary to the weapons mix they had now in that other history. By the time the other history had anything close to the AKs—even the AK3s much less the AK4.7s—they had machine guns.

Well, present day Russia had a sort of machine gun, but it wasn't even up to the standards of the American Civil War Gatling gun. At the same time, if not quite up to the 1903 Springfield, the AK4.7 was close in terms of combat effectiveness. As long as you had preloaded chambers, it probably had a better rate of fire than the Springfield. At any rate, that's what Tim assumed was the case. He had never seen a 1903 Springfield, not even one of the down-time made knockoffs. But he had experience with the AK4.7, and he knew what he could to with his. So far as accuracy and rate of fire, his AK4.7 was at least comparable to what the Springfields were purported to do.

But personal weapons were less than half the equation. There were also artillery and crew weapons that turned WWI into the monstrous killing ground that it was. What had yet to be tested on any significant scale was what happened when you had two forces, both of which had personal weapons with good range and rate of fire, but didn't have that much artillery or machine guns. Tim and Ivan and the war games they played and tests they did, even the battle of Rzhev, all suggested to Tim that tactically the defense was much stronger. But defense didn't win wars.

Meanwhile, the ice on the Volga was still there. But it was thin enough so that attacking across it would be suicidal. Kazan was safe, but still surrounded by Birkin's army. That meant that he couldn't possibly go to the aid of Ufa. He could defend Kazan now with half the troops he had in the city or less. He just couldn't get the rest past Birkin's forces.

Tim looked out at the Volga and muttered, "Melt, damn it, melt."

Moscow
April 3, 1637

News of the attack on Ufa by Kazakh warriors was met with public lamentation and private glee in the Moscow Kremlin. Director-General Sheremetev was still maintaining that Czar Mikhail was at best misguided, but more likely enspelled by up-timer magic. He publicly treated the attack as unfortunate, but probably God's mighty hand at work.

Then he sent orders—very private orders—to General Birkin to send a force to relieve Ufa, but to make sure that Mikhail didn't survive the attack of the Kazakh.

Boris Petrov took the message from Yuri and read it carefully. By this time the radio men were pretty circumspect about spreading the news, but also by now Boris had at least one radio man on every shift in his pay. So he was still getting the news, whether Sheremetev wanted him to or not. There weren't a lot of details. It was known that the attackers were the Kazakh Khanate, but nothing much about numbers or armaments on either side.

The next day, one of Boris' sources in Sheremetev's household reported that he had heard someone say something about Shuvalov when the radio message came in. It wasn't much and the man, a kitchen slave, was in no position to ask for clarification.

Goritsky Monastery
April 3, 1637

Only a week earlier, the sisters at the monastery had learned of the sack of Archangelsk.

Sheremetev's northern army had not besieged Archangelsk. It had destroyed the place. Most of the city had been burned to the ground. Half the population was dead or fled, and just about all the wealth in the warehouses that hadn't been burned was on its way back to Moscow to fill Sheremetev's coffers.

The sack had filled the radio stations, only displaced four days ago by the news that the constitutional convention had started in Ufa. The two pieces of news had made a very clear counterpoint to each other, Sheremetev's iron fist versus Mikhail's negotiations.

Now this. Ufa was under attack by Kazakh warriors. Most people assumed that Sheremetev was at least involved, but there was no proof. A lot of the upper-level players saw it as a clever move, indicating Mikhail's weakness and Sheremetev's effectiveness.

"I don't like him, either," said Elena Cherakasky, "but he's no fool. He managed to get the Kazakhs to attack Mikhail all the way out in Ufa. I don't see how Mikhail can survive against such a man."

Sofia felt herself going white. She didn't see how Czar Mikhail could survive, either. And Natasha was in Ufa. So was Vladimir now. And Vladimir's child, the baby Sofia might never see. She was very much afraid that she was going to lose the last of her remaining family and her czar, all at the same time.

"Yet," Tatyana said, "we got the news of the attack from Ufa itself. Their radio is still up and they fought off the initial attack." Suddenly, Tatyana laughed. "Never underestimate a peasant. They are a lot better at a lot of things than you would think." Tatyana made no bones about her past and, nun or not, she kept a lover in the town. "Ufa is still there, and so is Kazan. I wouldn't count them out yet."

Sofia felt the blood seeping back into her face at Tatyana's words. And even more, as Tatyana reached out and grasped her hand.

"The question we need to be asking is, what are the consequences?" Sofia said.

"The consequences of what? The successful attack or the failed attack?" Elena asked.

"Either," Tatyana said. "But let's start with what it means if the Kazakh are fought off."

"If they are fought off, Sheremetev is a dead man," Elena said with a fair bit of malice and satisfaction.

But Sofia wasn't so sure. "What if it turns into a siege of Ufa?"

"That's harder to say," Elena said. "The longer the siege, the more powerful Sheremetev will become. Mikhail will be seen as treed. At the same time, the sack of Archangelsk is sitting there as proof of Sheremetev's effectiveness. I don't like it, but if the siege lasts long enough, it might not matter if they actually take Ufa or not. Just the siege could let Sheremetev win."

Tobolsk, Siberia

General Shein again decided to stand pat. He had always been better on the defense than the attack, and the new weapons mix just reinforced that tendency.

However, that hesitation to take action had crossed from the tactical to the strategic . . . where it was a fairly severe error.

Ufa

General Izmailov looked out at the bow-armed Kazakh warriors with their iron breastplates and conical helmets. They were good cavalry troops—or they had been. But they had just suffered a severe shock to their morale, and they had to still be reeling. They had taken that shock in their precipitous charge of the first day and it had been reinforced in the following two days. It took him a couple of days to look over the situation and be sure. In the course of those two days, there had been four more attacks, all of them fought off with much slaughter among the attackers and surprisingly few casualties among the defenders. Though, from what he was hearing, over a million rubles worth of damages to factories on the outskirts of Ufa was done.

"We must attack, Your Majesty!" Izmailov said, turning back to Czar Mikhail. "We dare not give them time to recover from the damage your people have done them. With the AK4.7s prepared and plenty of chambers readied, we can sweep them from the field. I saw it at Rzhev when our own cavalry was decimated by the mercenaries hired by the Poles. Cavalry has no chance against massed pikes supported by rifle fire. And your people here were solid under factory workers. Under proper officers, they'll be like iron."

Czar Mikhail looked at the man. This was the general who had stopped the Poles at Rzhev. If any general in Russia understood war in this new time, it was Izmailov.

Stefan woke swinging. Luckily, all he hit was the wall. It bruised, but didn't break his hand and he sucked on his knuckles as he came back from the dream. He had been having a nightmare. A flashback. He was back at the warehouses, grabbed by—what

was his name—Ivan Petrovich Choglokov, a member
of the service nobility from Novgorod who had moved
out here to set up a leather works. From what he had
heard since, Choglokov hadn't been a bad man, aside
from being arrogant.

Stefan suspected that if the Kazakh army hadn't
been waiting just outside the hastily hacked together
fortifications, the trial might have gone differently.
And he was pretty sure that Sofia Choglokov wouldn't
be forgiving him any time soon. Well, he wouldn't be
forgiving himself any time soon either.

Stefan wiped the cold sweat from his forehead and
tried to get back to sleep. He'd been made a captain
of militia, a member of the service nobility. So that
there would be no future question of rank, he had also
gotten a talking to from Czar Mikhail, who pointed
out that if he disobeyed a lawful order given by a
superior officer, there would be severe punishment.

Stefan didn't want to be a militia captain. He
didn't want to be a member of the service nobility.
He just wanted to be left alone to do his work. But
that wasn't an option, not any more.

He wasn't getting back to sleep and, considering
the dream, he was just as glad of that. He got up
and started to get dressed.

"It's not dawn yet," Vera said drowsily. "Come back
to bed."

"I have to get ready." He pulled on his tunic and
felt the silver railroad tracks that he had been given
by Colonel Buturlin after the trial yesterday. His
company was to be part of the colonel's regiment.

April 4, 1637

Stefan and his company finished their time on the
improvised walls, then spent two hours at drill. Then
they went back to the new factory and made bayonets.
General Izmailov wanted bayonets for every AK in
Ufa, and long ones at that. The bayonet blades were
fourteen inches long, based on something called a spike
bayonet. No good for cutting, they were for poking.
Added to the length of the AKs, they made a long
weapon. Not as long as a pike, but moving in that
direction. And that was what they practiced, marching like pike companies and forming lines. Having
the first rank kneel and ground their rifles so that
there was a line of points. It looked impressive. Stefan
had to admit that because he had spent those drills
inspecting the lines, not standing in them. Then, back
to another stint at the barricades.

April fourth was a very long day for everyone in Ufa.

Stefan had more nightmares that night, with Ivan
Petrovich Choglokov ordering him to right face and
march into an oncoming army of Kazakhs, and Stefan
doing it. Then he would be ordered to left face and
his bayonet would plunge into Choglokov's belly.

Outside Kazan

General Birkin looked at his maps. They were good
maps, much better than anything he had before the
Ring of Fire. There had been plenty of time to plant
a forest of measuring stakes around Kazan, and with

the equipment and knowledge of the up-timers, he had mapped the area to a faretheewell. Why not? It wasn't like he had anything else to do but try to sneak a few troops away from Kruglaya Mountain.

Ivan Vasilevich Birkin realized that defense had gotten stronger, but he had no yardstick for how *much* stronger. Especially, he had no way of knowing how strong even improvised field defenses can make a position. He had field works in place around Kruglaya Mountain. Before the advent of the AKs, his works would have required the whole of his army and preferably another twenty thousand men to man them lest General Boris Timofeyevich Lebedev sally forth, break through his works at a weak point and roll up his entire force from the flanks. Now he felt fairly confident that the men manning his works were more than were needed. But he had no idea how much more.

Birkin looked at the counters on his maps again. He had, almost from the beginning, been sneaking troops out of the siege of Kruglaya Mountain. But he couldn't sneak many, because every time he pulled a company out, those damn Maslov rockets came falling out of the sky, reminding him that the baker's boy could see every move he made and warning him that if he moved too many, Colonel Ivan Maslov would follow the next rocket barrage with a massed assault and sweep his besiegers away. Then he would proceed to bugger his army while it was facing General Tim, who Birkin was beginning to think might be the second coming of Alexander the Great after all. How else could a nineteen-year-old—well, twenty now—general hold off the armies of Russia with a scratch force?

That last bought a grimace to the general's face, though there was no one there to see it. Little Timmy's twentieth birthday had been after Kazan was besieged and the whole city had made a celebration of it. That had been, as much as anything, to rub the noses of the whole besieging army in the youth of their general. They might not be fully convinced of the good will of Czar Mikhail, but the potentates of Kazan, Muslim and Christian alike, were in real danger of idolatry where General Tim was concerned.

Birkin's eyes fell on the radio message. It had been decoded. By now both sides knew to encode their radio traffic. That at least kept the radio operators from gossiping about the orders to the army. The message was an order from Director-General Sheremetev and the boyar duma to take—not send, take—a force to relieve Ufa, and an even more secret order to make sure that Mikhail died in the fighting. Birkin didn't like those orders, but he had a company of the duma's hounds in his army in case he should consider ignoring them. So the only real issue was how large a force he could detach. Word was that the Kazakh army numbered something like thirty thousand. In theory, Birkin's army was fifty thousand, but he still had seven thousand around Kruglaya Mountain. He'd lost over three thousand in assaults against Kazan, one on little Timmy's birthday. Most of the casualties were wounded, not dead—although many of them would eventually die of their injuries. But, if anything, a badly wounded man who needed care and attention was more of a drain on his forces than one who'd been struck dead.

That left less than forty thousand and he would

have to leave at least fifteen thousand here. So he was supposed to relieve Ufa against thirty thousand Kazakh warriors with less than twenty-five thousand troops, who would be marching through the spring mud to get there.

The good news was that the Kazakhs had gotten bloodied but good. And Izmailov was in command over there, so they were probably going to get bloodied some more.

Ufa
April 5, 1637

March. Work. March.

Stefan forced the food down at lunch and the orders came to form up again. Stefan had a hundred men under his command, in four groups of twenty-four each, with a *Streltzi* sergeant for each group. He hadn't met any of the sergeants before yesterday, and none of them seemed impressed by him. At least not as a military commander. Not that any of them were going to fight him. Word of the "one blow murder" had circulated widely in Ufa.

Stefan stood at the front of his company and called, "Company, right face. Forward, march." Then they walked down Zeppi Lane, and at Irina Way the barricades were moved aside and they marched out, Company B of the Second Regiment, to face the Kazakh in the open field.

Which, to Stefan, seemed a very bad idea. But he had had the chain of command made very clear, and he had already been on trial for his life once this week.

CHAPTER 27

Battles

New Ruzuka

Father Yulian looked out at the advancing patrol. He had never seen one, but from his reading these were from one of the successor states of the Golden Horde. There were several, the Zunghar Khanate, Kazakh Khanate, Bukhara Khanate, and more. He turned to the young man who had reported the attack on Ufa. "Are these the same people?"

"I think so. They're dressed the same."

There were perhaps a hundred of them. A patrol, not an army, but the army was close enough, should it be needed. Back in old Ruzuka, Father Yulian would have given them whatever they wanted and the villagers would have done the same to a man. New Ruzuka wasn't like that. New Ruzuka was their land. Owned by the New Ruzuka Company, with each of them holding shares. Nor were they the beaten down serfs of old Ruzuka. They were free people, protecting their homes.

The smart play was still to let the patrol have what

they wanted, but he wasn't at all sure that he could convince the citizens of New Ruzuka to see that. He wasn't even totally sure that he could convince *himself* to see that. Still, best to see what they wanted and maybe it wouldn't be too bad. "Get me a flag of truce. I'm going out to see what they want."

It didn't take long, and Father Yulian went out the gate carrying his flag of truce.

Abul-Fath noticed the flag, but also the black robes of a Christian priest. He might have respected the flag, but he despised the robe. As well, he was a captain of warriors and had no respect at all for peasants, and this seemed a peasant village, if a large one. He was offended by their wall, as though a stack of logs was going to keep his men out. And he hadn't been involved in the fighting. He was disgusted that the Kazakh army had been thrown back and wanted to prove it was a fluke. So he wasn't in a good mood to start with, and the guns that were sticking out of cracks between the logs seemed more an offense than a threat at a hundred yards.

Abul-Fath wasn't unfamiliar with rifles. He had two of them that he sometimes used for hunting. But his familiarity told him that rifles were a hunting weapon, not a military weapon. So he knew that the guns sticking out from between the cracks were smoothbore muzzle loaders. Knew it with the same certainty that he knew a man couldn't fly.

The priest reached them and held up his hand. Using two fingers, he made occult symbols toward Abul-Fath and his troops. Abul-Fath heard the Russian words, but didn't understand them.

Nor did he care. He drew his sword and cut down the offense to Allah.

On the wall, Makar watched. He wasn't the greatest fan of Father Yulian, but the man was a good priest—allowing for his peculiarities—and was as responsible as anyone for getting them here and keeping them together. So he watched with his AK4.7 long rifle braced on the wall. Everyone was nervous as Father Yulian reached out and blessed the Tatar. Then the Tatar, without even a by your leave, pulled his sword and cut Father Yulian down.

Nothing happened for a second, maybe two. Then, suddenly, any resentment that Makar had ever had toward Father Yulian was gone. Those bastards out there had murdered a priest! New Ruzuka's priest. Makar aimed his rifle and fired. So did at least half the men on the wall. Most of them aiming at the same man. There was no telling which of the hundred or so shots hit the Tatar captain, but they later got a count. Fifteen holes, most of them through and through.

The shots that followed almost immediately were more widely dispersed. But there were almost as many men on the walls as there were soldiers in the patrol. And the men on the walls were firing from cover, with perhaps eight square inches showing per man. Between men and horses, the patrol had almost as many feet showing. And the AK4.7 rifles laid down a devastating fire.

It was all over very quickly. The Tatars were dead or fled and, aside from Father Yulian, only four arrow wounds in Ruzuka, only one fatal. Three of the four wounds weren't even to the men on the walls. Liliya was one of the women loading chambers behind the wall, and was hit in the left leg by a blind shot. It wasn't serious, but the Tatars had fired several flights of arrows before they broke. More than they should have, but it had taken them too long to realize just how one-sided the fight was. There were two more flesh wounds from arrows falling inside the walls, and one poor fellow who had raised up for a better shot and caught an arrow across the side of his neck. It cut his carotid artery and he bled to death before anyone could get to him.

Proving once again that even very good cover is no guarantee of safety in a war zone.

New Ruzuka wasn't the only one of the villages surrounding Ufa that was attacked. Two were caught unaware, with no wall or defenses to speak of, and burned to the ground. Of the other five, most fought off attacks by small patrols, with some loss of life on both sides. All in all, supply by the raiding of outlying villages wasn't working well for the Kazakh army. This was only partly because of the weapons of the defenders. It was also because the villagers didn't have much in the way of food. No crops had been put in, and last year this had mostly been virgin forest.

Ufa

General Izmailov was confident, but not quite as confident as he would have preferred. His formations were ragged compared with what he had seen from the German mercenaries, but they went where they were pointed and shot what they were told to shoot. He wished he'd had more time to drill them, but the news had come in that the Kazakhs were raiding the countryside. Half the workers in Ufa had family in the outlying villages, and there hadn't been time for them to gather in Ufa. Besides, they would need those peasants to plant the crops once the Kazakhs were sent packing. The factors that decide when to fight aren't all military.

Izmailov had six regiments of three battalions each. That gave him almost fifteen thousand men. Granted, less than a thousand of them had any experience, but they had done incredibly well defending Ufa against twice their number. And by now the Kazakh warriors had learned to fear the AK4.7s that everyone in Ufa seemed to own. Still, he wished he had the *gulyay-gorod*, walking walls, they had at Rzhev. But *gulyay-gorod* took time and lumber to build and no one had thought of them before the Kazakh army had shown up and separated Ufa from the forests surrounding it.

That was another reason they had to take the fight to the Kazakhs. Ufa wasn't prepared for a siege. It was the end of winter and the supplies were at their lowest point of the year. They were short on everything from apples to vodka, and they couldn't use the ice-covered rivers to ship in supplies with the Kazakhs surrounding Ufa.

Izmailov hadn't studied at the war college in Moscow. He had been a general before it was set up. But he had listened to Tim while the lad had been his aide, and he was aware of the truism that generals always fought the last war.

On the other hand, that put him about two wars

ahead of the Kazakhs. Most of their army was still using bows and arrows. He also knew from the western European mercenaries that a pike and gun unit was proof against cavalry. If Tim had been here and told him the problem with his plan...

Artemi Izmailov had a lively respect for Boris Timofeyevich Lebedev. Not enough to make him a nineteen-year-old general, but considerable respect nonetheless. Unfortunately, Tim was in Kazan with his own siege to fight. Besides, they had a general right here in Ufa. A real general, not a kid bumped up before his time. The general in fact that had commanded and won at Rzhev. Arguably Russia's greatest general. Izmailov didn't think he was Russia's greatest general. That was General Shein. But he was a good, solid, workmanlike general who knew his business. He had talked to the commanders and to some of the men. Morale was good.

Besides, being the general who beat off the Kazakh attack would be very helpful in advancing General Shein's position in the congress. There had been plenty of time to think through this as his small army marched...well, walked...out of Ufa into the no man's land between the barricades and the Kazakh army.

It was cold. A little above freezing, but still cold. The ice started to melt in the day, then froze again every night. The no man's land between the barricades and Kazakhs was stomped-on mud that was frozen into place. It still hadn't thawed as they marched out. Stefan looked at his company. They were near the middle of the line and almost as soon as they had gotten out through the barricades, orders shifting them to the left came down. They were one side of an empty square. His boys were cheerful. They had kicked ass every time they were attacked.

Stefan looked out at the Kazakhs and wondered what they were doing. They were sure active, whatever it was.

"We will advance to bow range and shower them with arrows," the khan ordered decisively and Colonel Shuvalov nodded in agreement.

More orders were given and the host was organized. It would be a riding attack. They would fire while in motion, denying the enemy a stationary target. But it took time to organize, almost an hour, by which time the Russians were well out in the open.

"They're coming," someone from Alpha Company shouted—Stefan didn't know who it was. But it was true. Even obvious.

Stefan turned to the *Streltzi* sergeants who commanded his platoons. "Have the front rank kneel and have them load their AKs. But no shooting till they get close." The truth was, most of his men were not great shots. They got a lot more effective once the enemy was near. And Stefan wanted to pound the enemy once that happened. Really pound them. The chamber-clips he had been making had six shots preloaded, and each of his men had three chamber-clips. But he didn't want to be changing chamber-clips when the Kazakhs arrived.

The orders were given and Stefan looked over the lines then back at the Kazakhs. They had taken their time, but they seemed to be ready for the show. *Oh, Lord, there are a lot of them*, he thought.

Then he moved out from between his company and the soon-to-arrive enemy. But they didn't keep coming. They got to about a hundred yards away and turned right. Then they started shooting their bows. Great clouds of arrows flew up, and then a rain of arrows fell on his lines. His line was only four ranks deep and that was a good thing. It meant that a lot of the arrows overshot his lines and landed in the open space behind them. A lot... but not nearly enough. People were being hit, and these were not the hardened troops of the German pike regiments. These were farmers and factory workers. Not cowards, by any means. They had proved that. But not trained to stand in the open and take it.

People were looking to Stefan for orders, but no orders were coming. Colonel Buturlin had been very insistent that everyone needed to fire at once in a massive fusillade. Someone shot in his company and that was followed by a crackle of other shots. His wasn't the only company that was shooting without orders. There was crackling all up and down the line to no visible effect at all. "Hold your damn fire, you idiots!" Stefan shouted, though he wasn't at all convinced that it was the right order to give.

The crackling didn't stop, but it did slow. Stefan didn't see new smoke from any of his troops, but three more of them were sprouting arrows. Then the order came.

"By battalions! Fire on the order."

"Battalion!" "Companies!"

Stefan shouted, "Platoons! Ready! Aim!" He held up his AK like it was a baton, and looked to the battalion command group. When the flag came down, he shouted, "Fire!" and swung his AK down like it was an ax and he was chopping wood.

"Company! Cock! Ready! Aim!"

Stefan couldn't see anything except white smoke between him and the Kazakhs. He looked over at the command group and couldn't see them through the smoke. He waited. The smoke cleared a little, and he looked back at the Kazakhs for a minute and... nothing. Nothing at all. He couldn't see any gap at all in their formation and they were still sending those flights of arrows.

It wasn't true, what Stefan saw. The truth was that the massed fire had taken a toll on the enemy, especially on its horses. But they were the length of a football field from the guns and they were not tightly packed like infantry would be. There were plenty of gaps for bullets to pass through without doing any damage and that is precisely what the overwhelming majority of those bullets did. The Kazakhs took damage, but it wasn't as bad as they were expecting to take, and they were doing a lot more damage to the Russians. Perhaps more important, they could see the damage. When they had attacked the barricades, they hadn't seen the occasional hit they had made.

It didn't matter that what Stefan saw wasn't the truth. What mattered was that it was what the whole Russian army was seeing. They were shooting... and nothing was happening. Meanwhile, they were losing men.

It took General Izmailov a few minutes to realize just how corrosive to good order and discipline that appearance was. He had been so impressed by the way the peasants had held their improvised barricades against the Kazakh warriors, he had come quickly to think of them as seasoned troops. Seasoned troops could have taken this. Would have, and laughed it off, and kept right on pouring fire into the Kazakhs till they broke and ran. But these men didn't understand that appearances on a battlefield could be deceiving. Horribly deceiving. And the deceitful appearances here were telling every craftsman and street sweeper in his army that the battle was lost and that the longer they stayed out here, the more likely they were to die. First one man, then another, then groups, then whole companies, broke and ran. Some carrying their AKs, some in blind panic, throwing their guns on the ground to run faster.

Finally, though, he did see it. General Izmailov was a decisive general, and the truth was that he was quite possibly the fourth- or fifth-best general in Russia. Better, had he known it, than General Shein, if not as good as General Tim or the baker's boy. He realized that he had, in Bernie Zeppi's pithy phrase, "screwed the pooch." And the absolute best he could hope for was a rout that left a mostly intact defending force in Ufa after it was over. He started giving orders to try to produce a semblance of order to the panicked flight that was going to come.

There is a corollary to the axiom "never give an order that won't be obeyed." It's almost never stated, but it goes something like this: "You can exert some control by ordering people to do what they desperately want to do." It's analogous to steering into the skid on an icy road. Sometimes it works. The first regiment was gone. Second seemed to be holding. He sent an order to Buturlin to hold as long as he could, and ordered the rest of his army to fall back to the barricades.

✧   ✧   ✧

Buturlin cursed Izmailov, but gave the orders.

Captain Stefan Andreevich kept his company together by threatening to beat to death the first man who even looked back at the city. Company B held and Company A almost held, as did Company C. There was a clump of the army of Ufa, a clump of about four hundred men, who stood their ground because they were more afraid of their officers than Kazakhs. When the rest of the army started collapsing, the Kazakhs gave up their tactic of standing off and peppering the Russians with arrows. They charged in, lances lowered and flags flying. They charged right into the massed fusillade of the Second.

"By the rank . . . Fire!"

"Second rank . . . Fire!"

"Third rank . . . Fire!"

"Fourth rank . . . Fire!"

"First rank . . . Fire!"

A hundred at a time, with only as much time as it took for Buturlin and Stefan to growl out the orders.

It wasn't enough, not quite. But the defenders of Roark's Drift would have recognized them and called them brothers.

The Kazakhs rode them down.

The last thing Stefan saw was a lance coming at his chest. He swung his AK like he was parrying a sword, but it was too little, too late. He felt the shock and then there was nothing.

It bought time. Vital minutes of separation that let the army of Ufa get back behind the barricades in something almost like order. Close enough so that some of them were in shape to take position on the barricades. When the army marched out, the women

of Ufa manned the barricades. Now they stayed and
their presence stopped a lot of men who would have
kept right on running without them looking on.

It took a few minutes for the Kazakhs to exploit
the sudden victory. By the time they did, there was
enough force armed with AK4.7s to pour fire onto them.

It was a near thing, and it took three more hours,
but by the end of the afternoon, things were back to
what they were before.

Buturlin stood with his men to the last charge and
was wounded, but afterward he made his way back
to the barricades and slipped into the city while the
Kazakhs were attacking another section of the barricades. He almost got shot by the women defending
that section of the wall, but once they were sure he
was Russian, he was rushed to the kremlin where
General Izmailov was commanding the defense of Ufa.

Izmailov turned to him and, clearly looking for
men to man the barricades, asked, "Where is your
regiment?"

"Dead on the field, General! Dead on the field."
Buturlin spat the words. He once had such respect
for General Izmailov. Such certainty that the man
was a great general. And the cowardly son of a bitch
had left him and his people out in the open while
he ran back to the barricades. Hate was too mild a
word. Much too mild for what Colonel Buturlin felt
for General Izmailov now.

But he was a soldier, and loyal to the true czar,
and Czar Mikhail didn't need the sort of incident that
having one of his colonels shove a knife into the gut
of Shein's pet would cause. So he held his temper.

"I'm sorry, Colonel Buturlin. But your regiment was the one that was holding together best, and it was in the best position to keep their attention while the rest of the army retreated. It was my mistake, but the mistake was to take them out from behind the barricades in the first place."

It was just so much meaningless noise. Only a puffed-up peasant, making excuses.

Even Buturlin knew that he was being unfair, but he couldn't not be. Not under these circumstances.

CHAPTER 28

A Change in the Weather

Ufa
April 7, 1637

"That was stupid," Czarina Evdokia said, talking about the fast one that the commoners had tried to pull over the votes on the *Rukovoditel Prikaz* committee's report.

"It was," Anya agreed, "and they know it too, but that's part of the problem. They know it, but they won't admit it because they are convinced that if the nobles had pulled that sort of maneuver, no one would have gotten upset."

"That's ridiculous," Vladimir said.

"I'm not so sure, Vladimir," Patriarch Matthew said, then quickly held up a hand. "I'm not saying that it's unique to the nobility, but people are always more willing to forgive their own minor lapses than their neighbor's. If nobles had pulled such a maneuver it would have been resented, but not as much as when the peasants tried it."

"You may be right, Patriarch," Czarina Evdokia said, "but it doesn't change the fact that the convention could crumble on this issue if it isn't resolved. And the only way I see of resolving it is for the commoners to step back from their position."

"They won't," Anya said. "I agree with you, Czarina," she added quickly. "I'm just telling you how Vera and the others are going to react. Vera especially, after the battle and Stefan being killed on the field while Izmailov retreated. She and a lot of the others are thinking that the high muckety mucks are perfectly happy to leave the peasants out to hang."

"What we need," said Filip Tupikov, "is a new proposal."

"I propose," Czar Mikhail offered sarcastically, "that we select one peasant and one noble, chop them each in half, and sew the two halves together, peasant to noble and noble to peasant."

"Ah, but then we have the issue of which end of each becomes prime minister. Shall it be the peasant's head and the noble's ass, or vice versa?" asked Filip, equally sarcastically.

There followed a short but pungent argument between Vladimir and Anya about whether peasant or noble were more natural asses.

"Actually," said Brandy Bates, looking pensive, "I think Czar Mikhail's notion might be workable if the sharp objects can be removed. Didn't the Romans use a consulship in the republic? I'm almost certain that Ed Piazza mentioned something about that in our discussions."

"Yes. The consuls were elected by the *comitia centuriata* of the republic," Patriarch Matthew said. "But how . . . Oh, of course. One consul, a lord, elected by the house of lords. One a commoner, elected by the house of commons. And as the consuls of the republic, each would have veto power over the actions of the other. So that for the commoner to issue any directive, the noble consul would have to sign off on it. But the commoners would have a say because their consul would have veto power if the noble consul came up with something they didn't like."

"And we would end up with power struggles and everything being vetoed?" Bernie asked. "Sounds like the Republicans and the Democrats back home."

"That's what the czar is for," suggested Vladimir.

"I'm glad to hear it," Czar Mikhail said. "It's nice to think that I might occasionally be of some use."

"You know, this can work," Vladimir said. "The consuls together perform the function of the head of government. Chief of all the bureaus, but their actions even in concert, can be vetoed by the czar if he so chooses. But either consul, along with the czar, can issue a directive over the objections of the other consul, so that one holdout can't bring governance to a halt."

"That still leaves a question to answer," Anya said. "At what rank are you qualified to become the noble consul, and at what rank are you disqualified from being the commoner consul?"

"I would think the same social rank that would allow appointment as *dumnye dvoriane* in the duma," said Czarina Evdokia.

"That would work for the Russians, but what about the Cossacks and the tribes?" Vladimir asked.

"Leave it up to the house of lords or the courts," Anya said.

❖   ❖   ❖

They wrote it up and offered it to the convention the next day, making very sure that it was introduced as a single proposal, not something which could have parts of it voted on separately. It let everyone save face and, after half a day of debate, was passed by a narrow margin.

Kazakh camp, outside Ufa
April 7, 1637

Salqam-Jangir Khan walked through the tents where the wounded were being cared for. He was looking at the broken and mangled bodies of his men and the Russian prisoners who had been brought in because they might bring a ransom or a good price as slaves. He stopped as he saw a veritable giant of a man on a pallet. The man had bandages on his head, his left chest and left arm. "Who is that?"

"I don't know, Great Khan," the doctor said. "But he was a captain, so we assumed he was noble." The man pointed at the silver pin on the man's collar. "I'm told that denotes a commander of a hundred."

Colonel Leontii Shuvalov, who was following along at Salqam-Jangir Khan's heels nodded. "Not exactly, but close enough. It's one of the new rank insignia introduced by the up-timers."

"Is he an up-timer, then?"

"No. There are only a couple of adult up-timer males in Russia, and I have met them both. This will be a *dvoriane* or a *deti boyar* noble, but not high nobility." Then, looking at the long-healed burn scars on the man's arm, Shuvalov reconsidered. The man looked like a blacksmith. He might be *Streltzi*.

Leontii decided not to mention that possibility, as Salqam-Jangir Khan was talking again.

"No matter. If he doesn't have a ransom, he will make a strong slave."

The man stirred and the doctor touched his forehead with the back of his hand.

Kazakh camp, outside Ufa
April 8, 1637

Stefan opened his eyes again, then closed them to slits. "Where am I?"

"In the war camp of the Kazakh army outside of Ufa."

Now he remembered... the horse, the lance... he had thought he was dead for sure. After a minute or so, he got his eyes working and looked at the man who had spoken. He was well dressed in the Kazakh manner, which was similar to the Russian, but with its own flavor. He held a winesack to Stefan's lips but it wasn't wine or beer. There was a bitter taste to it.

Stefan's mind was sort of vague. He hurt, but it was a distant thing and everything seemed a step removed. "Why am I here?"

"You were wounded and captured. Now you must pay a ransom or be enslaved. Can you pay a ransom?"

Still vague, but starting to get worried, Stefan answered, "I don't know. How much ransom?"

"A thousand rubles," the man said judiciously.

"Not a chance," Stefan said.

"Too bad. Well, you'll make a good slave in the mines. Big man like you will bring a good price."

❖   ❖   ❖

The next time Stefan woke, his mind was clearer. He remembered the ransom of a thousand rubles and was terrified. Almost as terrified by the amount of the ransom as by the prospect of slavery.

Stefan understood mechanical things. A drop hammer was a simple and clear thing to him. So was a drill press. Even the induction coils and alternators made a kind of sense to him. Induction heating was, when you got down to it, just friction inside the iron. But Stefan didn't understand money. The rent on a serf's plot in old Ruzuka had been less than fifty rubles a year, and no one ever made the full payment. Fifty rubles would buy a good horse. A thousand rubles would put the whole village of New Ruzuka back into serfdom. At least, it seemed that way to Stefan's still somewhat opium-befuddled mind.

Concepts like economic boom and inflation were so much esoterica to Stefan. Even if they hadn't been, the factory on Alexis Street was gone now—even if they did get most of the equipment back into the city. The fact that the company still owned the land and had a good credit rating with the Czar's Bank never entered into his thinking.

Esim, the well dressed Kazakh, came to see him again and check his bandages. He learned that Esim was a doctor and knew a little—but only a little—of the up-time medicine. Mostly he knew down-time medicine from Arabia and China. He did look forward to meeting the famous up-time physician to the czar's family, Nurse Tami. "In fact, with any luck, I'll be able to buy her after the khan's warriors take Ufa."

He said it quite cheerfully, like he was hoping to be able to afford a prized pig. In a way it was shocking to Stefan, but the most shocking thing about it was its familiarity. It was as though the whole escape and trip to Ufa had never happened. Even more, it was as though the up-timers had never come and he was still pounding out iron nails one hammer blow at a time, and bowing and scraping to Colonel Utkin and that little bastard Nikita. Stefan wanted to feel rage, but as he thought of his wife and children in Ufa, any rage was buried under terror. He tried to think but nothing was clear, and he didn't know what had happened after the battle. Had the Kazakhs marched into Ufa? Stefan's heart was racing and his hands were sweating. And finally it penetrated, the tense of Esim's comment. *He* will *be able to* after *they take Ufa*. So they hadn't yet. And if they hadn't yet, why hadn't they? "How long?"

"How long what?" Esim looked at him for a moment. "Oh, you mean how long since you were taken? The battle was two days ago."

"What happened?"

Esim looked at him, then gave a shrug. "Well... your 'regiment,' is it? Your unit, in any case, held while the rest of the army ran back to the walls. And by the time you were ridden down, much of the army was back in its hole. But don't you worry. We'll dig them out soon enough."

"Not likely." Stefan was thinking now. Not as clearly as he would like, and his habit of reticence seemed to have deserted him just when he most needed it. Stefan still felt woozy, but he realized that if the army was back within the walls... the Kazakhs didn't have cannon. Hell, they didn't even have catapults. With the barricades to fight behind and the gunpowder in the Ufa kremlin, there was no way a cavalry force that size was going to take Ufa.

"You know war then?" Esim asked. "Someone said you were a blacksmith."

"That too. No. That first. War too."

"What?"

"Smithing first. War later. Not that I know much about war. Just what I heard in a few conferences. But General Izmailov doesn't think you can. Then again, Izmailov led us out there, so what does he know? I wish we'd had General Tim here. He wouldn't have screwed up that way. Met him, you know, once on our way through Kazan with young Alexander. Wonder where the boy is now? Oh, yes. He's the president of the convention." Then, with pride, "My Vera, she's a delegate."

"Your Vera?"

"My wife. She's a delegate to the constitutional convention."

"Really? Who is your wife?"

"Vera, I told you. Vera Sergeevna."

Esim nodded then, and went away.

Constitutional Convention, Ufa

"The delegate from the Tangu has the floor," Alexander said, and banged the gavel for emphasis. The delegate from the Tangu was trying to get Tangu declared a state, and get every square inch from Mangazeya to Tobolsk and from Moscow to the Bering Straits included in his tribal territory. He was being shouted down by the other delegates. Two days after the battle on the field, General Izmailov and the whole delegation from South Siberia were much weakened. Up until now, North Siberia had been respectfully yielding to South Siberia on most issues, and so had the tribal delegates from that area. But the coalition was showing cracks.

"These are the traditional lands and come down to us from the great Genghis Khan."

Alexander had to bang his gavel a lot that day, but he wasn't displeased. He wasn't nearly as rabid as, say, Anya or Princess Natasha about the freeing of the serfs. In fact, he could see the point delegates from the north and west made, that without serfs they would be left destitute. His family was likely to find itself in a similar condition if they lost their serfs. Still, the representatives from Siberia and points west had been playing the civilized westerners looking down their noses at the barbarian easterners, and it had gotten old fast.

Alexander was probably the closest in the convention to a moderate. He understood everyone's point of view, and mostly wanted to find a way where everyone could get enough of what they had to have to keep the wheels from coming entirely off. After the delegate from the Tangu finished his speech, Alexander called for a vote and the proposal was resoundingly voted down. The delegate didn't seem very displeased. He had to have known it wasn't going to get adopted, but he had managed to get his starting bargaining position on the record.

The day continued till the bells rang and they called the conference for today. Now the real bargaining would begin.

❖   ❖   ❖

Vera poured wine for Colonel Buturlin and tried not to think about Stefan lying out there in no man's land. This was the hardest thing she had ever done, but she had to keep going for the sake of the children. "Yes, we have the chamber factory sort of up and running. Not at full capacity, and we're stuck in a small building down by the river. But we are turning out chambers." It was important. Despite the soldiers' best efforts, the expensive chambers had a tendency to get dropped and lost in combat. With Stefan dead and so many of the factory men with him, the shortage of chambers was only going to get worse. But she couldn't think about that. She forced her mind back to the political maneuvering. "How do you feel about Natasha's amendment to the..."

Buturlin held up a restraining hand and shook his head. "I know Izmailov is weakened, but the issues that caused the delegates from Chudstok, Cherakaskistok, Novgorodstok, North and South Siberia to walk out have not disappeared. They won't give up their serfs. They can't. To do so would be to face utter and complete ruin.

"I saw Stefan hold his company together to the last, Vera. He was no man's serf. Even more than talking with you and Anya, what I saw Stefan and his workmen do has convinced me that serfdom must end. I have come to realize that serfdom is an evil that deprives us of the abilities of men like your Stefan. It must pass away if we are to ever become the great nation that both you and I wish us to be. But it's going to have to be a gradual thing. To try and—" He stopped and shook his head. "Right or wrong, if they take a constitution that abolishes serfdom back to their principals, it will be rejected."

Vera knew he was right. She knew it clearly in her mind, but she also knew that it was wrong. She turned away, trying to hide her anger and her fear. Fear for her children's future. Anger over the loss of her husband, who Colonel Buturlin had left on the field. The anger wasn't at Colonel Buturlin. The colonel had still been with them when the Kazakhs rode Stefan down. She knew that, but still...

CHAPTER 29

Buying Kazakhs

Kazakh camp
April 9, 1637

The level of opium in Stefan's system was almost
enough to counteract the pain. The lance had broken
three ribs and ripped open his left arm from shoulder
to elbow. He was bandaged and his left arm was held
immobile in a splintlike arrangement. He looked up
as Esim came in, leading a man much better dressed
than he was.

The new man was dressed in red velvet with gold
embroidery and lined with fur. He was introduced as
Prince Togym, a cousin of the khan.

Stefan listened as the prince, in accented Russian,
explained that he had been in command of the first
day's attack. "The first attack, the one that struck
between two buildings on the street you call Irina
Way. That attack met powerful resistance from well-
armed defenders. It would have been pushed back no
matter how swiftly we struck, would it not?"

It was pretty clear that the only acceptable answer

was that it would have been, though Stefan didn't have any notion of why that might be.

"Well, once we had the barricade up."

"So it's true you were in command of that defense."

"Yes," Stefan agreed hesitantly. The only reason he hadn't been executed for punching Ivan Petrovich Choglokov was that it was determined he was in command. But he wasn't at all sure that his having been in command at Irina Way would make him popular with these people. And at the moment he wasn't even in command of his own body.

"You did very well and must be a skilled soldier. You had more forces than we could see, did you not? Else you never could have held against so many."

Again it was a question whose answer was expected to be yes, and again it was clear that any other answer would not please his questioner. But the fact was that he hadn't had that many people. The rate of fire was because the AK4.7 had a tremendous rate of fire. "Well, we had a lot of good men and it was a limited front," Stefan equivocated. He was willing enough to lie, but he was starting to get the feeling that if he said something that he couldn't step back from, someone—not this guy, but someone else—would call him on it. This was sounding way too much like an argument between a couple of nobles, and the smart serf stayed out of those, because they never ended well for the serf. Stefan assumed that what went for serfs went double for a prisoner about to become a slave.

He was right. Prince Togym kept pushing to get him to say that attacking the gap before softening it up with arrow attacks would only have made things worse.

Stefan equivocated, but he wasn't good at it. He was forced into making increasingly firm statements and, in desperation, finally said, "The whole attack was stupid. Why attack Ufa anyway?"

"Because Sheremetev promised us guns. Ten thousand AK3 wheel locks with a hundred thousand chambers."

"Why not just buy them from us, then?" Stefan said disgustedly, "I had a factory that made chambers. It would have cost less than sending your troops up Irina Way."

"You had a factory?"

"It was a ways out, and when you attacked we gathered up what we could and moved it behind the barricades. I think your men burned the building we were in to the ground."

"So *you* know how to make the AK3s?"

"Well, of course." Stefan cut himself off, suddenly realizing that just like always, he had said the wrong thing. He had just made himself too valuable to give back. Not that they were going to give him back anyway, but now they were probably going to make his ransom even bigger and it would be harder to escape with them watching him. He had known since he was a kid that talking just got him in trouble, and here he had gone and done it again.

As he left the tent, Togym decided to keep this slave for himself. He certainly had enough rank for that. Only the khan could gainsay him. But as he walked a bit more, he had another thought. What about the attack? If they had sent a mission to talk to Czar Mikhail, they might have gotten the guns with a lot less bloodshed. They might even have gained an ally and a buffer between them and Moscow. If he could paint the whole attack as a mistake instigated by Colonel Shuvalov and offer the prospect of . . .

No. It was too late. Blood had been spilled. A lot of blood on both sides. It was too late for peace.

Or was it?

He turned back and went to have another little talk with Doctor Esim. He found the doctor checking on one of the other patients. "Doctor, have the captives questioned. I want to know everything about this Stefan Andreevich."

It wasn't hard. Quite a few of the prisoners had been from Stefan's company. There were even some who had been with him at Irina Way. The consensus was that Stefan was scary. The story of his killing a man with one blow was repeated and embellished. The story of his trial, ennoblement, and appointment as captain came out. There were also stories of how he held the army together when the Kazakh warriors had overridden them. There were stories about the factory, because three of the prisoners were actually workers at the factory and Vera and Izabella were better known in Ufa than Stefan was. All of which was recorded and reported, and made Stefan look more dangerous as a slave.

And, perhaps, more useful as an emissary.

Togym listened to the doctor as he retold the stories about Stefan, Vera, Izabella, Father Yulian, Alexander, the factory, and the village of New Ruzuka.

It all made Stefan seem a very important man. The president of the constitutional convention was one of his partners and his wife was a delegate. So were two other of his partners.

❖   ❖   ❖

"You should have attacked sooner," Colonel Shuvalov said yet again. "All the casualties we have taken were because of your hesitation."

Togym gritted his teeth. He knew that the khan was getting tired of hearing this, but he also knew that Shuvalov's tactic was still working. He stopped the spoon halfway to his mouth, and said as calmly as he could manage, "The issue isn't when the attack was made, but whether it was necessary at all." This was a dangerous counter because it had the risk of seeming to make the khan look bad as well as Shuvalov, but Togym was getting desperate. "We could, you know, have simply bought the guns here in Ufa."

"They don't have the facilities to produce them here," Colonel Shuvalov said.

"How strange, considering how many of them they have. Also, there is a prisoner in our medical tents who owns a factory to make them right here in Ufa."

"Can't be!" Shuvalov said, just a touch too emphatically to be completely believable.

Prince Togym smiled. "Why, then, don't we go see? The man is quite impressive, I assure you, Great Khan. He commanded the defenders at Irina Way, and killed a man with a single blow of his fist for disputing his commands. I dare say it was him, not the barrels, that made the difference there."

Stefan looked up, saw a delegation entering the hospital tent and wondered what was going on. They came over to him and Stefan started to get scared. This was Prince Togym and someone even more powerful...and what looked to be a Russian noble. A colonel by his collar tab. He didn't have the dog head on his other collar, but he did have the crest of the family Shuvalov embroidered on his tabard. And Stefan knew that the Shuvalov family, like the Utkin family, were retainers of the Sheremetevs. Suddenly it clicked "You're Colonel Shuvalov. What are you doing here? Oh. *You're* why they attacked."

"I don't believe I know you, Captain. What's your family?"

"Czar Mikhail ennobled me after the battle at Irina Way. I'm Stefan Andreevich Ruzukov."

"And you own a factory that makes AK3s."

This was apparently an argument between lords that a serf or prospective slave didn't want to get in the middle of. But Stefan was in it now, with nothing more to lose. "I am part owner along with my wife, Father Yulian, Izabella Utkin, and Alexander Nikolayevich Volkov. We own a factory that can make AK3s and AK4s. Up till the attack, we were making chamber clips for the AK4.7s. The factory across the street was making the caps."

This clearly wasn't something that Colonel Shuvalov was happy to hear, and that pleased Stefan well enough. "If you hadn't finagled them into attacking Ufa, we could have been making AKs for them by now."

"That's ridiculous. You don't have the tools, or the tools to build the tools."

Now at least they were in territory that Stefan understood. "A lot of the people from Murom followed Princess Natasha to Ufa, and even more from the Dacha. And they used riverboats so they could carry a lot. In the first weeks after Czar Mikhail escaped, there were several trips back and forth. We were still on the road while that was happening and I only heard about it secondhand, but I know it happened because there was already a steam engine-powered induction furnace ready to go when we started up our factory. There's an even bigger industrial quarter in Kazan."

"Well, at least it was honest error rather than lies that led us to attack Ufa," offered Togym with a smile.

Colonel Shuvalov looked like he wanted to kill someone—Togym by preference, but Stefan in a pinch. "It doesn't matter now anyway. It's too late..." Shuvalov stopped, and even Stefan who was no good at all at this sort of thing realized that he had only opened his mouth to exchange feet.

"I don't know. Maybe you can work something out. What will it cost you to send an embassy?" Stefan said.

"What indeed?" asked Togym.

"Director-General Sheremetev will not be pleased. It could disrupt the arrangement you have with Moscow and leave you with nothing."

"Or we might get a better offer if there is another bidder in the market," Togym said.

"What do you think, captain of soldiers? Will your czar make peace with me at this late date?" Salqam-Jangir Khan asked.

Stefan looked at the young man, who was more richly dressed than anyone, and was working just a bit too hard at looking wise and resolute. "I can't speak for Czar Mikhail, but he is a wise czar. It's worth trying, I think." Stefan wanted to explain that from all he had seen Czar Mikhail was a great man who was working hard to build a nation of free people, and that he would find a way out of this mess for all of them. Stefan believed that, even though the czar had only said a few words in his presence. Czar Mikhail had mostly sat back and let others debate the issues till it was settled, but that seemed the wisest course to Stefan. Unfortunately, Stefan knew that if he tried to explain, it would come out a jumbled mess. So he kept quiet after the bare statement.

"I will consider this, and decide," Salqam-Jangir Khan said, then turned and walked out of the tent.

Togym looked over at Colonel Shuvalov with what had to be the meanest smile Stefan had ever seen in his life.

The colonel glared back at him for a moment, gave Stefan a threatening glance, then turned and stormed out of the tent.

Stefan looked back at Togym and smiled. *This might work out.*

"Prince Togym," said the doctor who had been standing in the background in case he was needed, "you might want to have the outlander watched. Now would be a good time for him to leave, perhaps leaving knives in a few backs on his way out."

Togym nodded. "That's worth considering." Then he left.

"Togym, I'm inclined to try your approach," Salqam-Jangir Khan said.

The room was full of courtiers and officers, and there was a not-quite sigh of relief at this. The attack on Ufa had proven much more expensive than anyone had expected. The major exception to that collective sigh was Colonel Leontii Shuvalov, who hadn't made a run for it in the night. He was apparently planning to play the game to checkmate.

"But I still doubt that they will treat with us after we attacked them," Salqam added.

"We have the perfect gift for them, Great Khan." Togym hooked a finger at Colonel Shuvalov. "Clear proof that Director-General Sheremetev is plotting against the true and legitimate czar."

Shuvalov started to say something then, but Salqam-Jangir Khan made a sharp gesture and the guards drew their swords. Shuvalov was, perforce, silent.

Salqam-Jangir Khan nodded at Togym. "We shall also return them the prisoners as a gesture of goodwill." That was a large gesture. Most of the four hundred seventeen men who held the line had survived. One hundred fifty-two had died on the field, or later of their wounds. But five hundred seventeen more had been captured, hale or wounded, before they could get back to the barricades. That left them with a total of seven hundred eighty-two prisoners, including forty-three officers who might bring significant ransoms. The not quite sigh of relief was replaced with a not quite audible groan of dismay. Even with the khan taking the lion's share, that was a fortune. Not enough to pay for their losses in retainers, horses, and equipment...but it certainly would have helped.

Togym couldn't help a visible wince. The rest was bad enough, but in Stefan they had an artisan who could build them the guns they had to have even if the peace talks failed completely. He started to speak, then saw Salqam-Jangir Khan looking at him. Apparently he still wasn't forgiven for his hesitancy on that first day.

"We will carry this approach through. No half measures or..."

"Great Khan," said Shuvalov, "first send an embassy under a flag of truce, find out if there is any real hope of peace before you sacrifice so much advantage."

It was a brave thing to say. Speaking at all under the circumstances took more than a little courage. On the other hand, what did the colonel have to lose? Togym decided to speak. "Colonel Shuvalov is right in this, I think."

Salqam-Jangir Khan looked over at Togym. "Always so cautious, Cousin. Very well."

Constitutional Convention, Ufa

"The states must be allowed their own armies," said Yermak Fedov. "Otherwise, in a generation, the federal government will own us all."

"But that's what led to the American Civil War," offered up Filip Pavlovich Tupikov. "The ultimate must be the federal government."

"I agree with Yermak on this one," Brandy Bates said. "The ultimate authority must be the people, and an armed populace will keep that firmly in the minds of both the government and the people."

"Not the czar?" asked Yermak.

"No, not the czar, though he acts as a symbol for the nation," Brandy said. "Vladimir and I talked about this a lot back in Grantville and on the ship. And we talked to Czar Mikhail about it after we got here. The oaths will be sworn to the czar *and* the constitution. The constitution will give the czar and all the future czars certain rights and prerogatives, but Czar Mikhail—of his own will and for the good of the people—is conceding the right to rule themselves to the people of Russia and their posterity, now and for all time."

Yermak nodded respectfully, but Filip wasn't through. "In that case, what is there for the states to be concerned about?"

Brandy was about to answer, but there was a knock at the door which was immediately opened and a messenger stepped through. He turned to the president of the convention and said, "There is a delegation from the Kazakhs approaching under a flag of truce. Czar Mikhail asks, if they may be spared, that Brandy Bates and Vladimir Gorchakov join him."

It was noted by the entire convention that General Izmailov wasn't asked to attend. Apparently, all wasn't yet forgiven for the debacle of the sally.

At the barricades across Irina Way, they met the delegation.

"That is Prince Togym, the Kazakh khan's first cousin and senior advisor," Colonel Buturlin said. "I don't recognize the other two."

Czar Mikhail looked at the other men and recognized them, in kind if not as individuals. The one on the left looked to be in his twenties. Probably a personal friend of the khan; he was about the right age. At a guess, he would keep his mouth shut and then report back to the khan on what happened. There was also an older man, and Mikhail figured that he was probably not of the same court faction as Togym.

Bernie waved and some of the men started pulling apart the barricade. It took a few minutes and everyone waited while it was done, then they rode through and introductions were made. The young one was Count Nazar, and the old one was Count Tauke. There were a half dozen soldiers, but they weren't introduced.

"Why don't we go to the kremlin and find a comfortable place to sit and talk," Mikhail offered, testing the waters. If they agreed to go into the fortress, they would be putting themselves in his power, not that they weren't already. But it would indicate another layer of either trust or desperation.

Togym's smile was sardonic as he agreed. So, at least on the part of the delegation, it was desperation.

This was one of the small conference rooms in the Ufa kremlin, and had been built since Czar Mikhail arrived. It had actual glass windows. They weren't plate glass, but blown glass, and they were made of lots of small panes, but they were actual windows that let the sunlight in and had the room warm even today, without a fire. There was also an indoor toilet in the next room. It was different from what their guests had seen before, and Bernie made a point of showing them all the amenities. Mikhail knew why. These were inducements, examples of the advantages of joining the United States of Russia.

"Where does it go, though?" asked Nazar.

"There are pipes that take it to a brick-lined covered hole called a septic tank that holds it until the solids settle. Then the liquid goes into a leach field . . ."

"Ahem . . . Perhaps we can discuss waste management another time," Czar Mikhail suggested. "It's only one of the new techniques brought by the up-timers. And while I grant that it's an important one in the fight against disease, we are here to talk about making peace. At least, I hope we are, or we're all wasting our time." He looked pointedly at the three emissaries.

Togym nodded, and Czar Mikhail waved them to chairs at one end of the long conference table in the room.

Czar Mikhail sat in the rather ornate chair at the other end of the table and Bernie sat at the czar's right. Vladimir sat at his left, and Brandy and Natasha sat in the next seats. Colonel Buturlin sat on Natasha's other side. A young man came in and sat at a small desk against the wall, and set up with pen and paper. He would be taking down the meeting in shorthand.

Mikhail looked down the table and said, "You asked for this meeting. Why don't you start?"

"The Great Salqam-Jangir Khan is willing to consider calling off the attack if an adequate tribute is forthcoming," Count Tauke suggested belligerently before Togym could say anything.

Mikhail moved his eyes from Count Tauke to Prince Togym, then back.

Then Vladimir said, "Well, I guess we're done here. Thanks for your time. The guards will show you the way out."

Bernie checked his watch. "We can get back to the debate on interstate taxation if we hurry."

"Do we have to?" Brandy complained. But she was standing up as she said it.

"Wait." It was the kid Nazar who broke. But apparently only because he was quicker to respond than Togym.

Vladimir, who had started to rise like the meeting was over, sat back down. Then—pointedly ignoring Count Tauke—he said, "Count Nazar, if your khan has anything substantive to offer, we are happy to listen. We want peace. But we were attacked without warning."

"You sit in the territory of the Kazakh Khanate," Count Tauke said.

"Quiet!" Togym said. "This hasn't been part of the Kazakh lands for eighty years and you know it." Then he turned back to Czar Mikhail. "Still, the fact is that we control the land around Ufa. And if taking the city would be expensive, it is not beyond our means. Director-General Sheremetev offers us ten thousand AK3s and a hundred thousand chambers for aiding him in removing you. What can you offer us to counter his offer?"

"That assumes that you can take Ufa," Colonel Buturlin said. "The truth is, you can't. We have plenty of powder and shot. We have a factory manufacturing caps. We have built and improved the barricades, and we can hold this city if we need to till the spring thaws and then we will have access to resupply and reinforcement by way of the rivers."

"But you can't meet us on the open field," offered Count Nazar.

"Not at the moment. But those relief ships will be bringing *gulyay-gorod*," Bernie said. "We've talked to General Tim and Colonel Ivan Maslov, and they agree that we will be able to repeat the Battle of Rzhev once we have access to the new *gulyay-gorod*."

"And in the meantime, we can lay waste to the countryside," Prince Togym pointed out.

"Yes," Czar Mikhail said. "You can hurt us, but we will still be here when the ice melts and we will pay back every burned village with two of yours. Is that what your khan wants? We ravaged, you destroyed, and the traitor Sheremetev laughing at us all?"

"No. But we must gain something out of this. With the Zunghar Khanate and Erdenebaatar Khan to our east, we have to have those rifles."

"Well, you won't get them by attacking us," said Colonel Buturlin, "but you might get them by allying with us."

"How so? We should not face your AK4s, but Sheremetev's?" Count Nazar asked.

"Everyone is working out how the new weapons affect tactics," Bernie said. "According to Tim, we are somewhere between the American Civil War and World War I, with the strategic situation complicated by the fact that we don't have nearly the population density to support something like the Maginot Line." That brought nothing but looks of confusion. "Two wars that were fought in that other history, both of them very, very bloody. What it amounts to, at least in Russia, is that hard points and fortification are going to be so expensive to take that it's effectively impossible. But there aren't enough people to be able to hold a line that covers the country and blocks all attack . . ."

"Enough, Bernie," Czar Mikhail said.

"Rather more than enough," added Vladimir. Then he looked back at the emissaries. "To our allies, we are willing to share the knowledge of the future and all that it entails. But not to enemies encamped on our lands."

It was a long meeting, but gradually they reached a group of compromises. Czar Mikhail offered to allow Salqam-Jangir Khan or his representative to sit in on the constitutional convention, without obligating him to join the United States of Russia if he decided not to.

Prince Togym sounded doubtful, but agreed to pass on the offer.

April 12, 1637

It was no small party that headed for the barricade under flag of truce the next morning. Salqam-Jangir Khan, his bodyguards and some three hundred ambulatory prisoners were coming along behind. As soon as they reached the barricade, Salqam-Jangir Khan made it clear that there were more prisoners, but they would need help to move them.

Tami Simmons was called and immediately offered to go and examine the patients. By now Tami had a staff of medical people, some from the Dacha or Murom, but quite a few doctors, apothecaries and midwives from all over Russia. In a way, the rescue of Czar Mikhail had been Tami's release from a gilded cage. She had been the personal physician of the czar's family, not a practicing nurse. That position had limited her access to other medical practitioners even before the royal family was moved to the hunting lodge. After that, she and her family hadn't even seen anyone except the czar's family and the guards till the rescue. But once they arrived at Ufa, Tami found herself in a situation something like Bernie Zeppi right after he arrived at the Dacha. It was more specialized and Tami knew more than Bernie had, but it was very much one long open-book test as the down-time medics tried to pump her brain dry of every medical fact available.

Combined with the locals and the refugees coming in with all manner of ailments, it was like nine months in a MASH unit combined with a medical university, and Tami was due some down time.

What she got was several hundred wounded from both sides, and the opportunity to become a surgeon. She wasn't working alone. The Kazakh had excellent doctors, at least by seventeenth-century standards. But there were a lot of infected wounds to deal with after the ceasefire. Tami worked eighteen- to twenty-hour days, but she and her staff saved a lot of limbs and even more lives.

Stefan recognized Tami as soon as she entered the makeshift hospital. She was well known in Ufa and an acquaintance of his wife, as well as Izabella's midwife. She examined him and washed his arm in alcohol, then had the wound reopened and washed in 'alcohol. It wasn't pleasant but it probably saved his left arm, though not the full use of it. After that, he was shipped back to Ufa to convalesce in his own bed. He was consulted by both the Kazakhs and the government on the ability to produce actual AKs in Ufa. "It can be done, but it will take a while, especially with the damage done by the attack," he told Togym.

"But you said that you could make guns," Togym insisted.

"I said we could have, before the attack. And even then we would have to tool up. Look, up until the usurper's army invested Kazan, the main production of AKs was located there. We were making the chambers and chamber clips." Stefan paused. "All you need to do to get all the guns you want is relieve the siege at Kazan." *And pay for them*, he thought.

Togym went off then, muttering about the duplicity of Russians.

Salqam-Jangir Khan was better pleased. He entered the convention as though he had taken the city instead of being forced to the negotiation table. And he hadn't had to promise to join the USR to get a seat. Well, neither had many of the other delegates. Still, he had a great advantage over the others. He wasn't a delegate. He was the ruler of his own state. He had nobles and soldiers he couldn't completely ignore, but while someone like Izmailov had to report back to his principal, Salqam *was* the principal. It gave him a standing that was unique and he immediately became the center of the pro-slavery faction.

Moscow Kremlin
April 13, 1637

The coup attempt came out of nowhere, and was almost a complete surprise. They had gotten the news a few hours earlier that Salqam-Jangir Khan had made at least tentative peace with Czar Mikhail. And, worse, that Colonel Shuvalov had been turned over to Czar Mikhail.

Three of Director-General Sheremetev's guards were dead and the last wounded before he knew what was happening, but Captain Golokhvastov had seen the situation, and called a contingent of the *oprichniki* to the director-general's defense.

The good news was the bad news. The attackers had gotten into the Kremlin. That meant that Sheremetev's control was a lot weaker than he had believed. But on the upside, no one had heard the fighting.

Fedor Ivanovich Sheremetev dabbed a cut on his cheek with an alcohol-soaked rag and bit back a curse. "Who?"

Captain Golokhvastov looked at Sheremetev then back at the bodies on the floor. "I don't know, Director-General. I can think of three men right off who might try it if they thought they had a chance. But I don't recognize any of these men." Aside from Sheremetev's guards and three *oprichniki*, a dozen men lay dead around them.

"Romanov?"

"I don't think so, Director-General. Ivan Nikitich Romanov's venial enough, but he doesn't have the guts."

Sheremetev nodded and considered, but not for long. Fedor Ivanovich Sheremetev considered himself a decisive man and, in fact, he was quick to decide on most things. "I'll need..." He stopped. Best not to tell anyone his plans. "Captain, send a radio message to Bor. I need one of the new dirigibles here as soon as it can get here. Meanwhile, start with these men." He waved at the bodies. "Learn what you can and find me the traitors who bought them. Oh, and send Romanov to the Amber Room." Sheremetev had seen pictures of the Amber Room that Peter the Great had had made in that other timeline, and had something quite similar built.

"I will be gone for a few days. Perhaps even a few weeks," Sheremetev said, looking at Ivan Nikitich

Romanov, Mikhail's uncle. "I have arrangements to make. In the meantime, you will be in charge. I am naming you Assistant Director."

Ivan Romanov watched the small dirigible carrying Sheremetev sail into the clouds and be lost to the eye. He wondered if with Sheremetev gone he might be able to seize control of the duma. It was a tempting thought, but he wasn't sure.

CHAPTER 30

A House Divided

Ufa
April 14, 1637

"It's over," Anya said. "With Jangir to rally the pro-slavery faction, we'll be lucky to block slavery and serfdom in the free states."

"I agree," said Vladimir. "What about voting rights and representation?"

"We're going to have to have something like a house of lords," Brandy said. "We got stuck with that in the USE."

"Yes, surely. But what's the makeup of it?"

"What do you mean?" Bernie asked. "It's a bunch of freaking lords."

"Fine. But what level? Does Filip here get a seat? He's a member of the service nobility. If every member of the service nobility or the *deti boyars* got a seat in the house of lords, the house would never get anything done. And neither would the bureaus, because every bureaucrat and officer in the Russian army would be warming a seat in the house of lords."

"Didn't we already go over this?" Natasha asked. "It was in your original proposal, wasn't it? The bureaus would each get to appoint one senator, and the states would each get two?"

"Yes, we did," Vladimir said. "But there was some vagueness about who qualified as a lord. And if Kazakh comes in, we have this whole other set of nobility and the issue of what a title in the Kazakh Khanate translates to in the United States of Russia. What I plan to do is try to get Jangir to agree that the czar must ennoble all his state nobles for them to count. He won't agree to that. He can't. It would cause a revolution. But if I fight him on it for a while then give in, in exchange for limiting his right to make new nobles of the rank necessary to sit in the senate…"

They talked well into the night, determining what they would give to Salqam-Jangir Khan and what they hoped to get in exchange. And while they talked, the news of the truce raced across Russia.

Kazan
April 14, 1637

Tim took a bite of the mini lamb kabob, chewed, then swallowed. "We don't have many details, Abdul, but if it works there may be a Muslim state in the United States of Russia. Do you have any word from your cousin?" Abdul Azim's cousin was the chief of the Kazan delegation to the constitutional convention in Ufa. However, asking Abdul about word from his cousin was a polite fiction. If there had been a radio telegram for Abdul, Tim would have been notified by the radio crew. Not of the content if it was encoded, but of the fact of the message. Still, it was best to be polite when attending what Bernie Zeppi had christened a "cocktail party," a local get together where much of the business of governing Kazan was done.

"No, nothing yet, and that worries me." Abdul sipped his coffee and glanced over at the buffet table.

"I wouldn't be. They are probably pretty busy over there right now."

"No doubt, but Petr Milosevic is going to start claiming that the Muslims are keeping secrets again."

Tim hid a grin. Petr Milosevic was the leader of the Russian Orthodox faction on the Kazan city council, and had been less than pleased with the proclamation of freedom of religion in Kazan. He had been complaining ever since that the town was being overrun by Muslims.

From Abdul Azim's look, Tim was less than fully successful in hiding that grin, but he let it pass. "What do you think the truce means from a military perspective?"

"It's too soon to tell. Unless it produces some reaction from General Birkin or Iakov Petrovich reacts in some unexpected way, I don't see how it changes much. Ivan Vasilevich left way too many people here under Iakov Petrovich for us to consider risking a sally, when he went off to 'relieve Ufa.' Even if he pulled half of them out to add to his force, I still wouldn't try it. And his excuse has just gone away. Ufa is no longer under attack by the Kazakh forces. If he attacks Ufa now, it will be a clear attack on Czar Mikhail."

"Does that matter?"

"Yes, Abdul, it does. A fair chunk of his army is still

personally loyal to Czar Mikhail, and at least accepting of the notion that the czar is being influenced by evil up-timers. But if General Birkin orders them to attack the Ufa kremlin, they might well refuse the order."

Abdul considered as Petr Milosevic wandered over to join them. "What's the word from Ufa?" Petr asked in a voice that was more suited to a battlefield than a cocktail party.

"I was just asking the general that," Abdul answered. "The general here was just telling me how the director-general's hold on his army is less firm than I had thought."

"Then why don't we sally?" Petr Milosevic demanded.

"Because there is a very large difference between attacking Czar Mikhail and defending yourself when an upstart boy—" Tim pointed at his own chest. "—insults you by attacking. Also they have AK4.7s out there, and a lot of them. I won't send men out without cover to face that sort of fire. It might be different if we had *gulyay-gorod*, but my orders were to defend Kazan. I was more concerned with making sure that there was enough food and shot to defend the walls we did have, than to make portable ones." It was the same argument he had been making since the first attack was repelled, and Petr Milosevic didn't like it any better now than he had then. But military command of Kazan was firmly on Tim's shoulders and Petr's complaints to the czar had been met with expressions of confidence in Tim and instructions not to joggle his elbow. So Petr shut up.

"Well, if it's not going to have any immediate military effect," Abdul said, "what political effect do you expect?"

Tim didn't even try to hide this grin. "I think Sheremetev must be chewing the furniture about now. If he is successful, Czar Mikhail, while in exile, will add the Kazakh Khanate to Russia. That's more territory, and more civilized, than anyone since Ivan the Terrible has gotten, and Mikhail will have gotten it with much less bloodshed."

"That's what makes no sense to me," Petr complained. "Why on earth would the Kazakh khan even consider such a move? What would he gain in exchange for his rule?"

"Frankly, Tim, that bothers me too," Abdul added. "And you know how I hate agreeing with Petr about anything."

Petr laughed out loud at that. It was true they weren't great friends, but they had learned to work together in spite of that.

"I'm not at all sure . . . but I suspect that it has to do with our guns. And, perhaps, with the other up-timer knowledge."

"But they could get that by sending their own agent to the USE," Abdul said.

"Could they?" Petr asked. "They would have to either go through Istanbul and the Turks, or us and Poland, or all the way around Africa and Europe by sea to get their agent there. And the same again to get him back. If they need the guns now, or even if they expect to need them soon . . ." He trailed off, thinking.

Tim thought too. It wasn't just the knowledge. It was the tools, as well. The tools to build the tools. Old Russia had a lot of them. Five years of frantic work's worth. New Russia had less, only what the refugees could take with them as they ran or sneaked out later.

But that was still a lot in relative terms. Damn, he wished he had *gulyay-gorod*. He was starting to think he was going to need them.

Moscow
April 14, 1637

"So the weak, enfeebled Czar Mikhail, on the run and—how did the director-general put it?—'hiding in his hole in Ufa,' has managed to take the Kazakh Khanate with diplomacy." Prince Ivan Ivanovich Odoevskii snorted sarcastically. "While the great and powerful director-general, the firm hand Russia needed, has managed to lose half an army to take not so much as a town."

This latest news had made things worse. It was looking less and less like Sheremetev was going to be able to hold power. Not, at least, without a powerful ally. And it wasn't at all sure that Ivan could keep control with Sheremetev out there on a mission, wherever he had gone.

"We have more important things to deal with than laying blame, Ivan Ivanovich," Boris Ivanovich Morozov said, "This is likely to make the situations in the bureaus even worse." Boris wasn't a nice man and didn't try to be, but he was an efficient administrator and didn't like the way things had been going. In the period between the death of Ivan the Terrible and Mikhail Romanov's escape to Ufa, the rule of Russia had—in fact, if not in name—moved from czar to the bureaus, or at least in that direction. Since the escape of Czar Mikhail, there had been an almost continuous defection of the service nobility to Mikhail's court in exile in Ufa, to General Shein in Siberia, or just elsewhere. By now, defection was upwards of ten percent. And while ten percent didn't seem like much, it was often the most effective ten percent, people who would have been promoted except for the entrenched nepotism that permeated both the court and the bureaus. It was the go-getters who got up and went. That wasn't universal, but it was far more likely. The time servers had a strong tendency to stay where they were and continue with their routine.

That had given Czar Mikhail a smaller bureaucracy, but a more effective one. The defections had also led to increased corruption and decreased efficiency in the Moscow bureaucracy. Not that it could all be blamed on the bureaucrats. The corruption of the Moscow-based bureaus started at the top and spread down from there. Boris Ivanovich Morozov wasn't sure of all the causes, but he was starting to think he had backed the wrong horse. "What is the latest word from our ambassador to the USE? Will we be getting the new tubes for the radios?"

"I don't know," Prince Ivan Ivanovich Odoevskii said. "Check with my clerk after the meeting."

Grantville section, Moscow
April 14, 1637

"Are we getting the tubes?" Boris Ivanovich Petrov asked Yuri.

"I doubt it. Apparently Vladimir Gorchakov is one of the major stockholders in the company and he used his influence to get all of them he could. The rest are mostly tied up in USE government procurement. Ah, Boss...Alexis Ivanov is gone. He didn't come in to work this morning. I sent Stefan Alexandrovich to check on him, and the whole family is gone. And what about Sheremetev himself? Any idea where the director-general has gotten off to? You don't think he's defected to Czar Mikhail, do you?" Yuri laughed.

Boris didn't curse, but it was hard not to. The director-general going missing just now was a horrible sign. Though, as Boris thought about it, not a bad move on Sheremetev's part. With him missing, he couldn't be assassinated, and any potential coup would have to worry about his return. So everyone in the duma was afraid to blow their nose and nothing was getting done.

Meanwhile, Alexis Ivanov was one of their experts on electronics, in fact, the best one. Boris had tried to get him promoted to head of that section twice, but both times he had been stopped by incompetents with better pedigrees. The main job of the Grantville section was still the importation and organization of up-time technical data. By now they had a lot of books and articles and expertise. They also had a whole bunch of featherbedding clerks who were all desperately anxious not to rock the boat. Alexis had been one of the drivers of the Grantville section. He had been instrumental in finding the data that let the Dacha produce spark plugs that worked. Not the spark plugs themselves, but the coil. He was also involved in the Russian tube project that was located in the Dacha. His defection would delay Russia's making their own tubes. At least, this part of Russia.

There was oil in Russia. Rather a lot of it. And internal combustion engines were one of the goals of Sheremetev's five-year plan for the technological reinvention of Russia.

Yuri was looking at Boris, and Boris could see the question in his eyes. How much longer was Boris going to stay in place? How long before he ran east?

But Boris wasn't going to run east, for several reasons. First, three of his sons were safe, two in the USE and one in Ufa. Pavel was with Mariya, on the family estates, running the freeze-dried food factory. He had lost some of his serfs, but a lot fewer than he might have expected. And the farming villages were now almost completely dedicated to vegetable production, with most of their production freeze-dried. It was small enough to escape the notice of the Sheremetev family, but still quite profitable. Most important, Boris' position here, not in the direct line of espionage, but with access into the network of bureaus, left him in an excellent position to learn most of what he wanted to know, and was not so close to the power bases to make anyone nervous. Someday this was all going to break, and Boris didn't think it would be too long.

Goritsky Monastery
April 14, 1637

Click, click, click. The radio dotted and dashed out its message, and the radio operator took it down, trying to ignore the nuns crowding around his door. When the news of the Kazakh khan's truce with Czar Mikhail hit Goritsky, any trace of contemplative silence had abandoned the monastery. The nuns went into a frenzy, and a crowd of them hung around. For days now, he hadn't had a moment of peace.

"General Izmailov has endorsed Salqam-Jangir Khan's position on the slavery issue," said one of the old ladies.

"Why, it's virtually identical to Izmailov's position," said another.

"Izmailov is conceding leadership of the pro-slavery faction to the khan," said the first.

Petr wished they would go back to the monastery, but he didn't say anything. Over the last weeks, the messages the nuns of Goritsky Monastery sent and received convinced him that these weren't women he wanted to argue with.

Back in the monastery proper, Sofia went over the transcripts. "Do you think that Salqam-Jangir Khan will actually agree to join Czar Mikhail's United States of Russia?"

"I'm not sure it matters," Tatyana said. "Remember when Elena said that the longer Mikhail was besieged the worse it was for him? That's turned around now. The longer Salqam-Jangir Khan sits in Ufa negotiating with Mikhail, the stronger Mikhail becomes. Well, the weaker Sheremetev becomes."

"Which is not quite the same thing," said Elena. "Even if Sheremetev loses power in Moscow, it doesn't mean that Mikhail wins."

Sofia looked at Elena, trying not to show her irritation. Elena was the most depressing nun in the monastery. And even though Sofia understood the reasons for it, that didn't make it pleasant. Besides, the most irritating thing about Elena was that she was mostly right.

Russia was on the knife's edge and Sheremetev running off like that wasn't helping. If someone had killed Sheremetev—which was to Sofia's mind a distinct possibility—Russia could collapse into a dozen warring parts. It still seemed almost beyond hope that Mikhail could hold it together. There really was no reason she could see for Salqam-Jangir Khan to join the United States of Russia.

Dirigible Princess Anna, *approaching the Swedish fortress in Nyen*
April 14, 1637

Dimitry Ivanov cursed and sucked on his hand. The boiler on this dirigible was less protected, and burns from touching hot metal were quite a bit more common. Worse, the *Little Princess* as they called her, was only capable of carrying about a ton of useful load, or—if they overloaded with fuel to give them greater range—only a few hundred pounds. So Dimitry was captain and chief engineer, and he had two riggers for this trip. They had had to land in the hinterlands on the way here to chop trees to refuel. But they were carrying official messages from Ufa to the fortress, so it had to be done.

Princess Anna had a radio, a good one with tubes, so they could inform the fort they were coming. Even before they landed, the fort wanted to know if the khan of the Kazakhs had really joined the United States of Russia. "Not when we left. He had just entered the city, and they had barely started negotiating."

"Where have you been?" the radioman asked in dots and dashes.

"Crossing Russia. What's been happening?"

"The latest I have is the khan is new head of pro-slavery faction and they have moved on to voting rights. Oh, and the director-general has gone missing. Word is he flew off in a dirigible."

"I doubt it," Dimitry Ivanov sent back. "I have it from a reliable source that Sheremetev is terrified of flying. Spent his whole trip from Moscow to Bor in a stateroom and then wouldn't get back on the dirigible."

"You think he's dead?"

"Maybe. We can hope anyway."

Dimitry shook his head. The radios were fast. Much faster than the dirigible, and the network now reached all the way from Ufa to the Swedish fortress on the Baltic. Finally he sent, "I wonder if the world will have changed by the time I get back."

"Yes. China will have joined."

CHAPTER 31

Voting Rights

Ufa
April 15, 1637

"It's all falling apart. Salqam-Jangir Khan is threatening to walk out if we don't have slavery, and Fedov is threatening to walk out if we don't outlaw it," Natasha said.

"I don't think that he will, not with Sheremetev missing," Anya said.

"You don't think who will?" asked Czar Mikhail.

"Either of them, actually," Anya said. "But I was thinking of Salqam-Jangir Khan. With Sheremetev missing, walking out might leave him facing all of Russia united under you."

"I wouldn't count on that," Czarina Evdokia said. "We don't know where Sheremetev is. He might be out raising another army to attack us here."

"Put them in a room together," Czar Mikhail interrupted. "Salqam-Jangir Khan and Yermak Fedov. Vladimir, I want you there too, as a referee. And Bernie, I think."

The ladies in the room looked at the czar expectantly, and he shook his head. "Neither man is comfortable with women in that sort of meeting, so leave it to Vladimir and Bernie. Besides, I don't want it to seem like I'm trying to push the khan with a room full of abolitionists."

"What about Sheremetev?" asked Evdokia.

"I'll worry about that after we have a constitution," Czar Mikhail said. "For right now, the constitution is all that matters."

Meeting room, Ufa kremlin

"Thank you for coming, Salqam-Jangir Khan," Vladimir said. "Czar Mikhail was hoping that a private meeting between you and Yermak Fedov might yield better results than arguments on the convention floor that always seem to end in threats to walk out on the convention."

Salqam-Jangir Khan smiled. "I hope so, but don't expect miracles. My nobles depend on slavery. Slaves work the mines and the fields. Even many of the craftsmen are slaves. Were I to give Ambassador Fedov what he wants, I would face a revolution as soon as I got home. And rightly so. It would be the end of the Kazakh Khanate."

"And if I yield to Salqam-Jangir Khan," Yermak Fedov said as he came into the room, "my friends and neighbors would gut me like a fish. Besides, slavery is not the only issue. The Cossacks have always been the defenders of Christendom. Now you want us to be part of a Muslim nation."

"Not at all," Vladimir said. "The United States of Europe has shown us that individual states having

different state religions can work. All it requires is
religious toleration on everyone's part."

"And Sharia law?"

"That, I admit, is more of an issue," Vladimir said.

They talked about Sharia law and state law versus
federal law and managed to come to a compromise.
State law would be determined by the state, but
respect for the laws of other states must hold sway.
A Muslim with a harem must be allowed to bring his
family from Kazakh to the Don lands without being
arrested for bigamy. On the other hand, Kazakh would
be a dry state, though those laws would be invoked
by the state, not the church. And it was suggested
that Kazakh should probably want to decrease the
penalty, considering that a lot of Christians would be
traveling through Kazakh, or even working and living
there, and they must be allowed to practice their faith.

Oddly enough, everyone had aired their differences
on the subject of slavery, so that everyone was clear on
what they could and couldn't get. So slavery and serfdom
would be left to the states. The question of whether a
free state was obligated to return escaped slaves or serfs
to the state they had escaped from would be left to the
courts. It was a way of not having to take a stand on
the issue while they were trying to form a new nation.

"So, about voting rights?" Vladimir asked.

"If they are slaves, they shouldn't count," Yermak
Fedov said, more than a little smugly. "Since they
won't be allowed to vote, the representatives won't
represent them."

"But the representatives will represent them, just
as they will represent the women and children who
don't vote either," Salqam-Jangir Khan said. "Let's

not pretend this is not a matter of states' advantage. Clearly, it will be in my state's interest to have them counted, and against your state's interest, since we have slaves and you don't. Still, I don't wish to be unreasonable and am willing to compromise. One of my clerks tells me that in the up-time world, slaves were counted as three-fifths of a man. Personally, I think that four-fifths would be more fair, but I will yield to history if Ambassador Fedov will do the same." Then he looked over at Vladimir and smiled.

This was just the compromise that Vladimir didn't want.

Vladimir tried to explain. "That particular compromise is considered one of the most corrupt in up-time history, and one of the greatest shames of the up-time United States of America."

"Perhaps," Yermak Fedov said, sounding sad. "And perhaps history will condemn us for it, as well. But it worked, didn't it? For as long as slavery and serfdom lasted in this America, it worked. Czar Mikhail is showing great wisdom in not seeking a perfect document, but a framework."

Bernie, who had been sitting quietly throughout the meeting, suddenly spoke up. "What ever the advantage or disadvantages to the free states, they can't be as bad as declaring people three-fifths of a human."

Yermak Fedov looked at Bernie like he was a traitor. "So you want to make it so that people who aren't allowed . . ." He stopped and held up a hand, then he scratched his sideburns. Then finally, he said, "If Salqam-Jangir Khan wants them to be counted, then let them vote. No, that's not enough. They would be legally allowed to vote, then kept from voting. Make it by voting, not right to vote. The actual *voting*. If they don't vote, they don't count in terms of representatives."

"All that will mean is that they will herd their slaves into polling places and make them vote for their master's choice," Vladimir said.

"No," said Bernie. "We make the vote inviolate. Even if you own a man, you don't own his vote."

"Do you really think we can enforce such a law?" Yermak Fedov asked.

"Maybe not, at least at first. But it's better than being declared three-fifths of a human by the cornerstone of your nation's laws," Bernie answered.

"Mr. Zeppi is right," Salqam-Jangir Khan said with a smile. "We can make this work. Perhaps not everywhere, but if I have to—and I know I probably will—I can put enough heads up on pikes for interfering with a slave's right to vote to make the point."

"Would you do that?" Yermak asked, sounding both surprised and curious, but not doubting.

"The notion of janissaries is an idea of Islam, Ambassador, and a slave that has a vote seems to me one less likely to revolt. Let even a slave have some say in the government. Given some input into the laws that govern them, even the slaves will be on our side. Let them find out that the khan puts the heads of masters that try to interfere with that right up on pikes and they will be twice loyal." *Besides,* Jangir thought, *I have several examples in mind who are just the sort to attempt to try it. And aside from the good example set, it will help me to solidify my control of the khanate.*

"Not that I doubt you, but what about the others? Shein and the pocket states."

The pocket states were established by Great Families—and not-so-great families—fleeing Sheremetev's Muscovy. They were about as far east as they could get, which mostly meant the west side of the Ural Mountains. Some had sent delegates to the convention, others hadn't. The ones that had were the ones who had input into the borders of states in the United States of Russia, so some of the people who didn't send representatives to the convention were going to find themselves in other people's states. *Just like the Jungar Khanate is going to be a bit surprised at our border's new location.* "I can't speak for them, but you certainly have a point. Some of the representatives to the new congress who are 'elected' by mostly serfs will be the most dedicated to keeping the serfs in chains."

Bernie's usually pleasant, noncommittal face had a hardness in it as he said, "If necessary, I suspect the federal government will be able to find a gibbet. For this I would have no objection to heads on pikes, but Patriarch Matthew is probably going to go all soft-hearted on us and insist we just hang them."

Yermak nodded acceptance, then looked over at Bernie. "What happens when a bunch of slaves elect a slave?"

"Then the slave comes to congress," Bernie said.

"So anyone who can vote may be elected? Slaves, serfs, women, babes in arms, if they are allowed to vote?" asked Yermak. "And should such a one be elected, will he vote his will against the will of his lord or master? Will she vote her will against the will of her husband?"

"Some will, Ambassador," said Vladimir. "Certainly,

my wife will. Though, as my wife, she is more likely to be appointed to the house of lords."

"And others won't," said Bernie. "Surely what we have seen here in these last days is clear proof that this sort of government is full of 'sometimes.' Sometimes the voters, especially slaves and serfs, will be coerced in their votes, sometimes not. Sometimes that coercion will work, and sometimes not. A slave will sometimes vote his master's will in the congress, and sometimes his or her own conscience."

"I don't like the idea of women in congress," Salqam-Jangir Khan. "For that matter, I don't like them being able to vote."

Bernie grinned evilly. "Then don't let them. Don't let them vote and lose their representation in congress. Or let them vote and hold office and all the rights and privileges that go with it. If two-year-olds are allowed to vote, a two-year-old may be elected. Man, woman, child, noble, free, serf or slave—if you would have the representation for them in congress, they must be given the rights that go with it."

Salqam-Jangir Khan looked at Bernie, then over at Yermak. "And can you live with that?"

Vladimir spoke up. "It won't be just the number of representatives that is affected. Up-time there were all sorts of things that were dependent on population. Government funding for projects, for instance. If those things are apportioned based on the number of voters who actually vote . . ."

"Then you really will have infants voting," Yermak said. "And their parents beheaded for putting their little hands on the ballot to select the candidate?"

"It's not perfect," Bernie admitted, "but at least

it pushes things in the right direction. Leave the minimum age for voting in the hands of the court, but the states will want it low. As long as only voters get counted, they will want all the voters they can get."

Convention floor
April 16, 1637

Alexander banged his gavel and waited. There were a dozen copies of this new version of the constitution in the room, with all the delegates going over them and arguing. A lot. And loudly. With arm-waving and various other gestures, some not at all restrained.

Fortunately, no one had come to blows. Yet.

It was the voting rights for slaves that were causing the discussion. The free states objected in spite of Yermak Fedov's support of the measure. But the representatives of the states that had slavery and serfdom were taking offense at their objection.

"Are you calling me a liar?" Iakov Kudenetovich Cherakasky roared. He was the representative of his family and their new territory on the western edge of the Urals. "If we say there will be free elections, why do you doubt it?"

There was, Alexander knew, no good answer to that, because the truth was that the free states, especially the Cossacks, didn't trust the northern slave states. Or the Great Families and minor nobility that ran them. He banged his gavel again and Iakov turned back to him. Alexander knew Iakov moderately well. His family were clients of the Cherakasky after all, and Iakov wasn't nearly as upset as he was sounding. "Quiet please, everyone."

Once the noise in the chamber was down to a dull—if rather sullen—roar, Alexander called on Salqam-Jangir Khan.

Salqam-Jangir Khan rose with studied grace and bowed to the chamber. "I understand the concerns expressed by the Cossacks and the former serfs and slaves who represent Ufa in this chamber. I understand the concerns of my fellow Muslims from Kazan, and I do not task you for them. I can only give you my personal word that the laws against vote tampering will be enforced rigorously in the Kazakh Khanate, and that I, as the head of state for the Kazakh, will be signing that document and committing the Kazakh Khanate to statehood in the United States of Russia. I realize that most of you cannot make such a commitment at this time. You will have to consult with your governments and get their instructions. I understand that, and I respect it. But when you go home, taking the document before you and laying it before your leaders, take also this knowledge. There will be a United States of Russia and that nation will have at least two states, Ufa and the Kazakh Khanate. It will almost certainly have the Kazan Khanate as a state, as well. There is a nation forming here. A nation that will grow strong. Will you be a part of it?"

That brought silence to the chamber. Then Yermak Fedov rose. "Will you then, Great Khan, give over your sovereignty to this new nation?"

"No! The Kazakh Khanate will remain a sovereign state, but a sovereign state within a union of sovereign states. Still, your point, *Gospodin* Fedov, is well taken.

I propose one more change that we should make in this constitution of ours. Make it the constitution of the United *Sovereign* States of Russia."

There was general applause to that, which died down quickly. The delegates looked around and nodded to each other. Up till now this had been "a maybe," a possibility. They had been sent by their governments, just in case. The Kazakh Khanate, however, was a nation, and not a small or weak one. Combined with Ufa and the probable inclusion of Kazan, it was a real rival to Old Russia, that part of Russia that was still under the control of Director-General Shereme-tev. But with Director-General Sheremetev missing on some unknown quest, who knew how long Old Russia would last? And the United Sovereign States of Russia would be much more powerful than any of the rest of them, even the Siberian states, safe behind the Urals. This young man, with his signature, would turn "maybe" into "is."

He also effectively ended the debate. This document would be the ruling document of the new nation, because this was the document he had just publicly committed to sign.

General Izmailov signaled and Alexander recognized him. He rose and bowed respectfully to Salqam-Jangir Khan. "I cannot commit General Shein, but I tell you now that I will be recommending that he accept this constitution and join the union of Russian states." Then he turned to Yermak Fedov. "I know that this was a difficult compromise to make, and I respect the sagacity you showed in making it. I hope you can convince your fellow Cossacks to agree to it as well."

❖   ❖   ❖

Bernie leaned in to kiss Natasha ... and the door burst open.

"You didn't!" said Tami Simmons.

Every time. Every single time. Bernie turned with murder in his eye, but was interrupted by Gerry Simmons' bass voice, singing loudly. "Back in the U.S.S.R."

CHAPTER 32

The Relief of Kazan

Kazan
April 17, 1637

"They've got it!" The radio man rushed into the room.

"Got what?" General Boris Timofeyevich Lebedev asked, looking up from the map table. It wasn't a map of Kazan. Nothing was happening around Kazan except the cracking of the ice on the river.

"The convention in Ufa. They have a constitution and the Kazakh khan has signed it. His whole army is heading this way."

Tim stared at the man. Then he got up and ran for the radio room.

When he got there, they were busy. The whole constitution was being sent over the radio, one dot or dash at a time. It was going to take a while. But the initial message that the Kazakh army was coming to their relief, supported by a contingent of infantry from Ufa, was sitting on the desk. It didn't give their route and Tim couldn't tell them to sit tight and let the rivers melt. He had spent most of the siege arming and armoring a riverboat so that once the ice melted they would own the river, and the city bastions on the Volga River system would be able to support one another.

Unless, of course, someone at what was now the Sheremetev Dacha instead of the Gorchakov Dacha thought of doing the same thing. Then it would depend on the quality of the war boats. That was why the whole project was the most closely guarded secret in Kazan. It was about then that his thoughts caught up with themselves. Ufa was three hundred miles from Kazan, and at this time of year it was going to take weeks to slog through the mud. The rivers might still be frozen on their surface, but the land was thawing into mud every day. Long before the armies of Birkin and Ufa met, Tim would be able to act. After that realization, Tim just waited to read the constitution with everyone else.

Nizhny Novgorod
April 17, 1637

The city of Nizhny Novgorod received the news of the new constitution and the alliance—no, not simple alliance—the *statehood* of the Kazakh Khanate with mixed emotions. Not mixed in the sense that Ivan was of two minds about it or Boris was unsure. No, the problem was that Ivan wanted to cheer and Boris was ready to shit his pants. Fault lines in the city's political structure had become much more evident in the months since Czar Mikhail had sailed by, waving to the men on the walls. The Sheremetev faction was in charge, but that was because of the supply garrison that General Birkin had placed in Nizhny Novgorod when everyone thought they were going to take Kazan and move on to Ufa.

Some members of the city council had sent an observer to Ufa in secret. They wanted a seat at the table should the political winds change, and Czar Mikhail was offering seats at the table. On the other hand, they couldn't acknowledge that they were taking that seat. Not with the Sheremetev supporters in control of the city, with a garrison of several thousand men to support them.

The garrison was there because Nizhny Novgorod was way too close to the practical border between Old Russia under the director-general and the United Sovereign States of Russia under Czar Mikhail to be comfortable. Also because Birkin had filled the city with enough supplies to support a large army for a year. And the dirigible works just across the river in Bor meant they were a natural target. If Czar Mikhail—who seemed to be getting stronger every day—should decide to take someplace, this would be the place.

Taking advantage of that garrison, the Sheremetev supporters in the city had held a little reign of terror. They had the power and used it to consolidate their positions and remove their rivals. It had gotten ugly, really ugly, around December. Prominent citizens of Nizhny Novgorod had been executed when they were denounced as "up-timer sympathizers." There was now a violent Czarist underground that supported Czar Mikhail, mostly as an excuse to kill the people who had killed their friends and family. So Boris, who was in good with Sheremetev, was terrified. And Ivan, who talked about his loyalty to Czar Mikhail, thought he would soon have a chance to gut Boris like a fish.

Nizhny Novgorod was of two minds all right, but the city was schizophrenic, not thoughtful. And the question on everyone's lips was: "Why? What possible reason could Salqam-Jangir Khan have for giving up his crown to Czar Mikhail?"

"It must be the up-timer magic," claimed Boris, a little desperately.

"It's the righteousness of the cause," Ivan crowed. Quietly, because Boris' faction was still in charge.

Army forming outside Ufa
April 17, 1637

"Why did you do it?" General Izmailov asked Salqam-Jangir Khan. They were sitting on their horses, watching the army as the junior officers tried to get it into shape to move. It would be a few days.

Salqam-Jangir Khan looked back and didn't pretend not to understand. "What did I give up?"

"Your crown, your sovereignty, even if you did put sovereign in the name."

"Don't underestimate the power of a name. The court whose job it is to interpret the constitution will see first that it is the Sovereign State of Kazakh that is bringing suit against the federal government." The young man laughed an open, friendly laugh. "Besides, have you examined the state's rights clauses in the constitution? I have. There are restrictions on my power within the Kazakh lands, but they are not extreme. And, in exchange, I get a major say in the federal government. But that's not all. I get to make the laws of succession, so the possibility of rebellion from within is greatly diminished. Even should my nobles topple me, they must still face the federal government with its army. My nobles aren't going to like this new nation nearly so much as I do. But it is, as Bernie Zeppi would say, a done deal. Already signed and sealed. Rebellion against me is rebellion against Czar Mikhail, and that's not all. When I die, my son, who is now two years old, will be the khan. He will not be supplanted by a cousin because, again, rebellion against him would be rebellion against the federal government. 'Uneasy lies the head beneath the crown,' but mine lies a lot less uneasy than it did yesterday."

"And when serfs and slaves escape from Kazakh lands to the Cossacks?" Izmailov asked.

"Then they will escape. How is that any different than it is now?"

"The taxes? Import duties, export duties, much of your revenue?"

"That was actually my greatest concern. But while I can't tax trade with the rest of the USSR, I can tax factories that make things in Kazakh. And there will be more factories as the up-time tech and the New Kazakh Dacha get established. A richer Kazakh. A more secure Kazakh. I know that in that other history, eventually the United States of America became one nation, not a confederation. But who is to say the same thing will happen in this history? And even if it does, by then my granddaughters will be the mothers of the czar."

"Did Mikhail . . . ?"

"No. No promises were made. But why not? Kazakh is the first state of the United Sovereign States of Russia. It's the Virginia of the USSR, whatever they might claim here in Ufa. Again, General, what have I lost against what I have gained? Consider that when you speak to General Shein."

General Izmailov bowed from the saddle. "I will remember all you have said, Great Khan."

"Good, then." Salqam-Jangir Khan waved at the army. "When do you think we will be ready to move?"

"A week if we're lucky," Izmailov said. "And, by then, it's going to be marching through mud till the end of May. I don't see any way to relieve Kazan before June."

"And General Birkin knows this?"

"Yes."

"What will he do then? He is over a week out of Kazan, and if it will take us till June to get there, it will take him as long to get here. Do we meet him in the open?"

"Tim recommends that we spend the time fortifying Ufa, but that we use the forest to make *gulyay-gorod*."

"Tim?" Salqam-Jangir Khan's lips twitched in a smile.

"Czar Mikhail sent him a radio message yesterday, asking for his recommendations." General Izmailov tried not to let the resentment at that radio message show. In fact, he tried not to feel resentment. He failed, of course. He knew Tim and he had liked the boy when he was his aide. But sometimes he wished he had used the full Napoleonic technique. Medal, followed by firing squad. It was embarrassing to take instruction from his twenty-year-old former aide de camp. And that embarrassment wasn't helped at all by the fact that Tim had, in turn, consulted Ivan Maslov, also twenty. Still the advice was both deferentially worded and good. "Ivan Maslov thinks that the *gulyay-gorod* are the closest thing we can develop to a tank. And the tank was the technology that prevented trench warfare from dominating World War II like it dominated World War I."

"What about the up-timers' APCs?"

"Perhaps in a few years. We may even have some next year if we are very, very lucky. But not this year. Tim claims they have some project in the works that will allow them to break the siege, and if Birkin gets here, break that one too. But he won't put what the project is over the radio, not even in code."

Kazan
April 18, 1637

General Boris Timofeyevich Lebedev looked out at his relief column arriving. He could hear it. The cracking of the ice on the Volga. Spring had come to relieve the siege of Kazan and Tim was ready for the sally.

He turned back to Abdul Azim, who was still frowning. "It's going to be all right, Abdul."

"The commanding general of the czar's army shouldn't be on that boat," Abdul said. "You have nothing to prove, Tim."

"No?" Tim said. "Well, maybe not. But I do need to get to Ufa and talk to Czar Mikhail and General Izmailov. And, believe me, I am a lot more worried about meeting Izmailov than I am about meeting Iakov Petrovich Birkin's forces."

"Well, you shouldn't be," Abdul said. "I don't trust

your angled walls and the steel is way too thin. Sure, it will stop an AK4 round, but it won't stop a cannon round."

Tim didn't sigh out loud, but he did lose his smile. United Sovereign States of Russia Ship *Kazan*, built on the hull of a steam boat that had been trapped in Kazan more by winter ice than the siege, was an experiment. It had slanted oak walls, sheathed in thin steel plates. It had two gun ports that each had a Kazan-made breech-loading cannon behind them, and it had a launch pad for mortar rockets. It had a periscope for sighting and a steam engine for propulsion. It even had a false keel to break up any ice floes they ran into, assuming they weren't too heavy.

And from his tower in the Kazan kremlin, Tim had placed the locations of most of the strong points of the besieging army's fortifications. They could not be hit successfully from Kazan, but from the river, a lot of them were vulnerable. "I have to lead, Abdul. I can't just order. It's a matter of morale."

"And I say it's not..." Abdul ran down quickly. "But you're going to do it anyway, and my daughter Aamira will swoon over your courage and have palpitations over your danger, and I will be the one who has to put up with it." Abdul paused. "You know, Tim, there are several vital matters that I must discuss with our representative to the constitutional convention."

Tim laughed then, full and loud. "Not a chance. If you go, the rest of the council will go, and Fedor will insist on bringing his wife and all three of his daughters and... No. The USSR Ship *Kazan* would sink just from the weight of the diplomats, who just want to get out of the city for a day."

"Hah, I knew it. It has nothing to do with courage or duty. You just want out of tomorrow's reception."

"You've found me out, Abdul. But I will miss you while I'm gone." Tim reached out a hand and grasped Abdul by the forearm, then turned quickly away and headed down the dock to the *Kazan*.

Ten minutes later, the *Kazan* steamed out onto the Volga with Tim looking through the periscope at the army of Iakov Petrovich Birkin and waiting to take the fire that he knew would be coming. He didn't have to wait long. The rifles started firing almost immediately, and it was like hail on a tin roof. They were fifty feet from the docks before the first of Iakov's cannon started shooting. And they missed. They weren't used to shooting at moving targets, and they over led the shots.

The third shot hit, though, with a booming sound and a cracking of heavy timber. But by now the *Kazan* was behind the enemy ramparts and Tim ordered the gun port on the starboard side opened. And waited. The gunner watched and adjusted the gun, then fired. The shot missed. Not by much, but it missed. The gun crew started reloading and Tim ordered the gun port closed again. Reloading was fine, but they wouldn't get another shot at that gun emplacement, not unless they wanted to stop, and they weren't going to do that.

In ten more minutes, they were beyond the siege and on the open river. There was still ice on the river, but it was open for miles at a stretch and once they got past the confluence of the Kama and the Volga, it was open all the way to the Caspian Sea. In half a day, they passed General Birkin's "relief force" and

sailed up the Kama River at full steam. The Kama
River was a larger river than the Volga, and when
the two came together became the Volga. The ice
had broken up along the Kama a few days before it
had broken up at Kazan. The ice downriver of the
Kama had been broken up for two weeks. The siege
of Kazan was broken, unless the cousins Birkin could
get control of the river.

Army camp on the Kama River

General Ivan Vasilevich Birkin looked out at the
armored steam boat that chugged up the Kama River
and cursed. He didn't have a radio with his army,
but the dispatch riders had reported on the change
of sides of the Kazakhs, and they had also carried as
yet unconfirmed reports that Colonel Shuvalov was
captured or turned over to Czar Mikhail, as well as
the rumor that Sheremetev had sent him to recruit
the Kazakhs. Nothing of this was confirmed, but the
radio men had the information and that meant it would
be all over Russia in days. The armored steamboat
was just the punctuation at the end of the sentence.

There was no way that Czar Mikhail was going to
be killed in the fighting. It was at this point unlikely
that Birkin's army would get inside the walls around
Ufa. And by now even an idiot should be building
walls and ramparts about the city.

A man in a red and gold jacket and white pants
climbed out of a hatch on the boat and waved. There
was quite a bit of gold braid on the red jacket, enough
to indicate that Boris Timofeyevich Lebedev was

wearing the new uniform that the ladies of Kazan had made him. He took off his hat and waved it. The hat was fur-lined with ear flaps and a brim like the up-timer "caterpillar" hats and it had some sort of inlay on the bill. Boris Timofeyevich then ducked down into the steamboat before General Birkin could order his riflemen to shoot. Not that he was going to, as tempting as the thought was. He knew what it meant, that steamboat.

As of today, Czar Mikhail's forces still held the Volga below Kruglaya Mountain. And as long as that held true, that boat meant no city on the Volga or its navigable tributaries could truly be besieged. It would be next winter before they could move with any real hope of success. That wasn't all bad. Sheremetev's forces held the Volga above Kruglaya Mountain, and if they got a blocking force in place, it was unlikely that Mikhail was going to be able to do anything till next winter either.

The problem was that Birkin wasn't convinced that time was on their side. The longer Czar Mikhail stayed Czar Mikhail out here in Ufa, the worse things were going to get in Old Russia.

Birkin said one more unprintable word, then gave the orders that would turn his army around. All the while hating this new sort of warfare that was all shield and no sword, and wishing desperately that he had a radio.

Tim climbed back down into the bowels of the USSR *Kazan* laughing, only to be given a hard look by his aide.

His aide, Vasily Borisovich, was a grizzled captain

of the Russian army who had served in Kazan for years before Tim arrived there. He also seemed oh-so-respectfully convinced that Tim couldn't find his way in out of the rain without a keeper.

"It's all right, Vasily. I'll stay inside where it's safe," Tim said. "I just wanted to make a point. General Birkin is a smart man. I knew him before all this, and my uncle has great respect for him. I just wanted to be sure he got the message."

"If the general says so. However, I would think that the *Kazan* was enough to get the message across, if anything would be."

"Yes, probably. But there was some—I guess you'd call it subtext—that I wanted him to get as well."

"What would that be, General?" Vasily sounded curious now and Tim blushed.

"Well..." Tim hesitated, then blurted. "I wanted him to understand that I would be in Ufa before him, and there wouldn't be any more screwups like Izmailov's sally. Best to avoid battle if we can."

"How do you win a war if no one can attack?"

It wasn't a new question and it had been bothering Tim ever since the battle at Bor. No...ever since his time at the Kremlin academy before the Poles attacked Rzhev. He knew the answer in broad strokes—tactical defense and strategic offense. But the details were harder. You had to be able to break a hole in a line, or breach a city or town's defenses. And they couldn't make tanks; neither side could. "I think the *gulyay-gorod* will be the key, but in spite of Rzhev they haven't been tested enough for me to be sure. And I am very much afraid that a great many people are going to die while we figure it out."

Grantville section, Moscow
April 19, 1637

Boris Ivanovich Petrov read the dispatch from Nizhny Novgorod. The ice was broken up to Kazan. Combined with the new constitution and the Kazakh khan signing on, it meant that Mikhail was, militarily, about equal to Sheremetev. Weaker if Shein stayed neutral, but actually stronger if Shein decided to join the USSR. That was fatal news for Sheremetev because it meant that the momentum was shifting against him. And that would make his coalition of boyars harder to maintain. In fact, Boris was convinced that the only thing preventing a coup now was the fact that no one knew where Sheremetev was to coup him.

"Yuri, arrange for a message to the Goritsky Monastery."

"What's Lady Sofia Gorchakovna going to tell us that we don't know?"

"It's not just Lady Sofia. By now she has a whole network of old biddies up there. Old biddies, and not-so-old biddies, who are a real source of political intelligence."

"It will be risky. The assistant director has the *oprichniki* watching the radios like hawks."

"Talk to Petr Stravinsky. He's a practical man who can smell a change in the wind."

"You think the director-general is in that much trouble?"

"Yes."

Yuri didn't look pleased at that and Boris didn't blame him. As much as he wanted to think that

Sheremetev had taken a dirigible to some place of secure exile, Boris didn't believe it. Fedor Ivanovich Sheremetev was not the sort of man to meekly accept defeat, even if he had a good chance of surviving. And with what he'd done, there was no way out but victory. So he would bathe Moscow in blood before he gave up. *Where is Sheremetev*, Boris wondered, *and what is he up to?*

Goritsky Monastery
April 19, 1637

Some time later, Sofia read the radio message aloud to her friends, then asked their advice. She turned to the widow of Dimitri Cherakasky. "Elena, what do you think?"

"Fedor Ivanovich has to be getting desperate." There was a shortish pause, then she went on. "He can't be . . ."

"Can't be what?"

"Calling in the Poles."

"Why not?" Sofia asked. "He did before." Sheremetev had been part of the cabal of seven boyars who had invited Prince Władysław Vasa, now King Władysław IV of Poland, to come be the czar of Russia in 1610.

"Because if he does, all of Russia will rise up."

"If things keep going the way they are, all of Russia is going to rise up anyway," Katrina Chaadaev offered. "Did you read the constitution? Old Russia and the bureau men will be able to keep their serfs. That's going to cut the legs right out from under Sheremetev with the bureaus."

"Those who supported Sheremetev did so out of fear of Mikhail's reforms, but not entirely so. A lot of them were going with what seemed to be the winning side. Remember, at first Mikhail was just off in the woods somewhere and Sheremetev was running things in his name. That let Sheremetev put his people in position, so when Mikhail ran for it, he was already on top. Sheremetev never had what could be called real support. It was all about his position," Sofia said. "Now that position is looking weaker every day. If Sheremetev doesn't do something, someone is going to figure the best way to get back in the czar's good graces is to put Sheremetev's head on a platter and deliver it to Mikhail by steamboat."

"I think Elena is right. Sheremetev will invite Władysław to come be czar of Russia."

"But Władysław has Gustav II Adolf on his western border. Would he take it even if it were offered?"

"Perhaps not. But that doesn't mean Sheremetev can't get support from Polish or Lithuanian magnates. And they will come in, you know it."

CHAPTER 33

All Your Fault

Ufa
April 20, 1637

Vladimir stepped onto the dock along with Bernie. As it happened, he had never met Boris Timofeyevich Lebedev. And he wasn't convinced of the wisdom of depending on the lad, no matter how good—or at least lucky—he seemed to be so far.

That was the problem. Tim's success could have been nothing more than a combination of luck and caution. Vladimir had had opportunities to talk to real generals, experts in the art of war like General Lennart Torstensson and Admiral Simpson, who had cut his teeth in what he called a brown-water navy. River warfare, even if it was in up-time Vietnam where the rivers never froze, was still river warfare. Granted, nothing "General Tim" had done was exactly wrong, according to those men's advice. On the other hand nothing he had done had been particularly inspired either. Besides, he was a kid. Vladimir, near thirty-five, remembered how much of an idiot he had been at twenty.

The fact that Czar Mikhail and Bernie had faith in the lad didn't exactly fill him with confidence. They weren't military experts, either. The apparition that climbed out of the USSRS *Kazan* didn't put his mind to rest. The young man was wearing baggy white pants, a red coat loaded down with enough gold braid to support a small nation, and he was wearing a fur-lined baseball cap with enough scrambled eggs on the bill to feed an orphanage of hungry children. And his beard was not full. The words "callow" and "overdressed" came to Vladimir's mind... and Vladimir was not a man to dress in rags.

"I like the new look," Bernie said, grinning.

The lad winced and reddened. "The ladies of Kazan didn't feel the clothing I had suited the czar's general."

"Where did they get the idea for the scrambled eggs?" Bernie asked.

"Ivan!" Tim said. "It was his revenge for making him a colonel."

"Where is Ivan? I thought you were going to bring him."

"No. In my absence he's in overall command of the Volga forts at Kruglaya Mountain and Kazan." Then he turned to the grizzled captain behind him. "This is Captain Vasily Borisovich. He's in charge of changing my diapers."

The captain's expression was a study, Vladimir thought. A mixture of strained patience, affection, and respect. Suddenly, Vladimir felt a little less nervous.

In the Ufa kremlin, Tim looked over the plans for the walls and made a suggestion. "You should make your walls bigger. Cover more territory. In fact, my recommendation would be to run a wall from the Belaya River to the Ufa River, just north of the Ufa kremlin."

"That's three miles of front just along the wall and over thirteen miles in total," General Togym said. "Granted, right now the rivers offer protection for most of that, but next winter . . ."

"You're quite right. But I have been forced to reassess the number of men needed to hold a section of defensive works again and again since the introduction of the new rifles, the machine guns, and the rockets . . . not to mention the artillery that both sides will have next winter. And every time, the number goes down. Storming defensive works in a world of rapid-firing guns is a form of mass suicide. Even against hastily set up works, much less the sort of works that can be put in place over the course of a year."

"Fine. Perhaps we can defend so much. But why?"

Tim sighed. "Because what I haven't been able to figure out is how to defend the rest of Russia. We can defend hard points with very few men, but what about the fields, the outlying villages that we will need to feed ourselves? Those are the places that I see no way at all to defend. At the very least we need to have some place we can bring our people into when we are attacked."

"More than that," Vera added. "We need the room for industries to make things to sell so we can buy food if those fields are burned."

Tim nodded at her. "The strategic situation is complicated. Sheremetev has stabilized his control of Russia up to the west side of the Volga all the way to Kazan. He controls the northern Divina River, all the way to Archangelsk, but not much east of that. He doesn't control much at all of the Cossack territory to the south. On the other hand, he has an alliance with at least some of the magnates of Lithuania, so the Sjem is not going to authorize any actions against him."

"And for Sweden to act would take a miracle," Brandy said.

"Militarily, I'm sure you're right. But his political control of the territory is weak at best. If we just hold him off, he might well lose control of the duma. And we are getting defections. Granted, most of them are from the very bottom of the social ladder, but we are getting at least some representatives from most of the great houses now, and some of the mid-level nobility. If we can get greater support from the west, Sweden and the USE, that would put even more political pressure on him."

"Not very likely," Vladimir said. "The USE doesn't have access to us except through the northern trade route. And that is, at best, a very narrow tube to pull the sort of supplies we're going to need through, even if the *Catherine the Great* gets modified to handle the ice better."

"So we will get no aid from the USE?" Czar Mikhail asked.

"Nothing official. Ron Stone is sympathetic and gold is worth a lot. Have you found gold?"

"We have two mines, but so far the output is small."

"Well, Ron will provide lend lease for a while. I'm not sure how long."

"We need better access to the production of the USE, Your Highness," Czarina Evdokia told Vladimir. "Even if General Tim is right and they are stopped till next winter, a nonindustrial nation can't fight an industrial one for long and survive."

Ufa
April 21, 1637

Bernie's door burst open without a knock and Vladimir roared, "How dare you make free with my sister!"

Bernie blinked, and for just a second he bought it. Then he realized that Vladimir was just having a bit of fun at his sister's expense.

"How dare he?" Natasha screeched, and Bernie knew that at least for the moment Natasha hadn't realized that Vladimir was teasing. "How dare *you*! I am going to marry Bernie."

"I haven't given you permission to marry anyone."

Oops! Bernie thought. *That sounded real.*

"It's a new world. We have a constitution and I have rights," Natasha said. "I will marry who I want to."

Vladimir blinked. And while he was standing there, Brandy came in. "You tell 'em, sister," Brandy said in English. Then she punched Vladimir in the side.

The notion of male solidarity never reached Bernie's consciousness. The notion that he hadn't, in fact, asked Natasha, even less so. He was getting everything he wanted without having to say a word.

Vladimir looked at Natasha, then at Brandy, then at Bernie, and said, "This is all your fault."

Cast of Characters

Adams, John	Captain of *Catherine the Great* dirigible
Andreevich, Stefan	Smith in Ruzuka
Andreevich, Vera Sergeevna	Stefan's wife
Anya	Runaway slave
Cherakasky, Elena	Widow of Dimitri Cherakasky, monastery
Dolmatov-Karpov, Tatyana	Sent to monastery due to unfortunate incident with a groundskeeper
Eduardovich, Yulian	Orthodox priest of differing views
Gorchakov, Brandy (nee Bates)	Grantville up-timer, married to Vladimir
Gorchakov, Natalia (Natasha) Petrovna	A princess of Russia

Gorchakov, Sofia Petrovna	Natalia's aunt and chaperone
Gorchakov, Vladimir Petrovich	A prince of Russia, Natalia's brother
Izmailov, Artemi Vasilievich	General in the Russian army
Khan, Salqam-Jangir	Tatar ruler, attacks Ufa
Lebedev, Boris Timofeyevich "Tim"	General of Czar's army
Maslov, Ivan	Colonel of Czar's army
Metropolitan Matthew	Head Priest in Kazan
Nickovich, Petr "Pete"	Artisan and natural philosopher
Odoevskii, Ivan Ivanovich	Prince, with Sheremetev
Petrov, Boris Ivanovich	A bureaucrat of Moscow
Petrov, Iosif Borisovich	Boris' son, in Grantville
Petrov, Ivan Borisovich	Boris' son, in Ufa
Petrov, Mariya	Boris' wife
Petrov, Pavel Borisovich	Boris' son
Polzin, Stanislav Ivanovich	Commander of the "garrison" at Ufa
Polzin, Olga Petrovichna	Stanislav's wife
Romanov, Alexis	Son of Czar Mikhail
Romanov, Evdokia "Doshinka"	Czarina of Russia

Romanov, Irina	Daughter of Czar Mikhail
Romanov, Mikhail Fedorovich	Czar of Russia
Sayyeau, Guy	Engineer's Mate on *Catherine the Great*
Sheremetev, Fedor Ivanovich	Russian boyar, cousin to Czar Mikhail, takes over as director-general
Shein, Mikhail Borisovich	General of Russia, forms Siberian State
Shuvalov, Leontii	Colonel in Russian Army
Simmons, Gerry	Up-time husband of Tami
Simmons, Tami	Up-time nurse hired by Czar
Slavenitsky, Nikita Ivanovich "Nick"	Pilot
Trotsky, Fedor Ivanovich	A Russian spy
Tupikov, Filip Pavlovich	Artisan and natural philosopher
Utkin, Ivan Nikolayevich	Colonel of Russia
Utkin, Elena	Ivan's cheating wife
Utkin, Izabella Ivanovna	Ivan's daughter, about 16 or 17
Utkin, Nikita Ivanovich	Son of Ivan, soldier of Russia
Zakharovna, Valeriya	Crewwoman on *Czarina Evdokia*
Zeppi, Bernard "Bernie"	Up-timer hired by Vladimir, counselor to the Czar

1636: The Devil's Opera (with David Carrico)	978-1-4767-3700-3 • $7.99
1636: Commander Cantrell in the West Indies (with Charles E. Gannon)	978-1-4767-8060-3 • $8.99
1636: The Viennese Waltz (with Gorg Huff & Paula Goodlett)	978-1-4767-8101-3 • $7.99
1636: Mission to the Mughals (with Griffin Barber)	978-1-4814-8301-8 • $7.99
1636: The Ottoman Onslaught	978-1-4814-8298-1 • $7.99
1636: The Vatican Sanction (with Charles E. Gannon)	978-1-4814-8386-5 • $7.99
1637: The Volga Rules (with Gorg Huff & Paula Goodlett)	978-1-4814-8303-2 • $25.00
1637: The Polish Maelstrom	978-1-4814-8389-6 • $25.00

THE RING OF FIRE ANTHOLOGIES
Edited by Eric Flint

Ring of Fire	978-1-4165-0908-0 • $7.99
Ring of Fire II	978-1-4165-9144-3 • $7.99
Ring of Fire III	978-1-4516-3827-1 • $7.99
Ring of Fire IV	978-1-4814-8238-7 • $7.99
Grantville Gazette	978-0-7434-8860-0 • $7.99
Grantville Gazette II	978-1-4165-5510-0 • $7.99
Grantville Gazette III	978-1-4165-5565-0 • $7.99
Grantville Gazette IV	978-1-4391-3311-8 • $7.99
Grantville Gazette V	978-1-4391-3422-1 • $7.99
Grantville Gazette VI	978-1-4516-3853-0 • $7.99
Grantville Gazette VII	HC: 978-1-4767-8029-0 • $25.00
Grantville Gazette VIII	HC: 978-1-4814-8329-2 • $25.00

MORE . . .
ERIC FLINT

Mother of Demons   978-0-671-87800-9 • $7.99

Worlds   978-1-4516-3751-9 • $7.99

Worlds 2   TPB: 978-1-4814-8341-4 • $16.00

Rats, Bats & Vats (with Dave Freer)   978-0-671-31828-4 • $7.99

The Rats, the Bats & the Ugly   978-1-4165-2078-8 • $7.99
   (with Dave Freer)

Pyramid Scheme (with Dave Freer)   978-0-7434-3592-5 • $7.99

Pyramid Power (with Dave Freer)   978-1-4165-5596-4 • $7.99

Slow Train to Arcturus (with Dave Freer)
                    HC: 978-1-4165-5585-8 • $24.00

THE BOUNDARY SERIES with Ryk E. Spoor

Boundary   978-1-4165-5525-4 • $7.99

Threshold   978-1-4516-3777-9 • $7.99

Portal   978-1-4767-3642-6 • $7.99

Castaway Planet   HC: 978-1-4767-8027-6 • $25.00

Castaway Odyssey   HC: 978-1-4767-8181-5 • $26.00

Iron Angels (with Alistair Kimble)   978-1-4814-8358-2 • $7.99

The Alexander Inheritance   HC: 978-1-4814-8248-6 • $25.00
   (with Gorg Huff & Paula Goodlett)

Time Spike (with Marilyn Kosmatka)   978-1-4391-3312-5 • $7.99

The Warmasters   0-7434-7185-7 • $7.99
   (with David Weber & David Drake)

MORE . . .
ERIC FLINT

The Wizard of Karres   978-1-4165-0926-4 • $7.99
  (with Mercedes Lackey & Dave Freer)

The Sorceress of Karres   978-1-4391-3446-7 • $7.99
  (with Dave Freer)

THE BELISARIUS SERIES with David Drake

The Dance of Time   978-1-4165-2137-2 • $7.99

Belisarius II: Storm at Noontide   HC: 978-1-4165-9148-1 • $23.00
                     TPB: 978-1-4165-9166-5 • $14.00

Belisarius III: The Flames of Sunset
                     HC: 978-1-4391-3280-7 • $23.00
                     TPB: 978-1-4391-3302-6 • $14.00

AND DON'T MISS THE CLASSIC AUTHORS OF SF
EDITED & COMPILED BY ERIC FLINT—
NOW BACK IN PRINT FROM BAEN BOOKS!
Christopher Anvil
Randall Garrett
Keith Laumer
Murray Leinster

Available in bookstores everywhere.
Order ebooks online at www.baen.com.

1636: Commander Cantrell in the West Indies
978-1-4767-8060-3 • $8.99

Oil. The Americas have it. The United States of Europe needs it. Enter Lieutenant-Commander Eddie Cantrell.

1636: The Vatican Sanction
978-1-4814-8386-5 • $7.99

Pope Urban has fled the Vatican and the traitor, Borja. But assassins have followed him to France—and not only assassins! The Pope and his allies have fled right into the clutches of the vile Pedro Dolor.

STARFIRE SERIES
(with Steve White)

Extremis
978-1-4516-3814-1 • $7.99

They have traveled for centuries, slower than light, and now they have arrived at the planet they intend to make their new home: Earth. The fact that humanity is already living there is only a minor inconvenience.

Imperative
978-1-4767-8119-8 • $16.00

A resurrected star navy hero attempts to keep a fragile interstellar alliance together while battling and implacable alien adversary.

Oblivion
978-1-4814-8401-5 • $7.99

It's time to take a stand! For Earth! For Humanity! For the Pan-Sentient Union!

"[T]he intersecting plot threads, action and well-conceived science kept those pages turning." —SFcrowsnest